THE GATEKEEPER'S DESCENDANTS

Marrow Publishing
The Gatekeeper's Descendants
By Johanna Frank
© 2021, Johanna Frank. *All rights reserved.*

ISBN: 978-1-7777317-0-0 Paperback
ISBN: 978-1-7777317-2-4 Hard Cover
ISBN: 978-1-7777317-1-7 eBook
Fiction/Fantasy

Acknowledgements:
With sincere heart bearing gratitude to –
Those involved with critiquing and editing: 2nd Draft Critique Services, Writer's Digest Shop; Kevin Miller, Book Editing Associates; and Denise Harmer, Editing Services. Those daring souls who reviewed the advanced copy: Brenda N., Dottie Lu J., Jenn A., Jim J., John F., Linda S., Sylvia S. and Writerful Books. Sylvia Pond Photography – for snapping the author photo. DAMONZA – for cover design and interior formatting. And most important, to all those encouragers! My kids and grandkids, my husband, and dear friends. I am so grateful to have you all in my life, on tour as I am.

THE GATEKEEPER'S DESCENDANTS

JOHANNA FRANK

For Johanna, my great-great-grandmother.
We never met, but the story of your tour inspired this one.

And for Sam, my youngest.
Your tour was far too short, but such
sparkling light you left me with.

To my husband Joe,
I appreciate just who you are.

∽

He calls for patient endurance and faithfulness.
He gives mercy and grace,
all freely.

PROLOGUE
FROM THE DESK OF INTERVENTIONS

Somewhere Inside the Kingdom a File is Opened

THE WAY HUMANS track? I'd say 300 years, give or take. That's when Megs signed on, and he's never looked back. That job is his reason for being. He's the most thankful gatekeeper the kingdom ever had.

I know, I know, things were different then. Such long backups in processing and new arrivals were coming in by the droves. They were desperate to hire, so many jobs to fill. In those days people just had to be eager, show an interest in taking a job.

Now? There's so much competition, people have to stay "on track," as they say. Now they need to develop a particular character while on a humankind tour. As if surviving that tour, a lifetime on Earth, isn't enough.

Yup, those were the good ol' days, more jobs than there were kingdom citizens to take them. Most citizen folk know Megs as big, strong, and fearless—you know, the kinda guy you'd never mess with and yet the kinda guy whose heart still takes the prize as his biggest feature. But I know him better. I know what made the guy.

You see, Megs, or Megalos, as the king calls him, and I did our journey on Earth together. Actually, that's when we met. I was a few years his senior and a good deal taller, and back then, we were buddies. He was of the scraggly, timid, weakling sort, forever bumping into things. We were farming buddies mostly, friends by association, I guess you could say. When I was milking our cows, I knew he'd be milking his. When I was feeding our chickens, I knew he'd be doing it too. On those unbearably hot, humid days, I'd feel like a pig shucking all that corn, but somehow it was comforting knowing he was over there yonder, sweating it up just as much.

Our families didn't visit. My pa didn't like his pa much, told me to stay away. "Somethin's not right 'bout that man," he would say. "Keep an eye out for his boy. Let me know if he needs protectin'."

I had a perfect view of Megs' yard from the window beside my trundle. Barely a half field away, a stormwater ravine served as the boundary line. A bunch of lavender bushes grew wild on our side while a rotted-out date palm stood beside a big pile of stones on his. I saw Megs' pa kicking him in the behind now and again, and once I saw him get shoved into a patch of manure good and hard. Megs scrambled to get up and slipped even deeper. His pa offered him a hand and then yanked it away, causing Megs to slip again, headfirst. His pa laughed and spat out his tobacco, and Megs, well, he didn't even clench his fists.

I never told my pa. He had a temper, and naturally, I didn't want to start a feud. But I watched for Megs every day, making sure I caught a glimpse of him at least once, just to be sure he was alive and all. Poor kid, his head always hung in shame. I figured keeping an eye on him was enough, that I was doing good by doing that.

Therein something laid inside me, fresh as thick cement: a foundation of guilt. It was like a prison sentence for the rest of my earth years. *How could I have known what was coming?* I would ask myself. I had witnessed enough. I should have done *something*.

Megs was thirteen. I remember well because it was the year of mud, a time of trials, you might say. The horses and carts couldn't get through most roads. And the harvest that year? It wasn't much. In fact, most folks had diddly squat, including the farm next door. Megs' family's fields were akin to a swamp.

That was when Megs' pa took the beating and punching indoors. He caught me watching from behind our lavender bush once, just as he heaved a fist into Megs' temple. After that I couldn't look no more, was best to forget it all.

One night a couple of weeks later, I heard commotion and some banging around com'n from his way—some muffled yelping too. I did the only thing I thought I could do: I convinced myself all was good. But the consistent haunting *woos* of the eagle owl hinted otherwise. So, I snuck out of the house, crossed the ravine, and crept up to their kitchen window.

There was Megs, on his back, swinging his arms and legs like a wildcat, only his pa had one of his dung-caked boots pressed hard, squishin' his gut. Megs was yelling at him. "I hate you! I hate you!" His pa just laughed, called him a wussy mama's boy.

I'll never forget that shaky look on Megs' face. "Yer no pa. I *curse* you." Megs spat, but I gotta tell you, it didn't get far. "I curse you—and all yer relatives… to infinity. I curse you. I curse them all!"

That did it. Megs' pa didn't laugh this time. His eyes grew devil-like and red with hate. "Yeah, you'll never escape me. I'm yer family, but I'm gonna make sure *you* never get yer own."

His pa grabbed the cast iron pot, still full of hot fat and chops, and well, I didn't see anymore. Chicken that I was, I ran back home and cowered under my bed. Told no one.

The story 'round the village made no sense. "The boy didn't have a chance," people said. "Wolves charged straight through the gate. Jumped him whilst draining out the trough." The incredulous part, "Not a single calf got touched."

Megs' pa blamed the unnatural weather, said it caused wild animals to act like bats in the belfry. Know something? He got away with it. The whole village lapped it up.

But the way my pa looked at me, he knew better. That was no wolf pack; it was a cold-blooded killer, not the kinda pa any kid should have.

I pretty much blamed myself—for not intervening, that is. Things might have been different if I had done something. Maybe I could have stopped it, who knows.

For the rest of my tour on Earth, first thing each sunrise, Megs came to mind. That piercing sound when his pa shoveled gravel around, like it didn't matter. All I could do back then was score some lavender from our bushes and toss it over the ravine, hoping it would land somewhere close to that pile of stones, hoping Megs would know that I knew and cared his body was down there, rotting in the deep.

Now, I know the rule of time—it does not go backwards. But with the king as my ruler and witness, back then I pleaded with him over and over for a miracle, another chance to intervene, so I could somehow help my dear friend, Megalos.

Well, he heard me. 'Cause now, some three centuries later, Megalos came to me in my kingdom job as head of interventions and him in his kingdom job as head gatekeeper. He was all worked up, didn't know what to do 'bout a situation. He came asking for a favor. An intervention, something I'm darn good at now. And let me tell you, was I eager to pull a few strings!

Wanna hear the story?

CHAPTER ONE
IT'S HIM OR ME

In the Outer Courtyard of the Kingdom

*O*H, JUST LOOK at him. Pipiera squirmed in private adoration. Even now, as he gripped tight the edges of a page and read its message with dedicated focus, simply standing in his shadow assured her. A stern and peculiar expression washed over his face. But none of that mattered. To Pipiera, Megalos's presence was akin to a big, gentle bear hug.

"What's wrong, Papah Moolos?" her voice low and quiet, her eyes fixed upward in hopes to catch his. She knew he loved the nickname she invented, particularly the "Papah" part. It was a sure-fire way to make Megalos pause and grin. Plus, she loved the sense of belonging that came with the pretense she was his descendant, that he was somehow a grandfather to her.

But not today, no sheepish grin. *This is highly unusual. Stress, could that be stress I detect? No, that's strife. He seems worried.* No matter however dreadful the news, she knew he would overcome it in a matter of blinks. He always did.

She considered his face a bit longer, remaining silent and methodical. *Hmm, could it actually be that bad?* There was a serious crinkle between his thick, dark brows. *It almost appears to be fear. Almost.* She cocked her head a tad. *Surely not!*

She raised her heels effortlessly, shifting all weight to her toes and turning her attention to peek out the only window of Papah's humble living quarters, a single room held high atop the watch post. Nothing but an exquisitely carved bench to sit upon. She scanned the panoramic view. A pleasant aromatic breeze captured her senses and ruffled her bangs. Bored of debating which emotion was plaguing her papah, she decided to settle. Sad. *It's disappointing news. Therefore, he is sad.*

Head gatekeeper was not an easy job. The way leading to the kingdom's main gate saw a continuous hum of new arrivals. Nearly always there would be somebody on the edge of the horizon, heading in toward Megs. He truly shone. He was always prepared, always welcoming, always patient to answer questions and dispel concerns, and, when called for, he could shake his head in a kind and gentle manner. The latter inevitably meant the arrival was to go back. The rules were strict, the orders clear.

Pipiera loved being smack in the middle of the activity, a witness to it all. She teased him about how much fun his job was. He did his best to manage his concern that she did not recognize the seriousness of it all.

The other gatekeepers in the kingdom courtyard respected Megalos for his cautious analyzing, his calculated reasoning, and sometimes, though admittedly rare, his unenthusiastic kindness. But never, ever fear. His comrade, Roly, told Pip she was the only one Megalos would allow himself to banter with. That made Pipiera feel special and, in her own eyes, somewhat of an expert as to his inside track.

Her concern about him and whatever it was that stole his attention lingered. She crossed her arms and offered up some encouragement. "Papah, if you read it even just *one* more time, the words will not jump off the page and change clothes." With both eyebrows arched, Pipiera hoped her teasing would lighten things up.

The mood changed, but not the way she hoped. His facial expression was obvious; he was annoyed. It was the same discerning frown he employed when lecturing her about not taking kingdom business to heart. *I better back off, give him some space. I don't know why he lets himself get so disrupted by these letters from those authoritarians. What's the big deal anyway?*

Megalos often received information in the same manner—a message scribed on official kingdom letterhead, sealed by an authoritarian, and then delivered by that busy little book room keeper guy.

She put her mind on a serious track. *I bet it's an update on a gatekeeper recruit. Papah says it's a good job but really hard to get.* He had explained it to her many times. All his replacement recruits had to develop certain characteristics during their tour, a journey on Earth bookmarked with a time to begin and a time to end. It seemed so easy. All they had to do was recognize how blessed they were, cast their concerns on the king, allow him to keep their hearts clean, and stay loyal. Yet only a few stuck to that on account of all the earthly challenges and whatnots.

The ornate bench creaked as he cast a foot upon it.

Pushing her chin up, she dared a question, attempting to prove she could be serious. "Is somebody struggling?"

"It's a page from Matthew's book." He waved it high briefly before crumpling it up and shoving the ball of parchment into the pocket of his linen trousers.

So, it wasn't an official message; it was a page from a recruit's book. That can't be right. Since when do they rip pages out of one's book?

It was his turn to stare out the window.

Just being present and silent was the best way Pipiera could think of to support her papah at that moment. But her mind did swirl. Their paths had never crossed, hers and this Matthew's. *I knew it! You had him on a pedestal, you talked about him way too much anyway. I'm glad he's struggling.* Her Papah Moolos talked about him so much that anyone listening would come to know Matthew inside and out. That's if they wanted to. Pipiera preferred to ignore it because she couldn't bear the thought of Papah cherishing anyone more than her. *Just because this Matthew boy chose your footsteps to follow, you think he's so great. C'mon, Papah, he was barely qualified to take that assignment. You said so yourself.* Pipiera hung her head, attempting to hide her thoughts. *Dare I say it?*

"So… was doing a tour to become your replacement one day actually the plan for Matthew?" *There, I said it. Because truth be known, I think you want it more than he does.*

His back stiffened and his brows formed a perfect V. "What are you suggesting?"

Okay, here goes… "Well, what I mean is, I dread to think if it wasn't. I mean, if Matthew wasn't actually meant to be groomed for your replacement, his earth journey would be…" She sucked and tucked in her bottom lip, letting her words trail. She kept to herself the obvious—Matthew's journey would be an impossible one. *Besides, why do you need to retire anyway? What will happen to me? Did you ever think of that? Probably not!*

She could tell his mind was calculating away, surmising the situation at hand. "Matthew must be quite off track," he mumbled whilst rubbing his chin. "Otherwise, Bookie would not have come over like that."

"He's always in a hurry. Everything is urgent with him." She was trying to be helpful. The book room keeper was in charge of all the open books. If one was on a humankind tour, a book was certainly open in Bookie's special room under the special care of his countless scribes, scribbling madly, capturing every thought and action, particularly the details requested by the king.

"Yeah." His finger tapped at his temple while his chin rested in his large, solid right hand. "But he's never ripped out a page from anyone's book before, least not that I know of."

Pipiera watched as her papah continued to think. "Well, maybe he thinks you can have that page rewritten," she said. It was a genuine notion.

Megalos finally broke the silence. "Possibly." Then he shook his head, "I don't think that's it." He chuckled gruffly. "The law clearly doesn't allow for that." Then his lips tightened across his face.

I think that's a half smile. Pipiera took the relaxed muscles around his eyes as resignation to all this silly nonsense about some Matthew boy. *All will work out,* she wanted to assure him.

Alas, he gave the cue. "Let's get back at it." With that, he led the way.

The pair descended the interior circular staircase, seventy-three steps in all. She had counted them many times. Any other day Pip would have fluttered down those stairs, jumping two steps at a time, but today she followed obediently behind her papah. By the time they got to ground level, the heaviness had lifted. Megs paused briefly, flashing a curvy-lipped grin at his little sidekick. Then they stepped into the outer courtyard.

Ah, there you are. Back here with me. Where we belong. The two of us. She watched him head to his post by the gate only twenty something steps away. *Our closeness, this life we share…* She sighed. "I don't want anything to change."

Pipiera often wondered what drew her to Megalos, why she felt so close and connected, and why they made each other their closest of kin. At least six generations apart, they were quite different. Pipiera could only dream of adventure, but she wasn't certain what that might be, and she lacked the courage to find out. Megalos? Not so much. He wasn't into dreamy adventures. He realized his adventure in the here and now. Pip's bubbly spirit oozed out of her constantly even if her mind did flip in views. Megs stayed on track, by the book, with his inner thoughts tucked neatly inside a serious, all-business exterior. Nevertheless, the two were a pair, together all the time in the kingdom's outer courtyard—him working and her playing. Pipiera didn't take their relationship for granted; rather, she feared it could all disappear one day without explanation. She shuddered at the notion.

Glancing toward Megalos to be sure he was more than an earshot away, she vocalized her grief. "Why should I care if this Matthew boy is struggling? I don't want him, or anyone, to replace you. Why can't you just let the boy struggle and keep things the way they are?"

CHAPTER TWO
I BET YA

In the Town of Havensight, May 1973

I JUST WANNA BE freakin' normal." Matthew Mackenzie was disheartened. "Why do we have to live here, anyway? This town is squarer than a deuce." He backed himself up and got into position. Steady still for balance, he rocked his core back and forth and then wound up for the runoff. Leaping with his left leg, he sprinted, gaining speed, eight steps, ready for takeoff.

"Bogus." His footing was off, and he ran through the sand pit. *Least I didn't trip.* He was used to gladdening himself when it came to his jumps.

Andy Falcon, part-time track-and-field teacher and part-time guidance counselor at Havensight's one and only high school, jogged by hauling a net of batons and a pile of orange cones with the help of two students. "Keep goin', Matt! You can do it," he hollered as he passed, motioning five more minutes with his free hand.

Matt ignored him. Sure, he liked Mr. Falcon well enough, but Matt took so much mocking from being Vice Principal Decker's unwanted love child that showing acceptance of any teacher, or anyone in authority for that matter, would just pose another barrier. He wanted to be normal and for everything to be okay.

Matt arched his back. With a casual coolness, he scanned the sports field for the other students. Particularly one. There he was, in front of the worn, tiered set of wooden bleachers. "Figures." Half the class encircled Emerson. "Mr. Dufus Popularity, new and rich. That's all it takes." Matt conjured up a dose of spit and aimed for a patch of clover, then toed the glob into the dirt real good and hard with his spikes.

This was Matthew's first year at Havensight Collegiate Secondary School. He had hoped it could be a new start, a new feeling. But the old feelings steeped and swirled just the same and wouldn't disappear. He couldn't put his finger on the reason for his anger, but it was easy enough to figure out where to direct it: Marnie. Lately, he refused to call her "Mom," choosing to distance himself instead. After all, she was the betrayer. And as far as his pestering little sister Karo went, *she's the love child, not me.*

Matthew eyed a lump of grass growing through the sparse sand at the near end of the pit and positioned for another jump. The Tri-Town regional meet was tomorrow, and he was Havensight's top hope to take the running long jump prize. Problem was, the school had a self-reporting system, and Matthew had added more than just a few inches on his distance, then bragged heartily about his abilities. He loved white lies; they gave him a better life.

How could he possibly win? Good question.

Matt sighed. The way he figured it, just placing in the top three was his chance to become a regular kid at school, accepted, not a forgotten love child, no longer an outcast. He kicked the ground some more, chuckling about the previous week's big scene. Being strong-armed down the halls by the town fuzz didn't help. Apparently, smoking a doobie was cool. Getting caught wasn't.

The walls were closing in. *I've got to win.*

He angled his body forward this time and picked his landing spot. Ready... run hard... leap. Matthew's legs ran wildly through the air. Thud. He landed, fell backwards. "Bogus!" *Get it right,* this time he scolded himself.

"Get up, doofus." Emerson stood over Matt, grinning ear to ear.

Grody, whatta you doing here? "Get yer face outta here," Matt replied.

"Everyone says you're our best shot tomorrow. I say you're not good enough."

"Better 'n you."

"I'm not entering."

"Skinny arse."

"I beg your pardon?"

"You heard me." With ease and confidence, Matthew jumped to his feet then faced the kid at school he most hated. Instinctively his upper lip tensed and curled, his teeth clenched. As of late, this was a routine expression for Matthew. *Go for it, freak, I dare you!*

Emerson nodded to a threesome of jocks at his heels, pulling them into the act. Matt considered them groupies. His two child-hood friends, Josh and Nick, called them thugs on account of their muscular frames and their cowboy-farmin' man boots. Most of HCSS's students were bused in from farms north of town, includ-ing these Emerson loyalists. Matt could never figure out why they hung out and protected Emerson, who was as slick as a big city could conjure up. *It's gotta be a money thing.*

Head high and chin up, Matt speared into the eyes of the thug in the middle. He shook his head three times. *Tsk, tsk, tsk.* "Does he pay you to be his friend or just his bodyguard?"

Another nod by Emerson, and the thugs pushed Matthew onto his back, into the hardened and dirty sand.

"Buggers!" Matt would have stood up quickly to challenge the trio, only the taunting started. Taunting that struck a deep emo-tional chord, one that made him weak in every way imaginable.

"Go home and go cry to daddy. Oh, wait, little love child,

daddy's gone." Emerson, his thugs, and now a half dozen other students circled around Matt to enjoy the mockery and a good laugh. "Daddy, Daddy, don't go…" Emerson mocked.

Matt wished he could melt into the sand. Better yet, underneath it, be totally hidden, totally gone. *Who would care anyway?*

The bell rang. Perfect timing. Everyone left but Emerson. Apparently, he had more to say.

"So, you say you can do it. You better, kid, 'cause I'm a bettin' man." He narrowed his eyes and leaned in. "And I don't like to lose."

Emerson strolled back into the school building. Matthew slowly got up and shook himself off. Shook the dirt out. For a long moment he stared at the slow-closing double door to the gymnasium where the rest of the class had just finished entering.

He spied the sky for an opening in the clouds. No matter the day, no matter how cloudy, there was always an opening. He found it. An entrance to another world, one high above the school building and well beyond his life in Havensight. "Dad," he whispered while his throat tightened, "why didn't you take me with you?"

Matthew talked to his dad regularly each day. He was Matt's confidante, the only one who would listen. The problem is, Matthew's dad, his real dad, Franklin Mackenzie, died five-and-a-half years ago.

CHAPTER THREE
MARNIE-MOMMA

Two Days Later

MARNIE NEVER SLEPT a wink. Certain she heard every click, swish, and tick from her three alarms, she wondered if it was time to get a new clock. Just one, the digital kind. The kind that was supposed to be silent. *Darned squirrels. Too many power outages. I could never rely on those new plug-in types.*

Her fingers found the lever between the two bells atop the windup, her most trustworthy clock. She ceased the loud, continuous ring to not awaken the other two occupants in the house—her son, Matthew, and daughter, Karo.

Why on earth would that keep me up all night? She smothered a pillow over her face and groaned miserably into the package of feathers. *Karo going on and on about her bones…and her sloppy muscles…and how she's not fast like the other kids…and, oh my, what else? That's a job for me, isn't it, to ensure my children eat and grow properly? To be so competitive and so tiny. Oh dear.*

She pushed the pillow away and pulled up a cool section of her duvet. *Fifteen more minutes!* Her mind continued to race, away from her four-year-old daughter's persistence on nutrition, straight over to her job at Semi-Permanent Staffing. She had eight interviews scheduled for that day, all requiring reference checks and selection recommendations for Lance by the time five o'clock rolled around. It was late spring, and that meant Havensight's summer hiring rush was on in full force.

The long buzzer, the second alarm clock on her dressing cupboard, blared away, jolting her once again. Two steps out of bed, she slammed it down and then a quick jump to nestle back under the covers. *Where was I? Oh yeah, first interview at 9:15, that nincompoop, the police chief's nephew. Ugh, what a way to start my day. Hmm... I wonder if there's enough bread for Matty's lunch and my own.* She melted into another snooze.

The final alarm sounded off like a hesitant fire engine clang. It was seven a.m. She had strategically placed the clock on the floor in the only washroom upstairs, forcing herself to leap out of bed and shut its echo down as quickly as possible. Then there'd be no going back to bed. She'd turn on the taps, pull out the greys, brush her teeth, and slip into a tub of hot shallow water. The surrounding soft, minty tiles had become her place of refuge.

Marnie's single-family brick home sat along a tidy row with a dozen others on Warmud Street. Before becoming zoned for residential use, the area had been a field, a shallow stretch of unused land that coexisted with the main road into Havensight. The orphaned new development was a good three miles from town. In the back of the lots, an evergreen forest formed a corridor that nearly hid the hilly and non-farmable landscape. Despite water drainage issues—a regular complaint from residents—a heavy population of wildflowers, bushes, bunnies, squirrels, and field mice survived just fine. Unfortunately, so did the rats, particularly the night before weekly garbage pickup. The occasional deer could be seen meandering down the hills and through the trees to scour fresh buds from residential landscapes. Neighbors would shoo them away, but Marnie didn't mind them. To her, they represented peace and freedom. *Hmm... and grace*, another thing she wished she had. Seeing the deer also meant spring had arrived, stirring up a bittersweet emotion that was, quite frankly, better than just bitter.

In front, the one-sided row of houses appeared perfect, almost too perfect, much like something a hobbyist might build out of Legos; driveways curbed and graveled, each house with three to five concrete steps, iron railings leading up to aluminum screens, and freshly stained wooden doors with peek-a-boo pearl-drop windows, and black mailboxes with shiny even numerals, 1002 up to 1032. Who knew why those numbers?

Stretched out in front of the long row of houses and lined by the highway was a long, narrow grassy boulevard, not wide enough for a soccer game, but certainly long enough to play decent rounds of catch. And for kids like Matthew, it was perfect for running and jumping the whole day through. Warmud Street, "that stretch over yonder," as the locals called it, had been another of the town council's self-acclaimed brilliant ideas, a way to use up that useless unfarmable land and attract newcomers at the same time. It was oddly situated west of town, away from the schools, shops, and restaurants that provided all the basic services that residents of Havensight could ever want. "Typical," Marnie would say. "New-comers are welcome as long as they stay *over yonder*."

The tourist section, where mostly small owner-run businesses tried desperately to stay afloat season after season, was even farther west by the same distance. Marnie's little Legoland community was smack amid a much-gossiped-about nowhere, blanketed by a wide-open sky, a magnificent spot for those who were into stargazing.

Marnie had one of only three houses that boasted a second floor. That alone was enough to make it stand out. She would have much preferred it didn't. Out of all the houses, hers was the only one with the garage turned into a workshop. A workshop she never used but still housed all of *his* equipment—all kinds of observatory gadgets and whatnots that were no longer put to use or admired. That was another thing that Marnie knew stood out, a garage that wasn't used for their car, heavens to Betsy. But what topped it all off, separating her from all others on Warmud Street, was what ailed her the most. Her home was the only one on the street where the man of the house no longer lived. Neither of them. Marnie was reminded of that at the end of every workday. Each time she pulled into her driveway, she whispered his name and sensed a hollow chill, as if perhaps he were hiding behind the dusty black-out curtain that hung inside the garage door, judging her. Frank. Matty was especially touchy about protecting his dad's stuff in the workshop, so she left it be. The second man, Arnie, didn't count, at least not much. Arnie hadn't lived there very long.

Hugging her knees, she gave the sudsy tub water a swirl and held up an unusually large bubble. Early morning was her only chance for an exhale. Being dead tired was nothing unusual. Recently, she'd received a nervous disorder diagnosis from the one and only family doctor in Havensight.

"Bogue," she snapped at a bubble, imagining it to be her doctor. "I just lead a busy life. You try stepping into my shoes."

Raising two children on her own and proving herself at her job while managing a mortgage higher than she was comfortable with all weighed heavily. She shelved her own dreams for at least a decade, maybe two, though it wasn't clear if Marnie even knew what her dreams were. What was definite though, she was finished trying to fit into any of Havensight's trivial social buckets.

She grabbed the semi-clean towel off the rack and wrapped it around her. *Matthew. He's the one I should have been awake all night worrying about. What am I to do with him?*

She shuddered and tucked the towel end tight. Just thinking about that telephone call from the previous week, the one from Harry Cooke, and all the ridiculous drama that came after it. Harry had put his 'I'm-your-son's-principal-and-you-better-listen-to-me' voice to work—that was annoying enough. A stark contrast to the pathetic hinting that he'd like a turn to take her out. Perhaps since Marnie was married to his vice principal, Arnie Decker, for a brief stint, Harry figured a date was possible. He figured wrong. All that aside, on that dreadful call, he informed her the town duo of law enforcement, Constable Rusch and Detective Johnstone, were in his office, along with Matthew Mackenzie, her son. They were threatening to charge him with a felony offense.

Matthew was tall with oversized hands and feet for a thirteen-year-old. He still had a good four inches to grow if he was to be like his father, from whom he also inherited his mop of fiery red hair. His physique gave off mixed messages. A firm chin and neck suggested confidence, but slouchy shoulders begged otherwise. His eyes, one green, one blue, spelled trouble with the hope of honesty depending on which one you looked into. His recent practice of continuous fibbing and regular use of a sharpened tongue distressed Marnie. He had more energy than she could rein in, and he was far too easily influenced. That combination concerned Marnie, and his recent brush with drugs was justification enough.

He would turn fourteen in a few weeks. *Now that's something. I'll really be a mother of a teenager, no denying it now.* Matthew had fought her all of last year, claiming his independence as an official teen, but he lost on a technicality. *As far as I'm concerned, a teenager starts at fourteen, not thirteen.* Using her fingers to untangle her damp mid-length auburn hair, she chuckled, wishing she had argued it was seventeen instead. *I remember the day of your birth, my son, like it was yesterday. Overcooked you were with big ears!* A brief chuckle escaped before frustration returned. *But Matthew Sebastian, what do I do with you now?* Wrapped in her towel, she scurried back to her room before Matty woke and would come banging the bathroom door down with his fist.

By the time she tossed her towel into the heap of laundry on the bedroom floor, Marnie had switched emotional gears yet again.

She wanted to do something nice for Matty's birthday. *But what, what, what? We could really use a celebration, especially after yesterday.* Matt had fallen short and came in last at the regionals. So be it.

Marnie shook her head, as if that might shake her thoughts away. Using her fingers to separate the last tangles of thick hair, she exhaled. *What's next, Matty? Seriously, what's next?*

If only she knew.

CHAPTER FOUR
LIVIN' THE DREAM

MATT RUBBED HIS eyes with the back of his hand and cautiously perused his room. It was a small oblong-shaped bedroom, yet bigger than Karo's. The walls still a builder's beige— no one ever had time to apply fresh paint nor wallpaper. Some of Matt's crayon episodes were still visible and reminded him of his younger years, years when his dad was still alive. A tall single dresser sat beside a single closet door at the foot of his bed. The lamp on his bedside table was reachable if he slept on the lower bunk, which he never did. Fortunately, Matt didn't have to share this private space; he had that to be thankful for.

He awoke from a disturbingly deep and mindfully active sleep. *Am I awake?* His attempt to shake away the daze didn't work. *That was some dream, so freakin' real.*

The tail end of it echoed in his head. "All that matters," had been the reply from the tall, strong presence standing behind him. He hadn't even asked the question aloud, *What's all this?* Then Mr. Invisible's warm, heavy hand came to rest on his right shoulder. Matt actually *felt* it. The reprieve of the unity was salve to a wound he didn't know he had. And that voice—it penetrated a chord deep inside Matthew, the exact one which was suffering from a raw and chronic inflammation.

Matt leaned back and closed his eyes, urging his brain to recite more. He could picture it. A small, gleaming white door at the back of a long room that seemed to go on forever had opened. Even though a distance away, the details were incredibly vivid. The door frame was covered with ivy and speckled with tiny, perfect, white, aromatic blossoms. He could smell them, a delicious aroma. Matt was pretty sure one of the blossoms had winked at him. There were endless rows of perfectly spaced pedestals, each with an open book floating a few inches above it. Finished with padded gleaming white covers and pages edged with generous sparkles of gold, the books cautioned all things official. Tiny hummingbird-like creatures holding feathery instruments were writing furiously on the open pages, some faster than others and some resting and chatting.

A tiny man, a third of Matt's height though appearing a hundred times his age, rushed into the room, scurrying and waving his short little arms. "Enough, enough! We have work to do." The little man wanted Matthew out of the room and lickety-split.

It was a most profound dream. *Somebody's trying to tell me something. But what?*

Any other day, Matt would have jumped out of his upper bunk without thought and hardly awake. The thud of his fall purposely announced to the household that he was up, so clear the bathroom. This morning, though, he lay staring at his ceiling light. *All what matters?* He tried to catch more pieces of the mystery, but it quickly faded away.

The crescent moon light fixture on his ceiling glowed softly. *Mom must have switched on the light. I wonder when she did that?* It was the best gift he had received from both his mom and dad together. He was all of five years at the time and infatuated with the moon. Every gift he got had some type of lunar theme associated with it. Now he imagined his dad living somewhere up there, far beyond the moon, watching over him with some type of super-powered telescope. *Maybe you were the man standing behind me in my dream, Dad.* Matt wished it were so, but somehow, he knew it wasn't.

"Marnie!" he hollered loudly, getting no reply. *She hates it when I call her that.* "I know you're awake!"

He couldn't remember falling asleep with his track shorts and sweaty T-shirt still on. Then it all came flooding back. He had been so embarrassed that he skipped supper and went straight to bed.

Kicking off his blanket, he pulled off his crunchy Havensight knee-high sports socks and tossed them away as he maneuvered his legs over the bunk and wiggled his smelly toes. Before taking the leap, he thought again about his dream. He saw a secret room, he felt someone touch him, he smelled something delicious, he heard a distinguished voice. *Huh, so weird.*

Matt scratched his scalp as more of yesterday afternoon's events trickled into mind. *Doh. The Tri-Town regionals. I blew it. Of course you couldn't win, you idiot.* Scolding himself wasn't enough. He punished himself by yanking his hair above his ears, wishing he could pluck two fistfuls of it right off his head.

Yesterday had been the worst day in Matthew's history of school life, and he had no one to blame but himself. His shoulders slumped just thinking about what everyone would whisper today behind his back. Havensight Collegiate had taken the running long jump trophy in the Tri-Towns for juniors since 1966, seven years in a row. But not this year. This year they had to settle for ninth place. *Dead last. Thanks to me. Me and my big mouth. Why'd I have to go 'round telling everyone it was a bagger?*

He didn't have to explain what a bagger was, they all knew it well—a hands-down-for-sure thing. Matt had been jumping a consistent five feet, seven inches. He boasted his actual distance was an even six, and that would have been easy enough to take first. Secretly, he figured with practice, he'd easily gain enough extra inches in no time. Once the bets around the school got out of hand, there was no turning back. *Curse you, Josh, for taking wagers. Some friend.* But Matt blamed Emerson in particular, always flaunting his affluence. As if styling and having plans after school every day didn't present enough ways to show off, he was the one to drive up the bet value and blabber all over, like the entire universe needed to know.

Havensight was a community that, oddly enough, had attracted a half dozen successful entrepreneurs to the area. The hilly views of the winding Moon River north of town made perfect settings for large private estates. Close proximity to the regional airport meant fast and easy getaways. This kind of attraction led to another growing trend that the residents didn't like, particularly Matthew. Their kids—rich kids—attending the same school as him. They didn't belong.

Havensight was the only place he knew, although his mom told him they had moved to the sleepy town when he was three. From where, he had no idea. All Matt could remember was his dad watching, tracking, and measuring stars. Big-city scientists hired him to collect specific information on specific dates. With hardly much by way of artificial lighting, their location was perfect to observe groupings of stars given the nightfall gave way to idyllic deep darkness. The more observable the constellations were, the more jobs he'd get, and the more jobs he got, the happier Matt's mom was. What Matt liked best was when he and his parents shared a blanket in the deep dark of the night, so his dad could point out which stars he was studying from their yard. He spewed off measurement stuff and got excited about shifts and angles and historical movements. His work, he used to say, provided evidence about the truths of our existence.

His dad was proud of his work; the people of Havensight not so much. They thought him suspiciously strange and unconventional. That filtered into Matthew's school life, making it tough to fit in. Havensight was a town with families that made income from tourism and small businesses. They gossiped Monday through Friday, went to market on Saturday, and to church on Sunday. A family that paid their bills on account of the stars? Frank, Marnie, and Matthew Mackenzie may as well have been aliens themselves.

After some years, Matthew finally shed the forever hurtful "astro boy" label, thanks to nothing but the passing of simple time and the introduction of the "love child" label. He blamed his mom for that one, marrying and divorcing Arnie Decker inside a year and producing a baby sister, Karo, in record time. Why did it have to be him of all people? The high school's vice principal. Everybody in Havensight talked about it.

Matthew checked out the floor. He wasn't ready to jump off his bed, not just yet. *Not only will I be the biggest dunderhead at school, I owe serious dough. Josh and Nick can't pay up either.*

He reflected on the celebration he and his two buddies had shared just yesterday morning over the greatly anticipated "bagger windfall."

I let this happen.

He had been so successful at convincing Josh and Nick that he could jump the distance needed to keep the trophy that he came to believe it himself. After he won, he would bike to Hurley's Sports and buy that catcher's mitt he'd been eying. Nick yoo-hooed the plan and said he'd come along and get one too. The pair of them would have something exciting to do after school, figuring out who could throw the farthest. As for Josh, he tossed his options around secretly in his head, but whatever it was he wanted to get with the betting money, he was excited too. Now their much-chatted-about spending spree was squashed. And never mind that, fessing up to his bragging would be unthinkable. *They'll figure it out. I know it, they'll figure out I lied. What am I gonna say? Bugger off, I had a bad day? Bogus, they're not gonna buy that. How will I pay up? Borrow money from Mom? Yeah, right. I have no way to pay her back.*

Debating the grim consequences, he leaned closer to the edge. He slipped off and crashed with a heavy thud.

"Bogus," he yelped.

Matt was on the floor, feeling foolish and even more depressed, pampering the elbow that broke his fall. "I'm a doofus!" he shouted. He heard his mother's footsteps rushing up the stairs, obviously in response to the noise of his fall. "I'm okay," he shouted. "Just leave me alone."

He scratched his head and patted down the two patches of yanked hair. *I need to figure this out for myself.* He pondered while rubbing his gut. A burning sensation churned in the pit of his stomach. *Should I scoff it? Yeah. Yeah, that's my ticket out.* At that, Matt's no-nonsense attitude took over. Regrettably, he decided on the only way out of this mess. In no way would he fess up to his deceitful brag. And as for the betting money, he would snatch the funds from his mother's wallet.

"My life totally sucks!" he yelped, as if the universe needed to know that too.

CHAPTER FIVE
YOU DON'T GET ME

BREAKFAST STARTED OUT with nothing but quibbles in the Decker-Mackenzie household that morning. Marnie was not impressed with Matt's grumpiness. "There's no reason to taunt Karo. Leave her alone, you know better."

"She bugs me with her baby talk and her stupid blanket. What four-year-old kid walks around with a blanket, Marnie? And you don't say anything." Matt twisted a full stretch of his torso and groaned miserably. His back was still aching from the fall off his bunk. *You let her do whatever she wants. Makes me wanna puke.*

"I'm tired of this, Matt. Seriously. I hardly said anything about your... your... foolish choice last week." She had said it so casually with her back toward both of her children while fetching milk from the fridge. She was obviously conscious of Karo's big ears.

He knew his mom was referring to the doobie incident. Matt had sworn it was his first time. He wanted to test it out, so to speak. That's all. *Why do you have to bring that up again?*

"I said nothing either, when you gave your three-piece graduation suit away two months ago," she added. "Yeah, the one I could barely afford." She slammed the milk jug on the table, startling Karo.

Gaugh, she's on another rant. I wanted some money. How else do you expect me to get it?

Still annoyed, she continued to release, this time staring at him with her hands firmly planted on each hip and her upper body bent forward as if he might not figure she was talking to him. "And as far as yesterday goes, have I said a word about your boasting? Yeah, don't think I didn't hear you. You deserved to place last yesterday."

The scolding words pierced Matt like a dagger. *That does it.* Matt tossed his spoon into his still-empty cereal bowl, appeased with the clatter. He felt hurt and betrayed. Breathing in deeply to subdue the choke in his throat, he decided anger would be better than tears. He narrowed his eyes and gave a stealthy stare. This time he held his lips tight, careful to not show his clenched teeth. After all, she was his mom.

"Even you? I didn't expect *you* to be like that!" He slammed his chair onto the floor and then stomped out of the kitchen. His dramatic exit enabled the tears he couldn't control to go unnoticed. The monstrous, shadowy pain he knew so well but couldn't describe clothed him again. He braced himself in the front hallway, hidden with his back pushed hard against the wall, fists clenched. He needed to get a grip, pull it together.

"And it's *Mom* to you!" she called out, finishing the argument.

Karo sat still while digesting the scene. "Mom," she said, taking advantage of the moment, "I promise not to do that to you."

"Do what?"

"Be like that," she twitched her nose.

"Like what?" For four years of age, Karo sure knew how to be sly on the competitive front with her one and only sibling. Marnie wondered more than just a few times where that skill came from.

"You know. Say things and do things to get you mad and stuff."

"Thank you, honey."

Matt's chin quivered and his chest heaved. It took all his strength to keep from falling forward into a collapse. *Karo's the stupid love child. And Mom, you'll always be Marnie to me. You don't get me.*

CHAPTER SIX
SANDBAGGED

THE DRIVE TO school was tense and quiet. Matt stared at the window, studying his reflection and debating silently whether he liked what he saw. Karo sat in the back, peeking into her satchel, ensuring her blanket was tucked inside.

"Have a nice day, sweetie," Marnie said as she kissed Karo on the cheek in return for a big "I love you" hug before she ran through the carefully guarded gate of Havensight's Little Ones Day Care.

"Mom." Matt was seeking a truce. He'd already packaged up the morning's hurt.

She glanced at him before putting the car back into drive.

"Can I drive the rest of the way?" he teased, more so to lift his own mood.

With a roll of her eyes, Marnie pulled out onto the road. "Right. Of course you can, dear," she said sarcastically.

A good thing going for Matt was his mom's roller-coaster moods. When she got all huffy, detonating and being all accusing like, she could cool down even faster. Matt reveled in this.

He grinned. It was his best way to poke at his mom's demeanor. Matt wished he was sixteen already, thinking that might solve his issues, being more independent and older. Then he could quit school, drive a car, and even leave town.

The tension dissipated. His joking and grinning successfully lightened the mood, only to be replaced with empathy. Hers for him.

He could play that.

"I feel bad, Mom," he said as they drove into the student drop-off lot. "Today isn't going to be fun. I don't want to go into that building today."

"Face yourself first *and then* face your friends. If they are genuine friends, there will be no problems. You can sort this out." She gave him a warm, encouraging smile, which told him that no matter what he did, or how he behaved, she would always be there to pick him up. Even if she was rock'n mad.

He examined her face, now soft and sincere. Could their relationship ever return to a loving and blind trust? *If you only knew.* Matt had pushed the envelope too far on this one. *Emerson has reason now to have me pounded out. He's been waiting for this.* He thanked his mom. Usually he didn't allow kisses or hugs in the student lot, but this time Matt reached over and hugged his mom. "I'm sorry," he whispered, and he meant it.

He had caught her off guard.

"Honey, it's okay. You lost the jump. There are more important things in life. Look, you *can* get through this, and you will."

He wondered if he really would get through this. His instincts were jarring his soul, warning him otherwise. Matt powerlessly witnessed his hands twisting around each other on his lap, yanking his fingers from his palms. He imprisoned his emotions, particularly the guilt to steal from her. He wished she knew about everything—the taunting at school, the debt because of the previous day's disaster, and most of all, the deep monstrous sea he'd been drowning in since the day his dad died. But she didn't. Matt drew a deep breath and then got out and headed toward the school's side door, the closest to the locker he shared with a guy from homeroom.

Phil, a tall fellow with considerable extra poundage, was mostly quiet. He not only looked as though he preferred to stay out of the limelight, he usually went out of his way to avoid it.

"You gotta get out of here, man," Phil hissed with quiet but determined urgency as Matt approached his locker. Phil's eyes spelled out fear. If that wasn't signal enough, his tight neck muscles arched toward someone down the hall got the message across. Phil shut the locker door as if to scream "Now!" and then hurried down the hallway in the opposite direction. Matt watched Phil disappear while Nick and Josh came toward him with the same sense of urgency.

"Emerson recruited the thugs. No guff. He's callin' you phony and lookin' for a beat-down," Nick warned.

"You're finished, man. They're telling everyone *we're all* finished, Matt!" Josh shoved Matt's shoulder into the lockers. Nick put his arm between the two to stop the friends from getting physical.

"Freak me out, man. I didn't do anything. I jumped, and I didn't make it. Big deal." Matt turned his back on his buddies as if that would make the issue disappear. "He's just a doofus, anyway."

Opening his locker, he reached for his books on the second shelf and started sorting through them as if to concentrate on his morning schedule to see what classes were on tap. Josh forced Matt around and stepped close, so they were toe to toe, Matt's back against the locker.

Nick sighed. No sense intervening right now.

Ensuring the hallway was devoid of teachers, Josh scanned each direction before furthering his message.

"Chill, I'll come up with the dough," Matt said, holding tight to his position. "For all of us."

"You lied."

"I didn't make it. Big freakin' deal."

Matt could smell the cigarette stink from Josh's index finger in his face, which was totally gross.

"You couldn't do six, and you knew it. Emerson's right. You freakin' lied."

As Josh's face got even closer, Matt could smell the peanut butter Josh must have had for breakfast.

"You lied to *us.*"

Point made.

"Oh, go choke on your toast," Matt taunted.

"Cut it, man." Nick was always the peacekeeper, the referee, the, "Hey, let's just move on" kind of guy. Without Nick, Josh and Matt would have parted ways long ago. "Seriously, Matt. You gotta scram. Like, nowsville." Then he pressed a directive to Josh. "Chill. We'll figure it out."

Josh balked at first. He had a hot temper, but he cooled just as quickly. "Yeah, blow it, get outta here. Make like you're sick or somethin'. Stay home and chill till things cool down. We'll cover for you, but you're still a cheese weasel."

Stay home till things cool down? How long will that take? Matt didn't have to pretend he felt sick. He could produce vomit on cue—in fact, that might provide some relief from the burning pit feeling in his gut. A call to his mom from a teacher claiming he had the flu and should stay home for a few days could save the day, at least buy him some time.

The five-minute warning bell rang. Students scrambled to get to class. Josh and Nick left Matt at his locker, mouthing "scram" and pointing to the side door.

Matt hadn't wanted to bet any more than a five-spot, but Emerson spat a dare. A Benjamin. Nothing more, nothing less. Doofus Josh agreed, not even knowing what a Benjamin was. *Mom's not even gonna have that kind of dough in her purse. First things first. I better get outta here before I'm face-to-face with Emerson and his hideous gang. Emerson—it's not even a tough name. He's the phony. But his hired thugs sure aren't. They're all truck.*

Matt decided he would go out the side door and hoped no one

would see his urgent stroll through the parking lot. He would tell Marnie he wasn't feeling well. *Well, bogus, she'll know. She won't believe me. She'll think I don't want to face up. But facing up to Emerson will be worse than dealing with Mom.*

"I'm sorry, Mom. I really am," Matt whispered into the universe.

Across the parking lot, Matt already felt some freedom from his dilemma. It was a half-decent strategy, definitely worth a try. *Stay at home, lay low for a few days. This might just all blow over, up and away like.*

Dad. He searched the sky. Only a few clouds, no need to find an opening. *Can you make all this go away? I don't want to steal from Mom. I don't want to be like that. Help me out, would ya?* Matt imagined his dad giving an approving wink.

Feeling better than he had all morning, he sped up into a run and headed toward the rotten, collapsed picnic table at the end of the schoolyard. His pace got faster and faster, propelled by a sense of renewal. *Yes, this will go away, and I'll be a better person.* He felt a sudden urge of confidence and freedom. *I'm gonna clear you clean, you rickety old wooden jalopy!* Matt built up his run to top speed. *Two more steps...* Matt loved speed, and there was no better or more exhilarating way to do something with speed than to push off into the air with the force of his own body. He threw himself upward. *Yes!*

Thankfully, he had angled his body properly, just like he had trained. He made good height. And when he felt good height, he knew distance would happen.

Matt kept his feet in motion, running wildly through the air. He savored that brief feeling of an eagle in flight. He swept his arms forward and bent his knees, readying his body for the impact. *Made it!*

"Yes!" he cried. The jump felt great and solidified a boost of confidence.

But the fresh, invigorating rush ended abruptly. Before he sprang back to a solid stand, Matt collapsed because of a sharp, heavy-handed chopping pain in the middle of his back. His breath escaped him. *What gives? Was I just kicked?*

A bolt of pain jolted from his middle back up to his left jawbone.

Freakin' what? Another kick?

Matt was flat on the ground, thankful for the wood chips that cushioned his right cheek. Matt spat some dirt and chips from his mouth and focused on his breathing. Albeit blurred, he could make out a pair of steel-toed cowboy boots with two-inch heels standing inches from his face. He buried his face in the wood chips like a scared chipmunk, protecting it from what might come next, a straight-on face kick.

"Bugger off," he muttered. His heart was racing. He knew exactly what was happening. *Emerson, what a chicken. He has to pay a bunch of thugs to kick me around.*

Someone wrenched Matt's arms behind his back, so his wrists met and were tightly held with a pair of rough hands. Another body sat on his back. That heeled boot pressed Matt's head deeper into the dirt. *Freak me out, there's gotta be at least three of 'em.* The boot pressed harder. Panicked, Matt couldn't breathe. He struggled to turn his face sideways to get some air. He gagged and choked, struggling to loosen and spit out a mouthful of wood chips. His head ached, and the ground spun out of control. *Am I still down?*

Matt could barely make out the few words being thrown at him in rhythm with the pressure of the boot. "Nice jump, John Boy. Yer last." The heavy weight on his back lightened up as his wrists were pulled, yanking his shoulder blades up.

Uumph. Matt felt the weight of a body jumping hard on his back. His ribs felt like they split, pushing vomit up his throat. His head forcefully pushed and held again, face down.

"What's the matter, sandbagger?" another voice taunted. "Can't jump now?"

Matt could no longer hear their words, nor did he care what they said. He panicked and wriggled in his struggle to breathe. *Help, please.* His head was hot, and his ears felt like a tire that was about to blow. His screams were silent. He kicked wildly, producing some relief, but only for a fraction of a second. Two thugs picked Matt up, each holding him by his armpits. Matt gasped an inhale and for a moment eyeballed upward. *Dad, help me.* The guy with the boots kicked Matthew in the gut. Then again. And then once more. The other two released his arms. Matthew collapsed, receiving one last kick to the back of his head.

Matt's surroundings were spinning at an accelerating rate, his head throbbing. The light of day in his eyes dimmed till everything was black except for tiny lights that swirled like delicate sparkling stars. Then even they disappeared. His last thought was of an open gold-rimmed book with wings in a long, white room that had to be out of this world. *Seriously? What did that mean?*

Matt's body lay crooked, limp, and lifeless as the three thugs ran off toward the school building to sit in class as if nothing had happened, as if they had done no harm.

CHAPTER SEVEN
UP AND AWAY

"HEY, MATTY BOY, come on, get up. Let's get outta here!" A stranger stuck his oval boyish face into Matt's. His teeth, eerily perfect, only oversized, glistened when they caught the sun. "Here," he demanded, offering a firm hand. "Get up, I said."

Matt's mind was blank. He swiveled his head about. Instinctively, he applied pressure to his biceps, but neither would contract. He watched curiously as his right arm extended with such obedience to accept this kid's help while his left arm leaned on his right knee for added stability. *Geez, I'm separating.* Matt focused his brain on instructing his bones and flesh to move, but they wouldn't obey. All while a ghostly Matt leaped up with a spring-load of energy and peered around. *Freedom, oh this feels good.* The air was fresh, and his head didn't ache. He swished his mouth and gargled. *Nope, no dirt. Amazing. Quite amazing, actually! And what timing, I thought I was dying.* Matt turned his focus to the kid. *Kind of short and definitely disproportioned. Ugly,* he concluded.

"Yeah? So are you!" The kid's voice had an annoying pitch, like a whiny hydro wire. Matt didn't think he vocally announced his assessment. *Hmm... my lips didn't move. The kid must have super powers. Either that or he just read my face. That's likely it; he read my face. Karo does it all the time.* Matt reflected a moment, certain he hadn't spoken out loud.

"Look, do you want my help or not? Check around, Matty Boy. No one else is here to help you. You should be kissing my arse right now. A simple thanks and getting a move on will do."

Though disgusted at the gross suggestion, he ignored the insulting "Matty Boy" nickname—for the moment. "How d'ya even know my name?"

"We *all* know *you.*" The kid drew close to Matt, positioning himself so their eyes were level and just inches apart.

Matt eyeballed the kid's feet. *Yup, he's in midair. How else could this four-foot creepy-lookin' nerd look me in the eye?*

Matt checked out the lumpy hump of a body lying on the ground, flat-out and facedown with crumpled legs. The guy's hands just laid there, palms up and purple. Matt recognized the sunny-faced boxers sticking out of the Levi jeans. "Huh," he mused. "I have a pair of those."

It took a moment for the stunning acceptance to hit him. "I'm here. I'm fine. And I'm there, on the ground." Matt zeroed in for a closer examination. "Those jerks," he reveled in a proclamation. "They beat the crap out of me. Literally!"

"All depends how you see it," the kid egged Matt to size it up differently. "I'd say, rather, they beat *you* out of that heap of crap."

"And who are you exactly?"

"Who do you think I am? I'm here to pick you up. See? No one else is coming."

Though suspicious, Matt accepted the challenge. Everything was normal and different at the same time. A red Volvo drove past them and turned into the school parking lot. The school flag flapped in the wind. Curious birds chirped in the trees nearby. Nothing odd or even alarming, except perhaps for a flock of cawing crows. Matt was resigned to the obvious—he was dead. What amazed him the most, despite the absurdity of it all, was that he was not much alarmed. Not yet anyway, the news hadn't really sunk in.

He turned to the kid. "Got a name? And shouldn't there be a light or a tunnel or something?"

"Kasartha. No, I'm it. And we gotta go."

Matt had a fleeting thought. *Mom.* Oh, man, he couldn't leave her. *Dad's death nearly broke her. I'm all she's got. I'm the man in the house. No, I can't leave her.*

Matt narrowed his eyes at the kid with the odd-shaped head and oversized teeth. "I'm not going with you. I'm staying here." He hadn't given a great deal of thought to what happened upon the moment of death, but this wasn't what he expected.

Kasartha's jaw dropped, and his face turned a pale greenish color.

Oooooh, even uglier now. The whole transition thing intrigued Matthew. *Who is this guy, and why is he so panicked? I'm the one who should be freakin' out.*

Kasartha sighed, then took off his hat and patted down the few strands of hair on his head. He folded his arms together and forced himself into a whirlwind of color and light. Voila! His looks changed completely.

Matt watched with intense interest. Kasartha now stood the same height as Matthew. His teeth and hair were better than perfect. His eyes sparkled, and his mannerisms became gentle. "Matt, we really need to go. I have so much to show you. I want to share the beauty of the universe with you. And I promise to bring you back here...to this." He pointed at Matt's crumpled body.

Oh, so I'm not dead?

Without waiting for permission, Kasartha grabbed Matt's elbow. The pair rose, defying gravity, high above the school.

Shocked with the feather-lightness of his body and how freely he maneuvered, an initial tinge of fear turned to utter glee in no time. *I'm flying! So rad.*

"This is freakin' awesome!" Matt could barely contain his excitement. "Totally, totally cool." *Way better than jumping and catching a brief second midair.*

Matt saw the milk bus leaving from the school cafeteria's back doors and behind it the quiet schoolyard, everyone inside and no one running toward his lifeless body. *Huh, who cares? I don't.* Matt was too enthralled with his flying experience to worry about that package of bruised flesh attached to cracked bone matter all tucked neatly into the new pants his mom had just bought him, and his favorite T-shirt, now ruined with grounded in dirt. That made him think of his mom again. *Bogus. She's gonna worry.*

"I need to at least tell my mom I'm going," he hollered up to Kasartha, who was leading the way, taking Matthew higher and higher.

Kasartha's response was simple and firm. "No, you don't."

This is strange, Matthew thought as an odd sort of peace increasingly surrounded him the higher they went. He could see much of Havensight now—the town hall and the perfectly squared-off blocks around it hosting two churches, one on each side. Also in the same area was Mariam's Grocers, the Lavender Fields Café, Hurley's Sporting Goods, the movie theater, and several other businesses, one where his mom would be working, totally unaware of his whereabouts. The entire town sat one long block south of his school with several streets of modest residential housing. Mostly all of the rooftops were grey and from this height, he also noticed only a couple roads had cement sidewalks.

Matthew looked westward. *Wait, where's my house?* His eyes followed the highway, leaving the town's edge, past the field of wheat, past the three miles of lavender fields, and there it was. Warmud Street. Like an orphaned community, a single row of houses built on a narrow parcel of land between the highway and the edge of the forest. His yard was easy to spot, thanks to sheets waving from the clothesline next to it.

His eyes followed the highway even farther. He saw the lake and its gentle waves lapping against the shore. He had spent ample time on that long stretch of pebbly beach. It was the reason his community had become such a draw for campers. Although the town's advertisements pitched the aromatic air from the lavender fields as the attracting differential, the real reason was its unbeatable reputation for optimal stargazing.

For the first time, Matthew could see and appreciate the beauty of it all, a quaint community nestled alongside the winding Moon River that served as the town's border.

The thought of Karo distracted his focus. Matthew strained to find her day care, but he couldn't place it. He watched everything get tinier and tinier until what lay far below him was nothing short of a stunning crescent view of Earth.

CHAPTER EIGHT
EMERGENCY ROOM LONELINESS

THE WAY MARNIE felt emotionally was pretty much the same as how Matt's body lay physically—stock still. She breathed in and out with the same painfully slow rhythm as if that could make her one with her son, whispering a count for each breath. When she reached twenty, she'd wipe away a tear, take an especially deep breath, and then start again at zero. Intravenous tubes dripped. A heart monitor beeped. A blood pressure machine puffed up regularly. The clock ticked. Her mind kept a pace that her heart struggled to match. So she kept counting.

Harry Cooke had called her at work. It was just before ten a.m. He said a young man was found lying at the edge of the schoolyard and that Arnie believed it might be Matthew. "Could you meet me at emerg?" he had asked.

It seemed impossible. *I dropped him off at school just outside the front door. Why didn't they notice he wasn't in class? Why didn't I get a call earlier—like right after the attendance check? Did I misunderstand? Was he trying to tell me something in the car? Did I ignore his plea for help? Why didn't I ask more questions? Oh, Matty, what did you do? Who would want to beat you like this? Why didn't somebody—anybody—stop it? He can't possibly die... can he? Might he?*

Does he know I'm here beside him? Why didn't Arnie call me himself? Talk about chicken. Would his god do this to me—take my son? Really? C'mon. Man, you took Frank, and now you want my son? What about Karo? What do I tell her? Oh, gosh, what about Karo? Who will pick her up from school? Darn, I'll have to call Arnie. There's no way I'm leaving my son's bedside.

Marnie squeezed her eyes shut, still counting. She felt the wetness seep through the outer corners. The sounds of the hospital room were too surreal and hauntingly familiar. *Why couldn't Frank be here? Oh, God, why?*

A brief flashback took her to Frank's bedside. In his final weeks, he suffered terribly. Stuck in a room at the end of the hall in this very building. She shuddered at the memories. Doctors would hardly visit the terminally ill when there was no longer any hope. So, Marnie had taken on as many of the nursing functions as she could figure out. She stayed with him the entire time when visitors weren't restricted. Plus, the head nurse allowed her to arrive early and stay late, for which she was thankful. Home care was a new concept then and hadn't gained the required trust yet in Havensight. *Much has changed in just a few years.*

Marnie watched as a nurse entered to give her son a pain injection despite his unconscious state. *And much is still the same.*

An overbearing wave of emotion swept over Marnie, pulling her down into the warm, embracing waters of a comfortable sadness. She remembered too well the desperation for sleep, for healing, for answers to her prayers, for relief from Frank's pain. Striving to avoid those waters, she dove deeper, moving from lonely desolation into a freezing surge of anger—reminders of the miracle she thought possible for Frank and the anger when it didn't happen.

The head emergency nurse interrupted her thoughts with a gentle touch to the elbow. "Mrs. Mackenzie, this is Alan Pine, our chaplain. Alan's going to take you to our family room down the hall. Dr. Bonneville and Dr. Alexien would like to talk to you."

It was a long stream of words. *What? Okay. I don't want to go, but okay.* She cleared her throat but did not speak as she silently followed the threesome.

She felt like she was being escorted to prison, but instead the room had two loveseat-sized couches and two armchairs, all with miniature color-coordinated cushions. A pint-sized fridge with a brand new Mr. Coffee machine atop it sat adjacent to a plain bookshelf that was sparsely filled, mostly with various leaflets. A large painting of a red dirt walkway through a path of evergreen trees leading to a waterfront hung on one wall. Across from it hung a large photograph of a decorative iron gate. It was open and led into a courtyard full of potted greenery shimmering in brilliant sunbeams. Marnie could see "Madrid" followed by something else written at the bottom. *Yup, Spain is beautiful.* She had never had the luxury of travel herself, but she loved to peek at the travel magazines piled neatly in the lobby of her office. And the red dirt road, well, that was a dead giveaway. She knew that had to be somewhere in Prince Edward Island, Canada. *Are they travel agents on the side?* she mused sarcastically. She knew full well the artwork was intended to bring comfort should someone's loved one "move on," so to speak. *Well, Matthew's not going anywhere and certainly not through any gate. No business for you; not this time!*

A crocheted dove with an olive branch, likely crafted by a local church widow, hung behind the Mr. Coffee machine. It was more than just a bit worn. *And priests still subtly hanging their business cards too. Whaddaya know?*

Propped off to the side was a bucket on wheels hosting a rope mop in a shallow pool of grey water. *Well, that's smart.* Marnie chuckled inwardly. *They're already getting ready to clean the floor after wives and mothers like me puke, which will be right after they give me bad news, which will be right after they offer me a coffee from their stupid new fancy machine.* It was the same room where doctors had used the dreaded two words, "death" and "imminent," nearly six years prior. *Has it really been that long?* Marnie chose her spot, sat down, and daggered straight into the faces of the two doctors, one at a time. *Hurry up. Spell it out.* Her muscles held her gut tight against the inside of her rib cage. She knew she appeared angry, but she didn't care. Right now, who else did she have to blame?

After sitting on the opposite couch, Dr. Bonneville spoke first. "Mrs. Mackenzie—may I call you Marnie?"

She nodded nonchalantly, cherishing her guard of anger.

"Marnie, Matt took a few stresses to his body this morning. Two blows for sure. I presume they were blows or kicks of some manner. They are causing him some physical grief. On their own..."

Marnie felt a throbbing in her brain. *Blows... kicks... were things so bad because of other boys. Why would they be so cruel? What was so important they had to beat my son? Am I jumping to conclusions? Maybe they weren't kids. A random violent act from strange adults? That would be worse. Focus!* she scolded herself. She fought back the tears, but they still slipped down onto her cheekbones.

"... it appears he was kicked or punched hard in the stomach, and this caused..." Dr. Bonneville continued to give his diagnosis of the damage caused to Matt's organs. Marnie's thumb and forefinger were above the bridge of her nose, keeping her head from falling into her lap. She visualized her son hurtling onto the ground in pain. "And the other blow we are even more concerned about..."

Marnie sat up tall again. She had to be strong. *Crap. Come on, world, what gives?*

Dr. Bonneville paused. He needed to give her the state of the situation. Alan sat a little closer to Marnie and put his arm around her shoulder. "Can I get you some water?" he asked.

"No!" she said. Alan's arm dropped away as Marnie took a deep breath and regained some strength. Dr. Bonneville nodded to Dr. Alexien, and she took the reins.

Chicken, Marnie mused. *Leave it to the she-doctor to deliver the hard news with nice, soft blows. What, you don't think it'll hurt as much?*

"Marnie, this must be very difficult for you. Your principal, err, Harry Cooke, mentioned your sister was on her way to be with you when he left this morning. Will she be here soon? Mrs. Mackenzie?"

"No." Marnie had lied. Harry did not want to leave Marnie on her own at the hospital. Marnie urged him to go, to get back to his precious boy-beating school, saying her sister was coming. Marnie didn't have a sister. Or a brother or parents or a husband who wasn't dead or estranged. There was no one to call.

Alan nodded at the two doctors, then at Marnie, hoping to provide some comfort.

"I've got all day, Marnie. I'll stay with you and help you get through this. You can take some time and let me know if there's anyone you would like me to contact. I'm sorry about Matthew's father. I know you lost him just six years ago."

"It's not six yet," Marnie corrected without lifting her head.

"Pardon?"

"Five years ago. And change."

Alan blanched as if he felt this slight lack of accuracy was akin to tossing salt into an open flesh wound.

Dr. Bonneville leaned forward. "Marnie, we've placed Matthew into a medically induced coma. This will allow the swelling in his organs to subside and will enable his body to heal. He is in critical condition and it's possible that, well, you have my word we will do everything we can to keep him resting in a state where he can heal and get through this. Do you have any questions?"

Marnie knew she would have questions, but she did not have any right away. At least he didn't say "imminent" or "death."

"No," she muttered.

As Dr. Bonneville headed toward the door, Dr. Alexien clasped

Marnie's hands. "I've seen a lot, and I mean it. I have. You should know I've seen miracles. Beautiful, unexplainable miracles happen. So, please, Marnie, don't give up hope. Keep your faith."

Marnie couldn't help but like the brightness in the woman's face, but the word "miracle" only made her tense. "Thank you," Marnie replied tersely. Plus, she couldn't help but notice Dr. Bonneville watching from the doorway, frowning directly at Dr. Alexien as though he didn't approve of her hope-filled conveyance.

"How long have you worked here?" Marnie asked her.

"Oh, I just arrived this morning, temporary assignment. Doing some training. And perfect timing too, I'm so glad to meet you."

Oh, how convenient my son's beating is to your training, Marnie mused sarcastically.

Alan tried one more time. "Can I make you a cup of coffee, Marnie?"

"No," she replied adamantly. It was a good thing he couldn't hear her thoughts. *And go float.*

CHAPTER NINE
BOYS A' GALLIVANTING

Somewhere in the Cosmos

THE BOYS WERE moving fast. If it wasn't for the tattling streaks of trailing lights that Matt figured were stars, he could have easily believed they were floating in one spot. Were they gone for seconds, hours, or even longer? He couldn't tell, and it didn't really matter. Somewhere, somehow, he lost his sense of what's normal and exchanged it for something grander, something larger than life. He kept his eyes pinned to the inspiring round planet beneath his feet. He had never experienced such beauty and awe, so blue and green and now so very far away. The living ball grew smaller and smaller.

Dad, did you see this too? This is why you loved ogling the sky so much—I get it now. Can you see me? Watch. I bet I'm moving at light speed. You always said that would be so cool. Whooo it is!

He didn't dare let go of his guide, this kid whose image had already transformed back to ugly. Matt's hands remained clamped around Kasartha's right ankle.

"Hold on," Kasartha yelled.

Does he think I'm stupid enough to let go? Their flight became jerky as their pace slowed. Kasartha ducked and swayed to dodge thick clouds of dust. Matt instinctively did the same. He checked out Kasartha's expression between the pockets of dust, perhaps it might hint as to whether he should be frightened or gleeful for the adventure. "What the… What's happening?"

"I wanna show you something." Kasartha found a slight wave of pressurized gases and leaned into it. "Make like you're body surfing," he instructed.

Body surfing? Like I'm not already on the edge of my comfort zone. Matt was the athletic type; he was even close to earning his lifeguard level swimming badge. But the waves at Havensight's trailer camp beach never amounted to anything big enough to draw surfers of any type.

"Okay," he hollered back. He would have to fake it.

He watched Kasartha open his arms and relax into the invisible current. Matt also leaned in, relaxing his body so the two were like a single mass. He also loosened his grip around Kasartha's ankles and kicked his legs mechanically to help propel them toward another land.

Nothing for miles but shadows of silver and peppery greys. *Blimey.* Matthew held his breath as they glided across the surface, passing over a large, circular pit. Beyond the pit lay what appeared to be punched-down sandcastles, shellacked to retain a shameful look of destruction. Kasartha pointed ahead to a flat area, and the boys steered toward it.

Freakin, watch out, man. We're gonna crash! Matt watched Kasartha tuck his head and arch his back, and he assumed the same crash position. Both boys did somersaults and landed several meters apart on their backs. Kasartha laughed. After catching his breath, Matthew did the same, his eyes wide as he took in his new environs. That was when he realized they had landed on the moon.

Kasartha insisted this sightseeing stop was necessary, confiding that it was his personal favorite. They sat hugging their knees, tucked aside a rocky formation and watching a reddish orange glow off in the distance where the black horizon bordered the light side. Quite a show.

Matt wanted to pinch himself. *If only Dad could be here, just him and me with his telescope, he would flip out with excitement. All those stars he wrote and calculated stuff about, they're just as far away from here as they were from our yard.*

Matt reveled in a peace-filled triangular link, just he, his dad and this feeling of wonder. No surprise that he would return Kasartha's interruption with an angry face, teeth clenched and a glare stern enough to shrink Kasartha's ugly, protruding eyeballs. Literally.

"You traverse throughout the universe and see what that does to *your* body!" Kasartha scolded.

"Sensitive or what?" Matt was still suspicious that the guy could read his mind. *Do I truly read like a book cover, as Mom says?*

He turned his attention back to the solar system that now lay before him. The green, brown, and blue sphere peeked through whispers of stratus clouds. *Wow, can't believe just this morning that's where I was. That's where I live.* A haze of dark midnight blue, vast and endless, spread across the universe to Matt's left. Well-defined crescent-shaped glows of light outlined spheres lined in a jagged row, diminishing to mere specs eons away. To his right was a warm brilliance Matt feared to tend, though he enjoyed how it contributed to the view.

A sudden urge struck Matt. He jumped up and hollered, "I'm on the moon!" He screamed louder and louder. "Woohoo. Woo-hoo-hooooooooo!"

This got a laugh out of Kasartha. He jumped up and grabbed Matt's elbow "Waaahooooey" he shouted, joining in. After a bit of boyish hootenanny, the pair laughed uncontrollably until Matt settled into a concerned silence.

"Rad. Am I really… I mean, I don't feel like I'm… What I mean is… This…" He stretched his arms wide. "This is impossible!"

Kasartha grinned approvingly. He was enjoying Matt's company, something not totally unexpected. He had been watching and following Matt for several years now, planting seeds and urging transitions, particularly to boost Matt's ego and employing his anger to *harden 'im off*, as he termed it. So Kasartha knew Matt well, and he liked him. In fact, he was fond of him. Matt couldn't have known he reminded Kasartha of himself, that is, a wishful version from long ago.

Feeling uncomfortable with the long glances Kasartha was sending his way, Matt challenged him. "So what are you gawking at? Got something to say?" Kasartha did not respond, so Matt continued probing. "Why the rush to get up here? What happens now?"

"Don't be such a pill. You know I could leave you behind. Just take off and leave you here." It didn't matter if Matt's attitude resulted from Kasartha's fine work, he wasn't going to put up with it on a toe-to-toe basis. "Besides, I'm the one who made you what you are. I shaped you. You owe me."

What am I? This kid's talking gibberish. Matt's thoughts urgently reverted to his crumpled body, lying on the edge of the school grounds. *That's what I am.* He thought about his family, all two of them, and his friends, also just two of them, with one being just a sort of. What were they doing right now? They should soon wonder where he was. Would they find his body? *Seriously, Mom can't see me like that.*

"I need to get back. You said you would bring me back, so let's go now. I've seen enough." Matt actually hadn't seen enough, but he was now speaking from a place of fear and anxiety. He was in a vulnerable spot, trusting this weird guy. *What if he does leave me here?*

While Matt became increasingly obstinate and frustrated, Kasartha sat comfortably with his arms wrapped around his knees, responding with a slow, steady shaking of his head. "Nope. Not yet."

Matt stuck his chest out in his best bully stance.

"What are you gonna do, jump? Go for it, Bagger Boy." Kasartha enjoyed taunting Matthew. He particularly enjoyed watching him drop his body into a sulking position. "Over there's a crater. Jump that one." Kasartha continued.

Matthew cupped his ears. Bagger Boy. That would be his new nickname. *Ughhh. Guess it's better than "love child." Shoulda stuck with "astro boy". At least that one keeps you around, Dad.* His hands reached for the top of his head. *Do I really want to go back?*

Matt speared a scowl Kasartha's way. *This turkey needs to be put in his place.* With the lightweight feeling from the differing gravity, the stillness of the air, and the anger building in his body, Matt concluded he could do it. *I can if I want to.* He sized up the crater, calculating the distance in his mind. *Pretty sure I'd get more height here.*

"Enough." Kasartha stood up and stretched, ready to move. "Time to go."

Matt clenched his fists. "You think I can't do it!"

"Yeah, yeah, yeah. Blah, blah, blah. I know you can't. Don't matter. Come on, let's go." Kasartha assumed the position for flight mode.

Bogus. "You're wrong." As Kasartha leaped, Matt took a giant running step toward him and grabbed his ankles for dear life. Away they went, Matt sulking.

"Enough sightseeing," Kasartha announced as they headed toward a gassy hot stream that would lead the pair outside the galaxy and farther away from Matthew's home, the little town of Havensight on the miniscule sphere called Earth.

It felt like they'd been flying for hours. Matt's head felt dizzy and ready to explode. He tightened his grasp whenever they became engulfed in enormous waves of hot air. The blasts of heat arrived like clockwork, challenging his sweaty grip on Kasartha's bony shin. He was sure they were still winding their way upward on some kind of circular trajectory. *This guy obviously knows where he's going. He's been on this path before. But where does it lead? And why me? Why did he kidnap me? I'm clearly not dead, or am I?*

Kasartha pointed whenever a rock came hurtling toward them, instructing Matt to duck, twist, or dive. Matt had little chance to breathe in the fantastical beauty, all his energy was needed to focus on surviving this section of the flight. Wherever they were going, it seemed like it was taking too long, despite their incomprehensible speed. Matt was sure he'd taken a shape much like Kasartha by now—bulging eyes from straining and the need to be hyper-sensitive to his surroundings, an oval head from the pressure of traveling at high speed, noggin first, and a little green from all the changing atmospheric gasses—but he hoped not. His dad had told him all about the different gasses in space: nitrogen, argon, carbon dioxide, and other stuff. Who knew what all that did to one's form. It amazed Matt he could still think, and for that, he was very thankful.

A shadowy form appeared ahead, blacking out stars as it moved across the sky, revealing a frightening outline: the gigantic head of a dragon. *Or is it a snake? And with a helmet too small for its head? Really? It can't be...*

Matt's eyes glued with high alert to the silhouette. Bulging, focused eyeballs moving to and fro, as if scouting for enemies within the endless field of stars and blackness. *That thing could swallow the sun if it wanted to. I've never imagined anything so sky-scraping huge.* Matt checked Kasartha's reaction. *He's gotta be seeing this monster too.*

But Kasartha kept moving with no change to his in-flight, stone-faced appearance. A shiver shimmied through Matt from head to toe, like fear in its purest form. *We're tiny gnats compared to that beast of beasts.* He held his breath as they passed silently by the monstrous figure. *Maybe he can't see us.* Matt dared a glance. *Yup, that's an army helmet. Freakin' weird.* The straps from the helmet hung halfway down the dragon's head and dangled as its thick neck moved gracefully from left to right and back again. The beastly image peered into the blackness, still looking, watching, seeking. Its awkwardly narrow shoulders hinged short arms that wiggled and waved as the beast glided forward. The rest of the dragon's body was not visible, except for the tip of its tail that, in the distance, dragged along a wave of stars, leaving many more still behind to shake and swirl. *Freakin' man. We need to get outta here!*

A waft of hot, stinky air hit Matthew in the face, making him gag and cough.

"Get a grip," Kasartha ordered without looking back.

He's gotta be seeing it. How could he possibly miss a ginormous space beast? Unless its too big to know its there? Nah.

Kasartha motioned for Matt to cover his nose, and, with his index finger to his lips, suggested Matt keep as quiet as possible.

Ah ha, so he does know something's up, something's not cool, Matt thought. *That's good, whew.* The boys carried forward, eventually placing the space dragon farther into their rearview mirror.

Their speed slowed, mostly because of the air increasing in thickness. *Am I wet?* Matt noticed his form was glistening with moisture. He shivered as they went from a nauseating wave of hot air to a thick, cold, wet atmosphere. He could feel the resistance and debated whether this was better or worse. *I'm ready to land. Somewhere. Anywhere. Maybe then we can turn around, and I can go back home!*

Any sense of hope was short-lived. As the air grew thick, it also grew darker and colder. Matt didn't think the space wherein they traveled could get any darker or blacker. The dense atmosphere took the lead in their travels, its vacuum-like power pulling them along. Matt choked back a couple of tears. He would give anything to be back in his bunk at home right now. The black surroundings meant he couldn't see Kasartha's face any longer, but he could tell by the kid's limp movements that Kasartha was no longer in charge. He had relinquished control to gravity, which was drawing them near to something. Just what that was, Matt had exactly zero ideas. Based on Kasartha's comfort level, Matt deduced the guy had been there before.

Kasartha waved away the jelly-like darkness in front of his face, allowing for faint streams of metallic grey to shed a few glimpses. Matt squinted so hard his head ached.

"What are ya searching for?" he squeaked out.

Kasartha glanced back. "Hang on."

"Yeah, as if I'm not already," Matt muttered, wondering if he had any energy left to do so. He had never felt so powerless and weak.

"Oooh-whee, bogus, man!" Matt began spinning rapidly, sorry he had relaxed his grip even a little, now hanging on with only one hand. "Dude, stop already." To regain a measure of control, his grip needed to be a two-hander. Another swish, and Matt was spinning again. The waves were powerful. If the air wasn't thick like jelly stabilizing his form, he wouldn't have been able to regroup. Kasartha was laughing. *Nice freakin' guy. He's enjoying this.* Matt worked his anger to his benefit by maneuvering his flopping arm and grabbing Kasartha's other ankle with the tightest grip possible. Kasartha cracked an annoying grin.

The few doses of curiosity Matt rallied since meeting Kasartha were now used up. Scorned and called by his mom once a boiling pot of anger with impatience rolling over the sides, he admitted, in this instance, she's right. Deep down he longed to get back home, no matter how awful the consequences might be—picking up his life inside that thrashed body and facing what he left behind. That would be nothing compared to this space gig.

"I want to go home." Matt declared a demand.

"Almost there. Hang on."

They carried on for a while longer. As the air got thicker and thicker, the spinning slowed. Matt shivered, certain his lips were blue from the cold. He held on and dodged obediently.

Boulder-sized rocks of ice trapped in thick, dark jelly swirled unpredictably while large, hot, copper-colored waves advanced toward them, one after the other.

The chaotic, clashing energies and the confusing, contrasting temperatures caused Matt to vomit. *Almost there? Oh, this has to stop.* So exhausted and so overwhelmed, he had no choice; he had to let go of all emotions. It was the only thing he could dump to lighten his burden. He closed his eyes, hoped his heaving would end and that they'd land somewhere, anywhere, and soon.

"There," Kasartha pointed to something in the darkness. "We have to jump. Come on, let's go."

Jump? Up yers, I'm not jumping anywhere. Matt nodded anyway. He felt so vulnerable and homesick, but he had to do what this freak told him to. *Really, what are my options?*

"Ready?" Kasartha was full of excitement while Matt's stomach continued to churn and gurgle. It was still dark, though perhaps not as black as before. Matt doubted he could trust Kasartha, but here he was, handing his life over to the guy. He took a deep breath and felt a beat in his chest thudding with neither rhythm nor control.

Yup, I still have a heart. At least now I know that much. If I get outta this mess, I'll likely need a new one.

The pair jumped high, Kasartha leading the way as he clutched Matt's hand, velocity unknown. The descent was excruciating, like falling into black Jell-O. Down, down, down they went, nothing visible until they landed unexpectedly on a sturdy mass atop an icy current of water. Matt shivered as he kissed the large piece of ice bobbing up and down. He checked out his physique and gave his head a shake. *I'm not dead. Whew! This is getting outta control, way too crazy for me.*

Kasartha landed in the water. He flipped onto his back, held his head up with his hands. "Ahhhhh, now this is the life, wouldn't you say? You okay? Dragon got your tongue?"

"Not funny." Matt held on tight to his chunk of ice as though it were a life buoy.

"Oh, you're mad again. Tsk, tsk. No worries, Matty Boy. There's nothing to worry about. We're almost, pretty much, there."

The gloomy blackness lightened somewhat. An ominous mountain range lay ahead. Matt studied it and felt another chill run through him. "Is that *all* ice? Those mountains over there?"

"Pretty much," Kasartha sang.

Stunning and unforgiving, they towered majestically.

The closer they got, other ice chunks swirling haphazardly in the waters grew larger and larger, till they had no choice but to stop floating and start jumping from ice pad to ice pad to reach the shore, the foot of the nearest mountain.

Matt was proficient at this phase of the journey. "You know, if you were anyone else, this would be the most challenging part of the journey," Kasartha said. "You are special, dear Matty Boy. Just look at you… Whoo-hoo," Kasartha whistled. "You're good at this. You are *meant* to be here."

Matt might have cracked a smile, given Kasartha's praise, if it weren't for the revolting wafts of metallic tang that struck his senses. If there was an odor that could associate itself to centuries-old rotting metal that was bottled and aged into vinegar, that would be a way to describe the intense funk.

Loud screeches of scraping noised overhead. He strained to see what was going on. From a ledge high above, long, rigid rock chunks dove into the thick darkness. One by one, they shot off like rockets.

On each rock was a kid, much like Kasartha, leaning forward and hugging tightly, all spiraling outward without even a headlight to guide them. They blended into the blackness of the atmosphere, disappearing almost immediately. *Where are they going?* Matt wondered. So many questions, but, he admitted, surviving this journey was his priority.

With a thud and a jolt, the boys slammed into a rocky shelf of ice mixed with what Matt presumed was iron. *That must be what stinks—rotting iron.* He had felt no ground beneath his feet other than pads of ice since their quick sightseeing excursion on the lunar surface. This wasn't Earth, that was for sure, but there was some relief in being grounded and not dodging foreign objects in midair. He massaged his cheeks, which had taken a beating during the flight. Then he dared another check toward the stream of Kasartha-like kids rocketing off the ledge high above. *Who are they? They've gotta be on some type of mission. I bet they're picking up other people, just like Kasartha picked me up.*

The stench was overwhelming. Matt covered his nose and mouth to keep from gagging. "This island, err, planet, err, whatever it is, it blows." He waved the air in front of his face. *What kind of gas is it?*

Kasartha had busied himself with poking his head in caverns here and there. Lighting was minimal. Matt determined there were no trees or greenery of any kind, no vegetation to clean the air. There was nothing to challenge the foul smell.

Matt reminisced about the sweet smell of lavender and bushes and grasses in Havensight. Just the thought of the color green made him yearn, not that he ever actually took the time to smell the grass, of all things. But now he missed it more than anything. *When will this be over? It's gotta be a bad dream.* He seriously regretted his stupid bet and wondered, had he not made it, would he be safe back at home right now? He retraced his actions. *If I didn't lie about my jump records, if I didn't insist on taking bets, and if Emerson wasn't such a rich scheming bully, err, if I hadn't egged him on in the challenge, maybe I wouldn't have been kicked around so badly, and then, well, then I wouldn't be here, would I?*

He wanted to start fresh, to forget everything and just get back to his life. "I'm freakin' tired of all this bogus crap. Take me home. I want to go—" Before Matt could finish his demand, Kasartha jabbed his boney finger in Matt's face.

"Well, you shoulda thought of that before you let me into your life. You cannot, *cannot*, kick me out now. Kinda late, bucko."

Kasartha's comment stunned Matt. *What does he mean—I "let" him in?*

"Not only did you let me in," Kasartha continued, "you gave me the best seat in the house. Yeah, right down there, front row, center seat. Lights, action, camera. You friggin' bonehead. You have no idea how good you had it."

"Had it?" Matt's voice squealed. "What are you talking about? You've never been to my house, and I wouldn't open my front door if I knew someone like you was knocking on it."

"Ha."

"Ha what?"

Kasartha tapped his hands in midair, as if playing four piano keys. He took a deep breath before narrowing his eyes. Matthew could see he was refraining from saying something.

Kasartha's shoulders slumped and his face transformed. "If I were you... if only I had another chance... well... you don't, idiot!" Kasartha swirled to face away from Matt.

Matt strained to see Kasartha's face. *Is that a tear in the guy's heinous eye socket? No, can't be.*

Kasartha turned back to Matt and grabbed his forearm. "We keep going!" Matt felt a hodgepodge of burning emotions, the sickening regret of his actions that led him to this place, wherever it was, and with this guy, whoever he was. The shivering fear of the galaxy-sized space monster he was sure he saw, the deep pit of loss he felt for his mom, his sister, his life in Havensight, and the all-consuming fear of what could come next. And more urgently, right now, the biggest emotion of all—the sheer darkness and freezer-cold air made Matt shiver, feel so lost, lonely, and unwelcome. *I don't belong here. I'm sure I don't belong here. I can't possibly belong here!*

CHAPTER TEN
LET'S MAKE A DEAL

THE TAIL END of the galaxy space beast lurked ahead of the boys, flicking impatiently back and forth.

Sunk so deep into bitter thoughts and accusatory strategies, Matt hadn't noticed it, nor was he wise to the danger of the dragon's nearness to Kasartha. Kasartha swerved abruptly and took his traveling companion on a fast dive into a nearby cavern.

"Come on in here!" Kasartha had returned to that urgent voice, the one he used when Matt first met him in the Havensight schoolyard. That seemed so long ago now.

"Bugger!" Matt crash slammed into the ground, back end first. "What's the deal now?" He cautiously used a jagged, razor-sharp rock ledge to pull himself to his feet. *Good thing my head didn't hit that.* Weary and frustrated he pled again, "Just tell me. Why am I here? Who are you, and where are we going? Give it up. All of it. I mean it. I want some answers. This nightmare just won't end."

Kasartha climbed up on a ledge and guardedly checked the area around the cave's broad opening.

"Really?" Matt taunted. "You think I was born yesterday? You're using this 'fear out there, I'm protecting you' hand right now. Am I right?"

No reply.

"I am right, and you know it." *This freak is playing me.*

Kasartha climbed down off the ledge and put his hands on his hips. "You, my dear boy, are dead. I am your ride, assigned personally. You will like where we are going. It's just a pain to get there, and I need to keep you safe along the way." Kasartha forced a friendly smile. "That's my job, you turd. Your job is to trust me."

Matthew ignored the turd remark and dove in for more details.

"This smell?"

"It will be all gone."

"This blackness?"

"Lots of light."

"Friggin' ice and rock?"

Kasartha smiled with satisfaction. His habit of swearing had rubbed off nicely. "No rocks, no ice." Still somewhat distracted, he scouted the space above them, then continued. "The best part of the journey is in front of us. Tell you what, I'll be more of a tour guide. I'll explain as we go. Will that help?"

Only slightly encouraged, Matt figured he didn't really have any options but to trust this guy. His shoulders sank. "Okay then," he muttered. He surprised himself that he had no reaction to the reinforced news of his death. Frankly, he did not feel dead; it couldn't possibly be true. *After all, "dead" could mean a lot of things, couldn't it?*

Despite Kasartha's promises, he didn't teach Matt anything for the next stretch of the journey. Instead, from time to time, Kasartha would unexpectedly shove Matt under a rock, only to pull him out and brush him off. He claimed it was necessary, preoccupied as he was with checking out various cavern openings, determined to find one in particular.

"Ah, yay, here it is." They landed again, this time not so abruptly.

Matt stepped inside the cavern, hoping it would be an escape from the unsightly, unforgiving landscape and its metallic aroma. There was no relief in the cavern, at least not much. *This place I'm in, I'm trapped, like in prison, with no way out.* He closed his eyes and lowered his head to meet clasped hands. "Dear God, God of my mom, well, of Arnie, to be more precise, if you know me, if you can hear me, I can't take it anymore. Please let me die. Like, an actual death. This can't be real. This *can't* be real. I'm sorry, really sorry, for messing up so badly."

Matt remained still, facing the back of the cavern. He hadn't actually prayed and meant it before. Ever. *This can't be it. This can't be death.* His thoughts were like a painful plague. *Why didn't anyone warn me?*

A powerful wind swirled and twisted past the cavern, catching Kasartha off guard.

"No! No, no!" Kasartha flustered his arms. He beelined over to Matt and spun him around with alarming force. Then he shoved and held him up as high as he could against the shallow cavern's cold, smooth back wall. "Do not *ever* do that again!"

"Do what? Let me down. You're a wacko. Get me home."

Kasartha eyeballed Matt. "You don't know what you just did?"

"What's your problem? You're freaking wrong. I am *not* dead, and I wanna get home."

Kasartha maintained his stern glare, then relaxed and released it. "Sorry, bud. I don't know what got into me. I, uh, thought you threw a rock at me. Must have been the wind I heard."

Bud?

"You're a dork. No, you're a *doofus* dork." Matt scrambled free and then walked past Kasartha and headed out the cavern opening.

Kasartha sprinted after him.

Matt kneeled down and stared into space. He knew he needed this freaky kid to get him back home. *Strategize, think.*

"Look. Can we make a deal?"

Kasartha's eyebrows lifted. "Whatchya got in mind?"

"You take me home, and we can be buddies. I'll… uh, show you around. I'll stop calling you names too. You can… you can come and go as you please, but please, you've got to take me back."

Kasartha jumped at the offer. "Yeah, that's a splendid plan. I like the sound of that."

Matt exhaled a sigh of relief, happy with how he handled the situation. *How great is this? Got myself out of a pickle without involving my mom.*

"Am I still a freako in your books?" Kasartha asks. He raised a rock high above his head, ready to whack Matthew from behind.

Matt turned slowly to assure Kasartha, "Nah, sorry, you're not a…"

Crack!

Matt received a blow across the side of his head, rendering him unconscious to a whole new level.

CHAPTER ELEVEN
I WANT THAT

MATT AWOKE SOMEWHERE new. He opened his left eye, the right one swollen shut. He caught a glimpse of Kasartha. *Crapola, he's still here. Worse, I'm still here… wherever here is.*

Kasartha was concentrating on something other than Matt, his hands wrapped tightly around a telescope suctioned against one eyeball. Back straight, on his knees and with his neck outstretched, Kasartha was studying something high up. Hearing Matt stirring, Kasartha let out a yearning sigh and relaxed his position to lean back on his legs.

"Welcome back to reality, Bagger Boy."

Matty Boy, Bagger Boy, and bud of all things, I wish you'd leave me alone. Matt steadied his blurred vision on Kasartha, then took a moment to touch a throbbing ear. "You did this!" He scrambled to get up, but dizziness got the best of him, and he fell onto his back.

Matthew's chest heaved with one sob after another until it didn't. Kasartha posed a question. "Done?"

The seriousness of emptiness and regret consumed Matt, though the new surroundings grabbed his attention.

"Yes," he replied.

Stretching overhead was a watery ceiling, roaring in activity yet eerily silent in sound. Countless upside-down waterspouts fed liquid upward directly from the atmosphere. Presumably, it was water. Black water.

"Where are we?"

"Shhhh… listen," Kasartha strained to hear something in the distance. After a pause, Matt could hear it too, the sound of falling water, a distant waterfall.

Matt stretched his back and readied himself to listen and observe the body of water that stretched end to end overhead. *Intimidating* came to mind. A tiny but vigorous stream of shimmering lights pushed its way through thick murky areas. Then it divided into even thinner veins as it traversed around either sides of jagged rocks before rejoining to continue onward. Watery tornados that swirled ferociously at random caught Matt's attention. Inside the whirling storms were stones whipping around and colliding with each other. It reminded Matt of tornado alley and the fantastical stories of houses blowing around and around in the winds high above the farmland. Only in this case, the traversing light vein was attempting to reach into the center of those mini but mighty tornados. *Two water forces doing some serious battle. I'd hate to be trapped in those waters. Geez.*

Snatching the curiosity of both boys was a fierce beam of brilliance that suddenly separated the waters, forming a perfect, circular opening.

"There *is* more," Matt whispered in awe. He pried his gaze back to Kasartha, who was employing his telescope, straining to see something inside the newly opened and enlightening space.

"This is where dark meets light!" Matt impressed himself with his own version of the scene. He vividly recalled his dad kibitzing about such, even calling his stargazing colleagues fools for fantasizing about its existence. "They actually believe that somewhere beyond the edge of pure blackness, our galaxy butts up against pure white." He had said it was ludicrous and choked with laughter at the thought. "And get this, they argue its own light is its very existence. Like it needs nothing to light it up. Idiots!"

Dad, if you only knew, if you could be here...

"The point of no return, my friend. None, nada, nilly nah," Kasartha revealed confidently.

Yeah, sure, like you're my friend. Matt's sarcasm was brief, he shook it off quickly. It barely interrupted his admiration for the steel-like beams of purity bursting through a well-defined hole in the powerful, watery sky. *Yup, that's it, pure light, right there in front of me. Rad!*

Matt took the bait and fed into the conversation. "What do you mean, 'point of no return'? There's an opening that goes right through there." Matt pointed to the hole inside the whirlpool of ferocious light, which had increased substantially in size, as if it were trying to tell them something. "Please don't tell me you've never attempted to venture through it."

Matthew knew he simply had to get to the other side. *A passageway through the sea. I'm coming. I want to go there. I want to be there! I don't care if I can't come back.*

Kasartha abruptly interrupted Matt's private yearnings, his eyeball jammed up inside the telescope. "You really are daft. You know what really gets me?" He lowered the telescope long enough to ensure Matt connected to his glare. "You and all your friends down there think you're so smart. I'm telling you, you *know nothing.* Zero. Zilch. Nada." He resumed his spying activities. "You're the ones who are blooming idiots."

The kid wants a fight. "Well, excuse me for living." Matt jumped to his feet. "And you, you're so smart? Are you so freaking happy? Oh yes, wait a minute, you *are* a freak." Matt leaped over and grabbed the telescope from Kasartha. "What are you looking at anyway?" Matt's patience with Kasartha was much like wet tissue paper.

It took a few minutes before Matt's left eye could handle the intensity of the magnification. He stood there, twisting and turning as he attempted to capture whatever Kasartha was so interested in.

"Bounce it."

"Bounce what?" Matt asked, still struggling to see anything.

"Bounce the light. Direct it into the beam and then over to the left, atop the opening. Do you see a tall stone wall?" Kasartha was actually being helpful with his guidance. What a surprise.

Matt played with the dial, trying to catch a glimpse inside the opening. "Uh, not sure, err, actually I think so."

"Now hold steady and keep watching."

Matthew held the telescope steady. As he did, it began automation of its own. An image of a large white stone wall wavered inside the light, as though it were a sheet pinned to a clothesline. "Yeah, okay, I see it. It's kind of moving around." The telescope clicked and zoomed with more automation. "Oh, wait! I see something else. A gate? Looks like a gate… with a guard." Matt played with the dial, but the telescope continued on its own with snaps and clicks and all sorts of adjustments.

"Leave it alone. Just hold it steady."

"All right, all right, I got it, geez. Holding still." The view was clear. It was indeed a small gate and a large guard. *Weird,* Matt thought. *More people. Another planet, maybe? Life on another planet. Wow!* Lying before the gate was rolling greenery, lush carpets of grass flowing like ocean waves toward the gate.

"Keep looking," Kasartha urged. Obviously, Matt hadn't seen what Kasartha thought was so interesting, as if anything could be more interesting than this. This was the other side Matt hoped would exist. It had to be. It was not the dark, icy, rocky, inhospitable environment that left Matthew with feelings of anxiety and despair. Rather, it shone with brilliant light, emanating warmth and acceptance. A welcoming, stark contrast. *Perhaps Kasartha's not so bad after all. Not if he's going to take me there, to that other side.*

Matt was so relieved. "I knew this couldn't be death. There *is* more!" He was getting quite excited. "How do we get there?" Kasartha's silence prompted yet another query from Matt. "This is what you wanted to show me, right? *That's* where you're taking me, right?"

"Keep looking," Kasartha demanded, frustration embedded in his voice.

Surprisingly, Matt's previous distaste and distrust of Kasartha transitioned into concern and empathy. He repositioned the telescope and strained again. "Whoa," he exclaimed as he glimpsed two characters, each with long, wide wings and long, hunched necks. "Human arms, human legs, and an oblong human face... human eagles!" Bouncing on alternate knee hops in excitement, the telescope zoomed in even closer. In between the human-like eagles was an older woman, they hung onto her carefully as they came in for a landing just in front of that gate. *What a funky delivery. I'm in for that!* The guard stood with open, muscular arms wearing ancient soldier-like apparel—the ceremonial type, not the battle type. The guard's smile was far-reaching as he spoke to the woman. Matt couldn't tell what he was saying, but they certainly appeared thrilled to see each other. "Love those threads," Matt admired the guard's uniform. He felt like he had seen it somewhere, maybe in one of his childhood storybooks.

"Do you see her?"

"The woman who just landed? Are you kidding? I see her. And check out those delivery guys, part eagle, part human."

"No! Move to the right and down a tad," Kasartha instructed, still seething with frustration.

Matt was getting the hang of the telescope, distinguishing when he needed to make a manual adjustment and when it went into automatic mode. He scanned the view in the direction Kasartha instructed.

"Oh." He was not expecting something kind of normal,

someone doing something Matt loved. "Well, I'm a monkey's uncle." Matt gasped as he continued to study the scene. He witnessed the superb performance of a young girl, at least two years his senior he guessed, sail through the air in perfect toe-touching position and land upright, solid on both feet. "Far out!" The successful jump filled him with envy. He watched as she continued to practice. Her technique was unbelievably perfect, the run-up, the takeoff, the flight, and the landing. *And oh, what distance!* It immediately drew Matt to her. "Can we get closer?"

Kasartha smiled. "Huh. Bagger Boy wants to meet beautiful long-jumping girl. Go figure. I suppose a deal could be struck." Kasartha's lifted eyebrows suggested they were on track again—Kasartha's track, that is, not Matthew's.

Is he suggesting I have something he wants? Reluctant to respond, Matt shifted the telescope and resumed the snooping. The young girl carried out her running long jumps with precision. She was so efficient, so powerful, and so amazingly graceful. He felt such comfort, peace, inspiration just watching her. He desperately wanted to go where she was, to meet her, to hang out with her, whoever she was. Quickly forgotten was Havensight and anyone there who might have been important to him—his mom, his baby sister, and his buddies—well, Nick anyway.

"What could you possibly want from *me*?" Matt asked finally.

"Your stone," Kasartha replied in a calm voice while staring up at the watery, action-packed sky.

"My what?"

"Your stone."

"A rock. Is that what you want?" Fed up with the guy, Matt picked up a rock by his feet and chucked it at Kasartha. The thickness of the atmosphere caused it to mope, and the rock wavered lazily past his head. It was actually pretty funny, but Kasartha did not laugh or react, his face remained dead serious.

"I want your stone. Everyone has one, and I want yours."

Matt decided to play along. "I presume then there is a particular rock… or rather, a particular stone, that you want? And where might that be?" Matt displayed his empty pants pockets.

Kasartha pointed. Matt's eyes followed the path to which Kasartha's finger directed. He pulled the telescope close and pivoted toward the opening. The waters swirled angrily inside the circle until a new scene emerged inside it. There it was, the rushing sound of distant falling water that Matt had heard was now in crystal-clear view. Water growled as it toppled over an immensely tall cliff and fell with deafening silence before pounding into a pool of crystals. The pool branched out into many streams of light, each one twisting and swirling in midair and eventually dropped liquified contributions into a churning black sea. *This must be above the watery sky—has to be. Light flows down into it while dark flows up from below. Huh.*

"Is this the only place water flows into the sky?" Matt asked. "Or are waterfalls and these spirally things all over?"

"Just here." Kasartha was growing impatient with the Matt's curiosity once again. "Focus!" he commanded.

Annoyed, Matt focused on the new image zoomed in by the telescope. Midway up a rising mountain above the sea a waterspout shot out from beneath a rocky ledge. Upon the ledge, precariously situated, was a simple stone. It was as black as it was white, but alarmingly, it had a life of its own. It was jumpy, as though desperate to get back into the crystal pool below, likely needing the falling waters as an escape route. "Is that it? How'd it get up there? How do you know that's *my* stone?"

"It's got your name etched on it."

The telescope clicked and zoomed some more.

"And so it does. My whole name… in gold. Smackerals!"

Matthew Sebastian William Mackenzie

"Well, I'm a monkey's uncle." Regardless of whether Matt would give this stone, *his* living stone, to Kasartha was yet to be determined. And what good would it do for Kasartha to have it? "I want to see it. I want to hold it." Matt pulled the telescope away from his face. "Why's it such a scaredy cat? Shouldn't it just jump in, aim for the clear waters, have a little faith? Geez."

He could never understand his mother's choice of Sebastian. She told him it was the name of his great-grandfather, or maybe even his great-great-grandfather. Even so, it never convinced him that was reason enough to burden him with it. Most of the time Matt left it out of his identification papers. When someone or something important needed his whole legal name, Matt would state Matthew William Mackenzie. That was much more sensible and plenty long enough.

"So, how do we get there?" Still yet, no more burning desire to get back to Havensight. Matt was eager, curious, and ready for more of this whole new world. A new hope of something had entered his veins—a sense of familiarity, of true belonging, of something really, really good. Matt couldn't explain it, but he felt it. He even felt something for Kasartha—perhaps it was empathy. "Let's go, brother!"

Kasartha was enthused, one step closer to completing his mission, his *personal* mission.

Therein and after, the boys' relationship churned through a renewal. Buddies on a mission, they had in common an air of excitement about their next steps, albeit for each their own goal: Matthew's to get to that gate above and Kasartha's to take possession of Matthew's stone. They gave each other high fives and hip bumps, but their fun moment of camaraderie was short-lived.

Eyes tearing up, the pair covered their noses and mouths. The stench had returned, and so did the horror on Kasartha's face. A dark and mysterious presence filled the space above, blocking their view of the circular opening that, moments earlier, had given Matthew such great hope. Thick scales and spearheaded tentacles waved creepily. There was no question to whom the tail belonged—the monstrous space beast with the dragon head and army helmet. With a life of its own, the tail sleuthed its way into the opening, which by now had narrowed considerably, slithered up to the ledge, and wrapped a tentacle around the stone with Matt's name inscribed on it. Kasartha grabbed the telescope as if to change a channel and disregard the scene.

The tentacle tossed the stone up into the air as the tip of the tail firmed up like a baseball bat. *Whack!* The crack of the tail hitting Matt's stone was unmistakable; it was intentionally harmful. That dragon just declared a new battle.

"Oh, crap," was all a shrinking Kasartha could say.

Trembling from a loud rumble of thunder beneath the ground on which the boys stood, Matt choked in terror while his eye remained fixed on the scene above, the stone spinning madly toward the dark, unsettled waters. He was sensing the stone, his personal stone, had significant value. But what was it, and why the want for it?

Kasartha turned urgently, reaching out to grab Matthew. But it was too late, a single flash and Matt was gone. Sent back to rejoin his physical being in Havensight.

CHAPTER TWELVE
SLOW AWAKENING

In the Town of Havensight

MARNIE COULDN'T BEAR to accept any suggestions Matt would not make a full recovery. A groan or a mere opening of an eye right now would provide significant relief, even if it were ever so brief. Then she could take a deep breath and quickly recharge until the next signal of life came.

Her mind boggled. *What on earth's been going on, Matty, to make someone do this to you? Did you really do something so terrible? Would somebody please turn off that annoying elevator music!*

Matthew's comments in the parking lot yesterday morning replayed over and over in her head. Had she underestimated his fears and concerns? *Heck yeah,* she screamed inside, scolding herself and feeling guilty, like she could have prevented this. Not a word or a wink from Matty for the past twenty-three-and-a-half hours, an excruciating day. Like that was not punishment enough for Marnie.

At last, Matt stirred. Once. And then again. Marnie held her breath. *Yes! Good signs, good signs. I'll take that. Yes, yes, yes.* His eyes opened and shut six times, each occurrence producing bits of watery flow down his temples.

Marnie moved closer, so she could study all the details of her son's awakening face, her hand touching his forehead. She whispered his name, hoping the nurses wouldn't come running in just yet. She wanted this moment for herself. "Don't worry, son. Get better first. Then we'll talk about what happened. And no matter what, we'll figure out a solution. I love you. It's all gonna be okay. Okay? You hear me? I promise, son, I promise."

With eyes partially open, Matt responded with a slow blur of words, barely distinguishable. "Away… cold… bright… gate," was all she could figure from his mumbles. *Gate.* She clenched her teeth.

"Stay here. Stay here. No, don't go through," she commanded quietly.

The head intensive care nurse came busting into the room and repeatedly instructed Matthew to slow down and take it easy.

He is slow and easy. You're the one panicking with speed and fury, Marnie thought. She hoped Matthew had heard her plea to stay away from any gate.

"Breathe deeply. Come on, do it with me, breathe in. Good. Now slow release." The nurse had a firm hold on his shoulders and spoke with authority and directness. If she were any closer, their noses would have bonked.

Matt did as the nurse instructed, or at least it seemed so anyway. Then he blurted out a big, smelly belch.

Marnie took that as a sign of recovery. She moved in closer to stroke his cheek, smiling in relief. "Thank you, God. Thank you, thank you, thank you!" It was simply a default crisis response.

Another nurse returned, bringing along Dr. Bonneville. By then, Matt held a fixed and wild stare in his wide-open eyes.

"Matthew." Marnie's voice was quiet and serious. "You've been out of it all night. You were brutally attacked."

Dr. Bonneville gave Marnie the evil eye. Obviously, he didn't think she should spill those beans just yet. He motioned for the nurse to move Marnie a few steps away, toward the back of the room.

After what seemed to be satisfactory vitals results and a round of poking from Dr. Bonneville, two doses of something were administered, and in no time, Matthew was sound asleep again.

Marnie kept quiet, though her mouth twisted to one side. She had waited anxiously for Matt to wake up. Moment by moment, she watched his chest rise, fall, and rise again. She counted his breaths, watched the clock, sighed, and wondered how long it would be till he awoke. Now she was no further ahead, no new knowledge about what transpired at school or why. Nor did she know if she needed to be concerned for his mental or emotional state. And more disappointing than all, she had barely any further insight into his physical condition.

Dr. Bonneville stepped out of the room without even a glance her way or any type of explanation. So Marnie waited again, her on a hard chair beside his bed while he laid motionless inside stiff hospital bedding. Even with her eyes closed, the smell of those sheets commanded the environment. Poisonous bleach. Sheets that before today could have served as bed partners with an expectant mother, a dying elderly man, a puking child with a sickly flu, or an accident victim with blood and guts all over. Was it the smell she couldn't stand, or the fact she couldn't tame her racing mind? She decided to get up and get a fresh coffee. This time she would go to the cafeteria one floor down rather than the coffee machine down the hall, which offered only powdered cream.

"Just one coffee?"

Marnie nodded and paid the cashier. The water in her eyes caused her to question whether the stains on her why-bother-sized ceramic cup were there before or if she spilled somewhere along the lineup. Unable to hold back her tears any longer, they finally escaped. She didn't bother drying off the wetness that clung to her neck, soaking the collar of her blouse. Her head dropped, and her shoulders shook with the sobs. She tightened her grip on her cup. Maybe its warmth could somehow transfer into her veins. The walls had caved in. Marnie couldn't go back to Matty's room, not just yet.

Okay, just breathe. Find a place to sit, she instructed herself. She would pull it together and keep going. It wasn't just Matty; the déjà vu feeling was slowly taking over. The smells, the hard chairs, the long bedside visits, the needles, the bulletin boards with plasticized warnings and instructions, the hum of the bright lights that would never be turned off, the green-grey curtains that swung around the bed as if to hide and protect those inside from the outside world—or vice versa. The constant quickness of feet passing by on the other side of those curtains—knowing who was who simply by the sound of their steps.

"Frank… curse you anyway." Marnie felt so alone and didn't realize she had spoken until a passerby gave her a nasty look. She eyed a dark, empty corner and headed toward it, coffee in hand and tongue under control.

Moments later, Dr. Alexien caught sight of her. With her to-go sandwich in hand, Dr. Alexien headed toward that isolated corner of the cafeteria to offer compassion, the corner where Marnie had hoped to find solace.

"Hey," Dr. Alexien said quietly, placing a calm and caring hand on Marnie's right shoulder. She took the liberty of sitting down beside her and then waited until Marnie composed herself before continuing.

"This must be difficult, Mrs. Mackenzie. But good news, I just read an update. Matt is beginning the awakening process."

"It's, uh, it's Mrs. Decker. Mackenzie is Matt's surname. Used to be mine. I'm going to change back to it… I'm rambling. I was there. Matt woke up when I was there." Although scrambling for words, Marnie felt she was already coming around to what would have to be a new normal state. "Do you think he'll be okay? I mean, will he recover completely?"

"I believe there is a very good chance of that, Mrs. Decker. Basically, because I see nothing that prevents a full recovery—but we truly can't tell one hundred percent. Some things are not in our hands."

For some inexplicable reason, Dr. Alexien's voice and presence genuinely comforted Marnie.

Marnie breathed deeply and took a long-awaited sip. *Uph, cold coffee. Gross.*

She readied herself to leave behind her those moments of self-pity and sorrow for what she hoped would be a revealing chat about Matty's recovery. Pushing her cup aside, she pumped the doctor with questions. Although the answers were all couched nicely, Marnie felt more informed, more in control.

"Is there anything else?" Dr. Alexien asked finally.

She must have sensed Marnie was holding back a question.

Marnie had Matty's few words on her mind. "You know, he was blabbering a bit… about being away, being cold, bright light stuff. What do you think? Is that a sign of anything? Like, I've heard people talk about… stuff that other people experience when they are near… passing." The word "death" made Marnie shiver. "Passing" was far less harsh and less permanent.

Dr. Alexien folded her hands in her lap and studied Marnie's face. "Do you think he was remembering *another world*?" Dr. Alexien used her fingers to make air quotes around the term. "Was he frightened? What did he say exactly? What was the look in his eyes when he awoke?" The questions had turned the tables. Dr. Alexien was keen to know everything about Matthew's mutterings.

"Well, he wasn't frightened. Rather, it was like a quiet desperation. He was trying to tell me something. Think he could have had… an out-of-body experience?"

"It's not unheard of, Mrs. Decker. I'm interested to know what he remembers when he wakes up. And it may take a day or two or even longer for him to remember anything. If he starts talking about what may seem to be even a little weird, contact me. I'll be happy to talk to him and draw out what might be going on in his mind. Call me directly. Here's my number." She passed Marnie a crisp white business card with gold lettering. "It's not part of our typical medical response. We—or should I say, I—have done it before with other patients. It's a keen area of interest for me. It'll be helpful for Matthew to talk about it, and it's helpful for us. As members of medical teams, we ought to understand what patients experience in cases like this. It's part of the full recovery process—the *whole person* recovery process, which I take is a big concern of yours. And besides, it's quite possible there will be no more of this kind of talk... and then no worries."

Marnie sat with her chin resting in her palm. *No worries about what?* she wondered. She wanted to trust Dr. Alexien, and as much as she did not like the idea of her son being used for studies, she didn't have a better plan. "Okay. I'll call you directly if need be." Marnie hoped there would be no need for that type of assistance. But if Matthew did have experiences he needed to talk about, she vowed she would get him support.

Dr. Alexien walked away with her uneaten sandwich and left Marnie sucking in yet another deep breath of stagnant cafeteria air and releasing it before she headed back to the wooden folding chair at Matty's bedside. She stopped at the public telephone along the hallway and took another deep breath. She needed to ring Arnie and ensure Karo was fine and would be okay without her for one more night.

It turned out Karo was ecstatic to stay longer. *Ugghhh.* Then she called Lance, her boss, to let him know she needed the next week off and convince him that her assistant, Peg, could manage everything just fine. *Ugghhh again.*

CHAPTER THIRTEEN
A NEW FRIEND

Ten Days Later

"VITAL SIGNS ARE all normal now, thank heavens. But he's disillusioned; he thinks he's fine. You know he's been hallucinating, right?"

Matt rolled his eyes. He figured his mom must be talking to Arnie Decker, the bane of his existence—hers too, for that matter. *She has no one else to talk to. Who else could she possibly be explaining my condition to? Who else would care? She lectures and belittles him, and he just takes it.* Matt shook his head.

"He's napping now. I take him back for another assessment tomorrow. He needs a great deal of rest, so leave us alone for the next few days."

Yup, she's chatting with Arnie. She loves giving him directives to push him away, only to pull him back in when she needs someone to snap at. As much as Matt never cozied up to Arnie, he did wonder why Arnie kept silent in the face of his mother's continuous chewing outs. *It's like she blames him for Dad dying. Poor guy, ha ha. At least she's getting the school off my back for a few days.* Matt secretly thanked his mom for that. Right now, that was all that mattered—getting space from HCSS. Space from school meant space from Emerson and his thugs and more time to work on a debt solution. The message was clear—he'd have to replenish their loss. He wondered if they'd meet him halfway, fifty-fifty like.

By the next afternoon, Matt was lying in a makeshift bed on the couch in his downstairs family room while Karo intelligently and pridefully changed the channel on their Admiral console. "*I Dream of Jeannie* is up next, Matty," she said in her chirpy voice, her breath warm into Matt's ear. "Then my favorite." She did a little jiggle. "Buffy and Jody!"

"I'm not deaf. 'Sides, it don't matter. I don't care." Matt would be pleased if something funny could keep his sister preoccupied for the next twenty years so she wouldn't pester him. He just wanted peace and quiet so he could think. He imagined what discussions had been going on in Harry Cooke's office at school. Why hadn't there been any suspensions? Maybe that was good news. If they knew Emerson caused the beating, they'd have charged him and his thugs by now. But then, Matt moaned, *my arrogance and deceit would become the school's legend. Bagger Boy. Bagger Boy. Bagger Boy.* Matt stuffed his pillow over his head. *No. Hope they don't get caught. I'll manage the revenge myself.*

"You okay?" His little sister poked her upturned nose beneath his pillow. "Want Mom?"

"No, I don't want Mom. She doesn't listen to me. She just…" *Why the heck am I talking to this kid? As if my life isn't bad enough, my mom has a four-year-old watch over me? Why would she let this kid watch anything she wants on TV anyway? She should be watching stuff like Dumbo or Mickey Mouse or something stupid like that.*

"Just what? Just what? Tell me."

"No! Go away."

Karo crawled up to the console. Knowing exactly where the volume button was, she cranked it up a few notches simply to make a point. Fine, she would ignore him then.

Matt returned to his thoughts, as depressing as they were.

Once he heard Woody Woodpecker's cereal tune, he knew Karo would be wholly engaged at the tube at least for a few minutes. He flipped so his face could not be seen and tucked his pillow securely around his head. He melted into the fantasy world that Kasartha showed him. A world that crept into Matt's imagination whenever it pleased. Given that Matt had plenty of time on his hands these days, that strange world lurked into his mind a lot. He made the mistake of telling Dr. Alexien about it. After examining her notes, crisscrossing a bunch of things, and hemming and hawing, she advised Matt's mom there was nothing to worry about. "Matt's experiencing grief over the loss of his dad, and in his physical trauma from the attack, his deeply hidden emotional trauma found a way to escape. He's simply fantasizing about life after death. It'll eventually disappear as his life returns to normal." So, Matt stopped talking about it, which only seemed to validate the doctor's message.

His face nestled deep into the crack of the couch, Matt allowed deep, private thoughts to engulf him, that weird dream. He relished in its memory, so freakishly real. *A room full of floating books and a tiny man in charge. Shoo, get outta here, scram.* Matt chuckled at the stubbiness of his arms, recalling how they waved madly in the air. *And who was that with me? Never moved from my behind, never showed his face, never even said a word, or did he? He was tall, I could tell. And strong. And... comforting, really supportive. Oh yeah, I did hear a voice. It said, "All that matters."*

Matt shushed the words so he could say it without being heard. *What does that mean? All that matters.* A handful of potato chip crumbles wedged deep in the crevice were the only things close enough to hear Matt's mumbles. After checking it out and seeing no bugs, Matt continued comfortably, curious about his thoughts. *All what matters? After that small dude shooed us out, we vanished, just like that, both of us. That man behind me too. Huh, that was it. Till I woke up. Maybe someone's warning me, watching and writing everything down, everything I do.* Matt sighed as his mind continued to swirl. *Nah, that can't be it.* He refocused his thoughts on the weird green goon in the hat. *Funky name, though. Kasartha. Now he was totally and completely outta this world. And that trip through space! No one will ever believe me. Whoa, I wonder if I could do it again, so I could haunt the crap out of Emerson. Now, that would be cool!*

Matt pounded the sides of his pillow as if smashing something would help him remember more clearly. He had no trouble recalling Kasartha's image. *Freakish, the way he transformed.* His purple shirt and doofus-looking worn-out purple hat. His dirt-brown pants were only baggy because of his short legs. If not for the black leather-ish rope and big buckle, they'd surely fall right off him. *How did he fly in those things? Seriously? And those super-nerdy pointed shoes.* Matthew chuckled as the image came clearly into his mind. *Oversized teeth and bulging eyeballs. Who could forget that image? Yeah, that had to be a dream. Well, actually, a nightmare. No one could possibly be like that in real life!*

Matthew moaned and took a quick peek at Karo, who was still fully engaged. A good inhale of stuffy rec room air provided some relief. *Rad, I hope that's not me that stinks.* His face returned to the shallow grave of the couch, and he tucked in the pillow some more.

Despite surmising it all had to be fictitious, some sort of mysterious experience, he admitted it was pretty rad. One thing boggled him, though. *A stone with my name on it. And why would Kasartha want it?*

Matt turned to Karo. Her eyelids were flickering. *She'll be out like a light soon. And Mom will come in when she's sound asleep and yell at me, as if I should have kept her awake.* Frustrated but also happy no risk of interruptions would come from Karo, he returned to his thoughts.

My stone... my stone. Why is it so important? Straining his brain cells to the max, he vaguely remembered how his phenomenal journey had ended so abruptly. *A gigantic dragon slammed my stone with his tail. He whacked it! Yeah, like I could tell that to anyone— not.* Matt sighed deeply.

Just then, Karo shook his shoulder. "Josh and Nick are here." Matt glared at her for interrupting his private thoughts. He hadn't even heard the doorbell ring.

"I said, Josh and Nick are here. Can't you hear me?" She seemed impartial to the growl on Matt's face and darted up the stairs to catch some of the conversation in action.

I guess she wasn't as tired as I thought.

Marnie and Nick were exchanging sad thoughts about the recent news of Andy Falcon, their favorite teacher at Havensight Collegiate. Yesterday had been another shock for the community. Just as the news was settling over the brutal and seemingly sense-less attack on a thirteen-year-old boy, ten days later, one of the school's most well-respected and beloved teachers had died. Mr. Falcon interacted well with most students, probably because he was funny, attended most, if not all, the extra-curricular sports and arts-related events, and was an all-around nice guy. Few students could claim they had not received some encouraging or inspiring words from Andy Falcon. He had a way of touching lives. Just being near him, simply by osmosis, people felt more positive about themselves, like they mattered, really mattered. He was thirty-four years old. No one expected the sudden end to his life. The school and the community would be in mourning.

"Still waiting to hear the cause, eh?" Nick hoped Marnie would receive his partial statement as an inquiry. After all, she used to be married to the vice principal, so she might know something.

Marnie shrugged. "I haven't told Matt about this," she whis-pered. "He's still recuperating, and it just hasn't been the right time yet."

Always an opportunist, Nick wanted to be seen as the one in the know, the leader in charge—when there was no risk of danger, that is.

"Oh, would you like me to tell him, Mrs. Decker?" His hopeful eyes actually gave Marnie a reason to smile.

"Sure," she replied. "I'll join you in just a few minutes."

Marnie thought it might be good for Matt's friends to visit and give Matt something different to think about other than the attack or, heaven forbid, the long jump bet. Matt didn't want Nick and Josh to visit, but Marnie told him it was time to push forward.

"Matt's in the family room," Marnie said. "Karo will take you down. But..." She gave Nick a stern brow. "Wait for me before you share, you know, the news."

Karo leaped from behind the staircase to join her mom and the boys. She had kept out of sight, but she had heard everything. She loved knowing something Matt didn't.

"Come on, this way." She motioned to head downstairs to the tiny wood-paneled family room, a room the boys were quite familiar with and had spent many hours within over the years. Even so, they respectfully followed Karo as if going somewhere they had never been before. The boys stepped cautiously. This was the first time they would travel down the stairs to visit a trounced-up version of their friend.

The news of Mr. Falcon's death didn't really sink in. Matt's mind was miles away, in space and only partially present. He thought, however, this news could only be good. Now the school and the community had something else to think about. The glare of the spotlight could beam elsewhere, on poor Mr. Falcon. Matt might just make it out of this mess after all. Seeing his mother's cocked head and that familiar, concerned face made him nervous. "I'm fine, Mom. Don't go calling Dr. Alexien or anything."

Marnie's gears were turning. "I always thought you liked Mr. Falcon."

"I do. I did, everybody did." He shrugged carelessly, and they all dropped the subject.

Nick and Josh stayed for macaroni and cheese with a serving

of green beans. Although they hardly touched the beans, at least Marnie felt there was a green option on their plates should they reveal what they were served to suspicious parents, who were certain to ask. As if the way Marnie and Frank earned a living when they first arrived to Havensight hadn't given Marnie enough sideway glances, becoming a widow, a woman with a second husband, and then to top it off, a divorcee, well, heaps of scrutiny from the community at large came in regular doses.

The three boys chatted on the front step for a full hour afterward. It was the first time Matt had done something rather normal for days. Marnie was thankful, and hoped this would cheer Matthew up, particularly on the eve of his birthday. Finally, exhaustion appeared to get the better of him, and he announced he needed to go to bed.

His visit with Josh and Nick was a good dose of reality. That bit of normal existence provided the challenge he needed to doubt that any life other than this, the one he had in Havensight, could be real. His otherworldly experience may have been just a dream caused by a brain injury or concussion or whatever. Maybe there was a little grief and denial inside him, a desire to know more about what happened to his dad after he died, that made his brain think it all up. *I might never know*, Matt thought over a deep and loud exhale. But it was kind of rad, and he had to admit, he liked how it preoccupied his mind. Saved him from boredom.

With happy thoughts that Mr. Falcon's news would supersede his own headlines in the community and satisfied that likely he had just hallucinated the whole *outta this world* business, Matt settled comfortably onto the couch. He hoped his mom wouldn't let Karo stay up late and hang out in the family room. Content, he closed his eyes and rested his mind.

A high-pitched scream shrieked from the top floor.

Two steps at a time, Matt arrived in seconds. He and Marnie practically banged heads at the source of the shrill yell—Karo's room. Karo was crouched under the tiny dark-blue desk squeezed in beside her bed, her face white. The homework desk used to be Matt's. She refused to have it repainted in pink. She wanted so badly to have the same things as Matt right from the get-go. Matt was lightheaded from his running jolt up two flights of stairs, and he grabbed the room's doorframe to steady himself. Gasping for a breath between two simple words, he spat out, "What's wrong?"

"Some guy was in my room!" Karo cried. She pointed to her bed. "He was right there."

Marnie gave Matt a disapproving look. "No more talk about invisible people. Or flying people either." She turned to Karo. "Karo, so much has happened in the last few days. None of us are thinking straight just yet. If you like, you can sleep with me tonight."

Great, Matt thought, *she screams, and I get the blame.*

"Well, I'm not staying in here!" Karo marched out of her room and into the hallway. Marnie gave another disapproving glance at Matt and then left to prepare a spot for Karo in her room.

"Matty," Karo said in a matter-of-fact tone, "somebody really was there."

"Yeah, right." Matt didn't even want to hear about it.

"He said your name."

"What?"

"I said, he said your name."

"What did he look like?"

"A kid. Well, sort of like a kid. Kind of like a man too. He had big teeth."

Matt's eyebrows rose. "Go on," he said, urging his little sister to continue.

"He had a big purple floppy hat and a funny-shaped head. He was kind of on the ugly side."

Matt touched the sweat beads forming on his forehead. Whether from the anxiety that Kasartha had just visited Karo or from physical exhaustion at running up the stairs, it didn't matter. The drops on his hot, flushed head were real. He was beginning to think he couldn't discern reality from fantasy.

"He kept asking stuff about you," Karo continued.

"Like what?" There was no uncertainty in Matt's mind. Kasartha had been there, and he had talked to Karo.

Wait a minute. Matt eyed Karo with suspicion, suddenly switching back to doubting mode. "You screamed. How could you have possibly had a conversation with this guy?"

Karo had probably just taken the information she overheard and was playing a game. Darn Dr. Alexien; he wished he hadn't told her everything. How else did Karo come to know all the details about Kasartha's image?

"I didn't scream when I saw him. I screamed when he disappeared." Karo made a valiant attempt to snap her fingers in the air. It didn't work, so she clapped her hands, but only the heels of her hands connected. "He walked into my room. I thought he was a new friend of yours and I just didn't hear the doorbell ring when he came. He looked normal... at first."

"Why did you think he was a friend of mine?"

"Because he said so! He said, 'Hi, I'm a friend of Matt's. Well, is he?"

"No!" Matt dismissed any connection to Kasartha. This was all a little too much. Karo pushed Matt aside to head toward Marnie's room.

"Bring my pillow," she ordered. She clearly did not want to get close to the bed that Kasartha had sat upon.

It was 8:30 p.m., too early for bed. Back downstairs in the family room, Matt chose to turn the television on. He desperately needed to forget about everything, not just the last ten minutes, but the past two weeks. He wanted them wiped right out of existence. But no such luck, only a single burning thought.

He is real. I knew it! Karo could see and talk to him. But why bother her? What did he want? He really scared her. On purpose? To get back at me? Is he watching and laughing right now? Matt grew angry at the thought. "I need to find out what's going on!"

"Kasartha, wherever you are, get down here right now. Fudge nuggets, I mean it!"

CHAPTER FOURTEEN
GOT A PLAN

In the Outer Courtyard of the Kingdom

PIPIERA BREATHED IN the surrounding life. The view from where she played all the day long could make anyone forget about anything, particularly the whole we-need-to-help-some-Matthew-boy business. The kingdom courtyard stretched out in front of Papah's gate was heart-filling enough, satisfying beyond words. She could never drink enough of its delightfulness, nor would she ever tire of it. The courtyard was her home, and she loved it dearly.

She closed her eyes and stuck her nose upward. *Mmmmmm…* The fragrances were divine. She sucked in light aromas, one after the other, as they visibly swirled around: fresh buttery vanilla, deep grape berries, decadent chocolate, orange and peach blossoms, and finally, delicious hints of mint in earthy lavender. The swirls danced around in perfect choreography with the endless meadows of color. Hundreds of chimes rang together in unison in a gentle and breezy harmony. Pipiera was convinced she could hear every single pitch, even with the background of a distant waterfall which she believed to be invisible. She knew it had to exist because of the majestic sound, like thousands of water drops falling onto a horizon full of windowpanes—then falling and dripping some more. She heard rumors of a river catching all drops deep below the kingdom.

She opened her eyes. Crests of waves made of rich soil painted in a myriad of lush greenery ebbed and flowed inward. Their starting point was the horizon, but Pipiera knew the waves were born from afar, billions of miles away. They would have traveled forcibly and invisibly through the cosmos. She spoke to one that would soon reach the gate. "How I ache to know of your adventures along the way. What joy you must have, such a feeling of accomplishment now that you've arrived. That's gotta feel sooo good."

The kingdom's outer courtyard represented the ultimate destination. She watched as a wave dropped off its passenger and then took its final bow. The wave perked up, showing its face, and gave Pipiera a little side wink before making a gracious goodbye and melting into the fertile grounds.

Is that what will happen to me? Will I just melt into the ground one day?

She toed the soft grass beneath her bare feet. *What's the purpose of my existence?* She envied the colorful meadows of flowers that line her side of the incoming waves. From a distance, they could be mistaken for flocks of colorful butterflies with delicate wings. They fluttered and danced excitedly, which made such a pleasing show for the new arrivals. Even they had a purpose. The entire scene offered the delivery of a long-awaited promise.

Pipiera was a jumper. She loved the rush of running and leaping over the incoming waves. She had mastered the landings, but purposeful falls were such fun. Sometimes she hid between the waves and would simply roll along for a while before a last-minute surprise jump. Other times she surfed the waves, imagining they were fierce watery rolls, like the kind on Earth. But the feeling of a self-imposed race to beat the clock as a means of survival gave her the biggest rush. Sailing through the air, that was the exhilarating part. She wished she could freeze midway in flight and simply collapse into the willows of a wind.

The area also hosted and attracted plenty of picnickers, all citizens coming out of the kingdom and into the outer courtyard to wait for someone they heard would soon arrive. The picnic table section was tucked in closer to the kingdom wall and nestled in a forest of tall pine trees that carpeted the ground with soft, aromatic needles. Tall, ornamental tree trunks arched a portion of the way up, their branches curved throughout the woods creating a horizontal pergola-like structure. Large white roses and plump blue grapes wound artfully around the branches and dripped into the picnic area like delicate curtains. The waiting area was the place for citizens to gather and be safely out of the way of rolling waves but still in perfect view to witness the new arrivals in anticipation of that certain someone, inevitably a family member.

Not as many chose to wait in the courtyard as one might expect, as pleasant and pleasing as the picnic area was. It was a tense scene to witness. Of course, when all went well—scans and timing in particular—the waiting citizens celebrated and accompanied their loved ones through the gate and into the kingdom. When timing was off, it wasn't so bad, Pip figured. Often a few words of advice and a chance to encourage were permitted as their loved ones were sent back to complete their tour. The disastrous combination when the perfect timing of a completed journey met with scans boasting of a firm renouncement, therein lay the horror of it all. Pipiera had watched, too many times, such pain in the faces of waiting parties as they witnessed firsthand their loved ones being directed toward another path, one that took them away. Those citizens would sit there for a long time before re-entering the kingdom. They knew that once they re-entered the kingdom, this time their memory of that loved one would disappear forever, like they had never existed.

Megalos explained to Pipiera that was how the king protected the citizens from pain and hurt. "No need for tears inside those walls," he had said.

Pipiera grieved this haunting rule. It was harsh. She couldn't help but carry a grudging sadness about it all deep inside.

Rather than running and jumping, Pipiera meandered over to her favorite lavender patch and sat cross-legged, eyes fixed on the horizon. Cupping a twig, she resisted its gentle, resonant tune. "Shhh. Time to be serious," she whispered. "What if Papah's Matthew boy arrives one day, only to learn he had a key purpose, a reason for his role on Earth, and he never caught on to it, never learned what he was meant to learn, never grew any, you know, character? That would be a shame; he'd have wasted his life on Earth! Or..." She brought her face closer to the twig. "Would it really be that bad?"

She turned to face the kingdom gate and answered her own question. "Well, he would simply not be able to be Papah's replacement. That's all." *That's not so bad.*

She was distracted by loud, happy chatter and laughing at the picnic tables. Another outcome crossed her mind, and the entire lavender patch stood tall, keen to listen up. "Hmm... worse... much worse. What if that time came, and Matthew's family was right there, at those tables, wanting to witness him rolling in through the field from the horizon, having completed his all-important humankind tour and all set to join them. What if... my gosh, what if he gets so off track, he completely loses that deep sense of kingdom loyalty?" The twigs were horrified and already shaking their heads at what Pipiera would say next. "Ha, what if he forgets the king himself? What if the written code simply does not allow his entrance? His waiting family would be devastated, Papah included!"

Pipiera considered the thousand purple eyes blinking simultaneously. She choked and tapped both sides of her neck. Putting on a show of reassurance, she addressed her aromatic audience. "Don't be sad; the devastation won't last long. When his family walks back inside the gate, their memory of their Matthew will be totally erased." Another mass of purple blinked in unison. She sighed. "You don't like that outcome either."

The king didn't want that outcome for any earthly inhabitant. That's what kept the kingdom so busy in battles all the time, to avoid such scenarios.

The worst thing of all jabbed at Pipiera's heart. "If that were to happen, Papah would have to carry that pain continuously, for he works outside the kingdom walls. His memory will not be erased. How cruel!"

Purple tears were everywhere. An uncomfortable puddle grew beneath Pipiera, compelling her to stand.

"How can I be so selfish?" She glanced over at her Papah Moolos, who was busy with an arrival, a short man with ruffled hair and dressed in blue striped pajama bottoms with a "What's going on?" daze about him.

Stamping her foot and splashing purple all over, she declared a new conclusion. "This situation with Matthew is a crisis for you, Papah. And if it's a crisis for you, it's a crisis for me." Her lavender friends harped a tune much like a victorious march.

"Papah Moolos! Papah Moolos!" she called to get his attention. He heard her and quickly introduced the pajama man to his trusted colleague, Roly, before beelining to the grassy mid-section of the courtyard where she stood.

"Pip, what's wrong? You can't possibly be hurt. Did you fall wrong?" His feet swished in purple mud. He surveyed the slushy mess. "What happened here?"

Pipiera blushed with guilt. She should not have interrupted his important work like that, not when he was in the middle of a processing. "No, no, I am okay. Thank you. It's about..."

Before she could finish, he seemed to understand. He grabbed her hands and held them securely.

"I know," he replied in his calm, reassuring voice. "You're afraid for Matthew."

Actually, it's you I'm afraid for, not him. I couldn't bear to see you hurt.

"I was just thinking about what could happen—or might not happen—and..." She was too flustered to continue. She studied his face, wishing he knew what she was thinking. *What would be worse than losing you to a replacement would be seeing you sad and hurt all the time. Darn that Matthew. Either way, I lose.*

"Well, you'll be happy to know I've got a plan. I've already decided. I'm going to talk to a dear friend I've known for a great many years. He's now the big chief taking care of kingdom interventions."

"An intervention!" Pipiera pulled back from Megalos. "Aren't those dangerous? I thought they reserved that, you know, for when the rebels caused an interference. This business with Matthew, it's not like it's outside the code, is it? Surely, that's not the case here, is it?" She stared at him, knowing he would see the horror and fear in her eyes. "Besides, you told me interventions only happen in extreme circumstances, and lots of discussions and things have to take place first—with the king."

"It's the way forward that makes sense," he said, stroking her cheek. "I know you want him to succeed as much as I do. I assure you, I will do everything I can. But you know... free will and all. The code." He gave her that facial expression, the one she was most familiar with. The one that confirmed all things would work out as meant to, and sometimes they wouldn't work out the way we want.

Pip used gentle force to brush aside his hand from her cheek as though it were simply a caught strand of hair. She was not convinced. A burly lump in her stomach hinted otherwise.

Megalos turned to see how Roly was doing on his own. A threesome of arrivals was approaching just a few waves away. He smiled at Pip and patted her head before striding back to his post.

Barely moving, she watched her papah get back to the gate all while her mind churned. Interventions caused chaos and lawlessness. They were known to be full of battles and risks. She knew it, and so did Papah. "If that's the route he wants to take," she muttered, "then he's even more concerned about this Matthew than I thought. Darn."

CHAPTER FIFTEEN
THE BRIEFING

"MY, YOU LOOK nice, Moolos!" Pipiera said admiringly to her pretend, however many times great, granddad. She'd had time to accept his need to help Matthew.

"Big meetin', Pip. Gotta look professional." Megalos winked and grinned at her. She loved when he did that. It warmed her heart like honey butter on hot bread.

Megalos was dressed in his magnificent high-collared, dark-grey cape and navy balloon pants that tied up just above his ankles. A silky wheat-golden rope was tied neatly around his waist, the ends hanging on the right side. He wore ancient sandals that had been passed down to him from one of his own great ancestors. "These here sandals, Pip…" He had told her the story many times, "… one of the greatest patriarchs in my family wore these, I'm told. Yup indeed, for a long, long journey in the desert. They protected him from the scorching sand and sharp stones." He tried to make her laugh by pretending to shake out the sand trapped within the leather layers. He was proud of his ancestors. Well, most of them. Megalos flexed his toes and flashed another rare boyish grin. "More importantly," he leaned in to share a secret, "*they* lead the way." He took another deep breath. "These here sandals remind me I did not get here on my own and that I must continue to forge forward by following. Not by my own leading."

In his right hand was a walking stick, beautifully carved from a centuries-old date palm tree. Pipiera already knew its importance. Actually, it was nostalgic, made from wood harvested from his earthly parents' property. It was bendy enough to give Megalos the flexibility the journey along the outside of the kingdom wall demanded. It was a dangerous path. He shared with her once again how this walking stick also served as a mentor. It reminded him of the burdens he carried during his own earthly journey. "I never walked alone," he summarized, chin in the palm of his large thick hand, "but sadly, I didn't know it."

She often phased out in the middle of his story somewhere, not quite getting all of his metaphorical whatnots. But she made sure to straighten up and listen well when he finally arrived at his conclusion. Fortunately, that day's version of the story was brief, so she didn't have to phase out.

"Almost forgot!" Megalos disappeared up the stairs of his watch post and returned with a heavy chain made of one of the kingdom's precious metals around his neck. The head gatekeeper pendant sat perfectly against his hairy chest. Neither a shirt nor flowing garb was required for Megalos's uniform. He was expected to look the part of a strong, burly gatekeeper, one who would never allow an undesired trespasser through the kingdom's gate. He carried out his contributing part well, in appearance and in action. He rubbed his pendant. "I belong to our king," he said with conviction. "I am his." He leaned down to meet Pipiera's eyes. "Now, Pip, keep Roly in line," Megalos motioned his eyes over to his replacement, who was in charge for the afternoon. Roly was a keener and a little stressed already.

She was so proud. "I'll help him out, Moolos. As long as you promise to tell me everything!"

Pipiera wished she could go to the briefing called by the

authoritarians, but only key members of the intervention team would go. Everyone else would hear whatever was necessary on a need-to-know basis, so the kingdom could be prepared. A certain chain of communication had to be followed. Megalos would get his instructions regarding any intervention responsibilities for this Matthew boy direct from the authoritarians. She secretly hoped there would be none.

Megalos faced eastward. Beyond the chattering picnic area, well past the garden of trees and just before the sea of mountainous clouds lay a narrow opening camouflaged by brilliant orange and red bushes. He began, taking his usual long strides, leaving Pipiera behind with a pang in her heart. She did not like to be separated from him, and he knew it.

I hope your Matthew boy gets his life in order soon, because he's disrupting mine!

CHAPTER SIXTEEN
GETTING THERE

Outside the Kingdom

MEGALOS HEADED DIRECTLY toward the opening, knowing it led to a pathway so treacherous that only those with living footwear could possibly navigate it. The only views would be the ground beneath his feet. His sandals would take the lead once he pushed back the brilliant, oversized leaves and stepped upon the narrow, gritty path made of metals and gems, all precious and in various shades of black and blue. Soon he would be surrounded by a thick, luscious-smelling fog.

And, here we go. He thought of Pipiera's distraught face as he left. *Don't worry, we'll get everything sorted out.* He didn't like seeing her so downtrodden. *She's worried about Matthew just as much as me.* That thought made him smile.

Two steps away from the path, Megalos felt his sandals awaken. A mix of relief and anxiety kicked in, as it always did for the first leg of the journey. The adventurous climb would take him most of the morning. Megalos released a slightly nervous laugh as he wiggled his toes to prepare them. He knew that once he stepped onto that pathway, he would never see more than one or two footsteps in front of him at any given time until he arrived at his destination.

"You fellas down there are going to have one heck of a ride!" he teased his toes.

It was a mindful challenge as well. Steep cliffs and sharp turns with low visibility meant exerting a great deal of trust and faith. Megalos was thankful for his walking stick and not just to support his balance. It was the dear companion that reminded him of his past. Where he had journeyed in his own time and what his own path was like, it all helped shape and form who he was now.

A delicious woody, warm, and spicy aroma entered his nostrils. He was on his way. On his left side was the kingdom wall, the same wall that protected citizens from the harsh outer world and its rigid, dark coldness, which shouldered his right side. It had been almost a century since he had last taken this route. Fortunately, it was not a frequent demand of the job.

It took a good thirty steps or so before Megalos mastered the art of relinquishing control to his sandals, which were totally focused on the task. They fought his every step until he surrendered heart and soul to the groove and the pace.

Eager to get his somewhat anxious mind off the trek, Megalos focused on Matthew, whose protection was the object of the briefing. To gain the opportunity of taking up a life on earth was a privilege, no matter the purpose or tasks. It took tremendous courage to accept an earthly tour challenge, and even those who chose a brief lifespan were rewarded well. "I'm back! I did it!" some would exclaim in delight when they approached Megalos's gatepost to reenter the kingdom, fully charged with new energies, abilities, and insight. That is, of course, only those who remembered who they were—citizens of the kingdom. Some forgot, denied, or rejected their true identities. Megalos shuddered at the thought. But even the briefest of visits could bring the king such love and joy and satisfaction. All earthly tours were carefully planned to meet the king's overall objectives. Each tour was designed for those who accepted it, along with customized rewards. Few were up to the challenge, though. Most were happy to live simply and happily in the kingdom, that being their end goal. But this Matthew, he was after a lead role in the kingdom, as Megalos was centuries ago. The recent happenings could jeopardize Matthew's hope and deep desire, his true desire, which while on Earth was completely unknown to him. *If he only knew what was at stake.* Megalos concerned himself with possible outcomes that forced him to shudder yet again. *Am I to blame?*

Nearly at the halfway point, the path became even narrower. One foot in front of the other, the cliffs more jagged than before. The fog hung around his ankles. It was a tricky corner, an unforgiving sheer vertical rock on his right. *Get me through this, my King.* An aromatic scent of lavender flowed gently from his right side and encircled his head. The faith and love that Megalos beheld for his king kept him patient and steadfast on the path laid out before him, one step at a time. Only those who knew and acted on this were able to make such journeys. Others, leaning on their own steps, became frightened, tripped, or fell. The nature of the path itself was another simple form of protection surrounding the kingdom.

The scent transitioned to the distinctly sweet and gentle aroma of freshly sickled grain. Megalos was reminded of his earthly pa, who used to tell him, "Bow down like the wheat when the wind comes, 'cause if you don't, the king don't want ya." I suppose he had a point, but he used it all wrong. "Git rid of your pride, kid, and bend over," he'd add with overwhelming whisky breath. A severe walloping inevitably ensued. That sweet aroma saddened Megalos. His pa never did arrive at the kingdom's gate. If he did, he would have learned Megalos had forgiven him a long time ago.

Megalos vowed silently to help Matthew get back on track. He may not have had a parent who beat him, but he was allowing a dose of pride to get stuck in his head, and anger was building a wall in his mind. *I wonder if he senses discomfort for his own dad.* Megalos could relate to that. *But if he's off track already, he'll never get through his humankind tour, not given what's surely ahead of him.*

Megalos expressed his gratitude once again for his living sandals to accomplish the feat of the uphill journey. *Thank you, my King.*

On the next level up, the pathway curved inward toward the kingdom wall, creating a more secure distance from the steep edge. A gentle breeze brought a new and different aroma, a sweet, fragrant incense. A little less tense, Megalos switched his thought gears, this time back to Pipiera. He loved how she loved the citrus aroma from the orange trees located deep within the wooded area and how she never tired of expressing how beautiful and graceful the flowers danced, particularly the waving lavender fields. She almost always paused and smiled when new arrivals could be seen on the horizon. She had become the apple of his eye but also a stabbing concern to his heart. *Why is she so afraid to enter my gate?*

Pipiera became an arrival not long after she left. Her earthly tour was only a matter of weeks, although she arrived in the form of a young teenager. He could easily recall the day of her arrival; she was so inquisitive. The questions kept coming, one after the other. She certainly was a puzzle. Long story short, all these years later, she remained in the outer courtyard and was now known affectionately by all as Megalos's sidekick. He didn't fully understand it, but he accepted it just fine. Now he didn't want it any other way.

Guarding the gate with due diligence and grooming the other gatekeepers, Megalos understood his responsibilities and was good at it. Protecting, sensing, and greeting were all skills he had mastered. As for understanding everything else? Well, there were a great many mysteries still to be sorted.

Megalos silenced his mind, closed his eyes, and continued on. He slumped comfortably, fully submitting to his sandals. He could relax a little more now since the path had widened a bit. Brighter gems with added colors crunched beneath his feet. Just two more levels before he arrived at his destination, and that last bit of the journey would go fast.

His sandals stopped abruptly in front of a thick, green, forested frame. Megalos poked around until he found the opening. He stepped through, the bones and muscles below his ankles feeling like jelly as they started to arouse. He wobbled and shook his feet, wanting to ready them to resume the trek. *Ahhh, no more fog.* He wiggled his toes and glanced around. Before him was a perfectly circular clearing of thick, fresh-smelling moss. Century-old vines held back leafy branches from the surrounding trees. A vast dome of branches overhead provided a sweeping atmosphere of unity. Megalos figured there had to be at least seventy types of greenery intricately woven into creative patterns. The atmosphere was bright, cheery, loving, and welcoming. It was a pleasure to step into it.

But this meeting, will it be a pleasure? he doubted.

CHAPTER SEVENTEEN
A NEW FATE?

MEGALOS ACKNOWLEDGED JAMES, the authoritarian who arranged the briefing. He was busy sorting things out at the head of the space marked by three large rocks with sizzling red-orange wildflowers growing in front and in between. Megalos wasn't surprised to learn that James was in charge of the intervention, but he was surprised to see Bethany scurrying about. Bethany was a scribe, one of the kingdom's most well-known and most respected. Her thoroughness was nothing short of amazing, and despite her chubbiness, Megalos thought, she was ever so quick with her movements.

Like her scribe colleagues, Bethany was no more than two feet tall and had wings like a hummingbird that transported her to the most optimum position to study faces and hear all voices—whisperings included. Bethany's role, as much as Megalos could tell, was to capture the meeting's discussion for the kingdom's records, all of which were meticulously stored in the Book Room. *If she is assigned to this intervention, this is obviously a matter of considerable proportions, an even bigger concern than I suspected.*

Bethany didn't lift her head but acknowledged each participant with a buzzing kind of nod as they came through the same grassy opening as Megalos.

Three other participants had already arrived. Gad, the lead receiver, whose kingdom role was to capture requests sent to the king from earth tour participants. He and his colleagues would review, analyze, and determine whether and how responses might further the kingdom. *Huh, no one ever sees him, he's always behind the scenes. Wonder why he is here?*

Gad seemed to be quite chummy with Othis, the lead protector. Othis was an oversized guy with a mean, stern presence about him. His height stood out. *He's got to be at least eighteen feet tall. Is it possible he's grown since I've seen him last?* The breadth of his wingspan was double that. His helmet, breastplate, satchel, and knee-high boots were made with plenty of gold insignia. Megalos didn't have wings himself, his job simply didn't require them. But oh, he admired them, especially Othis's. He could not imagine how heavy that armor must be and how powerful those wings had to be for him and his armies to maneuver so expediently. Othis led armies of armies, all battling in *the deep*, all to secure and protect the kingdom from enemies lurking below. These armies did their job well, and Megalos deeply respected and appreciated such; otherwise, he may have strangers coming up to his gate rather than the expected and scheduled arrivals. Megalos gave Othis a slight nod, indicating a warm greeting.

Taking a seat on a log close by Gad and Othis was Aivy. She was the lead transition agent. *She and her colleagues have quite a fun job*, Megalos thought. Once his new arrivals were processed to enter the gate, they saw Book Room Keeper next, followed by the Gift Room Keeper. It was all coordinated by Aivy and her team, including the citizen orientation. Best of all, it included one-on-one time with the king himself.

Aivy's presence concerned Megalos though. If she had been called to the briefing, that could mean they were calling Matthew home early. And if they called him home early, he would not get the chance to accomplish what he was scheduled to learn, so he could assume any gatekeeper role, much less be qualified for the head role one day. Megalos hoped he was wrong, but why else would Aivy have been invited as a participant? Megalos rubbed his chin, deep in thought. *Perhaps asking for an intervention was a mistake.*

He absorbed the majestic presence of a rushing waterfall, allowing the pure enormity of its power to distract him momentarily. A series of crystalline drops fell from a level high above, through a clearing in the forest dome and straight through the floor of the mossy grounds where he stood. Megalos knew they fell farther and farther, cutting through all levels of the kingdom, even the lowest level. He had been there once at the heart of the lowest level where the falling drops, appearing as crystal flakes, each complex and beautiful, ended their vertical fall and entered the horizontal churning flow of the River of Times. Immediately their exterior hardened to stone, individual and unique. How could he forget the day he arrived not far downstream from that very spot to pick up his own living stone on the riverbank? *Now that was some place, some experience. A long time ago,* he shuddered.

Megalos snuck another glance at Aivy. Maybe he could glean a reason for her attendance by her facial expression. *Nope.*

He glanced again at Othis. What a job his crew had, particularly those stationed at the River. An army in never-ending, non-stop battles to slow the impact of intense waterspouts shooting up from the Deep underneath. Vortex upon vortex of deceptive waters with the sole purpose to blind the living stones, tricking them into corners where they become trapped and lost. *I bet our Matthew is stuck in the mud. Please, Othis, get him loosened.*

James was still setting up, hanging a mammoth, sheer, rectangular curtain made of the finest threads and woven by a group of talented kingdom citizens. Vines instinctively grabbed hold of its edges, and in no time, he could hardly tell it was there. It was virtually transparent. The curtain was a projection screen, but until the authoritarians put it to use, the endless rows of commanding trees behind could be seen with impressive clarity.

Just then the Book Room Keeper and the Gift Room Keeper arrived, busily chatting. The pair could pass for twin brothers, but Megalos knew they came from two different lines. They had so much in common, at least it seemed so. They were enjoying their kibitzing, their short arms waving excitedly at each other. They tended to get their messages across by using short, pointed phrases and often repeated themselves, which was sometimes annoying. They worked extremely close with the king, often referring to him personally by their favorite endearing nickname, Kal, short for Kalos. It meant "The Beautiful." These two beings had been in their roles forever, much longer than Megalos could comprehend—and Megalos himself had been around for quite some time. No one in the kingdom had ever identified a personal name to either of them. Oddly enough, they were only known as the Gift Room Keeper and the Book Room Keeper. However, there had been plenty of nicknames for the dynamic duo. Unlike the heads and leads, neither one had a team or even any colleagues. Rather, they worked in solo form, continuously and constantly. They never ran out of energy, neither did they ever take breaks. *Yet another mystery.* Megalos chuckled silently and wondered how they managed to escape their demanding roles to come to this particular briefing. Megs at least had Roly to watch over things in his absence. Their presence too was deeply concerning to Megalos. *If they are both here, along with Aivy, then there is no hope for Matthew to continue. They must be calling him back.*

Megalos sighed. "I've failed the boy before I even had the chance to help him." Sadness overcame Megalos at the thought of how young Matthew might feel upon his arrival, to learn and discover what he missed out on. He heard Bethany whiz away.

Shoot, she was behind me. She must have heard me mutter. So far this briefing hasn't gone well, and it hasn't even started yet!

From the wooded area behind the screen came Soogreese, the king's lead maintenance guy, along with Katakos, the kingdom visionary. They were an odd pair, but it was quite common for them to be seen together, likely because visionary work required immediate reporting. The two of them were rolling in three pieces of kingdom equipment—the Clock, the Pendulum, and the Scale. These three pieces represented basic equipment the authoritarians used to plan and measure all individuals since the beginning. The Clock outlined key events, including each earth journey's entrance and its conclusion. The Pendulum measured the variance between the height of faith and the height of doubt and was sometimes given a push for necessary increases. The Scale depicted the rewards secured for after the journey. Typically, everyone loved to check the Scale first.

The Scale and the Pendulum were just a little shy of twenty-one feet in height. The Clock appeared a bit more portable and was perhaps twelve feet tall by twelve feet wide. Soogreese, a tall, lanky fellow with bushy black hair, made abrupt changes to his walk, like he was trying to keep his stride up to the pace and direction of calculations that only he could understand. Back and forth, looking up, looking down, turning around, then back and forth again. It was dizzying to watch. He moved each piece ever so slightly, so they were in perfect position. Perfect to what, Megalos had no idea. What he did know was that Soogreese kept the kingdom's most precious equipment in perfect working order. There were no backups or replacement parts.

Katakos, on the other hand, had an even-paced stride. In fact, it was almost a float. His feet barely skimmed the ground. Any time Megalos had seen Katakos, he was smartly clothed in ancient garb and in deep thought, as one might expect from a visionary.

James scanned his audience, likely checking to see if everyone had arrived.

Suddenly, Serena bolted in through the bushes. "That journey gets me every time!" she exclaimed. She was a bit jittery from the journey, and Megalos could see her hands shaking somewhat. Managing a big exhale, she apologized for being late and grabbed a spot on the closest log. She was so thankful to sit down, her hands securely wrapped around the stump.

Megalos restrained the empathy he felt for Serena. He was cautious when it came to showing emotion, but a smile managed to crack. She reminded him of Pipiera. *Spirited and, well... quite spirited.* That journey was indeed an adventure, and it took full concentration to submit to living shoes. She had already slipped hers off and was pushing her toes into the soft moss, appearing to feel assured by it.

James straightened himself up. Satisfied everyone was present and accounted for, he clasped his hands together up high. Bethany fluttered into her ready position, scroll in one hand, pen in the other, and facing the audience as James was, her wings fluttering ferociously to keep positioned at just the right height. The attendees all settled into place. Katakos perched himself on the log beside Serena, likely to help her calm down a bit. Soogreese preferred to remain standing protectively close to the kingdom equipment. Othis stood near the back by the bushy entrance. The Book Room Keeper and the Gift Room Keeper unfolded a blanket out of nowhere and sat comfortably on the dewy moss. Megalos chose to stand in the opposite back corner where he could see everyone in clear view, as he suspected was Othis's preference as well. It was in both of their natures to be watchful and aware of all presences.

Megalos felt a call to glance again at the falling waters. He sensed someone from afar was watching. There were no spies inside the kingdom, and this was a protected place. All discussions held therein were on an open basis and entrusted to whoever needed to know. No one could escape the Deep and rise to the level where this private meeting outside the kingdom's walls was taking place. Megalos shook off the feeling, but his senses told him that someone out there was keenly interested. The preoccupation caused him to miss the opening. He presumed what he missed was a welcome and recognition of all who responded to the call for the briefing. Serena remarked about the incredible journey and how she had to admit it was tougher given the fog, never mind the living sandals and the keen awareness of being cliffside.

They were all thankful and expressed gratefulness to the king, their king. No one was surprised when Othis broke into song, a tune from his Germanic roots about how so many beautiful birds were perched in the woods. And they were—the wooded area was full of pure white doves. There were so many, it was shocking that one could have missed them. Their peaceful silence made them easily mistakable for white, flowery buds.

James motioned his hand and began to lead the next discussion topic, the reason for the gathering. "On this day and at this time," he began, "we are to become aware of the present situation of one of our own, currently a young lad in the fourteenth year of his humankind tour, to discuss and make recommendations to the king a new fate."

All attendees were still and quiet. They knew that "new fate" determinations were not common practice. In fact, they were quite rare. Revised fate determinations were only given when some type of rebel interference struck someone before reaching the age of understanding.

Fate had two simple determinations. The number of years—well, hours actually—that one's humankind tour would last and the categorical details upon the tour's expiry. In other words, how they were to shed and separate from their earthly clothing. Othis had fondly nicknamed them all. A journey of slow removal was called a *snake bite*, like a poisonous act. The *cliff fall* was a sudden unforeseen ending. The *axe* was a method reserved for the king to use at his discretion. And the fourth? Megs couldn't recall it, but it didn't really matter much to him. Regardless of method, if destined, they would arrive at his gate just the same.

Matthew had plenty of time left in his journey, certainly enough to enable a further continuance of the descendant line. That meant children and grandchildren. *If he comes home now, there will be no time to create his descendant branch.* Megalos knew this disappointment firsthand. *Will he be disappointed when he learns this?* Megalos sighed selfishly. *It also means he'll never be my replacement at the gate; no chance to learn the character. Two blows.*

"The lad is Matthew Sebastian William Mackenzie," James continued, "son of Marnie and Franklin Mackenzie, neither of whom are kingdom citizens as of this date. Grandson of Charles and Margaret Mackenzie, both still earth dwellers, great-grandson of Donald and Ruth Pichler, great-great-grandson of Sebastian and Eugenia Becker, great-great-great-grandson of John and Mary Evans, great-great-great-great-grandson of Malvina and Samuel Virtanen." Deciding to fast forward things, James glanced up at Megalos. "Matthew falls directly into the descendant line gifted to our dear Megalos." All the attendees nodded an empathetic smile toward Megalos.

Megalos himself had his earth tour interrupted prematurely, deleting the chance for children of his own. Upon his expiry, the king granted Megalos with a line renamed to call his own. *Something to do with cutting and grafting,* Megalos recalled. It was a precious gift, one he cherished, his very own adopted line. This gift, these descendants, however, were targets of rebel attacks, and those in the line suffered greatly. Matthew was not the first descendant gifted to Megalos to have gone astray. But if the boy came home early, with no descendants of his own, that would be the end of Megs' precious gift. *Another blow, only mine.*

"Young Matthew's true desire is to assume a contributory role in the kingdom, specifically, the head gatekeeper, to take us through the Time of Later. The significant sufferings he could very well be forced to endure would have prepared him specifically for this role."

Would have? They're packing it in already?

James looked straight at Katakos. "He would be perfect for that job. You know it."

Katakos remained silent.

Hmm... tension there.

Othis gave Megalos a slight empathic nod. The two of them had shared some of their plans upon the expiration of their roles. One could only be in a lead role for 144,000 days. Othis and Megalos were what some kingdom citizens might call "old school." They had started around the same time, and both were keen and knew their term would end in perfect timing for new, well-groomed leads to take the kingdom through the Time of Later. Both fully understood the importance of fresh energies and the value of highly groomed character needed for that day when the full rush of kingdom waters would fall with a powerful surge into the waters of the Deep, sanitizing the River of Times and forcing a catastrophic flood. Such chaos and disruption. Megalos shivered at the thought of the stones still journeying through the River on that day, even though handpicked to survive it.

"Matthew is not on track to meet the character requirements for this kingdom role," James said. "However, he has not arrived at the age of knowledge yet, so that is not the concern that gathers us here at this time." His audience sat perfectly still. They were waiting for more of the story, particularly Megs.

Oh, so you're not bringing him home? What are you trying to say?

"He's been the direct target of rebel interference," James said.

Megalos choked silently. *I knew it. Again. When will they leave my adopted line alone?*

Serena held her hand up, and James nodded for her to speak. "Did they discover the purpose of his humankind tour? Or was it... is it just being... in *that* line?"

It was a good question, although Megalos wondered why she was present. *What role does she play?*

James motioned his right arm toward the equipment. Bethany flew over to the mammoth Clock. "Matthew Sebastian William Mackenzie, son of Marnie and Frank," she announced. The Clock calculated speedily, showing four numbers: the moment Matthew became an earthly inhabitant, the number of significant experiences he was scheduled to have according to the kingdom plan, created with input by Katakos, and two countdown calculations—the number of hours till the next significant experience and the number of hours until his great separation. In other words, whence he was scheduled to come home. All would run according to the kingdom plan, providing, of course, he didn't drown and end up with rebel clothing upon him.

Soogreese crossed his arms and smiled, pleased the kingdom equipment worked so well.

"Tsk tsk." The Gift Room Keeper and the Book Room Keeper shook their heads at the same angle and at the same slow velocity.

Huh, Megalos thought. *In unison too. Wonder how they do that.* Unfortunately, he hadn't a clue what the numbers meant. *Why is what they are seeing so bad?*

"Oh dear," Aivy exclaimed.

Megalos tried to catch James's face in hopes of gaining another clue, but James's were glued to Katakos. There was obvious concern amongst the attendees. Megalos did not fully understand the results, only that Matthew's scheduled separation, with the king's grace, was not for another 554,332 hours. By then he would have incurred at least seven significant experiences. *Most of my arrivals endure one. Some, though, have three or even as many as five. It's rare to have seven scheduled. That must be the concern—the number of significant experiences our dear Matthew must endure and overcome, all to prepare him for my role. Guess I got off lucky.*

"He's got a tough journey," Katakos said. "We all debated

before he was given that assignment, and we all believe he could have done it."

"Could have?" James blurted. "You're really not going to give him another chance? It's a little early to reset the clock, don't you think?"

Tension rose between James and Katakos over the looming decision, though what the decision was about wasn't clear to Megalos just yet.

"Now, I understand the boy has not yet reached the age of understanding, is that correct?" Serena asked. Megalos knew quite well what that meant. Up until that point, Matthew was covered under kingdom citizen policies, but upon reaching it, he would be cut off and would have to find his own way back, all while experiencing whatever he was slated to experience.

"He has not," James replied. "You are right, Serena."

"Well, then, why can he not continue? He really hasn't been given a chance to shine. Certainly not where he's at. Not yet, anyway."

Othis, a man of few words, jumped in. "The rebels obviously discovered Matthew's purpose. What I'd like to know is, what'd they do to interfere?"

Looking down, James swirled the moss in full circles with his big toe as though to buy time. When he looked back up at the audience, he nodded a "go ahead" to Soogreese, who nodded firmly at the transparent screen.

A clip of Matthew's journey appeared before the audience, bearing a gasp from Serena, a pair of tightly clasped eyes from Aivy, a disappointed angst from Othis, and a crossed-arm, stern position from Katakos.

CHAPTER EIGHTEEN
THE REQUEST

In the Outer Courtyard of the Kingdom

"HELP HIM. ME? Why me?!"

Pipiera was a little excited. Not in a good way but in a most definite anxious way. She was being asked to do something totally out of her comfort zone.

Why did she like hanging out in front of the gate with Megalos? She would say it was her admiration and love for her Papah Megs, but it was also a calm and stable place to be, to simply exist, a place with a fantastic front-row seat. Pipiera could witness a great many things and experience many emotions there, all in the comfort and safety of Papah's presence. Her center square was Megalos—strong, stable, consistent, and reassuring. She admired him so much. As newcomers arrived, if they burst with excitement, Pipiera's heart sang along with them. If they broke down in tears, her heart shed tears along with them. All from a safe distance, ten to twenty large strides from her Papah Moolos at any given moment, mostly anyway, unless she was practicing her jumps or riding the waves for fun.

Megalos would grab an arrival's hands, partly to calm them and partly to give a genuinely warm welcome, but mostly because it was his duty. He inspected their palms, which somehow told the story of how they used their time in ways that forwarded the kingdom's purposes and growth. The information collected was not discussed at the gate, but the degree of cleanliness and the beams of brilliant color that streamed from their hands—some brighter than others, some stretching farther than others—revealed exciting hints. It was Megalos's job to scan the data and pass it along ahead of the arrivals' passage through the gate. Megalos told her over and over again that all arrivals had been required "to endure the number of days and hours requested of them," and each had their own "purpose or set of tasks" to accomplish between their set time markers. No matter what that was or however they managed it, Megalos's shining eyes of approval always comforted and reassured them.

Pipiera wasn't sure about the steps once the arrival actually went through the gate and into the kingdom. She couldn't see from the outside, though she'd overheard enough to confirm Megalos's story, that a book existed for every arrival—a comprehensive story that captured the words and thoughts of each person's entire earth journey. *Imagine, every single word and every single thought! My book would be so short.* That discouraged her despite her papah's arguments that the length of time in a tour was not a kingdom measurement. Rather, it was the value of what came straight from a heart that counted. He even hinted the king was more interested in how someone responded or reacted in various scenarios than what scenarios were imposed upon them. When Pipiera pressed for more, Megalos could only surmise, but he figured the king would want to know what choices one made, who they called upon for help, who they trusted, who was their confidant to walk alongside them, and what was going through their minds at different points in their journey. Stuff like that.

"You mean like did they depend on the king?" she had asked, and Megalos nodded in approval of her conclusion. *Still, I was far too young to make a choice.* She remained discouraged and curious, finding a kind of solace watching arrivals day in and day out.

To be truthful, she was a little jealous, and then very embarrassed, that she felt a little jealous sometimes. She didn't have the courage yet to be scanned. The more she came to love and admire Megalos, the more she was afraid her scan's results might disappoint him. *Yes, it is much safer to simply hang out with him outside the gate.*

To Megalos, Pipiera's innocent youthfulness served as a gentle reminder that some arrivals were afforded incredibly limited time for their tours. The shorter their journey, the cleaner and brighter their palms and the greater was the everlasting gift of impact they brought for the king. As far as he was concerned, watching Pip jump so gracefully and skillfully was another form of a fresh breeze. She never got the chance to carry out those skills on her earth journey, so it was satisfying to watch her enjoying it so much now.

The two were a pair, she and him. They had no expectations of each other, only joy and caring in being together. But now a challenge confronted them.

"I don't need to 'grow,'" Pipiera said defiantly, making quotation marks with her fingers. Her glare revealed considerable fear. It was a fear for both—the known and the unknown.

Megalos could only sigh. This was not his idea. The authoritarians had said this job—the next step with Matthew—would require Pipiera's involvement. Megalos was just as surprised. They explained her long-jumping activities were a common denominator with Matthew. She would be able to reach him better.

"Reach him better? Me?" Her voice cackled, an unusual screech, causing Roly to cast an eye of concern toward the two from the gatepost.

Megalos had, in fact, pushed that line of inquiry. That is, why Pip? But Serena had been so hopeful that Megalos would agree to the plan. Then Aivy and Katakos got behind it, both noting that perhaps it was time for Pipiera to grow, and this would be a perfect opportunity. James quickly shut the meeting down in favor of Serena's crazy plan. There was no further discussion given the absence of any other unanimous options. Nothing was ideal.

Aivy had rejected the plan to cut Matthew's fate determination to immediacy. She wanted him to have a fighting chance at his purpose, at what he signed up for.

Othis had been the opposition. He knew what kind of battle he and his crew would be up against. "Not fair to the kid. Too much collateral damage if you leave him there. When those rebels pin you as a main target, it gets messy," he argued. "Bring him home."

The third idea was complicated and concocted by Serena. She proposed a hybrid plan, actions for whatever it might take to wake up his inner self, so he might acknowledge and strengthen his ties to the kingdom. Othis warned the rebels would fight back with the same vigor and reminded all that an unwelcome relationship was already forming. They had witnessed it for themselves thanks to Soogreese and his perfectly maintained equipment. Serena argued they could make use of the rebel interference as though it were actually an intervention from the kingdom.

Not much made sense to Megalos, particularly the comparison chatter to tossing a living stone into a River of Times whirlpool to clean off the muck before it had the chance to blacken. The whole business made a spinning mess of Megalos's head. If Serena hadn't been so convincing and so hopeful, he never would have supported her plan. She promised, cross her heart, that she would devise all the details, the only caveat being that for the plan to work, Pipiera's involvement was a must. Katakos and James both voiced their concerns that the success of the plan would rest wholly on Pipiera's shoulders and Megalos's ability to support her.

Now he had to answer her.

"Why me?" she demanded of him again.

CHAPTER NINETEEN
OPEN UP A CLASSROOM

MEGALOS EXAMINED HER face. *I need to be convincing.*

"Pip," Megalos kneeled, so their eyes met. Despite being adequately tall for her age, he was much, much taller. "Look at this as an adventure. You've always wanted an adventure, right?" With hopeful and somewhat sad eyes, he pressed his finger gently into her upper-left side, suggesting a deep want from her heart.

Pipiera had avoided risk on her tour and even now was playing it safe. A drip of wetness dribbled down her cheek. "No."

"Pip? Come on." He urged a smile from her.

"I didn't know I'd still have to grow here," she said, sulking.

Megalos sat back a little, startled. Never before had he heard a whining comment about the kingdom come from Pip's lips. He had to rethink this a bit, re-strategize.

"Okay, I get it. Think of this as an act of helping. Or teaching. That's it, that's what it is, teaching! You know so much. How many arrivals have you witnessed here?"

"Oh, I don't know. I don't count." She twisted her mouth till it was a frenzied line across her face. "Well, actually, I do. Four million six hundred and eighty-four thousand three hundred and seventy-five.

Counting that last lady that just went in. Not counting those over there." She pointed to a bit of a lineup, three people, to be exact.

Megalos stood up and smiled at the threesome in line. "Amazing, isn't it?" Then he waved in an attempt to catch Roly's attention, but he was already prepared with arms open wide, ready to greet them. Megalos loved the teamwork.

Back to Pip.

"Don't you think you've learned a thing or two about entry to the kingdom? Hmm…?"

"Well, of course! How dare you think I don't pay attention."

"So, you could teach our Matthew."

"*Our* Matthew? I don't exactly *know* him." She shifted uncomfortably. "Is he coming soon?"

"Well, er, ah, here's the thing, Pip."

She narrowed her eyes to focus on his next words, as if they might be visible.

"We—the authoritarians and I, of course—want Matthew to remain in his earth life for several decades yet."

Pip's eyebrows rose. "So, why do you need me now?"

"Well, er, Pip, you could, er, still teach him… there."

Not just her facial features but her entire lanky body shrieked with horror. "What? No. No, no, no. No way, no how, not doin' it. I'm *not* going back there!" She reduced to tears. "No, Moolos, no. You know I can't go back there."

Megalos pressed his right thumb into his chin and grabbed onto the front of his neck with the rest of his hand, something he often did when he needed to think. He knew this wasn't a good idea. His heart throbbed and ached. Megalos desperately needed a solution. He sat back on his knees. "King," he whispered, "all things we bring to you. What's our next step here?"

With her head cocked forward, Pipiera transitioned her stance, indignant now. She shook her head and mouthed the words, "I'm not going."

"Ah yes!" Megalos clapped his hands joyfully to his cheeks. "The authoritarians said your role is to help, er, teach Matthew firsthand. But they did not articulate *where* you were to help, er, teach. So, we will bring our Mr. Matthew up here for lessons!"

Her curiosity was peaked. "Can you do that?"

"I'll ask, but I don't see why not."

She started pacing back and forth. She could think of several reasons why not.

Megalos could tell she was debating internally. *C'mon, Pip, I've never asked anything of you before. Can't you tell how important this is to me?* "What if we could? Would you consider it?" He tried not to appear too desperate. After all, she was already committed to the task, only she didn't know it.

Pipiera locked onto his pleading eyes. Her shoulders resigned to a slump. "Well, I suppose I would."

She seemed to have partially bought into the idea. Perhaps she'd latch on and run with it. Megalos could only hope.

"But only for short bits of time," she added.

"Short bits of time, okay." Megalos nodded. *It's a start.* Once she started, as long as she felt helpful, she would surely jump in with both feet. *No pun intended*, he thought with a grin.

"Here," Pip said, vocalizing her buy-in. "Only if it's here. And…" Her narrow eyes directed firmly at his, "Someone will have to pick him up and take him back." In other words, Pip wouldn't do the traveling part. She had made her point, all this teaching business will happen her way. "We can sit right here." She pointed to the picnic table area.

"The boy isn't to see any of this," Megalos said, circling his hands over the picnic area and the grassy waves flowing in one after the other, depositing their passengers in front of the gate. "We won't be able to show him too much. Faith in what he has not seen will still need some developing. We shan't just give it to him." He hoped this would not be a dealbreaker for Pip. "You will have to go over there to—"

"Over where? Over there? Not the banks of clouds! Oh goodness."

Megalos nodded, indicating she needed to look for a section on the side of the banks.

"The storage pit?" Pip was astonished. Surely not!

"It's a development arena. No one will bother you there. You'll practically have the place to yourself. Seems kinda fitting," he added. "Development."

Pip paced some more till she came around and stamped one foot firmly beside the other. "Okay, the storage pit it is. But over there farther on the east side, there's at least some cool cloud streets to gaze at."

Megalos smiled. He knew how much she enjoyed the manifestation of clouds mixed in with brilliant rays. He managed to hide his sigh of relief. "See, Pip? You already know a perfect spot. You'll be great at—"

"Nice and close to a main tunnel, not the little temporary ones," she said, doing a 360. "Those ones can close up without any warning. We must be close to a main tunnel, one we can count on, nice and secure—and guarded, I might add. We'll need fast access for secure getaways."

Megalos was in awe at her sudden ability to take charge, although he wondered why they might need fast getaways, it was a safe place to be. But he was happy for the ownership that his dear, young Pip was displaying.

She continued to list her needs. "A desk. A small one. There will be no note taking." She wagged her finger in the air. "The boy's got a good memory, I hope." She gave Megalos a sly stare. "You'll make sure of that, right?"

"Er, right, yes, Pip. Anything you say. I'll arrange a memory absorption for your teaching sessions." Megs hoped the authoritarians would approve this request, otherwise, that would be another bridge to cross.

"And a screen." She shot another firm glance at Megalos. "Like the one you talked about." She put her hands on her hips and stood tall, like her spine was pushing up, striving to get out of the top of her head.

Megalos pursed his lips. "Not sure I can do that one, Pip."

"You want me to teach, right? Then I must have a screen. None of this…" She wagged her finger back and forth again. "… no, no stuff. I need a screen."

"Er, okay, Pip, a screen." His shoulders fell. "Anything else?" He hoped not, but her wheels were churning, and he was sure there'd be more.

"The lesson plan. On my desk within the hour."

"Lesson plan?" But Pip was already walking away, off on a mission. She needed to prepare for this business of "teaching."

"Of course, Megalos, a lesson plan," she called back to him. "Whatever I'm supposed to teach this boy on my desk in one hour!"

Now it was Megalos who put his hands on his hips. "You don't have a desk!" he shouted, but she had already disappeared into the thicket behind the picnic area. *And since when do you call me Megalos? So formal.*

"I best call James," Megalos thought aloud, hoping all Pip's requests could be accommodated. "I'll just have to be firm with him. If they want Pip to do this job, and they want me to support her, I'll need them to support me."

The next hour of processing new arrivals went smoothly and joyously on cue, as predicted. The only difference was Megalos's struggle to contain the swirling of all the discussion points made at the briefing in his head. He needed to boil down one or two key lessons for Pip, and he had no clue what to suggest. *Why is this up to me? What learned things do I have to offer?*

Megalos kneeled and opened his arms wide. Gliding toward him on a grassy wave was a lovely young girl, not more than seven earth years. Megalos kissed her on her forehead. "Welcome home,

Greta," he said and then gave her one of his famous bear hugs. Greta's grin stretched from ear to ear, and her entire face burst with light. Hairless from nearly three dozen rounds of chemotherapy, she was wide-eyed and excited and surrounded by a dozen citizens, mostly all great-many-times grandparents. All were much too excited to wait for any scanning formalities but disciplined enough to stand back. Megalos held Greta's hands and captured her gaze. "We've been waiting for you, precious little one."

Greta blinked her large brown eyes twice. She had no lashes to disguise their curiosity.

Scanning completed, he patted her head. "Your beautiful curls will be back and bouncing in no time. Now go on inside and see that little man over there, the funny-lookin' one. He's got a special book all about you!" Megalos winked and shooshed his finger to his mouth. "Just call him Bookie, that's his nickname. Rhymes with cookie." As Megalos stood, still grinning, he motioned for Greta and her greeters to go through the gate.

Greta surveyed those surrounding her. Her maternal great-grandmother encouraged her. "No worries, honey. Mama's gonna come too, just later on. They'll all be here eventually. Let's go in. Come and help us get things ready for them." Off they went through the gate, the passageway into the kingdom.

Ahhhh... that's the answer right there, Megalos thought. Greta was a perfect example. She had endured a significant experience with such a brief tenure, and still she'd be a lasting, inspiring light to her family.

Yes, Matthew needed to understand that. And the better he grasped it, the more he'd allow the light to help him understand how to get through his journey. *And, heavens, the kingdom knows it'll be a long, arduous one.* So that would be lesson one. He had to focus on the true light, that's what mattered, no matter what whirlwind swirled him about.

Megalos scribbled some notes down, reviewed them, then gave

his scribbles a nod of approval. He headed over to the picnic area where families waited and where Pip liked to hang out. "This desk is as good as any," he said with a chuckle as he placed the notes on one of the picnic tables, tucking them under the weight of a lush and aromatic orange. That was her favorite fruit. Megalos smiled to himself knowing she would find his note without any trouble.

CHAPTER TWENTY
BIRTHDAY SURPRISE

In the Town of Havensight

MATTHEW OPENED HIS rheum-gunked eyes. Groggy as he was, he could still read the digital football clock across the room. 11:03 a.m. He figured he must have finally climbed up the stairs and into his bunk. That had to be sometime after 4:00 a.m. because he remembered tossing and turning in both body and mind on the rec room floor till then.

"Oh man." He grabbed a pillow and jammed it over the back of his head without lifting his face, which was still buried face down, becoming one with his mattress, thanks to gobs of spit and dribble. Since the traumatic beating, sleep was either nonexistent or disturbingly deep and fruitful.

"Matty!"

He heard Karo's footsteps pounding up the stairs followed by her hippity-hoppity voice. *Mom's let her loose to come wake me up,* he figured, and correctly so. He also predicted with perfect accuracy that she would make a valiant but failed attempt to jump up onto his bed and would nevertheless do the Happy Birthday thing. "Bogus." Slobbering and wiping it off with his bed sheet, he didn't feel like this was going to be a good day.

His mom wasn't too far behind Karo's thumps.

"Can't sleep all day, sleepy head. It's almost noon." She bent over to kiss Matthew on his forehead. "Ugh. You okay?" she asked. His spittle stank.

"What's your first clue, Mom?" Matthew didn't even try to keep his frustration to himself. His body was crooked and bent, his pillow soaked, and his sheets all over the place, his old blanket wrapped around his knees. "Do I look okay?" Without waiting for his mom's response, he rolled his eyes.

Marnie caught his super-duper bad mood. "Well, you've been through a lot. Happy birthday, Son." She walked out of the room. "Come on, Karo, leave your brother alone."

Matthew lay there for a few moments, feeling even worse. He knew his mom probably wanted to make a big deal out of his birthday, particularly in light of the past week and a half. She tried so hard. He mustered his way out of bed and scrubbed up as best as his energy would allow. Of course, the chirpy pair were waiting at the breakfast table, only it wasn't set, it was all cleared. All cleared, that is, except for a chocolate cake with dumb miniature football posts and players stuck on top, likely placed by Karo's sticky unwashed fingers, and who knows where those fingers had been.

"I don't even like football," Matthew muttered.

"Yeah, you do," his mother said.

Somewhere inside, Matthew knew he shouldn't make a deal out of his mom's traditions. She'd been using that same little football set atop his birthday cakes since he was about two years old. *She was so keen to have me in sports,* he thought, *anything but science or astronomy like Dad.* The little football, however, had disappeared many moons ago. Truth was, Matthew could throw a football quite well. He also had a keen interest in astronomy, but he suppressed it at every turn. He did not want to upset his mom. *All that stuff reminds her of Dad and all.*

The miniature football posts gave Matthew a sudden, deep

twinge of sadness. *Mr. Falcon.* He had been Matthew's favorite teacher. He was known in the community as the savior who brought back a high school football team to represent their region, but to Matthew, Andy Falcon was someone he could always talk to. The reality that he will no longer be in the halls of Havensight was unbearable, particularly right now.

Matthew sighed. The cake merely represented dead people gone from his life.

They had their fill of cake—yup, that was Matthew's breakfast. It was surprisingly good and probably the only thing that went well for him that day.

Karo was aloof and remained close to her mom. Early afternoon came, and Matthew was ready for a nap. Marnie encouraged it. The doctor's orders continued to prioritize lots of rest. Likely, he could go back to school for half days starting the following week.

Matthew was thankful his mom had made up his bed, fresh with new sheets. "Ahhh, rad." He settled in and fell asleep in no time. Till he was interrupted, that is.

"Sugar and sarcasm."

"Am I trippin'?" Matthew bolted upright. As he rubbed his eyes, it all came flooding back.

What the heck? "I knew it. You *are* real!" Matthew was annoyed and shocked to see Kasartha again, mostly annoyed.

Kasartha laughed. "That was some cake! Personally, devil's food is my favorite. Don't you wish it were more chocolatey?" He was met by a long silence from Matthew. "Hmmmm? What's the matter, Matty Boy, not happy on your big day?"

Matthew took a deep breath. "I have two things to say to you. One, leave Karo alone. And two, get out of here. Leave me alone."

Kasartha settled himself comfortably on the end of Matthew's bed. "Uh, you called me, remember?"

"Yeah, to tell you to split. Vamoose!"

"Well, that makes a lot of sense. Duh. Besides, it's wishful thinking. Believe me, I think you are a pain in the buttocks. You're not very nice to me, you know."

"Wishful thinking? Why is that wishful thinking? You got some kind of bounty on my head?"

Kasartha laughed. "Nope. That's a question for your Emerson dudes."

"One more time—get outta here, and don't come back. Do not bother my sister or anybody else in my life. Got it?"

Kasartha raised his head with great confidence. He turned away slightly as if to suggest Matthew's word was final, that Matthew held such authorization.

Kasartha produced a stone and proudly displayed it in his right palm. The name etched on it read, "Matthew Sebastian William Mackenzie." A hard black coating covered its bottom and one of the sides. It certainly appeared to be that same stone Matthew had witnessed in a dream-like scene that still plagued his mind—on account of it being so terrifying and surreal, the shadowy tail of an enormous, translucent dragon batting Matthew's stone into the swirling dark sea above them. Now Kasartha was sitting on the end of Matthew's bed proudly displaying what appeared to be that same stone.

Will this bizarre stuff ever end? Matthew wondered, not really expecting an answer to his wishful thought.

"You need to come with me," Kasartha said, tossing the stone up and down in his hand. "Now!" He held the stone inside his fist, his face scrunched into a threatening glare.

Matthew jumped down. With his own fists clenched, he stood up on the bottom bunk so he could be face-to-face with Kasartha. "No. And leave Karo alone. And leave me alone! Get outta here." As soon as these commands escaped his lips, he wished he could take them back. Well, not the words or the message, just the volume.

Sure enough, the loudness of his voice attracted Marnie and

Karo. He knew in a matter of seconds they'd be pounding up the stairs to check on him. Matthew reduced his next message to a whisper. "I don't know who you are or why you're bugging me. You and your stone and your bad breath and ugly face should just leave. I don't care. Whatever you want or need, I. Don't. Care."

"Matthew? You okay?" Marnie knocked on the bedroom door before opening it. She found him lying motionless on the floor.

"Karo! Call your dad!"

CHAPTER TWENTY-ONE
No Permission Needed

Somewhere in the Cosmos

KASARTHA HAD A good hold of Matthew's left forearm as they went up, up, and up. Past the hazy afternoon sky and the thicket of heavy, wet clouds, through a dark passage with vaguely visible stars in the distance, and past the crescent of a planet or moon or something, Matthew couldn't be sure.

This time there was no gazing at sights, no oozing of awesomeness over the amazing spectrums charging through thick curtains of darkness. No, this time it was simply a speedy surge of travel and a wiry tangle of emotions.

Ice-like rocks hurled against them at fastball speeds, first small and few, but soon enough, large and numerous. Matthew was thankful Kasartha dodged them all, undeniably an impeccable skill. Kasartha kept them on a steady track.

Matthew's face hurt. He figured it had to be deformed by now just from the speed they were traveling. *I'm gonna look like him, oooooeh.*

Kasartha headed directly toward the mouth of the very tunnel from which the charging rocks of ice were protecting. The eye of the swirl in the opening presented relief at first, only to lead to yet another brethren of terror.

Inside, the tunnel was narrow and claustrophobic, the air still and sticky. Eyeballs that bulged much like Kasartha's protruded from the wall's lining, watching their every move. Each pair had different features and portrayed a different personality, none of them welcoming and all of them angry. Matthew was certain that he and Kasartha were trespassing, but they continued farther inward at a painfully slow speed as if to not upset any apple carts.

A shriek of wind bellowed, freaking Matthew out. He shut his eyes tight. *This must be hell.*

The tunnel ended, and the space opened up. *Freedom!* Albeit still black.

Before picking up speed, Kasartha glanced back at Matthew. "Gotta love that shortcut, eh?"

Finally, they landed safely on a ledge halfway up an ominous landform. Matthew stood soberly trying to get his bearings—any bearing would do. It was a mountainous area as far as he could see, a long row of them. They would have been majestic if they were sprinkled with greenery or snow-capped and placed in a setting with a background of stunning blues. Instead, the background had lightened to an eerily grey fog. There was no color, just streaks of black variants. Ledges stuck out a little too far and unforgiving for Matthew's liking. He thought of climbing legends Urs Kallen and Brian Greenwood. *I bet even they wouldn't attempt these.* Matt felt like he knew them both on account of how he'd seen their close-ups and read their stories in a *Rock and Ice* magazine, the one he'd snuck into his coat while at Hurley's Sporting Goods. Matt surrendered to a wave of sheepish guilt. *When I get back, I promise to pay you, Mr. Hurley.*

Each mountain as far as Matthew could see was speckled with black holes, which he learned later were openings to countless caverns. Kasartha proudly took a bow, then pointed to the opening of his own cavern. "You're welcome."

Welcome for what? Matthew attempted a response, but his mouth wouldn't move. He was overwhelmed, mentally exhausted, and as far as his physical condition went, well, he couldn't figure that out either. His jaw was stuck. He kneaded his cheeks until his mouth finally moved. "What is it you need or want me for? Seriously, you're ruining my life."

Kasartha wasted no time and jumped right into argument mode. "Ruining your life? Ha! You don't need me to do that. Your life was not so tickety-boo."

"Correction. My life *is* not so tickety-boo. But look around you." Matthew motioned around the cavern with his arms. "This is better? It's freaky up here. Who are you hiding from? There's no one around for miles, except for those you spy on or check out with your binocular thingamajig. It's foggy. There's a freakin' dragon beasty thing up here. Do you even have friends? Do you eat food? Why don't you go find someone to play ball with or something instead of stealing people's stones out of… out of… out of whatever that is up there. A big, black, smelly lake!" When Matthew unleashed, he couldn't stop. This was a habit of his. His mom said it came from his dad, but she practiced it quite well too.

Kasartha grinned at Matthew, then turned around to face the mountainous lineup, pursed his lips, and gave a sharp whistle. In front of each of the black openings, shadowy figures slowly emerged and stood tall, signaling a sign of solidarity.

Blimey, how many of you are there? As far as the eye could see, lonely non-energetic shadows of people emerged from the thousands of caverns in the massive forms of solid rock. Matthew choked as Kasartha waved them a signal that all was okay and then turned to Matthew once again.

"You see? I am not alone."

Matthew rubbed his chin. From somewhere deep within, he

got rather bold, all things considered. "Give me a break. They're not your friends." The two exchanged hard glares. "They're just like you—losers. You're all losers." At that, Matthew released his anger. "You're all losers!" he yelled as loudly as he could.

The shadowy figures suddenly became energetic, growing straight and taller in height. Matt had certainly caught their attention.

Kasartha cupped his hands around Matthew's mouth. "You idiot! Do you not think I could toss you off that ledge, direct into deep nothingness? You think I won't do it? We'll see who the loser is then."

Matt pulled away and ducked in anticipation of whatever Kasartha and his thousands of lone ranger buddies might do. After all, Kasartha had whacked him before; he was sure of it. *I guess it was stupid to be so bold like that.*

But nothing happened. Instead, when Matt dared a peek, Kasartha's shadowy buddies had disappeared back into their caverns. Kasartha stepped away and sat down, his legs dangling dangerously over his private little veranda. Only it wasn't a veranda—it was a thin rock jutting out over a vast space of black nothingness.

"So, this is where you live?" Matt asked. "This is your home?"

Kasartha collapsed his head into his hands.

"Oh, bogus. Really?" Matthew did not like this game. *This guy really brings out the worst in me.* Matthew fought a deep natural desire inside, a pining for empathy to take the lead. He changed the subject, but that didn't work. It seemed strange to Matthew that empathy won over his anger and fear.

"What was the rush, by the way? Why did you have to bring me here so urgently? Without permission, I might add." Matthew attempted to encourage Kasartha by using a calmer tone and employing a, hopefully, pleasing smile. Matthew sat against the cavern wall and pulled his knees close to his chest. Even though he felt some empathy for this freaky fellow, he still did not trust him.

No way would he sit on the edge of that razor-thin ledge with his legs fishing into the black space where the living shadow of a mega dragon lurked. As he looked around, he wished he could escape, just snap his fingers and be home. *My home. My mom. Karo. My room. My friends, well not all of them, but some of them. I don't wanna be here.*

Kasartha interrupted Matthew's thoughts. He turned toward him, appearing quite distraught.

"Were you... *crying?*" Matthew asked.

"Don't be so shocked. You think feelings go away when... when... when you're here?"

That was an in. "Where exactly is *here?*"

"You know, I used to be just like you."

Matthew nodded to show even more empathy but still pressed to know their whereabouts. "Before you came... *here.*"

"I had everything. And I threw it all away. Just like you're doing." Kasartha turned away again, dropping his head into his hands. "I even had family."

"What happened... to them?" Matthew had a sick feeling he didn't want to know.

Kasartha could only blubber and sob. Matthew stepped toward him.

Kasartha blubbered and sobbed some more. Matthew stepped even closer, nervous about the thinness of the ledge.

"The king took my family."

"The king? What king? And why would someone take your family?" Matthew waited as Kasartha sobbed and blubbered some more. Matthew inched over and sat beside him, putting his arm around his shoulders. "Tell me what happened."

"It doesn't matter."

Matthew remained silent. He could not wrap his head around all this. Much worse, reality was setting in. He was now involved in two worlds that were colliding. Which one was real? Crazy enough, life with Kasartha in it seemed completely normal now, albeit a little bizarre and out-of-this-world impossible, but completely and emphatically real. Kasartha sitting there pouring out his woes on that ledge in deep space was just as real as his mom in their kitchen pouring cornflakes into a bowl. So was the empathy-to-anger sliding scale of emotions Matthew felt for him.

Matthew waited to hear more. Was Kasartha possibly a good guy? *I'm going with not*, he thought.

The period of silence was long enough. "What's the deal with the stone?" Matthew's tone was genuine and helpful. "And maybe... well, somehow... maybe *I* can help you." *Oh man, I'm an idiot.*

Another long pause. Matthew was wishing he hadn't put the offer out there, but it was too late. He felt something stir inside suggesting he needed to help this guy. He worked on convincing himself. *He seems to be a lost soul. That's how Mom would describe him. And Mr. Falcon too, for that matter. He would say the same thing. And maybe, just maybe, if I did something good for someone in the universe, my life back in Havensight will be better.*

Kasartha considered Matthew in a different light. "Naaah," he said, pulling away from Matthew's comforting arm.

"What's wrong with me? You're the one with the problem. I'm offering you help." *This guy's frustrating, to say the least.* "Do you even want your family back?" *What kind of king would do that anyway?*

Kasartha gave Matthew a sly look. "You'd have to give up... your life down there."

"What? I'm not going to do that!" There was another careful, cautious pause.

"There must be something *else* I could do to help." Matthew was beginning to believe this guy was emotionally deranged or disturbed.

While waiting for an answer, Matthew took in his

surroundings—the stark stillness of fog patches that he swore had eyes, hundreds of needle-like rock ledges, the lingering sight of all those sorrowful-looking figures hiding in the shadows of cavern entrances. He wasn't as freaked out as he had been on the first trip. All this made his earthly problems in Havensight diminish in importance. "Yeah, I'm not giving that up, no way," he muttered. He stood up and inched away from the ledge.

"Well, you could help me get *my* stone back," Kasartha said. "You distract the elevator guy, and I'll grab it. Then..." his face brightened with new excitement, "we'll go together up the mountain high enough to place both our stones, yours and mine, directly in the crystal stream!"

"Uh, elevator guy? Crystal stream? I don't know what you're talking about. Now there's two stones?"

"It's really quite safe, and it's pretty straightforward. We may have to break it up into a few trips—just to be safe and all. It's really just a timing thing. The first part's a challenge. The rest?... ah, it'll be a cinch."

"Uh, I'm afraid to ask, but what's the first part?"

"Below, way below, inside the earth. Ya know? C'mon, you gotta know. That's where the big pit is, heavy loads of stones dumped all the time. Categorized by time of commitment, so my stone will be easy to find. At least I'm pretty sure. It's dodging the elevator guy and the pit guards. Hey bro, that's nothin' for us! After that, like I said, it'll be a cinch."

Matthew pondered his proposal.

Kasartha urged, "Hey, I went outta my way to get yours. The least you can do is go with me to get mine. You owe me!"

"Down *there?*"

"Yeah, no biggie."

"And there's no chance I can lose my life down there?"

"No chance. In fact, you'll thank me. Your comfy life back with your Marnie-momma will be much better. Things will run much smoother. All your problems will be solved in the interim, and your future? Well, I'm telling you right now, it'll be *really* great."

"All my problems?"

"Yup."

"And you?"

"Hey, bud, I'll be even better than you—as long as we get my stone into that crystal stream too. Deal?"

Matthew wondered what other option he had. He had a sick feeling though. "You promise my life back home is safe?"

"Like a bug in a rug."

Could helping Kasartha really earn me some kind of reward? Should I be trusting my emotions so much? He doubted it, but considering his surroundings, he wondered what his options really were. He definitely did not want to stay here in this place of desolation.

"Well, sure okay, I think I can help you then. Deal. I mean, how hard can all that be? Picking up a stupid stone and tossing it in some river."

Kasartha grinned with excitement. "Pinkie swear? I mean it. Pinkie swear you'll help me."

"Pinkie swear?" *Is this guy five years old?* "How about we do a fist bump instead?"

"I need to hear you promise." Kasartha was intent on hearing Matthew verbalize those words.

"Look, Sarthie Boy, I'll do what I can. Don't push it. Do you want my help or not?" *Hah, if you call me Matty Boy, I call you Sarthie Boy!*

Kasartha shivered. Until then, it had only been Uncle who called him Sarthie. He eyed Matthew cautiously. "Okay, I guess that's good enough. But let's get you back to your mommy. I'll get a plan together and then come and get you. In the meantime, you must tell no one. And I mean *no one*. If my uncle finds out about this, I'm done for."

Yes! I'm going home. Matthew smirked. *Who am I gonna tell?*

Who's gonna believe me? He chuckled. Then, "Hey, if you have an uncle, you obviously have *some* family."

Kasartha stood and grabbed Matthew's shoulders, pulling him close, so they were eyeball to eyeball. "You don't get it. Buddy, you will have *no* life *there or here* if anyone finds out about this. Got it?"

"Okay, okay, got it." Matthew peered nervously over the ledge, wanting Kasartha to stop shaking him so they wouldn't fall. The deep vacuum of black nothingness caused him to shudder.

CHAPTER TWENTY-TWO
STEPDAD FOR SALE

In the Town of Havensight

ARNIE DECKER GRIPPED Matthew's shoulders, shaking him urgently. "Matt. C'mon, Matt, wake up!"

Matt recognized his stepdad's head. It was round like a soccer ball and red like an overripe tomato.

"He's awake, Marnie. I don't think you need to call an ambulance."

With Karo clutched in a tight grip, Marnie bent over Matthew. "Matthew? Can you hear me? Ohhh, my son, what happened? Did you pass out?"

"He bumped his head." Arnie pointed to a goose-egg-sized bump underneath Matt's hairline. He motioned to the bedsheet that was tangled around his ankles and offered the obvious and plausible cause. "I bet he got all tangled and fell when he tried to get up." He stood up to let Marnie take over.

"Can you get up? Are you hurt? You blacked out… what happened?" Marnie had a thousand questions. Most concerning to her was the blank stare in Matthew's eyes, like he had seen a ghost or something.

Matt gazed at the faces staring down at him. He quickly

scanned the room. *Huh, I'm back home.* Somehow he had crashed to the floor beside his bunk. He attempted to get up, only to collapse onto his elbows. "I must have fallen." He rubbed his forehead and scouted around again. No Kasartha. No journey back. Just kazam!

"I'm good, Mom. Really. Sorry you had to come over, Deck. You can go now."

"Matthew!"

Matthew looked at her. "I wasn't being rude. I'm just saying I'm good. You don't have to call him every time—"

"Matthew!" Marnie cut him off sharply and then looked at Arnie. "I guess he's okay. I overreacted. With all that's been going on and all…"

"It's cool. I always love the chance to have another moment with my little love bug." He winked and smiled at Karo.

"So *you* can be nasty with him but I can't." Matthew smirked at his mom.

"I'll walk you down the stairs, Daddy." Off Karo and Arnie went, leaving Marnie, who was annoyed, to help Matthew stand up so she could examine him. She made him hold his arms out and touch his nose to make sure he was all right.

"Of all things," he muttered.

CHAPTER TWENTY-THREE
NEED A LESSON PLAN

In the Outer Courtyard of the Kingdom

PIPIERA WAS PUMPED—AND stumped. "How do I build a lesson around a whirlpool, much less a *black-water* whirlpool?" Black waters were anywhere from five to 125 times heavier than crystal waters, depending on the intensity of its dark and murky composition. She felt a tinge of anxiety. "That's not what I would have picked," she confided to the precious orange snuggled between her palms while sitting at her makeshift desk/ picnic table. With a pencil tucked into her thick, curly blond hair and a crispy clean piece of paper to work on, she was determined to pull something perfectly relevant together—and perfectly effective. She had received word that her student, this Matthew boy, would be coming shortly after Earth's next sunrise, so she needed to be ready.

Pipiera flinched at the pressure within that was creeping up to an insurmountable level. A message had come direct from the king himself, passed on to the Book Room Keeper, who passed it on to James, the authoritarian in charge of this whole business, who passed it on to Serena, who had Aivy check it out before passing it on to Megalos, who passed it on to Pipiera, which basically reiterated that this particular intervention was of utmost importance.

And there were rules. She could answer all of Matthew's questions, but he would not be given generous memory privileges for her responses. She could arrange for dreams, but she'd have to use unique and suitable symbolism. Pipiera wondered how she might come up with a way to reinforce her lesson with dream language. "I am so out of my league." She sighed and wrung her hands. "I don't want to let anyone down."

She studied the orange, inhaled its invigorating aroma, and then placed it back onto the table. *Here goes…* She started scribbling some notes. Her scribbles came fast as good thoughts and ideas flooded her mind. *Thank you, King!*

Soon everything was set. All Pipiera needed was her student to arrive.

CHAPTER TWENTY-FOUR
NEED A STUDENT

In the Town of Havensight

MATTHEW HEARD HIS mom's first alarm clock—such an annoying ding-ring. He covered his ears. *Jeepers, get up already, would you?* Long gone and almost forgotten were the days when Matthew woke up happy. He waited patiently, tapping his fingers on the wooden bed frame that was split from his abuse. Next on deck would be the buzzer. That one was not so bad; it gave Matt a sweet kind of achy feeling, reminding him of the times his dad shaved his sideburns. But after that? A fire truck might as well come slamming through the entire top floor. That was Matt's reality alarm. The third alarm meant time was up. *Life sucks.*

His mom moved slowly that morning, like many others lately, so Matt decided to scamper into the washroom to relieve himself and get out before she had a chance to draw her bath. He had to admit, that day's wake-up equipment was a reprieve from the punishing exhaustion that came from trying too hard to sleep. The anxiety of going back to class was daunting. His mind tossed all night from one boggling topic to the next. The surreal haunting notion of the other world he had somehow fallen into and the wild ride within it. The likelihood that Kasartha was some kind of threat—and might he really come back to pick him up? Maybe that was a good thing. It certainly felt distinctly personal. Was that a bad thing? Or was this whole business just from trauma, like his mom and that doctor thought?

It had been a quiet, uneventful few days, but Matthew couldn't quiet the storms swirling in his mind. If he couldn't dismiss it, what then? What was next? Would there even be something next? Had he actually committed to doing something for Kasartha? Would he be sorry for offering to help? That particular question was the only one he could answer for certain. A definite *yes*.

Matthew thought he would have heard from Kasartha by now. *Maybe the guy is already done for. He was kinda paranoid. Hmm... maybe I'm going to be done in by Emerson's thugs today. Huh, maybe there's some kind of funky connection.* Josh and Nick had warned Matthew that Emerson was playing it cool and innocent with Harry Cooke but made it crystal clear on separate occasions that Bagger Boy was not off the hook.

They'll be waiting for me.

Maybe I should just come clean with Mom. But then she'll go to dingle-nut Decker, and that'll just make it worse. "My life is freakin' over!" he yelped. Fortunately, neither Lieutenant Marnie nor Battalion Leader Karo heard his outburst.

He threw the covers over his head and was reminded of that gold-edged book with wings he had envisioned the day his life was ruined. *Right there, it was just floating around.*

What was it someone was trying to tell me?

Maybe it was a "time for a rewrite" or an "it is written" kind of message, whatever either of those meant.

Matthew picked a pair of jeans from a pile on the floor and pulled them on. With a sudden urge of conviction, he realized he needed to fix his mess at school. *I gotta do something! I can't avoid them forever. I gotta pay up, at least half for now. I'll ask Mom for a loan. But what excuse can I give?* Since money would be his best remedy, he would ask Marnie for some fast cash to settle this score.

I'll tell her I need it to start a business. So… I'll start a business! Hmm… just what, though?

He had at least fifteen minutes to figure that out.

On the drive to school, Matthew rallied his nerves. "Mom, you know how I love books?"

She made a quick glance his way. "You love books? Really? I mean, er, that's great. I love that you love books." Her face remained puzzled.

"Yeah, totally. I spend lots of time in the school library. Well, I used too—before, er, you know. Anyway, you know the guys are always asking me to recommend books to them." *Oh this was a dumb idea.* He encouraged himself to keep going, to stick with it.

"Really? Wow! I did not know that. I am impressed, young man. What kind of books?" Matthew skirted her question, the fewer details the better.

"I've been thinking. You know how you keep telling me I should consider doing something to earn a bit of cash?"

"You mean like maybe a paper route and chores around our house?" She narrowed her eyes, wondering where this was going.

"Yeah." He turned away for a moment, gazed out the window as they drove past Havensight's pride and joy, the fields of lavender. A few were striving to bloom, but it was still early in the season. "I'd like to set up my own library. A resource library. You know, to buy books and lend them out." Suddenly, the idea wasn't sounding as smart as he thought it would. He felt his mom's laser-like gaze cut a path from one ear clear through to the other side.

"That's so doofus. Just go to the central 'brary," Karo said.

"Shut up," Matthew muttered.

"Matthew!" Marnie scolded. "Really!"

Well, that went over well—not, he scolded himself internally.

"Just forget it."

"Forget what?" Marnie asked.

"Dr. Alexien said we should keep an open mind to each other, think about the big picture and the future and where we wanna be and all that stuff." *Good one,* he thought, congratulating himself for that brilliant line.

Marnie remained quiet; Matt took it as an open door. "There is an entire set of encyclopedias, really good ones, at school. They're selling them. I'd like to buy them. Cheap. Fifty bucks. I'll loan them out. I'll even share with Karo when she gets older. They'll be really helpful." He turned and looked at Karo, hoping she'd add a little excitement to the idea.

"Fifty dollars! Matthew, I don't have that kind of money to spare."

"It's Daddy's school," Karo said. "Can't he just give them to you?"

Bogus, Matthew thought. "No, this does not involve *him.* It's between me and the librarian, the book lady. Please, Mom. I don't want you to get Arnie involved. Promise me you won't."

"First, I haven't said yes," Marnie replied. "I need more information about these books. Second, I won't raise this topic with Arnie—Mr. Decker to you. He's your VP!"

She recognized he needed space from Arnie, his ever-so-brief stepdad. She took a deep breath as she did whenever she felt this balancing act with Arnie and their intertwined lives toppling over.

"And Karo, you don't say anything either," Matthew said, hoping she'd keep quiet about it. It would be a full five days before she saw her dad next, so at least time was in his favor. If he played his cards right, the matter would be resolved by then, and Karo wouldn't even remember the conversation.

"So, Mom, you'll think about it?"

"Get me more info, and we'll chat tonight. Bring me one of the books, so I can have a gander through it." She sought confirmation from her son with an inquiring look.

"Uh, sure. Of course. Tonight. Gandering." Matthew was quiet the rest of the way to school.

The hallway seemed different to Matthew, narrow and claustrophobic. Perhaps because he had been absent now for several weeks and wasn't sure he wanted to be there. He was convinced everyone he passed eyed him suspiciously.

Yeah, I'm a liar, a bragger, and practically a professional thief now.

He kept his screaming responses to himself. His guilty attitude resulted in a twisted-up face, which was maybe why kids were looking at him funny. But something was different; something felt wrong. Josh and Nick weren't there to meet and hang out at his locker.

Matt's locker partner smiled at him. "Welcome back, bro."

Matthew didn't usually take much interest in Phil, but he was thankful for the warm greeting.

"Good to see you too, buddy." Matthew was surprised at his own reply. It had just fallen off his lips. Normally, he would have merely shrugged in Phil's direction. *Hmm… maybe he thinks my getting reamed puts me in the same loser club as him. Except he's there naturally, and I'm not gonna be a member for long.* Matthew grinned. It was a nice moment, but his day spiraled downward from there.

Two of Emerson's thugs walked expediently toward him and, without breaking stride, picked up Matthew by his armpits and continued down the hallway and into the boys' locker room. They maneuvered his upper body as high up as they could against the wall, struggling to hold him given the slippery, glossy grey paint that covered the cold bricks. Matthew kept his composure, which surprised him. Already settled in his mind was the need to keep his promise. A bet was a bet.

"You win. I've got your dough, well, half of it." From his position, Matthew could see one of the guy's hair was thinning on top of his head and the other's greasy roots, but he dared not comment. *I'll save these nuggets to insult later,* he mused, still composed mentally but entirely uncomfortable physically.

After what many would consider an unusually calm discussion given the scenario, Matt's feet still dangling and all, they agreed that he would meet them on Wednesday night in front of Havensight's movie theatre at seven p.m. sharp. Matthew would provide three envelopes of cash, one with four five-spots and two with three. No one was to know about the arrangement, and he was to come alone. "That means none of your doofus friends," they instructed. Matthew had fifty-eight hours to come up with three envelopes of cash.

"So, give it a rest now. Let me down!" Matthew was becoming lightheaded and dizzy. Discouraged their victim hadn't displayed sufficient fear, the thugs pressed in harder, just for fun, thrusting Matthew upward until his head slammed into a caged wall clock. What they didn't know was that the bottom wires of the cage had been cut and bent open, giving Matthew a sharp stabbing slice atop his scalp. Poor Matthew; he immediately went limp and blacked out. The thugs were shocked when they saw blood squirting. They dropped Matthew's unresponsive body and raced away fast.

CHAPTER TWENTY-FIVE
FIRST DAY AT SCHOOL

Outside the Kingdom

IN LESS THAN an instant, Matthew came around. He sat up, finding the locker room wall unusually soft and the perfect temperature, like an oversized, overstuffed fresh, clean pillow. Instinctively, he reached for the wound on his head, but by then the pain had already fizzled out.

"Hi there." A chirpy girl around his age squatted to check out his face. "We've got lots of work to do." She could hardly contain her anxious excitement. "Well, get up!"

Puzzled, Matthew watched as two odd-looking characters walked by, waving nonchalantly at the girl. They had human torsos and legs, but their feet were oversized and had bird-like claws. Their humped backs and ostrich necks were remarkably eagle-like. One was bald, and the other had bushy, overgrown hair, but both had smallish egg-shaped heads. Their stride was casual as gigantic, folded wings hung off their shoulders like capes. White bands tied around their biceps with red symbols reminded Matthew of something an ambulance driver might have on his uniform.

"Our delivery boys, heh heh," the girl said. "Come on over here." She urged Matthew to take a seat at a tiny desk, assuring him he'd be "more comfy." She patted the back of the chair and gave him an "It's okay" kind of look.

No, it can't be. Matthew cupped the top of his head with his hands in disbelief. *Not again. Now where am I?* Still on his butt, he turned a careful 360. Thousands upon thousands of arcs, like miniature rainbows, bright white and without color, breathed easily in playful piles, some even chasing each other the way butterflies might. Sections of clouds, neatly segregated by size, dimensions, composition, and whatever else in every direction he looked. Bright light was streaming through some, while others were totally opaque. And the taste of it all; he savored uniquely different aromas. Refreshing spring rainfall, an angry storm, and the security that all was well were new flavors to Matthew's palate. "Is this... *heaven?*" he asked meekly.

Pipiera chuckled. "Well, not exactly. This is just a working area for stuff in progress. The storehouses are over yonder, and the city, well, you can't see it from here. It's thataway. It's the best I could do, short notice and all." She studied him for a moment. "You okay?"

Matthew was certain he didn't have the capability to instruct his body to move, much less get up. On account of a thick wave of fog that had rolled in, much like the waters that rolled into Havensight's beachfront, only warmer and the folds mellower, he couldn't see much below his waistline. "Are we on a cloud?" He fixed his gaze upon the young girl's face. Her skin was so clear and bright. She had rosy cheeks and a tiny bump for a nose. Her eyes sparkled with mischief. She looked surprised, and her response proved even more so.

"Duh, we're on solid ground."

He detected a definite dose of sarcasm in her voice. He watched her mouth twist till her cheeks buckled up, like she was contemplating something. "I've been called to teach you a few things," she said in a gentler tone. "Things that will help you during your humankind tour."

"Humankind tour?" He laughed. "C'mon, seriously?" *She's pretty funny, whoever she is.*

But she did not laugh, she squinted instead. "You know you're on one, right?"

"A humankind tour? Are you for real?"

She blinked a few times and then offered an alternative. "An earth journey? C'mon, you gotta know! Like, seriously." Hands on her hips, she looked astonished. "Exactly how foolish are you?"

Matthew thought of Kasartha and the reality of his existence. And now her. *Who is she?*

The girl continued to push. "It's your time to walk the earth. Can you at least fathom that?" She paced and pointed a finger at her chest. "I'm in charge of helping you overcome."

Matthew was insulted, then hopeful. "Is my dad here?"

"What? No! Uh…" She stalled. Obviously, she hadn't anticipated this line of questioning.

Kasartha's dire warning not to reveal their plan *to anyone or else* came to mind. Matt straightened up to deliver a firm reply. "This is a joke. Don't know how you did it, but hey, love the cloud effects. But seriously, I've had about enough. Really. I just want to live my life. I'm fine. Take me home." *Help me overcome. Give me a break.*

"Uh, what?" She circled him. "*You've* had about enough? We haven't even started! No. You're not going back, not yet. Go." She directed Matthew to take a seat at the tiny wooden desk. "I've got lots to show you, and you will stay put till you've seen all that I've prepared."

Her command resulted in a display of astonishment from the delivery boys who were waiting behind a nearby pile of "stuff in progress" for the "take him back" directive.

Matthew blinked and then reached a likely conclusion—he

was being tested. "Ahhh… Kasartha put you up to this." *That's something the little freak would do.*

That startled her. She straightened her posture as if to stand on her tiptoes, but he could see through the dissipating fog that she remained flat on her feet.

"Kasartha?" she inquired.

"Yeah, Kasartha."

"Never heard of him. No such being exists."

"Well, yeah, trust me, he does."

"Trust you? You've been here before? You met this being?"

Matthew didn't know how to answer that question. *Either she's playing some kind of game, or I am definitely going crazy.*

"Well, have you met him? Look, if I've never heard of him, trust me, he doesn't exist here. You better hope he's another being on an earth journey himself 'cause if he's not, I'm telling you, he's bad news!" She eyed Matthew with firm suspicion. "Bad, bad news. Capiche?"

Matthew stood up. "Who are you and why should I listen to you?" *Don't all these super-being, non-earthly, outta-this-world people just automatically know each other? Aren't they supposed to just all get along?* Matthew chose to stand his ground and wait for an answer from this young, bossy girl.

Instead of a reply, a teardrop fell.

"Oh, crap, now you're putting on the waterworks." *What is it with these people? So sensitive.*

"That is no matter." She choked and regained composure. "What does matter is that you need my help even more than I imagined."

"You think I need *your* help? Kasartha says he needs *my* help. How about the two of you get together and… hey…" the sarcasm grew in Matthew's voice, "*you* could help *him*… and leave *me* outta all this. When I see him next, I'll get his number for you. Better yet, I'll have him call you directly!"

Well, he had done it. Stunned and offended, her tears won the battle this time, flowing generously.

Holy crap. I'm outta here. Matthew inspected the surroundings for an escape, a way home. He spied a large tunnel in the distance and suspected that was where he arrived from. He ran toward it and gave his best high jump ever, disappearing into the opening.

The two delivery eagles swooped into the tunnel behind him.

CHAPTER TWENTY-SIX
GIVE IT UP

PIPIERA WAS HORRIFIED. Why would Matthew say such things, and why would he do that? Jump into the tunnel *on his own*? Such an unthinkable and dangerous move. She wondered if the delivery boys would grab him and bring him back against his will or if they would simply ensure he got back to his earth home safely. She presumed the latter.

She sat for a moment in the desk chair authorized for Matthew, hoping to rein in her scattered thoughts. *Boy, did I underestimate how that was gonna go.* Her head hung heavily between her knees. This was a serious project, not just a little adventure. "That Matthew boy is in danger, and wow, he doesn't have a clue what's at stake." She felt foolish for putting the situation into a box that she thought could be managed with a desk, a screen, and a simple lesson plan. *I just messed him up even more.* She wiped her eyes and tapped the desk with her fingers before deciding she'd best go back to the checklist of rules that Aivy had given to Papah to give to her. *I think I left it on my desk,* she thought, so she headed to the picnic table area.

The delivery boys returned with Matthew in hand and plunked him into the chair. This time the chair snuggled around Matthew's body and held him in place. The delivery boys left him sitting there, his eyes free to investigate his surroundings.

Pipiera returned in time to witness Matthew on all fours, vigorously shaking his buttocks and kicking to free himself from the desk. It wasn't working.

Now that's funny!

"Testing out the chair?" she teased.

"Your eagle dudes locked me here."

She noticed his face was red. *Embarrassed? Him? Was that possible?* It was, after all, a compromising position, him on all fours wagging his buttocks to get out of the chair. She giggled again. That just annoyed him.

"What is it with you people?" Matthew barked.

"You don't have to be a prisoner." Pipiera was genuine, but Matthew was still red in the face.

"Just come and go, disappear and reappear whenever it pleases you," he responded angrily, likely to cover his embarrassment.

"And I suppose you think this pleases me?" Pipiera asked.

"Very funny. Ha ha. How do I get outta this thing?"

"You find it uncomfortable?"

Matthew stood as far as he could, his body bent forward, the chair still affixed to his buttocks. He crossed his arms. "Actually it's quite fine. Any other questions?"

"So, being confined is comfortable?"

"Yeah. Uh, no. Is that some kind of trick question?"

"You're in charge. Release whatever's attached itself to you."

Matthew felt around. Perhaps there was a lever or a button he could press to release the chair and desk.

"No, silly. Relax. Breathe deeply... Let it go." The boy looked dumbfounded to Pip, so she encouraged him some more. "Focus. Simply focus on what really matters. What *should* matter."

Matthew followed her lead. He closed his eyes, even though

she hadn't told him to do that part. Before long he opened one eye and peered at her. "Now what?"

"Change what you acknowledge inside."

Matthew wiggled around some more and eyed Pipiera suspiciously.

"Matt," she continued, "you don't have to be trapped, no matter your circumstances. Release the desk. You belong to the kingdom. You're free."

"Huh? You mean like, let it all go?"

"Mmmm, more like, give it up."

"Oh, like, forget it all."

"Uh, no, no, no forgetting. Just *release* it, give it up. To the king." *No wonder you got problems,* she thought. She hoped she didn't sound as sarcastic as she felt. Would he be thankful for the results? She doubted it. That lesson would have to be another day.

Matthew stood the rest of the way up, slowly. The chair came along with him initially but then toppled off. He was free. "Whew, looks like I can get up and out of the dang chair whenever I want to after all." He chuckled. He wouldn't mind a chair like that back home. He sat down and leaned back in the chair as it hugged him lovingly, twirled around in the air, let it flip him topsy turvy, then spun him like a top as fast as he could handle before settling back onto a fluffy carpet of thick, sweet-smelling fog. To end his little performance, he jumped up and took a bow. His display earned amused head shakes from the two eagle guards. That made Matthew smile.

"Now you're just showing off," Pipiera teased. For about three seconds, she admired his grin. *He's not so bad*, she thought. "We got off on the wrong foot. For that I am sorry. All my fault."

"Aw, that's okay," Matthew said. "But is this normal, all this stuff? I'm kinda confused, and no one I know ever talks about… you guys, er, you, or this place or other places that are… not in Havensight, not on Earth even, as far as I know. Well…" he added, "except for heaven. You know, talk about clouds and stuff." He stumbled for words and looked hopeful she might shed some light.

"As far as your question goes, you already know the answer."

After blinking a few times, he gave Pipiera a hesitant nod.

The writing face of the tiny desk interrupted their little relationship renewal. It grew five times its size and transitioned into a superb, highly defined digital screen.

"Whoa!" Matthew exclaimed. "Super sleek! Can you play 8-tracks on this thing?" He settled back into his chair to check it out.

Phew, I think we're actually on track now, she thought.

CHAPTER TWENTY-SEVEN
REMEMBER?

A FARAWAY TUNE BEGAN to fill Matthew's ears. It was a familiar voice from long ago. He had forgotten that he had forgotten it. A close-up of a young woman cuddling a baby in her arms played on the enlarged desk screen. *What? Whoa, so rad.* Matthew gasped. He recognized the woman.

"My mom, that's my mom. Is that me? It has to be. That's me. Oh my gosh, my old room! I remember. Mama, I remember." It wasn't much of a melody, more like a whispered set of words in a quiet, repetitive way. Matthew could feel his mom's love. How she felt then was inside him now. It was almost painful, such a deep feeling of connectivity. Suddenly, he felt horrendous guilt for deceiving her. "Turn it off!"

"Can you recall what you felt as a newborn?" the young girl asked, ignoring his request.

Matthew nodded, surprised he could. "Uh, just surrounded… by good… no, by perfect harmony. All was right." He felt close to tears.

"What else?"

Matthew didn't have to think too hard. He allowed the words causing a lump in his throat to escape. "Not a care in the world. I felt safe." He touched the screen, amazed that he could really feel the moment, like emotions on steroids. Glad the bossy girl didn't turn the screen off, he straightened up a bit. "Ooooh, but my chest hurts a little. What's that all about?"

"Reflux," was all she said.

One of the eagles cuffed his beaky lips to keep from eliciting a giggle.

"And man, does my head feel heavy. It's exhausting holding that thing up. I can actually feel a stretched muscle down my arm!"

The video skipped through his first five years in a flash. The emotions dizzied Matthew till he held up his hand, motioning for her to stop. *Too much too fast.* "Slow it down, would ya?" Matt was nauseated with all the fast-moving glimpses of his childhood. "My dad…" His stomach swallowed his heart as he pointed at the video. "Slow it down."

She stopped the life scan but told him they had to press onward. This was not a social visit or a healing session. He was getting the benefit of a gate scan way before his time was up. She spoke as if she were delivering a lecture. It was way over his head.

Whatever.

"Do you remember your childhood message?" She proceeded with her unusual line of questioning while queuing something new up on the screen.

He frowned. "Childhood message?"

"Well, it probably felt like a nightmare or something along those lines; they often do. Unfortunately. When you were about, say, five to six years of age?"

"Which one?"

"Five or six, in that range."

"No, I mean which nightmare?"

"There was more than one?"

"Yes. Quite a few, actually."

"Huh," was all she had to say at first, then, "Okay." She pressed on the screen. "Well, the one I would like to review is the main one, or at least I thought it was the first, the most fundamental one. The one you had over and over."

Matthew did have one dream over and over, at least a couple dozen times. "Yeah, you're right. I was about five or six years old. Went on till, well, dunno, a few years ago, I guess. My mom called them nightmares. I get why. I'd wake up kinda stunned, but I wasn't actually scared. Wait… what are you doing?"

"Yes, that's the one. We're going to start there."

Before Matthew could say anything else, that nightmare began to unfold in front of him. He held his breath, not so sure he was as brave as he made himself out to be but certain he didn't want to experience it again. *At least it's on a screen and not real.* The young girl positioned herself behind Matthew, so they could watch it together.

The screen presented an eerie grey image. Matthew was so focused on what he knew would come next that he didn't notice the atmosphere around him transition to the same eerie shade. The clear, baby-like rainbows had zipped away, keeping a safe distance.

"Tell me what you see, Matthew."

At least she used my name, he thought. She hadn't up till that point. He didn't know her name. He threw a suspicious glance her way. "Why am I doing this again?"

Pipiera must have realized she blew the whole proper introduction thing. It seemed awkward but necessary that she restart. "I've been asked to help you. My name is Pipiera. I live here. Well, not here," she motioned to the surrounding area, which was now thick with grey shadows and black, thanks to the image on the desk screen.

"How about we go through this childhood message? Following that, I will answer all your questions about me and what you're doing here. Is that good with you?"

Matthew nodded. "Like I have a choice," he mumbled. He focused on the images that began to formulate on the screen.

Sucking air as deep as it would go, then letting it exhale, he began. "I was locked out of my home where I lived with my mom and dad. You can see it there." He pointed. "I'm in the side yard of my house. I suppose I was frightened. I had nowhere to go. It was dark, pitch black, and it was cold and kinda rainy. Well, more like fog, a moist fog—a dark, moist fog. And I knew things."

"What things?"

"They were coming to get me."

"Who was coming to get you?"

"An army. Militia. I knew they were on their way. Big army tanks. Ruthless soldiers. They were coming to get anyone and everyone who was on the street and not in their homes. I didn't see them, but I *knew* they were coming and that they weren't that far away. It was seriously urgent, like a time's up sorta thing. I didn't want to get caught outside."

"So," Pipiera prodded, "what did you do about this *urgent* situation?"

Matthew turned away from the screen. Bizarre how it displayed the same vision burned in his memory from so many years ago, standing barefoot on the east side of his house in the pitch dark, bending down to peer inside the basement window. He was astonished at Pipiera's question. "I was five!" he exclaimed.

"Were you five in your dream?" she persisted.

He looked back at the screen. "Oh. Not sure. I guess so. I didn't really feel an age, except maybe that I was older, like the age I am now. I was deathly afraid. Er, rather, I knew I *should* be deathly afraid. I knew if they got me, it would mean death for me. I *knew* my life was in danger. Like a life-or-death kinda thing."

"Did you know what death meant at age five?"

Matthew paused and reflected. "Likely not, I suppose."

"Do you *know* what death means now?"

He straightened up. "Uh, yeah. My dad's dead." He couldn't help himself, the temptation of angry sarcasm was irresistible.

Pipiera held her breath and ignored his abruptness. "Okay. Continue."

"Well, there I am peering into my window at the unfinished basement where I played all the time. Great cement floor to bomb around on my trike," he added light-heartedly. "There was anywhere from, oh, I don't know, twenty to thirty men dressed in flowing pants and bare chests circling around, waving and spinning machete-like swords in the air, like some war dance or something."

Matthew gasped as the image carried out on the screen. "Yup, them. I just *knew* they were all watching and waiting for me—ready to slice me to pieces should I attempt to re-enter."

"So, you yourself were not in the room."

Matthew watched the way the Arabian knight-like characters swirled around, carrying out some sort of ceremonial preparation for a battle they were sure to win. Swords high and slicing the air in perfect precision, no one could possibly enter the room without being sliced to bits, shedding plenty of fresh, red blood. On the screen he could also see the image of his own back crouching and peering in the window to watch. *Rad, here I am watching myself.*

"Uh, what did you ask again?" Matthew was quite taken with the idea of watching an old nightmare on a screen built into a tiny school desk with a chair that hugged his buttocks.

Pip rephrased the question. "Did you join those crazy sword-wielding guys?"

"What? No! I was outside. I *wanted* to be inside, but… there's no way I could've gotten in there."

"Did you find that frightening?"

"Uh, duh, yeah! Those goons were waiting for me. They were waiting patiently, like they knew I'd try to step back in sooner or later."

"And why do you want to get back in?"

"Well…" Thinking that was a silly question, he gave her a glance. "It was my house! I'd be safe there. It was where I belonged.

It was the *only* safe place. Of course I wanted to get back in!" Matthew wondered when such enemies took over his domain, forcing him out.

"Does the same hold true now?"

"Whaddaya mean?"

"Are you in your house now? Or outside watching in?"

"How the heck should I know?" he gave her his best *I'm annoyed* face.

"Who do you think those guys with the swords are?" She nodded at the screen to encourage him to return his attention to it.

"Well, they're enemies for sure. They hated me. Totally. It was some kind of personal thing. They wanted me personally, that is. Not sure how I know that, but it's really disturbing. They wanted to cream me, slice me to pieces *inside my own house*. And they knew eventually I would have to deal with them. Otherwise the other guys, the army that was coming outside, would get me." Remembering that moment, he looked her way, this time with an expression of horror. "Anyone still outside their house when that army came would be done for!"

"They barred you from your true self, so you'd be forced to stay out and unprotected by the coming army," she whispered.

Matthew took a deep breath and sat still for a moment before slouching back, his chair easing along with him. He regained a sense of normality and seemed almost proud of himself. "A true terror this was. I woke up all sweaty. It never got better. I never got used to it. Eventually, I just stopped having them. I'm not really sure why though. Guess I just grew up."

Annoyed that he wasn't getting it, Pipiera ignored his last comment. "You said at one point you weren't afraid. Then you said you were. Which is it?"

He hesitated. "I guess I was."

"What else?"

"What else? Well…"

"What stood out the most for you?"

"Those swords being twirled, they were *sharp!* I just knew it."

"What else?"

"Well, the army coming up the street, they were dressed in camouflage uniforms. And they were *mean*. They had equipment. They were well protected with army gear, the full deal—tanks, loudspeakers, commanders, men outfitted with boots and helmets and guns and marching in unison. They were like the military, organized with leaders. They had maps and names. They weren't going to miss anyone. Anyone. People couldn't possibly hide from them."

"Unless..." Pipiera prompted.

"Unless they were safe inside their houses."

Pipiera exhaled, appearing thankful for the answer. "Anything else?"

"Hmm... it was dark. I said that already, right?"

"How did you know it was dark, and what about the dark fog you mentioned? Could you feel it?"

"Well, I could see the fog swirling by the light of the lamppost. See?" Matthew pointed to the screen, which zoomed in on the lamppost. Fog swirled inside the limited circle of light.

"Any emotions other than fear?"

"I was puzzled. Not just kinda but a lot." Matthew knew Pipiera was going to ask him *why* was he so puzzled, so he figured he might as well continue. "It was like someone wanted to show me what was happening in my house and in the world outside my house. He was explaining it to me."

Pipiera exhaled another sigh of relief. "Who?" she asked. "Who was explaining this? Someone was with you?"

"As a matter of fact, yes. Someone who knew me and who I knew I could trust was standing behind me. He never said anything, and I never turned around to look at him. But coming from him was light, a warm buzz. It made me realize the light from the lamppost on the street was artificial, you know, temporary. One day it would go out." Matthew paused. "Huh, I just figured that out, just now." He crossed his arms, quite pleased with himself.

The screen ended its show and turned blank before shrinking and returning to a normal old wooden desktop.

"And you don't know what this so-called *terror* means?" This time Pipiera's sarcasm was sharp and cutting. Her hands firmly planted on her waist didn't help.

Her tone made Matthew feel small and angry. That was it, he'd had enough. "If I want to be insulted, I can get that at home. I don't need to be here being grilled by you!" His chest swelled up and tightened. *Enough of this crap. First Kasartha, now this know-it-all girl.*

His head fell into his hands. Once it started, he couldn't stop the sobs. "Dad? Where are you? Please stop all this craziness, I can't take it anymore. Stop, stop, *stop!*"

A bewildered Pipiera watched as her student simply fizzled away into nothingness.

CHAPTER TWENTY-EIGHT
ENCYCLOPEDIAS APPROVED

In the Town of Havensight

MARNIE WAS THANKFUL for the on-call doctor's report. He wasn't concerned. No nausea, no vomiting. Matthew would be fine, he had simply passed out. She tucked her son into the bottom bunk, not wanting to risk him falling out of the top bunk and striking his head, not again.

Marnie sat crouched on the end of his bed, wishing she knew what to do. Sure, she'd get him the medical care he needed, but something else was wrong. He had seemed so stressed that morning. *Guess it was just too early; he wasn't ready to go back. And encyclopedias?* She wondered where that sudden and urgent interest came from. "Honey, I'm sorry," she whispered to her sleeping boy. *I've failed you. I'm so sorry.*

Believing she was inadequate was her greatest flaw. So, it was no surprise she took the blame for Matthew's emotional and physical state.

"I should be paying more attention to you. Instead…" She hung her head and fought back tears. She decided right then and there that she would make it up to him. She would start by giving him whatever funds he needed for this set of encyclopedias, and she would encourage his young entrepreneurial spirit by respecting his idea to start a business. And finally, she thought, *I'll grant you more space from Arnie.* She was the one who had pushed a stepdad relationship, only to toss the concept in the trash as she had their marriage a short while later. *You shouldn't suffer for my mistakes.*

She patted his feet and headed downstairs to call her boss. It wasn't often women got beyond the secretarial pool and Marnie didn't want to end up back there. *What am I going to say this time?*

CHAPTER TWENTY-NINE
NO MORE BAGGER BOY

WHEN MATTHEW AWOKE, the first thing he felt was a ferocious hunger. But with his vision still foggy, he lay still, attempting to overcome the morning's events. He put into practice the breathing exercises Dr. Alexien had taught him to help him relax. All that did though was make him more aware of a throbbing pain at the back of his head. He rubbed it, discovering no wound and no bump, only a memory of the Emerson thugs thrusting him upward and then a stabbing feeling.

Someone was rubbing his feet. "Thanks, Mom," he whispered without looking.

"Oh, you're welcome, my baby poo poo boy," a high-pitched voice said.

Alarmed, Matthew sat straight up in bed.

"Hey, poor bro. Another rough day, huh?" Kasartha grinned ear to ear. "I told you I'd be back with a plan." He jumped excitedly into bed with Matthew. "And boy do I have a plan!" Kasartha's eyes sparkled mischievously. He could barely contain his excitement.

For a split second, Matthew liked the moment. He missed that feeling of fun camaraderie that he and Josh and Nick used to share not so long ago, and boy, would a fun adventure be a good thing at that moment. But during the second half of that split second, reality set in—whatever reality was. His secondary reaction won the battle. He slouched back under the covers. His last adventure had gotten him beat up and in huge debt, and he really wanted this green goon, Kasartha, to go away for good. Besides, his head was throbbing, and his stomach was growling.

"Oh, cheer up, mate, I've taken care of your little predicament."

Matthew eyed him cautiously. "What do you mean? What did you do?"

"I mean Marnie-momma is a…" Kasartha popped out of the bed and over to the dresser lamp. With his index finger, he pushed the lamp over. "Pushover." Matt jumped out of bed and caught the lamp before it hit the floor. He did not like how Kasartha had referred to his mom.

"Guilt. She's an easy pushover with guilt. You, my dear boy, will have your money *very soon*. Your debt will be cleared. Thanks to…" Kasartha took a bow, "me."

"Really?" Matt had to admit the idea was invigorating. He could put this whole stupid Bagger Boy business to bed. No more thugs. A fresh start. *A normal life.*

"Totally. So, you are going to help me now? In case you forgot, you did promise."

"Well, it's not all settled yet. The money isn't exactly in my hands." Matthew sure liked the idea of not having to thieve the funds from his mom's purse.

"Tsk tsk, boy. No worries. It will be. Look, I'll make you a deal. I'll make sure the money you need is in your hands in time to meet your goons. And you promise me you'll help me as soon as you pay off your goons. Deal?"

It seemed too easy, but feeling hesitant and dizzy, Matthew was eager for a quick solution. "Deal!" he said, and just like that, Kasartha disappeared.

The rest of the afternoon and evening went well for Matthew, thanks to a couple Nurofens from his mom. Matthew was able to relax, believing the harassing business of his looming debt might very well be resolved, putting Bagger Boy in the rearview mirror. Could Kasartha actually do that though? Influence someone to hand over money like that?

Between snoozes he gobbled up his favorite Marnie-made dinner—fried ham steak, baked beans, and fries.

True to Kasartha's words, the next morning she smiled and handed him an envelope of cash. "Good luck. I know you'll do your best with this little business venture of yours. You know I believe in you, Matty," she said.

Matthew stayed home from school that day and the next, but when due time came, he convinced his mom he was well enough to go out to the movies. That would be a good break and a test for him. He assured her that he would be okay. After all, he would be with Josh and Nick, who could assist him if he got lightheaded, feeling like he might pass out again. He begged her to believe he was in fine form and that any and all such passing-out stuff should never happen again. He was convinced of that as he cast the blame on Emerson. Squaring up with him and his thugs would solve all his issues.

Matthew was trying to please Marnie, so he teased his little sister playfully about her crocheted Ernie vest while ruffling her hair. He was in a good mood. He had a good handle on a fresh start. Meanwhile, his three carefully sealed envelopes with the dedicated funds were neatly folded in the pocket of his secondhand dark blue Levi's jacket. He was anticipating the victory of getting all this business behind him. He would take care of the envelope exchange before catching up with Josh and Nick, and then together the three of them could enjoy a super-large bag of buttered popcorn and have some good laughs like in the old days, way before the days when Bagger Boy was a thing. Marnie dropped him off in front of the theater and then headed back home with Karo.

The night passed just as Matthew hoped it would. It couldn't have gone smoother. And the movie *Battle for the Planet of the Apes* caused an excited flurry of chatter among the three boys right up until Nick's dad drove by to scoop them up. Things really went Matthew's way once again. Once the thugs were paid, they ran off, and finally Matthew could chill. He was off the hook. Nick and Josh were tight with Matthew's cover story of encyclopedias to Marnie. To be totally cool, Matthew brought the leftover popcorn home for Karo.

He was happy as he settled into his top bunk, so much so that he whispered a message of thanks to the universe.

CHAPTER THIRTY
TROUBLED ABOVE

In the Outer Courtyard of the Kingdom

"IT'S NOT BAD, Pip," Megalos said as he followed Pipiera, who was distraught and pacing. He was having a hard time calming her down. "Really," he said, trying to be as convincing as possible.

"I blew it. I totally blew it. Something so simple. Duh, yeah, I can do this. Not! Evidently, I am a mess-up."

"You're no such thing. You are a blessing, a gift. I know you know that! Look, Pip, these are not easy assignments. Everything—well, practically everything—seems like it's the opposite. Upside down even. It's a whirlwind. It's, it's, it's…" Megalos sighed as he tried to find the right word. "Complicated."

"Complicated? That's the best you got?" She held her hands to her ears. "I don't want to hear any more." Her sobbing grew louder as she collapsed to her knees. "I ruined his life!"

"Now, Pip, you did no such thing."

"You can't know that for sure. I pushed him too far. What if I pushed him away from the king instead of bringing him closer? He didn't warm up to me at all. I… I… I should have been more patient. Kinder. Gentler. I just… I was so surprised he didn't know much." Her wide eyes glared at Megalos. "He knew… like, in his own words, duh… nothing! Can you believe that?"

"Pip, broadly speaking, many don't know much. I like to think of them as little babies on a long journey. Lots of growing up to do." He gave her an odd look. He hadn't known her *not* to be patient, kind, or gentle. He scratched his head, his confusion over the entire situation continuing to grow.

Pip stood up. "And *some* people don't take the journey," she snapped.

Megalos realized he had said the wrong thing. Pip was pretty sensitive to the fact she chose to accept an early exit offered during her own journey. He decided a bit of silence between them might be a good idea.

Eventually, however, he needed to speak. "He didn't warm up to you at all?" Megalos had a hard time believing that. How could anyone *not* warm up to Pip?

"Well, we had a couple of moments."

"A couple of moments? What does that mean?"

"I think maybe he warmed up to me, but he didn't want to show it. Maybe? Oh, I don't know!"

It pained Megalos to see Pip so frustrated and upset with herself. "Well, then you did make some type of connection. You must have."

"Yeah, but my job is to make a stronger connection between him and the king, and I didn't do that. I didn't even get to that part where I could help explain things, tell him what really matters. I only reminded him of his so-called nightmare, and he didn't understand it. So, that's what he will recall, a feeling of confusion. Great." She let out a sigh.

"Is it possible you're overreacting just a teensy bit?"

"Well, even if I am, I still don't know what to do."

Megalos motioned to Roly to continue taking charge and then led Pipiera over to one of the picnic tables a distance away from any waiting or gathered citizens. He sat her down and then sat across from her. He stretched out his hands to hold hers, remaining focused on her face. He hoped this would send a clear signal to Pip that he was serious about helping her get through this. "We are not going to leave this table until we have a plan. We're in this together, and you're not alone. I thought you knew that. You must believe it yourself if you want to share that message onward."

Pipiera was so disappointed in herself that her face fell. She wondered how she ever got to be so lucky to be where she was and with whom she was with. She forced her chin up and smiled. "Oh my gosh, you're right. I don't know how I could doubt. I've been so silly, and yes, I'm overreacting. Oh, Moolos, I'm so sorry."

"No need to apologize, Pip. It's okay. Perhaps you needed this… this… this immediate little setback to remind you just who and what you are representing. We get scratched up from time to time, gouged even. Those nicks, well, they hurt, but that's when we have the chance to deal with some of our rough edges, you know?" He shook her arms. "Smooth us out a bit. Make us a little more whole, a little closer toward perfect."

"So what you're saying is, I need a sandpaper scrub?" She actually cracked a half a smile.

"Yup. Hey, I'm pretty sure we can arrange that!" He was glad she was getting to a place where they could start to brainstorm next steps without the self-blaming accusations. "So, tally it up for me. What do we got?"

She sat up tall. "Okay, well, first we have a young man—well, boy, actually, fourteen years old, aggressive eternal goal, off track to attain it…"

"Yes, we know that. I mean, what are the facts coming out of your meeting with him?" Megalos was as gentle as he could be with this question. He believed progress had been made, there had to be something they could work with. "What was his attitude like?"

"Curious. Angry. He ran away… literally took a running long

jump into the tunnel. The boys got 'im and brought him back. He got stuck in his desk, then he got free, then... then... he just *disappeared*."

"How'd he get free?"

"I told him he could free himself."

"And he did?"

"Yeah, you know he's a fast learner."

"That's good. That's great, actually. Okay, he was quite receptive to your message, by the sound of it. So, he freed himself quickly. That—that's a good thing, my dear. Don't you see? He has inadvertently learned the association between the king and freedom."

"Oh," she said, pondering his words. "I guess you're right... I think." She looked up, attempting to recall the conversation about the king she and Matthew may have had, then sadly shook her head. "Nope. No, I never told him about the king or the kingdom, for that matter."

"You didn't happen to mention where he was? Or did he not ask?"

"He asked, and well, uh, hmm... nope." She shook her head. "I don't believe I ever *really* got to answering that question, at least not properly. I wish I had. I didn't realize he would just disappear on me!"

The sudden disappearance part was not alarming to Megalos. "Timing has to be exact in terms of his coming and going. Don't be alarmed; you do not have control over that. Unless, of course, disappearing meant he ran away on you a second time." He eyed her cautiously. "Did you say he jumped into the tunnel?"

She shook her head. "No, I mean disappeared." She snapped her fingers. "Into thin air. Didn't think *he* could do that." She shrugged. "But as far as that tunnel jump goes, I mean, before he disappeared, yup. Eyeballed it, took a running leap, and plop! Dead center."

"Hmm... that's extraordinary. Unless he's done that before." Megalos pondered if that could be possible.

"I know, right? I thought the same thing!"

"He may have done that instinctively as a result of some sort of training *prior* to his earth journey. And if that's the case, he has good instinctive memory cells. That's another plus, another thing we have learned, my dear, thanks to you."

"Oh, well, maybe I didn't do as badly as I thought. Although I really don't know how that will help. Not much to add to anybody's memory cells."

"So, continue. What else?"

"Well, I think he started to trust me a little." She eyed Megalos cautiously.

"Really?"

"I'm not certain, to be honest. I thought he was kind of funny and sweet. When he wasn't sarcastic and mad or anything."

"Hmm… okay, so then…" He frowned at her. "Then you *did* make a connection of some sort. He *will* remember you, Pip."

"Will he?"

"Not sure. If he has a need to, and he actually tries to recall you, he might."

"And so, that means what?"

"Well, if, hmm… perhaps rather *when*," he looked at her sternly to emphasize there would, in fact, be another meeting, "he visits you again, he will remember you and what the two of you talked about. It's during the course of his earth journey that things get a little… fuzzy. But his mind will have been impacted. It's like, hmm… like you have planted some good seeds inside of him. They will grow. That's just what he will need. These things take great patience, lots of watching and watering, of course."

Pipiera studied Megalos's face as if she might gain more insight. "What exactly might… grow, as you say?"

Megalos shrugged. "Whatever needs to. It'll be something good. I'm sure of that."

Pip pondered his words and then sadly reported that she didn't think he would have taken away any type of "good seed" over the repeating of his childhood dream. They hadn't gotten that far to talk about it. But after Pip laid it all out, Megalos disagreed. He felt Matthew's comments about his dream were quite insightful and that Matthew and Pipiera did, in fact, have a good place to springboard from.

Pip and her Papah Moolos took some quiet time to thank the king and ask for continued guidance. "You know," Megalos said, breaking their united meditation, "you might consider—"

"Messaging him while he sleeps!" Pip shouted before he could finish his sentence, having been struck by the same idea. "Yes, of course! Brilliant idea."

Megalos chuckled. "My dear little Pip, you are the brilliant one in my eyes." He liked how she could switch quickly into a clearer stream of thought when fished out of her own muddy waters. They got down to business and created the beginnings of a sleep message that Pip could work with.

Then she was off again, pacing, this time with a renewed sense of excited energy to figure out the details. "First, he won't like it," she warned Megalos, "but I think it's important. So he knows it's from us, we'll start with what he's familiar with, his childhood terror. But then quickly, so he doesn't get all freaked out," Pip waved her hands in the air to accentuate the freaked-out phrase, "we'll add messages to help confirm and expand his understanding. As he gets it, we'll keep building his knowledge with more messages. Yes, I think this could work! Brilliant! Thanks, Papah Megs." She smiled at him.

He grinned, relieved and pleased she was happy and ready to jump back in.

Pip got straight to work. *I have to make this work. The king has never asked anything of me before. I must make this right. I must do good!*

Not only *must* she do this, she *could* do this, and she *would* do it.

CHAPTER THIRTY-ONE
C'MON, LET'S GO

In the Town of Havensight

A FRANTIC CRY THRUMMED from up the stairs. Marnie shivered; a teabag jolted from her cup. She wiped the hot splashes off her face. So much for a stress-relieving beverage. This time the scream belonged to Matthew.

Karo got there first, gasping for speech. She stared, wide-eyed, and held her stuffed dinosaur tight to her chest. She watched in horror as Kasartha kneeled at the end of Matthew's upper bunk with her brother's foot in hand, yanking his leg as hard as he could. Matt held his body up on his elbows, his fingers clenching the mattress.

Marnie bolted in and straddled the bottom bunk, so her arms were free to grab her son. "What is it? What is it?" Her panicked voice matched the fear in her eyes. She showed no inkling whatsoever of seeing or even sensing Kasartha at the end of Matthew's bed.

Karo must have wondered how her mom paid no attention to this freaky un-human-looking guy who was trying to rip off a leg.

It took Matthew a few seconds to get a grip. He had had a nightmare, the same one from his childhood, but this time he was awakened in the midst of it. Was it a coincidence Kasartha was yanking his leg at that moment? If he told his mom about Kasartha, she would surely send him back to Dr. Alexien, and he would be treated like an imbecile.

Smirking, Kasartha released Matt's leg.

"A cramp in my leg," Matthew said. "Sorry, Mom, didn't mean to scare you. Just a cramp." His right leg was aimed upward and bent. It was a plausible story.

"Oh, thank heavens! You scared me. I mean, I'm not saying your leg cramp doesn't hurt." She smiled. "Whew, I'm just glad it's nothing more." She rubbed his shin as Karo watched in speechless terror. The boy with a slightly deformed face was laughing and mocking their mother's movements. Marnie offered more Nurofen to Matt, which he gladly accepted without saying a word. After kissing him on the forehead, she escorted Karo out of the room. "C'mon honey, let's get you and Dino back to bed."

"Mommy, can I sleep in your bed?"

"Uh, well, sure, why not."

Karo glanced back. "C'mon, Matty, you can sleep with me and Mommy."

"I'm okay, Karo," he said. "Really. Go tuck yourself in, and forget about this." He attempted a smile. "Sweet dreams."

Reluctantly and pale-faced, she went off with Marnie.

Matthew gave Kasartha an annoyed look. "You know she can see you."

"Yeah. Sorry, I forgot to turn myself off to her."

"You can do that?"

"Of course I can." Just then, Kasartha flickered on and off like a dying light bulb.

"Okay, okay, I get it."

"So, what were you screaming about?"

"A nightmare."

"Whooo, I *love* nightmares! Do tell." Kasartha cozied up to Matthew under the sheets.

"Really?" Matthew asked sarcastically.

"C'mon, don't be annoyed with me. I just came to pick you up. Then you started screaming. I thought you were pulling a joke on me. Ha, did you see the look on Marnie-momma's face?"

That made Matthew smile. "This is getting too weird," he said, and they both laughed. "But promise me one thing."

"What, bro? Anything."

"Tonight, this trip, it's our last, right? One little mission tonight, then all back to normal tomorrow, right?"

"Of course. Let's go. You can tell me about your… oooooooh, scary nightmare along the way."

CHAPTER THIRTY-TWO
THAT'S YOUR UNCLE?

Somewhere in the Cosmos

B Y NOW MATTHEW was a veteran. He knew what to expect, what was coming, when to brace himself, and when to gaze in awe. Within what felt like hardly any time at all, the pair arrived at Kasartha's cavern. Matt gawked around. *Huh, it's not so bad up here, I guess.*

"We just need to pick up a few things, then…" Kasartha nodded toward the ominous Mount Skia.

"We're going up there?"

"Yup!"

"I take it you've been up there before?"

"Nope."

"You're kidding me."

"Nope."

"Didn't you say something 'bout an elevator guy?" For some inexplicable reason, Matt thought that sounded a tad safer.

"Changed my mind."

Matthew surveyed the section where the watery sky clashed against Mount Skia. A flash of lightning revealed thin, arm-like waves reaching angrily around the peak, as if it were forming a seal where the mountain's spike punctured the sea. It was a hostile scene.

"No freakin' way. I'm not going up there. You're crazy." *Why do I do this? I might as well have just backed into a corner and said, "Hey, everyone, come get me. I want to die."*

"Yup."

"Yup what?"

"I'm crazy. Isn't that what you just said?"

"Look, man, I didn't sign up for a *no returner* kind of job."

"What did you sign up for then?"

"What did I sign up for?" Matt's agitation was growing. "Dude, I'm doing *you* a favor. To get you off my back. I want my life back to normal!" He paced in a circle. "I felt freaking sorry for you! I'm trying to help you. And this is what I get? Ooooh, ah, I changed my mind kinda crap?"

"Calm down, bro. You're going back from where I picked you up. As long as my plan works, all will be good. It's rather simple, actually. We just have to be sure no one sees us."

A tad more relaxed, but not by much, Matt had questions. "No one? Like who? Who cares about this? Who's going to see us? And stop calling me *bro*. I never said that was okay."

"My uncle."

"Why do you let your uncle push you around? What's the deal with this guy anyway?"

"He gave you the heebie-jeebies when you saw him."

"Me? I've never seen him." Matt embraced a horrid notion. "Wait, that space beast guy? *He's* your uncle?" *Please say no!*

Kasartha hung his head and swallowed slowly. He affirmed with a nod, barely wanting to acknowledge the relation himself, for his uncle was a great deceiver, the worst of them all.

"You know that army, the camouflaged army coming to get you in your nightmare?"

Matthew didn't know whether to be annoyed or nervous. He

wished he hadn't shared the details of his nightmare with this guy. He was anxious. What was coming next?

"Well," Kasartha looked Matthew square in the face, "that was a warning. It's my uncle's army that's coming after you."

"What?"

Kasartha let out a huffing sigh of relief. Matthew could see he had been struggling with this.

"Don't mess with me, dude." Matthew's face was strained with equal doses of fear and anger.

"I'm not. Don't you get it?"

"What is it with you people? What am I supposed to *get*?"

The question caught Kasartha's undivided attention. "Wait, what? *You people*? Who else is visiting you? Man, you gotta tell me." Kasartha was horrified. "Who else?" He grabbed Matthew's neck and picked him up off the ground. "Are you duping me?"

Matthew kicked his feet furiously, then got it together enough to kick Kasartha in his knees, hard enough for Kasartha to release his grip. "Boy, do you turn fast."

"Now who's messing with who?" Kasartha challenged. The awkward and meager trust built between the two disappeared.

"Nobody else *visited* me. I was taken somewhere."

"Where?"

"Chill out. She's harmless."

"She? Who's *she*?"

"It was weird. Actually, it might have been a dream. I blacked out, and suddenly I was in… well, it wasn't even a room, just a big expanse of whiteness, sort of."

Kasartha paced and tried to collect his thoughts. "What did she want to know?"

"She didn't want to know anything, really. She showed me a movie of my nightmare, which was pretty cool. But then she got a little miffed when I didn't get her version of meaning. Then next thing you know, I was back in the locker room on the floor with Principal Cookie breathing down my neck."

"And then you had that same nightmare again tonight. The same one?"

"Yes. What am I supposed to *get*?" he repeated, annoyed.

Kasartha continued to pace. Then he held his hand up, signaling silence. "I need to think," he insisted. Suddenly, he walked into his cavern, into a second room, then into a third room. Curious, Matthew followed him.

When Kasartha breathed fire into a lamp, Matthew was aghast. But then he challenged himself. *Why should I be surprised?*

The cavern walls were illuminated, exposing a full circle, a spotlight dome shape around them. The walls were engraved with grooves and scratches, large, detailed drawings that resembled a map. Perhaps of a city. Matthew stepped up to have a closer look. Asterisks and Xs marked specific locations. Numbers resembling clock times were jotted down here and there. Arrows scratched their way from one location to another. A deep circle was etched around a rudimentary drawing.

"What's that?" Matthew inspected it closer. "A picnic table?" He stood back a bit. "PU 8:58:05 was written alongside it. Matthew followed what marked like a path carved into the rock. He cocked his head back and forth until it hit him. "You jerk. You've been following me. This… this is a map of my life!"

"It's not your *life*."

"Of course it is. Look!" Matthew pointed out each location. "There's my house. There's the hideout in the woods where me and my dad would go. There's the town square. There's my stepdad's house. And look! That… that right there, circled by *you*, is where I was attacked. The day *you* showed up. Right then. Right there! You *have* been following my life."

"I've been watching where you go, but that's not your *life*, bro."

"I already told ya, don't call me 'bro.' How long have you been watching me? Wait, did you cause that fight to happen? Was that you behind everything?"

"No! And I find the question insulting. You, my dear friend, are responsible for your lickin'. It was your own pride. You asked for that one."

Matthew was upset and confused. "This whole thing is getting complicated."

"There's nothing complicated about it."

"You didn't answer my question. How long?"

Kasartha shot a glance at Matthew. "Since the night your dad died."

Matthew stepped back. "What's this got to do with my dad?"

"Look. Can I be honest with you?"

"Oh, please do." The sarcasm was oozing out of Matthew.

"Can we sit down? Over there." Kasartha pointed to the cavern opening. Matthew went first. He felt he had the winning edge to this argument, but he also recognized he was vulnerable. After all, consider where he was. How would he get home if Kasartha chose not to take him back? *I'm walking on a tightrope.* He shook inside but instinctively coached himself not to show it. *I need to hear this.*

"Okay," Kasartha began, "that night…"

"The night my dad died?"

"Let me finish please. You don't know how lucky you are that I'm spilling the beans."

Matthew wasn't sure he really wanted to hear this story. It was certain to be unbelievably bizarre and might cut deep into an unhealed wound. The memory of that night was not something he wanted to relive. "Keep going then."

"That night, well, I met Frank. By accident, actually. I was just an orderly." He eyed Matthew. "Down there. Not down there where, you know. Down there, down there. Down yonder."

Matthew was frustrated. He stood up and took a couple of

steps toward the ledge, over which Kasartha had dangled his legs the last time they were there. It felt like eons ago already.

"Well, I worked one of the elevator shafts," Kasartha continued. "We brought him in—er, some of the guys brought Frank down for an assessment. He, um, uh, he was pretty feisty. Said he didn't belong there. Said he did a lot of good. Said he was smart."

"He *was* a good man. My dad *was* smart. You didn't believe him?"

"It's not up to us as to what their stories are. If we get 'em it's because we get 'em."

Matthew didn't think that made sense, but nonsensical had become his new normal.

"He got used to seeing me all the time, and he confided in me, as if I reminded him of family. My son this and my son that. I could tell he loved you, you must have been his whole world."

Matthew struggled to keep his chest from heaving and his cheeks dry.

"Well, long story short, I'd been wanting to get out for a long time. Out from down below. I wanted to be up here where all the action is."

Matthew glowered at the black-and-greyish atmosphere. Desolation everywhere. "Yeah, I can see this is a happening place," he said.

Kasartha frowned, tired of Matthew's sarcasm and ignorance. "Don't you see? He saw something in me. In *me!* I reminded him of you. He saw something in *me!*" Kasartha's face flipped from hope to guilt. "So... so, I set out to switch places with you. I thought maybe I could have another chance."

"What?" Matthew thought he had seen and heard everything, but this was unbelievable. "Is that even possible? Do you guys *do* that? Actually steal people's lives?"

Kasartha shook his head sadly. "No. It's not part of the rules."

He cast a sideways glance. "But I can still *want* it. I still have feelings, you know."

Is he really expecting me to feel sorry for him? Matthew's thoughts swirled. *This guy's got serious problems. Does he know he's confiding in me, admitting he wants to take my life?* He looked around. *Freakin' crap, I'm the one with the serious problem.*

There was no escaping, at least not on his own. He remained silent, not sure what his next step should be or even what his next step *could* be. A shiver went through his spine. He was in the very spot where he had witnessed the ghostly outline of that space dragon's tail batting his stone into the murky waters of the expanse. *Who has a relative like that?*

Kasartha strapped his telescope to the side of his waist buckle along with a wiry contraption that he referred to as his lifesaving cane. "I'm sticking with the original plan. Come with if you want."

Not knowing what the original plan was, nor having an understanding as to why they were going to climb Mount Skia toward the overhead sea, Matthew obeyed out of fear, however, his mind swirled nonstop.

If he's telling the truth, Dad, you're out there somewhere. You're alive! I knew it. But how might he get to him? Where could this "down yonder" be?

CHAPTER THIRTY-THREE
TAKE ME TO MY DAD

KASARTHA'S WIRY CANE proved to be a valuable tool. The climb was treacherous, but the pathway itself was worn, which meant others had traversed it. That fact gave Matthew some comfort.

Mount Skia was one of two mountains that poked through the bottom floor of the watery ceiling. The other mountain, far in the distance—Kasartha couldn't recall its name, perhaps on purpose—was surrounded by smooth, unruffled waters. Kasartha evaded Matthew's probing as to why they didn't take a route up that mountain instead.

The roar became deafening as they climbed. It wasn't a pleasant roar like a soft rush of waters falling from great heights. It was more like a gurgling drain pushing its way through a clogged-up sink with a nest full of hair, only a thousand times louder. Kasartha's cane offered light as well as a measure of solidity, so they could be sure of the terrain with each step. Thankfully, Matt was skilled with his own footwork and able to keep up.

At the point where the water met the mountain, there was no more climbing to be had, at least on the outside.

"What happened to the storm?" Matt asked. It had settled

down. Certainly, that was in their favor. Kasartha didn't reply. Curiosity begged. Matthew reached up into the underbelly of the sea. He could hardly tell the difference between the air and the water because the two substances and their temperature were exactly the same. He couldn't even tell if his hand was wet. The moisture felt different from anything he had experienced before. He felt a current inside the water though. He could tell that if it caught him, it'd be awfully tough to fight it. Darned impossible, actually.

"Feel around!" Kasartha yelled over the gurgles. Visible at eye level across the horizon were hundreds of watery spirals feeding upward into the sea. Matthew braced himself and dared to probe the water again. Surprised, Matthew beheld three small, sticky stones that had been swirling around in circles.

"Ooooh gross!" He quickly tossed them back up.

"Ha ha. Yeah, those ones sitting in the murk at the bottom are pretty gross. Let's keep going before we're spotted."

"Where? We can't go any farther." Matthew looked around. "And seriously, who's gonna spot us?"

"Tsk tsk, think, bro. If we can't climb up on the outside, how do we continue to go up?"

"Swim? Gross! I'm not going in there." *And stop calling me "bro".*

"Ha! You wouldn't survive long in those waters, bro. We're gonna climb *inside* the mountain." Kasartha rooted around a little bit. "There's an opening somewhere around here." He glanced at Matthew. "So I've been told." He pulled out his wiry cane and fished around the rocky ledges until he found it.

The opening was, in Matthew's opinion, not too promising. It was small, and it was hard to tell what part was hard rock and what was sand cemented with muck. It was all the same shade of black. They would have to feel their way around to crawl inside the mountain. However, Matt thought that if the path ended there, others before them must have continued on through that opening. *Can't be that bad, can it? I've made it this far.*

After an examination, Matthew shook his head. "No way, man, I am not going in there." Matthew was never one to sweat over claustrophobic enclosures, but this was clearly a trap. The tunnel was much too tight. He squirmed. Again, he thought of death. The suffocating kind.

Kasartha switched positions, encouraging Matthew to take the lead. "We've got to do this. Don't be scared. You got me. I'll be right behind you."

"Oh yeah, that gives me oozes of comfort." Matthew felt a tightening in his chest and prickly chills circling his neck. He turned around, brushed past Kasartha, and bolted down the mountain path.

"I wouldn't do that if I were you." There was a song-like tune to Kasartha's words.

Oh crap! Matthew lost his footing and slid down the side of a pebbly bank. There were no oversized tree roots or bushes to slow his fall, only loose stones smattered with spiky juts of rock.

Kasartha flashed his light downward. "Matt? You blockhead. I told you, you're safe with me. Now look what you've done." After moments of echoes, Kasartha repeated his call. "Matt? You shouldn't have left me."

The water gurgled even louder, swallowing up any audio other than its own deafening pitch.

"Matty Boy, listen up. You are not hurt. You might think you are, but hear me out. *You are not hurt.* You got no body here, buddy. Think, no bones and no flesh. You *can't* be hurt. It's all in your mind." Kasartha used his cane to detect different densities, giving a hint of where Matthew was—or at least, where he was not. "Where are you?" he hollered. "Either you've fallen a long way, or you're hiding. Kid, what are you gonna do?" A haunting echo repeated Kasartha's taunting sarcasm. "Head home? On your own? Come on, use your noggin. Strategize. Think. Jump. Climb. Whatever you gotta do, get back up here."

Head home? Head home? The echoes of Kasartha's words played a sarcastic tune in Matthew's head. However, nearer and more threatening were the sounds of the battling waters, a powerful downward thrust gurgling with attacking bolts of upward spirals. Neither force was reassuring, like two types of darkness duking it out. He had indeed fallen but not too far, just enough to be out of sight. He crawled onto a shelf of rock and scouted for a place to hide. At least he was dry. The thunder of the water creeped him out. He was thankful he didn't feel pain, physical pain anyway. He curled up and wondered about dying. *Right here, right now.* He sobbed internally, careful not to make a sound. *I'd rather have a thousand brawls with Emerson's thugs than be here in this predicament. In fact, I'll kiss their feet if I ever get to see them again.* He was so sorry he had listened to this Kasartha freak in the first place— and the second and third time, for that matter. *And why did I? What was I thinking?* He racked his brain, trying to get his head around how on earth he had ended up here.

"Oh, God, help me. I hope you're out there somewhere. I hope you can see me. I hope you can hear me. I'm sorry. I shouldn't be here. Please, God, please help me."

Matt heard the echo of his name as Kasartha called out again. He took a deep breath, realized he didn't even need breath, then called out, "What was the original plan?" *To kill me, right? To take me away from my family. But what does he gain from that? Surely, whatever the deal, it's not good, and it's not in my interest. Only his.*

Kasartha scampered down toward Matthew's voice and found him curled up like a snail and neatly tucked underneath a craggy ledge. He stared at him before he finally looked away and started to climb back up. "I can't tell you."

"So, you're going to just leave me here?"

"You know you're a real pain."

"Did my dad really tell you he loved me?" Matthew's emotions were running high, and his voice was squeaky.

Kasartha scampered back down and wiped Matt's cheeks with the back of his hands. "Yeah, he did." After another silent pause he continued. "You were lucky, man. I never had that kind of love." Choking, he lowered his voice to a whisper, causing Matt to lean in closer. "I never gave it. I wanted another chance. Now do you get it? I wanted to be you. I wanted your life. It was stupid, I know."

Matthew tried to remain guarded. "Where's my dad now?"

"Well, er, that." Kasartha shrugged. "Like I know."

Matthew sat up, wondering where his renewed energy and courage came from. With a commanding new mission, he challenged Kasartha. "You know! I know you do. Take me to him. I'll have none of your plan until you take me to my dad. I want to see him."

Kasartha started to climb. "Okay, bro, stay here if you want. Alone. See if I care."

"You can't do your plan without me. I've got your number."

"You don't have my *number*," Kasartha grumbled. "But boy, I've got yours. Let me see, hmm… ah, oh yeah—bolstering pride, angry hate, selfishness, dishonesty, and such and such. That's what you got inside ya. And you know what? You'll be easy picking." Kasartha supernaturally stretched his long neck to position his face upside down in front of Matthew's. "When the time comes, my uncle's army is gonna scoop you up like doggy doo."

"True colors flying now, eh?" Matthew turned away and out of habit, let out a breath. *This is not good.*

"Look," Kasartha's voice became quiet and genuine. "I don't want to fight, bro. I just want us both to get up there," he motioned upwards, "across the waters. I've never been up there. I got this feeling, this knowing, that a really good solution to all your problems and…" Kasartha hung his head as if shameful, "maybe mine too, are up there."

"My problems? What exactly are my problems? You know nothing about me. A big zero, a big double-O zero!" Matthew's anger took charge.

"I know you."

"You do not."

"Oh yes, I *doooo*," Kasartha broke into a stupid song-like tune again.

Matthew stood up. "Take me to my dad."

"I'm taking you home. Right now. You're not behaving."

"Okay, hotshot. Take me home then. Now. And stay out of my life. Do you hear me?"

Matthew was amazed. Kasartha actually responded to his directive. It was an incredibly long, silent journey, as though Kasartha purposely went slow in case Matt might change his mind along the way. All Matthew could think about was his dad. How wonderful it would be to see him again. He wondered if that were even possible. *Seems anything could be possible now.* He shook those thoughts out of his head, knowing that the most logical thing to do was to get back to safety, back into his bed, at home, with his mom and Karo.

As soon as Havensight was in view, Matthew tugged at Kasartha.

"Why won't you take me to my dad?"

Kasartha stopped in midair. "You wouldn't like it. Plus… I'd get in trouble."

"I want to see him."

"It's dangerous."

"More dangerous than what happened tonight? C'mon."

Kasartha sighed. "Pinkie swear. If I take you to see your dad, you'll take me above the waters."

"Why me? I've never been above the waters. Why do you think I can take you there? I just… I just don't get all this."

"Because you, Matthew, you're still open in their book room. I am not."

Matthew thought back to the gold-rimmed book floating in midair. He scratched his head. "Uh, what does that mean, anyway?"

Kasartha gave Matt a "Can you be more stupid?" look. His explanation that Matt's age of understanding was fast approaching was received with a perplexed "I don't get it" look in response. Employing a sincere tone, Kasartha offered additional and even more confusing info. "You, uh, soon you have to make your own choices. You know, get stuff sorted out. Like, who you gonna follow."

"Get stuff sorted out? Follow?" Matthew was losing his patience. "Well, my choice is, I want to see my dad."

"Okay. But do you pinkie swear?"

"Pinkie swear what?"

"You will take me above the waters."

Matthew sighed, figuring he'd have plenty of time to figure out all this other business later. Seeing his dad was his first priority, a burning one at that. Everything would come somewhere after that. "Yeah. I pinkie swear." A new deal was made all while he scolded himself privately. *I'm gonna be sorry for this, I know it. But, Dad, here I come!*

"Okay, okay. But first take a few breaths in that there body of yours." Kasartha pointed to Matthew's lifeless form strewn across the upper bunk."

"No!" Matthew replied. "I know your tricks. Take me now!" He wasn't going to let Kasartha fool him again. *I want to see my dad, even if it means giving up my own life.*

Kasartha shrugged and then off they went, up and away from Havensight.

CHAPTER THIRTY-FOUR
A MISSING MATTY BOY

In the Outer Courtyard of the Kingdom

FIRST IT WAS horrid frustration. Then it was wild panic. Pipiera never even knew she was capable of such states of mind.

"You *must* call the authoritarians. I'm telling you, *he's gone.* And if he's not here," she pointed to the greeting area in front of the gate that Megalos so carefully guarded, "then I don't even want to imagine. Where *is* he?" Her fists clenched tight as though they gripped the hope necessary to find him.

"Calm down, Pip." Megalos urged her over to one of the empty picnic tables and signaled for Roly to take his place. "Okay, tell me, event by event, what happened. Why do you feel our Matthew is in danger?"

Pipiera looked a bit annoyed. She still struggled with the "our" part in front of the boy. Nevertheless, she felt a keen sense of responsibility for his welfare. After all, she was handpicked to intervene with his so-called "off-track-ness." And after meeting him in person, she did feel a tiny bit of connectivity to him.

Appreciating his calm demeanor, she took a deep breath.

"Okay. We…" She paused, wanted to explain the *we*. "Joyce from the Night Messages Team—she sends her greetings, by the way."

Megalos nodded in acknowledgment.

"Well, Joyce came to help me; she queued up the dream—you know, the one we talked about. It was his childhood message."

Megalos nodded again.

"The message was interrupted. I understand that happens a lot. Someone wakes up, either for physical reasons or mentally charged reasons. Anyway, Matthew did not get the whole message. It was interrupted. We tried a bit later, but then we couldn't even get him open enough to receive the message. At first I thought, well, he's awake, maybe, you know, getting something to eat or whatever. It was a physical barrier—the message kept showing the target as unapproachable. Unapproachable!" She inspected Megalos to determine if he found this shocking. He didn't, so she continued. "Then Joyce said, 'Let's wait an hour's worth of earth time and try again.' We did that, but still, unapproachable! Joyce set about their usual process of investigation. She inquired about the urgency, and, of course, I said this was an urgent matter. Otherwise, I think they would have just waited for another opportunity. So glad I said this was urgent! Know why?"

Megalos shook his head.

"Because they sent a messenger to check on him physically, you know, to determine what the physical barrier might be. Oh my goodness, Moloos." She cupped her head in her hands.

He comforted her but remained silent.

By now her racing words were slowing, she could barely get them out. "He was gone. Gone! His body was empty. We've got to find him and get him back before his family finds out. They'll freak! So, please call the authoritarians. They've got to hear about this. I'm sure they can do something!"

She could tell he didn't like where all this was going. But rather than reacting urgently, he simply comforted her. "Pip, first, the authoritarians know full well what is happening. They know far more than you and I, including where Matthew is right now. So, we must have faith. Now, I'm as concerned as you are. I don't like this, and I clearly do not understand why we are so actively involved in this one. So, let's just think about it for a moment before we decide anything."

She leaned in, flashing him a beady-eyed look. "Uh, may I remind you that an intervention was *your* idea? Or did you conveniently forget?" Her lips were tight, her eyes mean. *Yeah, I'm blaming you.*

He kept quiet, obviously deciding to let it go.

The pair sat on the picnic table for a long moment sizing each other up. Megalos could see that Pipiera was totally despondent. He spoke first. "Look, Pip, you're not responsible for what Matthew chooses to believe or what actions he takes. Remember, he's on a journey, *his* journey, and he has much to learn. People learn best through experiences. Sometimes they need a real knocking on to figure it out." He chuckled, hoping to lighten up the mood. "And I forgive you for releasing that hurtful arrow."

She hung her head. "I'm sorry," she whispered. He nodded, still smiling, as she continued. "It's just that I was called in—handpicked—to help, but I've messed up every single step so far. I'm afraid he's with that Kasartha guy."

"We don't know that."

"Who else would he be with? Who else would come to pick him up?"

Megalos shrugged and assumed a serious face, one she knew meant she was right. He faced the arrivals field. It was a picture of hope fulfilled. "Look," he said, pointing. "Look at all the people who do make it." He smiled grandly. "So many have come across those fields in absolute awe and wonder. I'm sure they had countless doubts during their journeys. I bet they had scary moments too, moments that helped them discern better."

"Discern?"

"Yeah, that's one of the basics."

"What do you mean?"

"Well, to understand and accept guidance, you must first be willing to listen, to have a kingdom worldview. When you make our king the center of your life, well, then you take listening more seriously."

"More seriously?"

"Yeah, like striving to learn the mysteries." Megalos goggled around with his hands high in the air. "C'mon, Pip! So many awesome, amazing, life-changing mysteries. Just look around!"

"I guess Matthew wouldn't know about all this." She also motioned to everything around them. "How *do* they figure it out?"

Megalos moved closer to Pipiera and took one of her hands. "That's all part of their earthly journey." Her head hung as she slumped her shoulders, and a tear dripped onto her lap.

"I'm so inadequate."

He put his arm around her. "Whatever happens next, you need to be ready. Just know that whenever you're called to do something, you can do it."

Pipiera always appreciated how her Moolos could pick her up out of any slump. He was right. She touched his face with her free hand. "You always amaze me. I love you, Moolos. Thank you." She forced a smile, still feeling she was a disappointment to him, to herself, and worst of all, to the king she had yet to meet.

Megalos kissed her forehead and then hurried back to his gate. A large crowd was approaching on the horizon.

Pip concluded she must have faith in the authoritarians and wondered what she could do to prepare for what might happen next. *Who knows what that might be?* "Hmm…" she muttered, "I didn't get the sense that Matthew understood much of his childhood message. He couldn't have, not if truly considered it a terror." Because if he really understood it, he would be thankful of the warning, she was sure of that. Pip decided the best next thing to do was to study that message and find a way to spell out its meaning to Matthew. She would review it, make some talking points, then go down to chat with Matthew herself. "Yes! I will go there myself."

She turned back and smiled at Megalos, who was busy preparing for a coming group of excited chatters. "I better not tell him I'm going to Earth myself," she muttered, "it might set him up for hope, and I could fail again. But I'm gonna do it. Papah, I'm going to make you proud!" Pipiera convinced herself she had the courage to do it.

She headed to the section of the "works-in-progress" field where she had positioned the desk for Matthew near one of the primary and most secure tunnel openings. *I should have positioned the desk farther away from the opening,* she thought. *Then Matthew never would have seen it. And if he never saw it, he wouldn't have been tempted to jump.* "Emotions and temptations, clearly not a good mix!" She sighed and decided she must be more careful not to make any more mistakes. There was a great deal riding on this intervention, and it was already going sideways.

She stood where the desk once sat. "This may help me to recall the terror, as he called it, and figure out what his interpretation was." From that position, she would develop corrective messages to help his mind adjust to new thoughts that could get him back on track. *Yes,* she thought, nodding approvingly, *this is a good strategy for my next step.* She sat and hugged her knees to help her focus.

CHAPTER THIRTY-FIVE
PLAIN AND SIMPLE

Outside the Kingdom

NOW, WHAT WAS the first impression Matthew had? Pipiera tapped a pencil on her forehead, then scribbled some notes. He had talked about feeling alone and, worse, about fear and confusion. It was definitely an uncomfortable environment for him. "I nearly had to pry it out of him that someone was there with him, a presence, a being who made him feel safe." She waved her pencil at a rainbow as it scooted past her head. "Why did he forget that part?" The white baby rainbow wasn't at all interested.

Standing up, she pulled a notebook out of her skirt pocket. "Rather than feeling safe, the fear was stronger. Hmm… first point to note, he must remember that, first and foremost, he is not alone, so there's no need to fear."

Pipiera paced. "Okay, that's number one. What's the next point?" She surveyed the area. It was a pleasant yet chaotic place, domed with every cloud formation imaginable, even dark, ominous ones on the far side, threatening a storm.

"That's it! Coming to get me. He said that. There was a feeling of urgency, a ruthless army coming to get him. Again, lots of fear."

She paced some more. "Hmm… he did seem to understand that had he been inside, the army could not touch him. But I get it." Pip continued her thoughts aloud; there were many obstacles. "All those enemies lurking inside, ready to slice him to pieces. Did he think it was impossible to get inside, where he belonged?" She gave her pencil a victory shake. "Okay! That's point two. I'll tell him it's not impossible. No matter what it looks like, no matter how many rebellions are going on inside or how big those monsters are, it's not impossible! He needs to understand this if he wants protection from the approaching army. Whooo, on a roll."

Pipiera eyed upward and imagined her Moolos for a few moments. "Thank you, King, for providing Moolos to watch over me. How lucky I am. My heart is so full of joy. Thank you for you, for all of this." She felt a tear of joy roll down her cheek. Placing it on the tip of her finger, a baby rainbow swooped by to pick it up. "I am truly happy. Thank you for this opportunity to serve you. Thank you, thank you, thank you." Pipiera smiled. Life felt so good right now.

She switched to a cross-legged position. "Okay, let's continue," she muttered happily, her forehead wrinkling with concentration. Of course! How many times had she seen Megalos shake a finger to reinforce a common kingdom message: *Admit and submit.* "Yes, indeed, that'll be it. He must admit to the king that he has those rebellious enemies inside and offer them up, submit to him, and let him battle against those swirling swords. Then Matthew can get in and not worry about that approaching army. Do not refuse the king. Admit and submit; that's what he needs to do."

Pipiera was enjoying this so much that she almost had to pinch herself. *I'm going to make a difference in someone's life!*

She continued to think aloud. Voicing her thoughts gave them wings. "At least Matthew sees these knights with swords as enemies who want to harm him and capture him. And for certain they are." She sighed. Matthew had some major internal battles ahead of him and couldn't conquer them on his own. He needed these messages, to know he wasn't alone, that it was possible to beat his inner enemies, but to do it successfully, he had to admit and submit. "I'll have to explain to Matthew in more detail. He must learn to understand this, to focus, and to overcome. It's all that matters, really." Pipiera scribbled a big star beside that point.

Usually, three points were sufficient. Megalos said it was about the most any earthling could grasp at any point. Nevertheless, Pipiera decided she had to validate Matthew's understanding of that lamppost and its temporary light and how the ever-present being standing behind him was the permanent light, the one he really needed for his journey.

"I must be sure to toss that into the conversation somewhere. I guess this is what Megalos was talking about when he said discernment was fundamental. It's dark there, and Matthew must learn to discern which light is which. One is temporary, and one is eternal. Okay, lesson plan done. For now, anyway. Next, I must request an escort to Earth."

She underscored the learning points she wanted for Matthew, took a deep breath, and committed herself to carrying out this mission. To go to Earth, straight to wherever Matthew was, and give him these learning points, plain and simple. "If I go in person, he will listen—he'll have to! And he'll pivot back onto the right track."

Pipiera sat back, pleased with herself. "Yes, this is a good plan." She smiled. She knew, however, she had to move urgently, there was no time to waste. If he was soon to be capable of understanding and yet still chose to spend time with and listen to Kasartha, then… *Oh my, I can't even bear to think about the outcome.*

CHAPTER THIRTY-SIX
A LIGHT SHINES

In the Town of Havensight

PIPIERA WAS THANKFUL her escort agreed to stay with her. She figured he had likely caught on to her continuous shake.

"Relax. I'm on watch. You just focus on what you came to do," he assured her. He was tall, nearly twelve feet, she figured, but not as tall as the width of his wingspan. She smiled gratefully at him. Not just because of his comforting words but also because he never complained when the job called for him to scrunch down really low and arch his back to fit into Matthew's bedroom closet alongside her mere five-foot-two-inch frame.

She cocked her head and, with a puzzled grin, focused on her escort, who was quite effective at calming her nerves. "I haven't even asked you your name."

Eyeballing Matthew's room through cracks inside the closet, he chuckled. "Yeah, I already told you. Actually, you've heard my name mentioned three times." He tried to hold back an enormous teasing grin. Pipiera released a slight laugh.

"Three times? No way. Not true!" She held her head high. He had to be incorrect. "Oh, goodness, really?" she started to doubt herself. She was extremely preoccupied, considerable energies already spent on preserving the courage needed to make this trip. Any remaining energies were directed to the mission itself. Her overly rehearsed messages to help Matthew didn't help. She already felt sapped. She looked at his bright face, embarrassed she still didn't know his name, and wondered what expression she might get back from this character who seemed able to make her laugh and put her at ease. *Thank heavens they assigned him as my escort,* she thought.

So far, she was pleased. *I'm here, aren't I?* Despite some new-found self-assurance, truth be told, she was barely coping. *On Earth. On Earth, in this Matthew's bedroom! On a mission. A mission assigned by the authoritarians! I am truly amazed.* Through a giggle, she gained a renewed feeling of excitement, thankful to be on an adventure. She could hardly believe it. She just wished she had shared her plans with Megalos. *He would be so proud of me right now.*

"Guess."

"Guess what?"

"My name! You want to know what my name is, right?"

"Yes. You're a tease," she said on account of his big, cute grin.

"Okay," was all he said. He started to rise above the inside of the closet as if the ceiling wasn't there.

"No! No, no. Okay, okay! C'mon, get back down here. We have work to do."

He sat back down, this time cross-legged. His wings bumped into everything and even pushed Pipiera around a bit.

"You're like a bull in a china shop."

He mocked her words with a bit of an adjustment. "You're like a china doll in a bull shop."

He was right, mostly. "Pen. Pen, not shop." She studied him briefly. That grin, that cute grin, it made her laugh, and when she laughed, she became more at ease.

"Jophiel. My name is Jophiel."

"Well, pleased to meet you, Jophiel." Pipiera extended her right hand to offer a proper greeting.

Jophiel took her hand into his two and smiled. "Don't get your hopes too high," he said in a more serious tone.

Pipiera was surprised at his words. "What do you mean?"

Jophiel nodded toward the crack in the closet door where Matthew's bunk beds were in perfect view. "A seed must germinate *before* it can start to grow," was all he said prior to a commanding, "Shhhhhst!"

The moment they had been waiting for had arrived. Pipiera's plan included being right there in Matthew's room the exact moment Kasartha brought him back.

Giggling like they're grand 'ol buddies, Pipiera thought, dismayed at what she was witnessing. The two boys were play fighting, butting their heads into each other's non-physical bodies. Matthew's head was sticking right through the other side of Kasartha's back. They laughed as they took a couple more turns before settling down. Kasartha finally shoved Matthew back into his physical body, which had been lying in his bunk during his galaxy gallivanting. No one knew he was missing. The shove was considerably rough compared to the play fighting.

"Hey! Take it easy," Matthew said. Then they both started laughing again, although Matthew was now visibly pale and weak.

"Darn, they obviously bonded." Pipiera sighed but raised her chin once Jophiel gave her a "don't be discouraged" nudge.

A sharp glimmer soared into the bedroom from the crack in the closet door, catching Kasartha and Matthew's attention.

Kasartha gasped. His immediate reaction was to whisper into Matthew's ear. Pipiera couldn't hear what he said. Then Kasartha stood tall and descended straight down, disappearing into the floorboards.

Matthew glared at the spot on the floor as though he'd never seen Kasartha disappear into the floorboards before. Then his gaze transferred to the light sword shooting out from his closet. He appeared to be in a fear-frozen state.

Pipiera's mind was stuck on the whisper. Her heart sank. She knew the danger of a rebel's whisper. "It's one of the worst weapons ever," she told Jophiel, who knew exactly what she was referring to. The deceit of even the tiniest, slightest whisper from the dragon's forces conjured upon earthlings has potential to cause a widespread or even generational wave of destruction. The gentlest ripple could create tsunami-like chaos. Seedlings planted could germinate and grow deep roots that tunneled and burrowed down to descendants unless someone with proper knowledge lopped off the growth. Pipiera knew Matthew's heart was full of anger, hurt, self-righteousness, and more recently, a growing boastfulness and even thieving. Plus, he was vulnerable, still grieving, a perfect target for a dragon whisperer. This was exactly what she was afraid of, what she and Jophiel had just witnessed. Once this seed, inevitably a lie, took root within Matthew's heart, that pesky, poisonous weedy plant would grow, particularly if that danged Kasartha kept coming around to water it.

"Oh my." She sighed again, only to be pushed aside by Jophiel, who chose that moment to step out of the closet. His light and sheer presence created a silent "light boom," and for a full second or two, nothing could be seen but white, bright nothingness.

Matthew scrambled as far back as he could against the wall and cowered beneath his raised arms. "Don't hurt me!" he squeaked.

"Don't hurt me?" Still positioned unseen behind Jophiel, Pipiera was flabbergasted. "Is he serious? The guy romps around with the dragon's own, and he asks *us* not to hurt him?" Jophiel shushed Pipiera with a slight but unquestionably commanding wave of his hand behind his back. Pipiera decided she better be quiet and just listen, although she was sure Jophiel had to know how sarcastic and bizarre this situation was.

Jophiel spoke a single word, one that Pipiera was certain could be heard by the entire population of Havensight.

"*L i s t e n.*"

Matthew rubbed his eyes, still looking stunned. Anyone would. Jophiel was an enormous, illuminating figure, and he easily dominated the room. Choking down a lump in his throat, Matthew's eyes followed the sprawling width of wings from one end to the other, and that was with Jophiel keeping them folded. And his height! How he fit into Matthew's tiny bedroom, much less the closet, well, that was a head scratcher.

Matthew swallowed hard and nodded nervously, his entire body shaking.

Jophiel stepped aside and spoke in a low voice that only Pipiera could hear. "Okay, kid, you're on. Go."

Oh crap. Really? She was panicking. *Did you have to make this such a big deal? Such a grandstand opening? So grandioso?* Pipiera was beside herself. *Why would he put me on the spot like that? What right does he have? Now what am I going to say?* She was so nervous she had forgotten her talking points. And besides, Matthew and one of the dragon's boys had bonded, and there had been the mouth-to-ear whisper. *What can I possibly say to change this scene, to turn it around?* Pipiera felt sick to her stomach. *Oh, I wish I was just hanging with Moolos, jumping and watching and chatting and all. But nooo, I have to be here.*

Jophiel stepped aside, and his knee pushed her forward. Pipiera was beginning to think this Jophiel guy wasn't the greatest escort after all. He obviously didn't understand that interventions were not her thing. She was just here on a favor, a duty, a mission from the authoritarians. He obviously thought she had more to offer than she actually did.

At first Matthew couldn't see what was happening. He squinted and crawled slowly to the foot of his bunk. All he could see was the top of a head full of blond, curly hair.

"You!" Matthew exclaimed once he leaned over close enough to recognize the young girl who had held him captive and made him watch his childhood night terror.

Pipiera was taken aback, a nervous shake rippling through her core. *This is not how I envisioned this would go.* Her mind felt like a jumbled heap. She didn't know what she should say first or how to say it. Should she be commanding like Jophiel? Could she be like that even if she wanted to? Her sarcasm and lack of patience had driven Matthew away once already; she did not want to make a habit of it.

A calm, steady, reassuring voice came into her head. *Be yourself. Say what comes to you.*

Oh, thank heavens, Pipiera thought. A reminder that she wasn't alone in this. It wasn't just her and her escort there in Matthew's room. She was supported in the utmost of ways. *Okay,* she whispered in her head and stood a little taller, enabling the crown of her head to rise at least an inch. She looked up at the boy who was causing such a disruption in her life.

She studied Matthew's face. She did not like how suddenly annoyance replaced the fear he had displayed just seconds earlier. *Ha, he remembers me. Hmm… I thought he wouldn't.* She wanted to tell him how cross she was at his eagerness to listen to someone like Kasartha. On the other hand, she wanted to tell him she could see in his eyes how very lost he was. Hurting and grieving. Desperate for guidance. *And, I think,* Pipiera concluded, *desperate for some serious friendship. Friendship with the kind of being you could trust, to tell them how you really feel and, in return, know that you'll be encouraged and not judged. Friendship that always goes without saying, "Hey, I'll always be here for you. Always."* She smiled at this thought and realized the dead silence in the room was pining for her to speak. She didn't have anything on the tip of her tongue that she thought would sound intelligent though.

"Uh, you have quite a collection of jumpers in there." She

pointed back at his closet. Matthew just blinked. "Well, I suppose I should have said runners. That's what you call them, right?" Matthew nodded slightly and blinked again.

Without moving from his commanding position, Jophiel peeked down at Pipiera. "What are you doing?"

"I'm bonding," she whispered confidently. He seemed satisfied with that.

"Unusual tactic. I hope it doesn't take all day."

Pipiera wasn't sure what to say next, so she kept things casual. "I like to long jump too, you know. You should think about some extra cushioning. You know, protect those heels. Those spikes look a little heavy too, if you ask me. I like them nice and light. I can run faster with no spikes. Barefoot is best, actually."

She noticed Matthew still looked stunned. *Okay, this is awkward.* She decided to switch topics. "By the way, what's the deal with all those cans of spray paint? You've got at least seven of them in that back corner." She pointed into his bedroom closet. Then she narrowed her eyes and glared at him. "Are you defacing community property?" Hands on her hips, she demanded an answer.

Matthew finally regained his vocal cords. "You came here to give me a lecture on *what's in my closet?*" He was cheekily bold.

"Silence!" Jophiel boomed.

The wind from Jophiel's voice blasted Matthew back up against the far wall. Even Pipiera shook, but she calmed herself in time to appear in command and in charge. She had just been reminded of the sarcasm and annoying back talk Matthew was capable of.

"Well, now that I have your attention, Mr. Matthew, tell me, what are you doing with Kasartha?" She crossed her arms across her chest for added authority. "We've caught you red-handed."

All Matthew could do was gape and blink. Then he wiped the top of his sweating forehead with the back of his right hand. "I'm... uh... er..." He glanced toward the door.

Could he possibly be thinking about escaping? She noticed he purposely avoided Jophiel's gaze before he spoke again.

"I'm confused," he said slowly.

Pipiera was concerned. No doubt, he was quite distressed, even more than when she had seen him last. Then he started to cry. *Oh, dear.* Pipiera hadn't counted on that either.

Jophiel nudged Pipiera ever so slightly. "I'm impressed," he said, winking at her. His job was to impress fear upon Matthew in a sufficient dose that the boy would begin to contemplate the seriousness of the messages Pipiera had come to deliver. So, having Matthew full of fear was good; it set the stage nicely. Jophiel also knew that job came second to his first, which was to protect Pipiera. As her escort, he was to ensure her safe return to the high kingdom. As far as Jophiel knew, this was a one-time and straight-forward mission.

Seeing Matthew reduced to tears caused Pipiera to let her guard down. She watched him sob. His face was surely a confession of guilt and a deep, deep sorrow. He *was* lost. She wished now she had spent more time learning about Matthew's history, to familiarize herself with what he had encountered on his earthly journey to that point. Instead, she had concentrated on what her messages needed to be, how to position them and how to phrase them, all to better align his future. She knew hardly anything about his past. In fact, she didn't know much about it at all other than he was somehow considered "our" Matthew, so there was a sense of belonging, to Megalos anyway. This boy was to have a great future in the kingdom. She knew that. He was going to be Papah's replacement in due course. That was clearly nothing to discard. She could hardly believe this kid would qualify for such a prestigious role—protecting the kingdom gate.

Humph, him? Welcoming kingdom citizens as they come home? For heaven's sake, look at him, weak and weeping, confused, and romping around with one of the dragon's boys. Pipiera sighed and then stood as tall as she could. Even so, she was still challenged with facing the height of Matthew's top bunk, where he sat now all crumpled up. She suddenly realized the conversational ball was in her hands. *Be yourself, and say what comes to you*, she reminded herself.

"Maybe we can get together and go long-jumping some afternoon?" she said. In her upbeat, encouraging manner, she checked to see if her words would bring a calmness to his demeanor, maybe even a smile.

Jophiel scrunched his face to hide his puzzlement. "You operate quite differently than others," he noted quietly for Pipiera's ears only. He tried not to chuckle. Instead, he needed to keep the pressure of his presence in good form to retain a serious and enlightening atmosphere. He was becoming rather curious about Pipiera, in a fond way. He couldn't help it.

Matthew lifted his head, surprised at her response. He appeared cautious yet interested. Truth be known, he would like nothing more than a friend, a good friend. Someone he could jump and hang out with and who would accept him for who he was.

I bet he doesn't even know who he is, Pip thought. *Even less how special he is.*

Matthew wiped his wet eyes and cheeks before rallying enough courage to examine her face. "I-I w-would like that." He appeared surprised to hear his own voice accepting her invitation.

"Then it's settled. I'll call you, and we'll set up a date."

"How will you do that?" he asked, still a little bewildered by their conversation. "Call me, that is."

"Yeah, just *how* are you going to do that?" Jophiel murmured as he lifted an eyebrow and peered toward Pipiera, spilling a bit of sarcasm. "I'd really like to know."

Pipiera stood and felt as tall as ever. "You just leave that up to me. In the meantime, Mr. Matthew, no more defacing public or anybody's private property for that matter. Got it?"

"Er, yeah, okay, got it," Matthew replied. On a dare, the

Nick-Josh-Matthew trio had defaced the bus stop benches on the tourist side of town the previous summer. He must have wondered if she actually saw them do it.

There was an awkward silence for what seemed an eternity. Jophiel decided to break it by edging Pipiera with his lower-right wing. "Are we done here?" he whispered.

"Yes," she replied without moving her smiling gaze from Matthew. With that, Jophiel and Pipiera and the illuminating light that set their stage dissolved upward through the ceiling, leaving Matthew to sit there blinking until his head became so heavy that he finally fell backwards into his pillow, sound asleep.

CHAPTER THIRTY-SEVEN
SO, WHAT'S NEXT?

THE RELATIONSHIP BETWEEN Pipiera and Jophiel was about to take a turn.

"What was *that?*" He seemed annoyed. Jophiel no longer looked cute to Pipiera. He obviously expected the visit with Matthew to be more profound, more kingdom-business-like, more... effective maybe?

Why is he challenging me? she thought. *I did my best. At one point, he was actually impressed.*

The pair stood without illumination atop Matthew's roof. She sat down and snuggled her knees up to her chest. He could tell by her move that they weren't leaving Havensight, not yet anyway.

"So, this is what I missed," she whispered. She glanced back. She knew Jophiel was expecting an answer, or more likely the signal it was time to go back. But she wasn't in the mood to defend herself or give a signal of any kind. She was confused. "I need more time," she said.

"Well, my dear young one, if it's time you need, you have come to the right place."

Young one? She wondered what prompted that label.

"Earthlings are big on time," Jophiel continued. "They've got lots of that here. Too bad they don't use it very well."

"Whaddaya mean?"

"Instead of a precious resource—a limited, nonrenewable resource—which it is, it's forgotten." He shook his head. "To them, it's just a measurement stick. They measure everything! From one point to the next—years, days, hours, even seconds. Instead of just markers in the dirt, it's meant to reflect on the seasons between them. *That's* what truly should be measured. No, my dear, what you need is to let your thoughts be loosed in your mind, so you can organize the chaos. That has nothing to do with *time*."

It was obvious this scene had been hard on Pipiera. He was trying to be helpful.

"This is your first mission, isn't it?" He raised his eyebrows, perhaps hoping to alleviate some of the heaviness that surrounded her. Facing the back of her head, he saw her nod. "Okay, I take that to be an unenthusiastic yes." She shrugged. "Well, you, my dear, have a very unique way about you," he stated.

Pipiera waited for him to go on, eager to receive some encouraging words, possibly maybe even a "Job well done".

"Look, you wanted to bond with him. You are indeed well on your way, right?" Jophiel plopped in front of Pipiera so he could see her face. Awkwardly, he laid himself down across the rooftop, and his eyes aligned with hers.

For a flash, his actions reminded her of her dear Moolos. *Oh, I should not have kept this trip from Moolos*, she whined to herself.

Jophiel was adamant, he needed to lift her spirits. This was not normally part of his escort responsibilities, but he could tell this visit, this young lady, this mission… it was all a little different. Even the process to arrange him did not go through the normal channels.

"If you want a plant to grow, where do you place its seed?" he inquired of her.

"Here, you mean? Well, in the ground," Pip replied.

"Anything special about the dirt?" he asked.

"Dirt... er, soil, soil that's good for the seed." She knew where he was going with all this. "I wasn't born yesterday. I know the soil must be good soil, so the message, which is what you're really getting at, will stabilize by establishing and growing roots, so it can grow externally, up out of the ground and into the sunlight. It needs good roots, so the plant itself can grow as it should and really mean something, be really meaningful."

She had to admit, she was amused at this oversized guy strewn across the roof simply to reassure her. She held back her grin and decided to play along.

"What constitutes good soil?"

"Anybody knows that!" she said. "Willingness to listen, eagerness to learn about the king—"

"And *before* an earthling will listen, *what* needs to happen?" Jophiel asked.

She was stumped. What was he driving at? "Uh, a need to listen?" she guessed.

"Yeah. A good reason. Something that causes one to wonder, to search further than they normally would. Sometimes that desire is a gift. Nice. But sometimes it comes from being backed into a corner and having nowhere to turn."

"Do you think Matthew is backed in a corner?" Pipiera wondered what Jophiel was getting at. *Is Matthew stuck in a corner? Am I representative of his hope, or at least the one to help him navigate that hope?* That was a little more pressure than Pipiera could bear.

"Well, he was certainly backed up against his bedroom wall."

The pair looked at each other and then broke into laughter. "Did you see his face when you told him to listen? Oh my, was he flabbergasted!"

"I had to do that, Pipiera, to put some fear into him. The fear of the king is fundamental to planting a seed of wisdom. And you know that's my job, right? I carry considerable authority. You do realize that, don't you?"

"Oh. And yes, of course I do."

"He, this Matthew boy, I presume he's some sort of relative of yours and that's why you're on this mission. He needs to trust someone. And you saw his face."

"It was a face of stone."

"No, no, Pip. May I call you Pip?" She nodded. "I saw something different. He was delighted to hear that you wanted to hang out with him, puddle jumping or whatever. He *needs* to trust someone. He needs to grow out of this phase he's in. He's lost and hurt. I'm sure you could tell. He needs to learn and experience that your interest in him is for his own good… for his eternal future. There's nothing, and I mean nothing, more important than understanding the life that follows the broken curse of death."

Pip nodded slowly.

"And then," he added sternly, "you will need to disappear from his life, watch perhaps, but leave him alone. He mustn't learn to depend on *you*."

She nodded as though she understood and agreed with all he had said. "Yes, I really want to be his friend. I felt his pain, his fear, and I want to help him." She lowered her head and started to cry.

This puzzled Jophiel. "Why are you crying?" Pipiera upgraded into an uncontrollable sob. He decided to let the tears drip from her cheeks. Sometimes it was best to let the waterworks do their thing, wash and then let the emotions hang out, like freshly washed laundry in the breeze.

When she got a grip, Pipiera tried to explain. "Because—all this." She stretched her arms out, motioning all around them. They had a nearly 360-degree view apart from the wide chimney. "It's a community of people, families, homes, mothers, fathers and…" She sobbed some more but pushed it out. "Babies! Little, helpless babies that are gonna grow into little people and people

Matthew's age. They all have journeys and learning tasks for all kinds of things." She faced Jophiel, her face soaking wet. "And I missed all of it. All of it!" Her voice was loud and determinedly mad. "My journey was so short. I copped out. I fled as soon as I could. I was scared. I was never walked in a stroller, and I never had a birthday party. Heck, I never mouthed a single word!" Her voice was sounding angrier and angrier. "I left way too early, and I can't take it back."

"How long have you been holding on to *that*?" Jophiel was surprised at her confession. He didn't know the circumstances surrounding her "quick getaway," but he decided not to inquire, thinking it would be best to move toward a comforting approach, one from which she could springboard. She wiped her cheeks as her sobs subsided. It gave Jophiel a moment to decide how to enter their next discussion. Now *he* was the one totally out of his comfort zone.

"Want to tell me about it?" was all he could come up with, hoping she would say no.

She assessed his face. It was full of compassion and wisdom. *I bet he's ancient, just like my Moolos,* she thought. If there was anyone she should shed her inner feelings with, it should be Megalos. But here she was, this was the moment of her great, long-awaited spill. She sat up tall and took a deep breath. "Yes, it's time... er, I need to do this. Now is as good a chance as any." She tried to avoid using the term *time* given his little lecture on the topic.

"You see, I signed up for a tour. A short one. I really wasn't thrilled about the whole earth journey thing." She looked at him and wondered if he would judge her for that. He did not, so she continued. "There was an opportunity on the sign-up wall for a short stint, a mere few weeks, to a young couple who were just marrying." Pipiera realized her heart was pounding, and her breath was short. So much bottled up inside for so long. She got her grip and continued. "I was supposed to be on this continent, close to here, actually. Zero physical and mental pain. Sounds like an easy gig, right?" She studied his face again. Any judgment there? Nope, so she continued. "Somebody has to take those tours!"

"Sounds like you're convincing yourself it wasn't much of a job."

"Well, truth be told, I could have—and perhaps I should have—signed up for something longer term. Looking back, I think it was a bit of a cop-out. I had more to offer, but I didn't, for whatever reason, feel that I wanted to." Pipiera's eyes fell into her lap. She didn't need to study Jophiel's face for judgment; she was judging herself now. He reached out to hold her chin up.

"Pipiera, look at me. Those roles are key. They bend and shape directions for future paths, right? You must know that. Just because they're short doesn't mean they're simple! They are highly emotional, very strenuous, *and* sacrificial! You lose out on your opportunity to hang out here and learn. It's tough, but it's an opportunity that many, many beings take. Every single tour posted on that sign-up wall is critically important. *Every single one.* One is not greater than another because of its duration. You, Pipiera, gave your earth journey to help a couple reach their eternal destination. You accepted a predestined and sacrificial tour. The king had a plan, he knew the what and why. That role was developed, and you, my dear, dear Pip, filled it. You completed your role beautifully." He smiled at her. "I bet you were one beautiful baby."

"Yeah, well, I *was* pretty cute." She was so appreciative of his view. He would know how this part of the process worked, given the important job he carried out for the king. Then she became serious. "Do you really think so? Do you think my time—er, my journey here—served a good cause?" She dared not ask about the purpose of the king's plans.

"I can't believe you would even ask such a thing. Of course it did. Otherwise, that job clearly would *not* have been posted." He had to change positions, given the awkwardness of his size, her size, and the pitch of the roof. "That was the job you signed up for, and that was the work you completed. Done. Nothing further to say, except, my dear Pip, good work! Not just anybody will sign up for those roles."

"I felt a calling to it. I really wanted to experience the whole, you know, growing up and high school thing. I always dreamed that when my turn came up to journey, I would get to be an all-star long-jump champion, you know, like a known-around-the-earth champion." She laughed. "I don't know why, but my heart was stuck on it. Then on a whim I changed my mind, was accepted, and off I went, knowing I would never be able to fulfill this silly little fantasy of mine. I didn't think it was important, but I couldn't let go of it." She looked at his face again, hoping this was not too much for him. She was spilling a lot of beans. She had held this in for such a long stretch, nearly sixty earth years, in fact.

Jophiel delivered an admiring beam as a light bulb flashed in his mind. "Of course, this is why you were assigned to this mission. This Matthew kid likes to long jump. Well, there's no question Pip, you're meant to have that date you just made with this young boy living under this roof to go long-jumping together. So, go do it!" He paused for a moment. "But please remember, dear Pip, the king and his mission is not just central to your life, which I know you know; it *is* your life. He *is* your life."

She wasn't sure what he meant, but she sighed happily. "Good talk, thank you, Jophiel. I'm so glad we met. Really. You've been very helpful. Thank you." She was incredibly relieved.

Jophiel sat up, cross-legged to match Pipiera's seated position, although he still towered well above her. They both surveyed the street. The night was still and quiet. A dog barked a few houses away, and a few bedroom lights turned on here and there. Stars were still visible, and the moon was a crescent shape. Several bicycles leaned up against backyard sheds, some locked, others not. It was a bicycle commuter neighborhood for sure. The town center was only a twenty-minute bike ride away while the tourist area was a good twenty-five minutes in the opposite direction. Pipiera noticed the wagons and strollers parked beneath carports and sighed. She wondered how her earthly parents were doing. They would be in their late seventies by now. To her knowledge, they had no other children. Pipiera had been their only hope.

"They were so devastated when I left," she whispered. She knew, however, she had to remain focused. Her job right now was Matthew.

Jophiel heard her whisper and put his arm around her. They continued to sit quietly in the stillness of the night as the community began to awaken and the Earth turned to greet the full brilliance of the sun.

Once again, Jophiel was about to speak, to suggest they get started on their way home to the kingdom. He would escort her back to the gate level. But Pipiera spoke first, wanting to engage in more discussion, this time about Matthew. "What do you think he whispered in his ear when he saw us?"

"Who?"

"Kasartha."

"Oh, you mean when he saw my light? He didn't know it was you there. Nor me, for that matter. Rather, he saw the undeniable distinguishable brightness that peeked through the crack of the closet door. He knew we were of the kingdom, and he *knew* we were there to visit Matthew."

"How do you figure he knew it was Matthew we were there to visit?"

"Because we were in Matthew's closet."

"Right, of course. Silly question." Pipiera chuckled. "I know how much havoc a whisper from a dragon boy can create. What do you think he said once he knew we, er, kingdom visitors were present? What could he have said in that split second?"

"Anything, I suppose, but whatever it was, it was to ultimately discredit the messenger and the message."

"Well, he didn't have to do that. In case you haven't noticed, I never actually delivered my message. And so, he wasn't able to discredit us!" They did a high-five to celebrate. "Matthew actually seems okay with getting together again, hanging out with me. I made that first step. He seems interested in starting a relationship—well, at least it seems that way."

"Make detours when you reach trouble spots. Wait for instructions, then keep going, Pip. You're gonna be fine." Their definite next step was to get back home. He knew there would be a lineup of other escort responsibilities—there always was. They would be placed in an impeccable order, a system he did not want to mess with. Besides, this visit had concluded. There might be more visits for Pipiera to complete her mission, but this visit had reached its conclusion, more or less.

"Would you mind if I stayed a little longer?"

Another unusual request. "While I'd love to stay, I cannot. I must get back. And my job is to deliver you home. Safely!"

"Is it not also your job to take orders from me?"

Jophiel frowned at this commanding half-pint standing in front of him, challenging his role. "No, it is not."

"Oh. Well, then." Her shoulders drooped. "Will you do me the favor of allowing me to stay? We could arrange a pickup *time*." She jabbed at the word.

"You mean we could agree on an *arrangement*?"

"What's the diff?"

Jophiel sighed hesitantly. "Well, when you have completed what you are intending to complete, wait for me, and I'll come to you." He looked straight at her face, "And exactly what do you want to complete before going back?"

"Well, it's been on my mind forever just how my earthly parents might be coping. I've been wondering and waiting. I'd like to go and visit them. Just to see... to see for myself how they're doing."

"That could be quite emotional."

"They won't even know I'm there!"

"Of course they won't. I mean for you. I don't like the idea of you going by yourself."

"I won't be long. I promise. What do you think?"

Jophiel was not in a position to deny her request, although he did not want Pipiera to know that. After a short contemplation, he agreed. However, he warned her that another escort could be assigned to meet her and lead her home. Pipiera was feeling quite brave and agreed to all the terms he laid out, all for her safety.

"Just one more thing," he said, becoming quite serious.

"What?"

"The boy, Matthew. Yes, he's backed up against a wall, but remember, he's not blocked into a corner yet. And it's not you he's listening to—not yet."

Pipiera nodded. "Yes. I get it."

Off he went, leaving Pipiera on the roof of Matthew's house as Havensight continued its gracious bow to the powerful sun.

CHAPTER THIRTY-EIGHT
ANOTHER PICNIC

"MATTY. MATTY." MARNIE shook Matthew's shoulders again, this time with a little more vigor than the first three nudges. "Matthew!"

Hugging her ragged pink rabbit, Karo was alarmed to hear panic in her mom's voice. Not again! "What's wrong with him, Mommy?" She stared up at her mom, who was balancing on the bottom bunk's mattress to get a close-up peek at Matthew, trying to figure out why he was not waking up. She shook him hard. Matthew opened one eye slightly, then the other.

"Mom?" As if he wasn't sure it was her, Matthew attempted to sit up and lean back on his elbows. *Where am I?* He shook the cobwebs out of his head. "Oh, man. Did I have one crazy sleep." He focused on his mom's face as it transitioned from white to its usual dull pink. He could see she was recovering from fear. "What's wrong?" he asked, his voice curious and tinged with panic.

Karo clutched her rabbit even tighter. Whatever fever of fear was going around, she didn't want this week's sleep buddy to catch it. She gazed around the room for any sign of the ugly green visitor. *Nope, thank heavens, not here*, she thought with relief.

Marnie stepped back onto the floor. "Whew, Matty, you scared me. I couldn't wake you." She had also had a hard time waking up that morning, and now for certain they would all be late. *I'm giving you too many of those painkillers*, she thought. Matthew would be late for school, Karo would be late for day care (which really didn't matter that much), and Marnie would be late for work, which mattered a great deal.

"We really need to move it. C'mon. Get up and get dressed. I'll throw a package of Pop-Tarts in your lunch bag for your breakfast. Let's go!" Her voice got louder as Matthew fell back into his pillow. Grabbing Karo by her free hand, Marnie marched out of his room.

The morning drive had been fast and dead quiet. Matthew insisted his mom let him out of the car a block away from school. Then it would be easier for her to turn left and head straight over to Karo's day care. His head was spinning. The walk and a bit of fresh air might help clear his mind. Once in the schoolyard, he stopped and sat on the rotten picnic table at the edge of the property, wondering why it was there anyway. He reflected on that dreaded morning, the morning of the attack. He was thankful he had a place to sit still for a moment. The same overgrown clump of lilac bushes that kept the attack out of the school's view provided him with much-needed solace from nosey teachers and onlookers. Absent-mindedly inspecting the globs of purplish buds on branches grown wild and out of control, he wondered why no one ever trimmed them. He recalled his dad trimming their own all the time—when he was alive, that is.

Matthew felt an intense sadness, like a black cloud settling over his head. He wanted to cry, but what was worse, he didn't know why. An incredibly real battle raged within. He didn't understand it, never mind knew what to do about it. He didn't know who he should listen to, who he should talk to, or who or even what he should believe.

Nobody knows me, and nobody gets me, he thought. *I don't even know me.* He wanted to yell that to the universe, but why and what good would it do? *Maybe you, Dad, could hear me then. Maybe you'd be sorry you left.* His head hurt from his raw and swirling thoughts.

I'm glad I let those bets roll, and I'm glad I took a beat-down, I deserved it. I wanted it. I want everyone to see I hurt.

But they didn't.

"Can you see me, Dad!" he cried in a cracking voice of desperation.

Matthew broke off a splinter from the picnic table and threw it into the lilac bush. It also ignored his feelings.

He vowed never to do sports of any kind ever again. *Yes, that'll fix me.*

CHAPTER THIRTY-NINE
MAN TO MAN

ARNIE DECKER SLOWED his car right down. *Matthew? What's he doing there?*

He pulled over in front of the picnic table and jammed his car into park. *Looks like he's stewing real good, but I'm the last person he wants to see.*

Arnie's thought was validated when, without even looking up, Matthew flipped him the bird. But Arnie had already stepped out of his car, already committed himself to walking over. He had always felt an immense sadness for Matthew along with his own sense of helplessness. It was quite surprising that Matthew was coming back to school so quickly, given he had blacked out in the boys' locker room the previous morning. He knew the boy wouldn't want his help.

His own relationship with Marnie had been a tumultuous one. Oh, at first, it was great, but they married too soon. Had Karo too soon. Everything fell apart just after Karo was born. Arnie realized Marnie was stuck inside a bubble of immense grief and didn't want it to burst. Her grief was her refuge. Perhaps it was the emotion of having another baby. He really couldn't figure it out. Although he suspected guilt of some sort somehow wound its way throughout her head, totally unnecessary and uncalled for. When she insisted it was over, Arnie was devastated. All he ever wanted was a family in a loving home. A family he could cherish and provide for. A wife he would dote on. Children he could care for, hang out with, and teach. Oh, how he would love to teach all sorts of things to his family and to be there for them as they grew and matured. Arnie was a man with a heart for the kingdom and felt a passion to pass it onward. He envisioned a long line of descendants. That was his purpose, and he believed in it.

Matthew never wanted any part of Arnie. Not when they lived under the same roof and quite clearly not now.

Do I approach as someone who once played the role of dad, or should I approach as his vice principal? Pulling his chin, he voted for neither and settled on simply approaching Matthew as a friend. *Yes, I'll try that. A buddy, even.* He doubted that would work, but he had to try. He couldn't leave Matthew sitting there, despondent.

He headed toward Matthew with a casual stride and his head bent down. He didn't want to appear as though he was coming over to demand why he was not heading into class.

"This is my picnic table," Matthew said. "You're not welcome."

Arnie sat down anyway.

"I'm not feeling well. Mom's coming to get me," Matthew said, knowing if rudeness didn't work, this would be the next most suitable message to get rid of the guy. Arnie meant nothing to Matthew, just a guy who had interfered with his family, nothing else.

Arnie stared down the road, the opposite direction of the school. He knew that was a lie, and he knew Matthew said it simply as a technical student-like response. Marnie preferred Arnie not to have much contact with her son. She had said it time and again, claiming no matter what discussions they had, it always upset her Matty. "Just stick to school business," she warned him, "particularly when at school."

But today, there was no more appeasing her and no more appeasing the boy. "It's time we talk, Matt, I mean really talk. Man to man."

"Man to man." Matthew chuckled. "Yeah, right, more like doofus to… to me."

"Don't hold anything back." Arnie stared at the streetscape again, wishing Matt didn't have to be so sarcastic. "Look, you don't want anything to do with me. I get it. Really, I do. I can't change the past. Your mom and I entered something we thought would be a good thing."

"Yeah, like you getting to use all my dad's stuff. Who was that good for, apart from you, that is?"

"Is that really what you're mad about? A lawnmower? A pair of hedge clippers? C'mon, Matt."

Matthew turned his back on Arnie, refusing to answer.

"I don't expect you to understand. Things didn't turn out the way I had hoped. Your mom wasn't ready and needed her space. She didn't want me around anymore. Ever, for that matter." Arnie seemed to be talking to the air in front of him now.

"More like *you* didn't want to stick around!"

This reaction startled Arnie.

"Is that what you think? That *I* didn't want to stick around?" Suddenly, Arnie realized perhaps he was treading on one of Marnie's emotional "borders." Perhaps that was the story she had told Matthew, that it was he who wanted to leave. Might Matt have been thinking that all this time? Obviously. Perhaps Marnie thought that would make the transition easier for Matthew. After all, it hadn't been that long since his dad died. Arnie wondered whether it would be worth explaining the truth to this lost, hurting young boy or leave it all for his mother to sort out.

Arnie sat up and decided he needed to be straight with Matthew, thinking that maybe there might be a chance at some sort of father-son relationship. For heaven's sake, who else would play that role?

The boy was suffering, he had to feel doubly abandoned. Arnie felt he could help. It would be wrong for him not to try. Arnie decided to throw Marnie's request out the window, the request that he stay away from her son because it "stressed him out". That was a ridiculous conclusion, and if there was truth to that, Arnie was determined to change it for good.

"Matty."

"You don't get to call me that," Matthew scolded him.

"Okay, Matt." Arnie regarded the school building, then focused on Matthew. "Let's get out of here. Let's go for... uh, I know. Let's go into town for a nice plate of bacon and eggs. We can chat. You can tell me how you feel, and hey, don't hold back any punches. Good?"

Matthew looked at Arnie, his face scrunched with curiosity. Surprisingly, he nodded his acceptance.

Arnie grabbed the opportunity, "Let's go then."

As they walked toward the car, Arnie glanced back at Matthew, who was two paces behind him, and chuckled. "It's been awhile since I've played hooky." He winked at Matthew.

Matthew looked back at the school hoping none of his buddies or any of Emerson's thugs would see him disappear into Principal Decker's navy, rusted-out Chevette.

CHAPTER FORTY
FOOD FIGHT

MATTHEW POKED AT his scrambled eggs. At first he had a ferocious appetite, tapping his fingers on the table and waiting for the "hungry man" special to arrive. He had dived into his waffle, but then his appetite disappeared when Doofus Decker made fun of his mom.

"Guess I shouldn't have brought that up," Arnie admitted with regret.

It might have been an okay comment to make except they both knew Marnie's cooked breakfasts were totally nonexistent. Strictly Pop-Tarts, Buc Wheats, packets of strawberry instant breakfast drinks, and Tang were housed in Marnie's kitchen in the morning food department, alongside countless brands of breakfast cereals and, on shopping days, fresh donuts. Now dinner, that was another story. Marnie made a fantastic roast pork dinner with whipped mashed potatoes and gravy every Sunday afternoon. Getting back to Arnie's comment though, Matthew didn't much care for the sarcasm.

"Insulting Mom is off limits," he held his lips tight, but his thoughts managed to escape nevertheless.

The tightness in Matthew's jaw told Arnie he would have to be more tactful.

He leaned forward, starting again in a gentle voice. "You know, Matty..."

Normally, just hearing Arnie use the personal family name "Matty" totally irked him, but somehow, at that moment, Matthew warmed up wearily with the personalization. Not many people were left who called him that anymore, only his mom and sister, and Matthew was feeling alienated even from them these days. *But then so does that creep Kasartha,* he thought. *He abuses the "Matty" privilege too.*

Arnie continued, switching back to his bulldozer-without-brakes voice "... you gotta know, I tried really hard. Your mom... er... it's just that... er..."

Matthew's eyebrows rose, his emerald eye threatening with red as did the blue one. "What? It's just that *what?*" After all, this was a man-to-man chat right?

Arnie flubbed around some more. "Matty, none of what happened... or didn't happen... or should've happened has any reflection on you. Your momma, she's a great woman. I loved her. I still love her. Just in a different way now."

Matthew's opportunity for a cheeky response was golden. "You mean like the kind of love you have for one woman when you're married to another woman?"

"No! And..." Arnie switched into his vice principal role, shaking his right index finger to drive this next point home.

Matthew already understood this habit. Every time Arnie got a little angry or annoyed, rather than his voice getting louder, his face would fluster, and he would employ that finger vigorously. It was actually quite a skill and he was well known for it. Kids at school would poke fun by shaking an angry finger at each other while using calm, sweet words to send a message. It was his trademark, and Matthew and all of Havensight Collegiate's students knew it all too well.

Arnie spotted a smirk on Matthew's face. "Not like that. And you know it. Like someone who is in my life and I care about."

"Well, duh, she's Karo's mom. Of course she's in your life. And besides, only Karo calls her *Momma*."

Arnie was growing impatient. Matt could tell because his face was getting red, and he grabbed his right hand tucking it into his left, as if keeping his finger from shaking would help him keep his voice gentle.

"You try too hard. You should let it out," Matthew advised.

Arnie sat back to take a deep breath before crossing his arms. "Let's get serious, shall we? I know you're more mature than you let on. Am I not right?"

Matthew shrugged his right shoulder.

"I'm not going to explain or defend how we got to this point. But I do want us, you and me, to be friends. More than friends."

Matthew bit the inside of his cheeks.

Arnie leaned forward, his elbows on the table. "I know you miss your dad. You loved him. You love him now, and will always love him."

A tear began to choke up inside, one that Matthew would not let out.

"I'm so sorry for your loss."

Each word penetrated Matthew's core. "That's what everybody says. It means nothing." It escaped. The tear fell directly into his cold eggs. Just then the waitress appeared to see if everything was all right with their meals.

"Oops," she said, "your toast. Coming right up." She observed it had not come out with the scrambled eggs, sausage, bacon, huge pile of cubed, deep-fried potatoes, and waffle. "I'll be right back." She pretty much ran away, obviously sensing she had interrupted something sensitive.

Another tear fell. Matthew felt a bubbling up inside his chest, a battle of emotions. Then it started. He began sobbing uncontrollably. He kept his back straight and his head pressed against the booth's vinyl back. His cheeks were wet, and drips fell onto his lap. He breathed in and out of his mouth, feeling his chest rise quickly to inhale and fall, quivering to exhale. It felt like time stood still. A dome of silence covered him and Arnie. Those close by glanced over but pretended not to notice. One woman tiptoed over and discreetly dropped a lavish lime puff on the bench where Matthew was sitting, close to his hands so he could grasp it easily enough. The empathetic waitress chose to watch from across the room rather than sweeping busily from table to table. Matthew was certain the entire restaurant stood completely still, and he felt the stares of countless eyes. His mind swirled in grey nothingness like it was caught in a whirlwind. His heart ached like it was cracked in half, and something heavy lay inside of it. He focused on bringing his breath lower into his abdomen to get a grip before he could tend back to Arnie.

Arnie hadn't budged his position. He was still leaning across the table on his elbows and he hadn't modified his gaze. It was still fixed on Matthew's eyes, only now it was loaded with empathy.

After a nudge from the Lavender Fields Café owner, the waitress came back. "Honey, I'm going to make you some nice fresh eggs."

Matthew grabbed his plate and shook his head. "No need to." She topped up Arnie's coffee cup and then scampered off again.

"Still no toast," Arnie said with a chuckle, hoping to lighten the mood.

Matthew didn't like how Arnie used insults as humor. Still, he was relieved his sobbing session had passed. The air felt a bit lighter, and he felt good, but only for a moment. Looking around the restaurant, he felt embarrassed. Had he just made a fool of himself? Yes, of course he had. Anger began to stir. *This guy messed up my life, and now he's made me look like a fool.*

"Leave me alone. In fact, leave all of us alone." Matthew's voice was loud as he scolded Arnie. "We would have been better off without you. You don't know shite about me or my dad!"

As Matthew exited the booth, he decided to finalize his little performance with a spit of saliva aimed at Arnie's fruit plate, but he missed by an inch. He grabbed his gym bag and headed out the front door, passing the onlookers and the waitress, who stood ready with his toast.

Arnie leaned back and crossed his arms. "Well, that went well," he muttered. It was his turn to cry, but he would keep that pool of salty water deep inside.

CHAPTER FORTY-ONE
BACK TO NOTHING

MATTHEW NEVER LIFTED his head once during the entire twelve-minute walk to school. He felt foolish for sobbing in public, especially in front of Arnie, but he had to admit, it felt good afterwards. It felt even better to embarrass Arnie in front of all those people. After all, he deserved it. "What a guy," he mumbled, "blaming Mom."

His anger trickled into other thoughts that dripped into his mind like rapidly melting ice. "Stupid Mom for marrying the guy." He kicked a rock down the center of the street. "Sucky baby Karo. Now I'm stuck living with her for the rest of my life." He kicked the curb before stepping onto the sidewalk. "Freakin' thugs. Now how am I gonna pay Mom back?"

Arriving at the school property, he kicked the picnic table, splintering fragments of rotted wood. "My stupid friends, they don't even really know me."

At the front door to the school building, he kicked the kick-plate and entered quickly in hopes of disassociating the vehement bang to himself.

Matthew went straight to history class, leaving Arnie to deal with the whole late slip deal and quite possibly having to call his mom.

Despite the stink-eye look from his teacher, he flopped into his seat. His 500-plus-page history textbook slid out of his grasp, making a slapping noise on the floor. *The only reason I'm here,* Matthew thought, *is because I don't want to think about last night's ghosts. I can't think about that. I can't tell anyone; they'll lock me up. I can't go home right now. My life sucks.* He picked his textbook up off the floor. He wondered if Kasartha and the ghost girl were his only true friends, the only people in the world interested in him. *Even they don't get along. Should I be choosing which one is real? Which one to believe? Everything sucks.*

The class was long and arduous. Who really cared if armies still battled after their respective authorities signed the Treaty of Ghent? Matthew figured more wars should have taken place on account of the natural thing people did was break promises and hurt each other. That happened all the time. And no surprise, the innocent people were brutally smacked and left for dead. *Like anyone cared for their well-being either. It's all bogus. This whole world.*

Matthew was the first one out of class when the bell rang. He had worked himself into an even greater frenzy, if that were even possible. A bad mood, angry and anxious, it was surprising he paid attention through an entire lesson, his way of punishing himself.

Josh was waiting at Matt's locker. "Phil said he saw you get into Decker's car this morning. That true?" Matthew was irked even more by the stupid grin on Josh's face.

"Get outta my way."

"So, it *is* true. What the heck did he want? Where did you go?"

Matthew wasn't having any of this interrogation. He hauled off and punched Josh in the nose. Remorse filled Matthew's head immediately, but what he needed more than forgiveness was space, a place to be alone.

He ran out of the school, across the yard, past the picnic table, and kept on going. Had he really just sucker-punched one of his two best friends? Realizing he was heading toward home and not wanting to go there, he turned north up Simcoe Street and found refuge behind the Bowl-O-Rama. He sat on a large rock hidden by a large waste-disposal container with a backdrop of seven-foot weeds. The spring sun had been plenty kind to plants that year. By the dozen or so cigarette butts on the ground, he figured he was where the Bowl-O-Rama employees took their smoke breaks.

Out of breath, he crumpled his body into a folded position and held his head down past his knees. He wished he had more control over his emotions—and his mouth and fist. Tears wouldn't come. Matthew believed he didn't deserve to cry.

"An amazing punch!" An excited and familiar voice came out of nowhere.

Matthew turned around, and there was Kasartha, bobbing up and down in the weeds shadow boxing with a make-believe opponent. "Poof! Poof! And he's down!" Kasartha started jumping around, waving his arms in the air. "Man, that was good!"

Matthew was disgusted. He started to say something, to argue with Kasartha. Instead, he reverted to his head-in-hands position. "What's the use?" he mumbled.

"What's your problem?" Kasartha came around to approach Matthew face-to-face. "C'mon, what's a little punch? The pip-squeak was into your business. He had it coming."

Matthew swallowed hard. "He's my buddy. At least he was."

Kasartha shook his finger. "No, no, no. I heard you." He mocked Matthew kicking a curb as he did earlier that morning and employed a high, squeaky voice. "My friends don't even know who I am." Kasartha rubbed his eyes to add a dramatic effect. "Ha! Right? You said it yourself."

"You heard that? You followed me? What gives?"

"Don't matter. You said it, and you are right. Your friends don't know you as well as you want them to. That's true. It's a fact, and you declared it."

"What are you, some kind of recording device? Going around

listening to people's conversations?" Matthew stood up. "Is that what you do? Eavesdrop and then throw things back in people's faces?" Matthew focused his angry energy into a mean stare at Kasartha. "Besides, Josh knows me well enough. And if he doesn't, Nick'll set him straight."

"Oh yeah? Then why don't you tell either of those so-called buddies about me? Think they'll believe you? Tell them about our little trips to the edge of the universe. Can you share that with either of them?"

Matthew pulled back. He knew he couldn't and wouldn't tell anyone about that. They'd think he was crazy. In fact, Matthew was having trouble absorbing the whole business himself.

"Life sucks," he proclaimed to the stinky cigarette butts at his feet. "I am so done with it."

Matthew had never felt so alone, like his life didn't matter. Hoping for even an inkling of sympathy from Kasartha, instead, he caught a glimpse of his hat disappearing into the ground.

Kasartha had made an unusually quick exit downward upon Matt's declaration of his desire to be done with life, like he had to report something somewhere urgently.

Matthew sniffed. "I can't even count on him."

CHAPTER FORTY-TWO
A LAMP STILL SHINES

In a Town Next to Havensight

MAGGIE'S HAIR WAS thin but still long enough to be tied neatly into a tight, tiny bun atop her head, secured with at least twenty dark brown bobby pins. Her hair must have been darker in her younger years, otherwise, why would she use that shade of pins? Such a contrast to her now-sterling-white color. Pipiera finished scouting around her once-upon-a-time home and decided that her earthly parents were frugal. *Not a bad thing.*

The kettle's whistle settled down. Pipiera watched as Maggie slippered from the turquoise boomerang countertop, balancing one porcelain hummingbird cup filled to the brim. The short path on the floral linoleum flooring was well worn and darkened with yellow compared to the rest of the floor, which still had a golden sheen. She placed the cup carefully on a kitchen table barely large enough for two. Five unmatched placemats full of diverse colors were spread out, overlapping each other to protect the table's precious veneer. Back for another pour, this time into a cup decorated with red cardinals and yellow daisies, she filled it, gave the instant coffee a stir and shuffled back, placing the morning beverages opposite each other. Maggie was somewhat flustered upon accidentally knocking over a cane as she pulled out her kitchen chair.

Pipiera's heart swelled up at least ten sizes, it might as well have stopped. *Oh*, she kept thinking to herself over and over while jerking back tears. Was it guilt, love, regret, or sorrow? Pipiera would analyze her feelings later. Right now she just wanted to absorb these surroundings as much as she could. She'd been imagining this for so long.

Maggie added milk, then carefully measured and added scoops of sugar for each cup. Without raising her slumped shoulders, she turned her head. "Well, are you coming?" Maggie redirected her focus to her cup, which was still much too hot to hug with her hands.

Pipiera attempted to clasp her mother's face. "Mother, I'm here," she whispered. "I wish you could know how much I love you." Pipiera could only hope the breath of her whisper might miraculously sink into her earthly mother's ears and seep into her heart.

"Mother, I'm waiting for you, you and Father, okay?"

Maggie was unaware of anything unusual in the room, most certainly not the presence or whispers of her long-passed infant daughter.

Pipiera studied Maggie's eyes. Despite her weariness, the lamp within her shone. Her eyes glimmered, though not with sadness.

Aren't you sad?

Pipiera backtracked through her thoughts to the day of her departure. She had been a few weeks old and suffered a heart condition, something Maggie and Charles were told later to be an atrial defect, but for Pipiera, it was the first of three pre-established exit avenues provided for her. She recalled the horror-stricken gape in her young mother's face as Pipiera lay comfortably cradled in her arms. It must have felt like a mean trick. How could Maggie have known there was a plan, a strategy to it all, one the king had carefully crafted, even knowing they might never understand? It was those eyes, the horrible sadness in her mother's eyes that Pipiera had carried for all those years.

Megalos had tried to put it into simple terms for Pip, explaining that pain in earthly journeys enabled the king to burrow closer into the sufferers' souls. Closer relationships had great power to do things that could touch the lives of others, not just in the present, but quite often in the future too. Megalos had gone on and on about weaving a web and fetching far into roots and such. Pipiera had once again phased out of his ongoing lecture. But what she did take away from it was that there was indeed a master plan. Pipiera had been assured over and over that she had carried out her role perfectly. It hadn't mattered which of the three avenues she chose to exit, but if she had more courage, she could have stayed longer, could have brought more joy to her parents and exited later in her childhood years. The vision of Maggie's face emboldened with horror and grief had stained Pipiera's soul. It was the real, unspoken reason why she would not allow herself to enter the kingdom.

But now Maggie's eyes were bright with a grin stretched across her face. She looked up as the love of her life, Charles, shuffled into the kitchen. They would share this morning time together, inquire as to the quality of each other's sleep, and then discuss possible reasons for whatever—restless tossing and turning, noises late in the night from passersby on the footpath beside their bedroom window, of how they might have gained a stiff neck or what could have caused that charley horse. Charles commented on the consistency of his bowel movements, which would always rouse a chuckle from Maggie, and he so liked to trigger that smile in her eyes.

That morning nothing was unusual or different, except that Maggie was already offering a grin without Charles having to work on her.

"What's up you? What are you chuckling about?" he asked as he tucked himself into his chair and drew it closer to the table.

"Oh, nothing. I was just thinking about our Penney this morning. Not sure what made me think of her just now, but you know, she'd be going on sixty next week. Imagine that. Just think what a party that would be."

That made Charles smile too. They loved to talk about their beloved Penney. Around this time every year, the pair would scheme about what they might have done for their precious daughter's birthday. What fun they had. The year Penney would have turned five, they envisioned a country pasture with seventy white ponies, each decorated uniquely using the colors of the rainbow. The ponies would prance in circles with grace and efficiency. Seventy or so five-year-olds dressed in cowgirl and cowboy outfits would ride for hours, laughing and calling out to their watching parents, whom Charles and Maggie decided should be there also. For her thirteenth birthday, they envisioned jewelry making and giggling teenage girls. For her eighteenth birthday, they dared to wonder what chaperoning a mixed party might have been like. For her twenty-first, they imagined a dinner, just the three of them, and gifting her with Maggie's mother's special pearl pendant, which was meant to be passed down the generational lines. At twenty-eight, they imagined possibly gifting her with a weekend away because she might have been married and maybe even had children of her own by then.

"Hmm… sixty years, my dear Charles what would we do?" Maggie asked.

Charles grinned. "Well, I suppose we could dye each other's hair. That would be quite a party."

"Oh my, I haven't done that for some time. Wouldn't that be a party indeed!"

Both still had a touch of dance left in the sparkles of their eyes, his a translucent blue, hers a deep green. Indeed, given the gene pool, Penney would certainly be totally white-haired by now too if she had lived.

Hands on her hips, Pipiera scolded the pair. "Uh, hello, I'm still blond."

The light shining through the tiny kitchen window got a little brighter and captured Pipiera's attention. Sudden brighter sun rays usually meant activity of some sort, typically the arrival of a kingdom messenger or a host. A moment later, she heard Jophiel's teasing whisper behind her. "Looking for someone?"

Pipiera jumped a bit, startled. "I thought you weren't coming back for me."

He shrugged. "No one else was available."

Pipiera knew that was not possible. She tilted her head to one side and let out a little "Oh?"

"And so…?" he asked.

"And so what?"

"What have you discovered, my dear?"

"My dear?" She laughed. He was full of surprising remarks and approaches.

"Seriously."

Jophiel had been scolded for leaving Pipiera alone and sent back with stringent goals. She was to feel independent and in control of her mission, and he was to support, protect, and encourage. But the mission, as Jophiel learned, was less about Matthew and more about her, unbeknownst to her. It was a delicate scenario. That was all Jophiel was told. He knew he needed to get more involved, to get a deeper grasp on what was going on inside this unique creature's heart and mind.

"I'm in love! They're so cute! I guess I wasn't expecting them to have aged. But, of course, duh, yes they have. But look, aren't they the cutest couple?"

Jophiel nodded and motioned her to continue. "And…"

"And?" She really couldn't figure this guy out. Why did he probe so much?

"What have we learned?"

"We?"

Jophiel grinned from ear to ear, enjoying the half-teasing, half-serious interrogation. He felt this was his best shot at getting some good two-way communication going. "Spill the beans. Tell me about them," he nodded toward Maggie and Charles. "Are they not what you expected?"

Pipiera wasn't sure how to answer that question, nor if she wanted to. "I told you, I think they're cute. Just look at them." Maggie was putting two slices of soft white bread into the toaster while chatting about the likelihood of a thunderstorm sometime later that day. Pipiera was a little discouraged they had moved on from conversing about her so soon—and for what, the weather of all things.

"They love each other," she said. *And I think they loved me— still love me*, she admitted to herself.

"And…"

Oh, you are so annoying. "Well, and, to be quite honest, they're not as sad and broken up as I remembered."

Jophiel gave her an empathetic smile. "Is that okay?"

Pipiera hugged and rocked herself, "Yeah, that's okay. Actually, it's good. All good."

"Oh, you're related!"

"Of course we're related. They're my earthly parents."

"No, no, not them. I knew *that*. Him!"

Jophiel was practically on top of Charles, bending and twisting his oversized existence to see straight at a tiny, framed photograph of a young boy, a toddler posing with a grown-up telescope. Pipiera hadn't even noticed the long horizontal shelf. She hesitated. She would have to climb over Maggie to have a closer look.

"Mother," Pipiera whispered, again hoping that somehow her mom could sense her presence. "I'm here. I'm waiting for you. I wish you knew how much I love you. I wish… I wish… I'm so sorry for leaving you. I regret it. I should have stayed longer. But it wouldn't have mattered. My leaving would still have hurt you and Father so much." While Pipiera kneeled beside Maggie's chair, murmuring her confession, Maggie continued to spread plum butter onto her toast.

Jophiel was concerned, realizing Pipiera had been hanging onto such deep guilt for so many years. He decided to speak to her in the most effective manner he knew to get a point across: scolding. "You shan't blame yourself. You had an assigned journey to fulfill. And you fulfilled it."

Pipiera just stared up at Maggie, wishing their eyes could somehow meet and connect. "There's no use. She'll never know."

Jophiel grew impatient. "Of course she'll know! When it's the appointed time for her to know. Is that what this trip is all about? You reconciling unnecessary guilt?"

Now he's being belligerent, Pipiera thought. "No. Of course not. And you weren't supposed to hear that. I wasn't talking to you. I'm here for Matthew. Papah Megs is concerned about him. He's off track. I'm going to help him get back on track. Somehow. I think. I hope. Anyway, *this* was just a last-minute side trip."

"Connected?" Jophiel asked.

"Connected? What do you mean?"

"You and them and the kid. How are you all connected?"

"Uh, duh, we're all connected."

"Yes, but that is not what I mean. This Matthew kid is off track, but you are here. How are these two things connected?"

"They're not!"

Jophiel pointed. "Then what's this photograph of Matthew doing here?"

CHAPTER FORTY-THREE
KASARTHA CHOOSES

Somewhere in the Cosmos

"YOU BETTER BE right. You've failed miserably before." The behemoth Uncle eyed Kasartha. "If you are truly *in*, as you claim, stay put. Firm. Do not let him kick you out."

The height of Uncle's eyeballs alone were taller than Kasartha, and when those pupils narrowed into blood-red slits, Kasartha's innards melted into a gooey pit of angst. Uncle was no one to mess with.

"Do not disappoint me, Sarth. I want this boy's commitment, more than a thousand others. More than I need you, if you catch my drift."

Catch your drift? How can I not? You reek.

Uncle's frame disappeared into the black background, leaving a trail of hot metal stench to torment Kasartha's nostrils. A telltale sign that Uncle had indeed departed was the illusion of stars twinkling. They weren't really twinkling; they were simply temporarily hidden as Uncle's perfectly black frame disappeared into the void.

It was safe now for Kasartha to mumble his complaint, stifled with disappointment. "I can't win. You just want what you want."

Kasartha second-guessed himself but fought the urge to flee. Where would he go? There were plenty of places, actually—a good choice of galaxies, thousands of planets, and trillions of caverns. He could keep jumping from one to the other. Kasartha slumped against a tall, jagged piece of rock. He knew there would be no sense in that. Slumping even further and sighing, he debated his grim options.

He had been down this path countless times, always arriving at the same hopeless conclusion. His idealistic goal to be free, to cross that treacherous River of Times and seek refuge on the other side, the side he had heard stories about, the side he had scoffed at and rejected vehemently so long ago, the side he loved to spy on. Kasartha watched carefully, as often as he could, the goings on in front of that kingdom gate. He could only imagine what it would be like to make an approach and be allowed to enter, to be like a family should.

But it was time to let that dream go. The risk of scheming to get across was too high with zero guarantees and no success stories that he knew of.

The best Kasartha could do now was try to pull in his own kind, so that he too could have a family, only on his own side. Heck, he'd be happy with one good friend, even a sort-of friend or a sometimes buddy, someone like Matthew.

Is there some kind of special deal with Matthew? he wondered. Uncle practically admitted there was. *I want him more than a thousand of you, blah blah blah.* But what was it? Why was everyone so interested in him? Uncle wanted him bad. The other side clearly wanted him bad too. Why else would they send a visitor? But why did they want him?

Kasartha paced. *Crossing that dang river just ain't gonna happen for me. So, so, so... what if I could deliver Matthew to Uncle? He'd have to be pleased, and what could be better than that? He wants him bad, and I've got the kid's ear. I can do it. I can really do it. Yeah, that's it! I will hand Matthew over to Uncle like a gift, a prisoner. Uncle can do with him what he wants. Hmm…I wonder what he'll do with him? Poor kid. But why should I care? Heck, I don't care. I need to think about me… maybe then Uncle would give me a promotion, a better job. More than likely though, he'll just let me keep my targeting job.* He kicked a rock off the ledge.

Even with the uncertainty of rewards, there it was, Kasartha's plan. He would do what he needed to hand Matthew over to Uncle like a prized catch. As much as he had a liking to Matthew, Kasartha had to make his own way in his world and this would be it. *Besides, maybe, just maybe, Uncle will let us work together, the kid and me, let us exist in the same cavern and scheme strategies for targeting. Now that would be cool. To have my own assistant. We could go jumping in our spare time.*

It was possible. And there could be benefits to this plan. Kasartha vowed to do everything he could to deceive Matthew. It was the most secure of all his grim options.

CHAPTER FORTY-FOUR
WHAT TO TAKE OUT, WHO TO PUT IN

In the Town of Havensight

"NOTHIN'S WRONG. I dunno. How many times do I have to tell you?" Aggravated and slouched, Matthew exhaled nothing but frustration as he leaned back into the comfortable, overstuffed chair made of soft, deep-orange velvet. The room was dark mostly due to the color of the floor-to-ceiling paneling. Matthew was surprised Dr. Alexien hadn't cleaned the orange marble ashtray from cigar ashes her previous patient had left behind. *What a stench.* He envisioned Dr. Alexien with a cigar in her mouth. *Ha, what if it was hers?* He cracked an unintended smile.

"Until you tell me the truth. Talk to me, Matthew. I can be here all night, and your mother said you could too." She leaned toward him from her own chair which, while identical in texture, was designed quite differently. Hers had a straight back and was square with no arms. His chair was triple the size with wide arms and a rounded back. There was nothing straight about his chair and nothing straight about what he had shared so far. The desk behind her was large, shiny, and smooth with only a tissue box sitting atop it.

"What kind of doctor are you again?" he asked.

"The kind you need." She did not move her gaze from him, nor was she about to let him off the hook. She wanted... needed him to talk. "Matthew, let's try another angle. Say you really don't know what's going through your mind, as you state is the case. If I were to present you with a... hmm... a toolbox. A special, maybe even a *supernatural* toolbox, what would you want inside of it to get your mind in a good place?"

"A gun" was what he impulsively felt like saying, but he didn't. He pondered her question. Rather than dismissing it with sarcasm, he decided to probe. "What do you mean by *supernatural?*"

"I mean anything at all. Don't let reality hold you back. Use your imagination—no boundaries at all. That is, of course, if you consider your life here as Matthew Mackenzie to be your reality?"

Matthew suddenly sat up. Did she know? How could she? He hadn't spoken of Kasartha or any of his other odd, unearthly visitors. Not since the early days of his recovery, and that was all packaged up as mumbo jumbo. "No," he said, denying her suggestion quickly with a voice that was deeper than normal. Then changed his answer just as fast. "I mean, yes, of course my life here is my reality!" In truth, he had indeed been wondering about that as of late.

"Fair enough," she replied. "So then, I'll ask again. Here... " She motioned as if giving Matthew a large, invisible box, then unlocked it with an imaginary key and opened the lid. "What's in there right now? Are you scared of it...or does it make you happy? I mean real joy. What could you put in there that you like so much, that you'd climb right in after it."

Okay, this is weird. Matthew stared at the spot where the toolbox was supposed to be. "It's not what I would put in," he said after a long pause, "but what I need to take out."

"What will you take out, Matthew?"

Her question frustrated him. "It's not that easy. It's what I *want* to take out. I can't just, like, do it automatically, just because you say so."

"Okay, so what would you *like* to take out?" she continued calmly.

Matthew changed his position in the comfy chair, leaning forward, like he was indeed putting his mind to work. It hurt; it was hard to do so. He scratched his eyebrow. *Okay, I'll play along.* "I'm mad."

"All the time?"

He shrugged "Mostly."

"So, you would like to remove your anger?"

"Yes."

"Who are you mad at?"

"Mom."

"Why?"

"Because Dad died. And Karo."

"Why Karo?"

"Because Dad died."

"Karo didn't know your dad."

"Doesn't matter."

"Does Karo remind you of losing your dad?"

"Yes."

"Do you want to get rid of Karo?"

The very question horrified Matthew to the core. "Of course not!"

"Then what do you want to get rid of?"

"I'm *mad*. I don't want to be mad like that."

"Why?"

Is this lady a dork or what?

"Because it makes me hate people! There. I said it. Happy?"

"You yelled it. And no."

"No what?"

"No, it doesn't make me happy. Does it make you happy that you said it?"

Matthew slouched back and let the soft, cushiony puffs of orange velvet embrace him. He wasn't sure how to answer. If he said *yes*, did that mean he hated his stepsister? If he said *no*, he'd be lying. Dr. Alexien saved him by asking another question.

"What exactly would you take out of the box? Karo? Or being mad at Karo?"

Okay, that makes sense, he thought. He could answer that. "Being mad at Karo."

"How will you do that?"

Matthew shrugged. She continued her expectant gaze right through a long pause.

He wondered if hating Karo was really hitting the nail on the head. *Do I really hate Karo?* But it was too late. It was already out there, and this lady was working it.

"Um, well, I'll just stop."

"Can you? Just stop hating her?"

"I don't hate her! I just said I'm mad at her. I guess I like to be mad at her. But I don't *hate* her." Matthew didn't like how Dr. Alexien was twisting his answers.

"Okay, so we've determined that A, you are mad, that B, you are mad that you lost your dad, that C, the very presence of Karo reminds you that you lost your dad, and, therefore, D, you're mad at Karo—not because you hate her but because she reminds you that you lost your dad. Does this capture it accurately?"

Matthew scrunched his face up. *Please, somebody, get me outta here.* "Yeah, I guess that's it."

"So… the toolbox?"

"Oh, um. Well, I dunno."

"What if you were to put something into your toolbox to remind you of your dad, a favorite memory, one when you felt special, like a gift of closeness was given to you. What do you think?"

Matthew said nothing.

"Perhaps then, rather than using that hammer of frustration and targeting Karo or your mom, you could stop and pull out the special memory instead. Feel gifted rather than a need to direct your anger toward someone."

This is stupid. Matthew thought for a bit. He wasn't sure if she had it all wrong or if she was actually making sense. *I never really thought of it this way.*

He had an idea to get her off his back. "What if I get something of my dad's and carry it with me in my pocket at all times?"

"Might that make you mad at all times then?"

Matthew had to think about that. Maybe his idea would actually trip him up. Discouraged, he tapped the armrest with his fingers.

After another long, arduous pause, Dr. Alexien suggested they had covered enough for the day and that she would call his mom to pick him up, but not before he was clear about his homework. "Think about your toolbox," she said. "What's in it that you need, what's in it that is harming you and should be tossed out. Then we can chat about what you think is missing and how we can address that, including who can you trust." She raised her eyebrows to an all-time high, expecting a response.

Matthew scrunched his face again. *Seriously?*

"Think of it as a toolbox of emotions," she said. "Which ones help you? Which ones are missing? And, of course, which ones do you want to get rid of or at least learn how to use better?"

His twisted face grimaced even more.

"What matters, Matthew. Just think about what matters most to you. Can you think about that?"

Happy the session was over, Matthew agreed.

CHAPTER FORTY-FIVE
ALL YOUR FAULT, FRANK

MARNIE WAS HAPPY that Matthew's session with Dr. Alexien appeared to have gone well. She was so thankful this young lady, a stranger in town, had come out of nowhere to study at the local hospital. The fact she was interested and willing to help Matthew, at no cost, just out of the goodness of her heart, well, that was one good thing in their lives right now. Dr. Alexien had been the first person Marnie called when the emergency room nurse reached her at her office. And thank heavens for Josh. He followed Matthew to the Bowl-O-Rama when he thought something was wrong. He said Matthew had sucker punched him at school and then just took off. Josh had found him alone, mumbling and screaming with clenched fists, "Leave me alone! Leave me alone!"

Frank, I hate you right now. It was easy to blame Matthew's dad. If he hadn't left her, their lives wouldn't be falling off the rails, Marnie was convinced of this. She allowed the attacking thought to repeat over and over again, particularly when it was convenient for assigning blame.

"So," she rallied a smile of encouragement for Matthew on the drive home from Dr. Alexien's office, "how was your chat?"

"Um, it was okay, actually."

"Oh, that's great!" She hoped he would share some details, but he remained silent as he stared out the car window. "May I ask what she suggested? Is there anything *we* need to do? Does she want to see you again?"

"Nope."

Marnie sighed heavily, hoping for more conversation with her son. She would have to be satisfied with the little information she got. If her mother were alive, she would call and ask for advice. If she had a sister, or better yet, a girlfriend, she would have someone to yak to and confide in. Yet again, another moment surfaced, serving up a reminder that she had none of the above. Frank was gone, and she had pushed Arnie away, hard.

As soon as she pulled into the driveway, Matthew bolted out the passenger door of their Pontiac. She stared at the dusty black-out curtain in the garage before turning off the engine. For an instant her breath got stuck in her chest, and a tear leaked down her cheek.

CHAPTER FORTY-SIX
WORKIN' THE PLAN

Somewhere in the Cosmos

KASARTHA PACED BACK and forth inside his cavern, going from room to room. He stepped outside to peer over the ledge, then walked back inside to review the map etched in the back. He eyed the path Marnie took regularly from her house to Matthew's school, to Karo's day care, and then to her place of work. He focused on the building that housed Semi-Permanent Staffing and studied its surroundings. He walked back out to the ledge to contemplate his next move.

Perhaps I can influence boss-man Lance to layer on extra pressure. That would make Marnie-momma spend less time at home, create more alone time for Matty Boy, and make their household tenser. I can also heap on her another load of guilt. He chuckled at the thought as he walked back inside. Then he debated the drawbacks. That plan could be a long, drawn-out one. He walked back out.

"Possibly, I'd be better off working on Matt's goofy boys, Josh and Nick, so the three of 'em get in some serious messes," he said, rubbing his hands together. "Now *that* would be fun."

Back inside he studied the map and the travels of those in

Marnie's life. "That darned Arnie Decker is sure to be in my way." Once again he went back out to the ledge.

"That nuisance of a sister Matty Boy has perhaps? I could raise a great deal of havoc there. Increase the jealousy and hatred levels for the kid, so much that Matthew starts to... hmm... physically harm her?" Kasartha pondered. *Would that be enough to make Matthew keep me close, maybe even run to me for guidance? Maybe I should employ a good mixture of all three strategies.*

Kasartha moaned. The latter would take a great deal of effort on his own, and he had no interest in recruiting others. This was a personal battle; Kasartha wanted to collect the full reward. He wanted to single-handedly deliver Matthew to Uncle. He needed to move urgently though. He had to get to Matthew before this young female kingdom visitor could walk him out of whatever he could talk Matthew into.

Kasartha hadn't recognized Matthew's visitor on account of the blinding light, but thankfully, Matthew did, and he spilled the beans. This girl, this person Kasartha spied on and admired, the same girl he dreamed would one day help him obtain the refuge he so desired if only he had the chance to get across that river to tell his story... *Well, dang her anyway. Now she's my number-one enemy. If she wins, I lose.*

Kasartha paced until he had convinced himself that this was how he must move on. There was no hope of crossing the River of Times ever. He had to stick to a win for Uncle, and that meant influencing Matthew to hold Uncle's values and someday commit his stone to him. *Then, if Uncle will let him stay with me, Matty Boy and I can be buddies. It makes so much sense. The kid has inside information about people in Havensight. We'd be great partners. Uncle will think it's a brilliant plan.*

But even that hope of a future, the next-best outcome for Kasartha, was a stretch.

He gazed across the grey mountain range and feasted on this

new hope. They could target people side by side, egg each other on with competitions even. *I won't be so lonely then.* He felt better about his new direction and was even starting to get excited. *Heck,* he thought, looking toward his cavern, *I should start hacking out a few more rooms to prepare!*

Kasartha spent the next while pulling together the final details of his plan. He identified two hurdles. First was a time marker. He no longer had the luxury of chipping away at Matthew's attitude at a slow but sure pace. He'd have to move fast and drastically. He needed Matthew to be full of hate and hopelessness as soon as possible, so much so that escaping with him permanently would feel like an opportunity of promise. Second, how could he prevent that pain-in-the-butt kingdom girl from contacting Matthew? She could thwart his plans. He sighed at that one, kicking a rock over the ledge. She had represented his secret dream of refuge for decades.

He beheld the dark, swirling waters overhead and instantly got an idea.

CHAPTER FORTY-SEVEN
PIP DEMANDS ANSWERS

In the Outer Courtyard of the Kingdom

PIPIERA'S MARCH OF determination was unstoppable, until she reached Megalos from behind, a don't-mess-with-me index finger stretching firm and pointedly pressed into the crux of his shoulder. She had interrupted him smack in the midst of an arrival process—this simply could not wait.

Roly jumped in to complete the welcome and scanning of the twosome who had just arrived and were already bewildered.

Megalos wasn't pleased. She had been missing for hours at a time and, worse, elusive about it. For that, he was concerned, but clearly, she was out of place to interrupt his important work in such a manner. This would be their first, and quite serious, argument.

"Is there something you need to tell me?" she asked loudly.

Unimpressed and huffy chested, Megalos pointed to the picnic area. The tables were full. Apparently, the two new arrivals were popular. Four large family groupings were waiting anxiously to greet them.

Pipiera pointed up at the watch post.

Annoyed, Megalos headed up the stairs, eager to get whatever this was over with quickly. By the time he reached the top stair, he had already convinced himself to calm down. After all, this was Pip. He felt he was angrier with her for abandoning him and not sharing what she was up to more so than he was about the interruption.

"What is it?" he asked as he sat on the bench beneath the small window with the never-ending view. He could see for miles what was happening out there, but he couldn't see what was bothering Pip that would make her behave like this.

"I visited my parents."

He could only respond with a questioning ogle.

"Yes. I did it. Don't look at me like that."

Megalos was a little offended. "I'm not judging you. Never have."

"I saw your Matthew's picture on their kitchen shelf." She tapped her fingers on her hips; that was her nervous twitch. She watched Megalos's head drop. "You knew. All along. You knew we were related. Must be a close relation. Otherwise, his photograph would not be around like that, not in *my* parents' house!"

"Look, Pip, I told you he was part of my tribe, and you know you are too. That's not new news. I've never hidden that."

"Moolos! Tribes are huge, enormous!" She held her arms open wide. "That's not the same as a close relation." She choked on her last two words.

Megalos was quiet for a moment. Then he took a couple of deep breaths. He motioned for Pip to sit beside him. "He's your nephew."

"My nephew? How can that be? Matthew?"

"Your parents had another child after you... you... came home here. They, well, Maggie thought it would help them overcome their loss. They loved you so." He smiled at her, realizing his smile would not be returned. He continued. "At first it was good. Charles and Maggie were thrilled, but they also held on to a deep sadness. Maggie coped better than Charles."

Pipiera continued to sit still, wide-eyed, and leaning forward, not wanting to miss a single word. Megalos was using his quiet voice, and Pip strained to hear over the loud throbs in her chest and the excited yelps outside.

"As the child, a boy, grew, so did Charles's unreconciled grief. He couldn't let go of you, of his guilt. You see…" Megalos hated to tell Pip this next part, but it was time. "He was the one watching you when you left. He fell asleep. Of course, any parent would when they are so exhausted and their newborn is finally resting quietly. When he awoke and found you in your cradle, not moving, he believed it was on account of him. He believed if he hadn't fallen asleep, if he had checked in on you more often, well… You and I know that wouldn't have changed things, but Charles didn't know, and he couldn't reconcile himself to it." Megalos sighed. "Some earth journeys have significant struggles. Some assigned, some not."

He looked up at Pipiera with hope in his face. "The amazing news? He came out of it. He was still remorseful, but he let go of his anger and his guilt. Well, most of it. He's still hanging on to a touch. That's what I hear anyway."

Pipiera felt her ribcage collapse into her stomach. Her shoulders slouched, and she forced an exhale. "How does Matthew fit into all this?" Her voice was also quiet now.

"Their son grew into a teenager, then a young adult. They never really, uh, connected, Charles and him." Megalos shook his head. "Their bond, it just wasn't what it could have been. Charles and his son—Franklin, they named him—they argued. Through the years they said a great deal of hurtful things to each other, Charles out of unreconciled anger and his son out of not feeling close to his father. Rejection, you know, that's a tough one. Then one day Franklin left and never returned. He chose to live a life without fighting all the time. He was determined to live without anger. That meant a life without Charles. It also meant a goodbye to his mother. Franklin left Charles and Maggie's lives on his seventeenth birthday."

"And Matthew?"

"I'm getting to that part. Franklin moved to a much larger urban community. That's when he shortened his name to Frank. He had a love for big-picture things, a mathematics kinda guy. He worked three part-time jobs, studied his passion, astronomy and such, courted a young lady, married her, and together, they had a son, Matthew." Megalos decided the puzzlement on Pip's face meant he needed to continue. "His love of astronomy brought him and his little family to Havensight."

"Oh!" Pipiera clasped her face. "So close to Maggie and Charles, to where I was born."

Megalos nodded. "We were all hoping he'd approach his parents—er, your parents too—and maybe start a new relationship. He actually tried."

"What happened?"

"He and his dad, well, in a matter of minutes, they got into an argument. Frank stormed out, but not before telling his mom he had a son. The Christmas after that, Frank mailed a photo of Matthew to his mom, but the relationship part never materialized. They had no idea their son lived just one community away. And Frank never told Marnie, his wife, about his parents, about any of it. He took all that stubborn, silent unforgiveness to his grave."

"Oh my gosh." Pipiera was overwhelmed with sadness. She sat still for a few moments to digest it all. "So, Matthew's dad... Frank, was... *is* my brother."

Megalos nodded.

"Then I want to meet him. They've buried him. How could I have possibly missed him at arrivals?"

Megalos shook his head. Pip glared at him.

"No!"

"I'm sorry, Pip. He didn't make it... here."

Pipiera sobbed uncontrollably as she thought about her earthly dad carrying all that guilt and the brother she never knew she had and had already lost.

Megalos didn't even try to console her, even when she quieted down. She needed this emotional release, and he felt he was her enemy right now. He had just stuck a knife into her heart. He was only the messenger, and he had waited for the right time to deliver the news.

CHAPTER FORTY-EIGHT
MAYBE FOR GOOD

In the Town of Havensight

AS DISCREETLY AS he could, Matthew bypassed Karo, who was crawling beneath the kitchen table chasing her Baby That-a-way doll, and slipped downstairs into the rec room, his own private cavern—that is, when he had it to himself.

If Karo was home already, that meant dorky Decker must be in the house somewhere. Sure enough, Matthew heard his voice instructing Karo to stay put, then the sound of his footsteps heading out the front door. Matthew reached for the basement window lever and heaved it open a crack. If Decker and his mom were going to have a powwow, he wanted to hear it.

The Chevette door opened, and Decker's car keys jingled. *Good, he's leaving.* But then came his mother's sobs. *Oh, for crying out loud, Mom!* Matthew wanted to yell at her. *Don't go crying to him, of all people.* The two were too close for Matthew's comfort. He could tell by their shoes, their covered toes having a stare down. He heard mumbling—him, then her, then her some more, then him.

"What are they saying?" a voice behind Matthew asked.

"She *should* be saying get lost! Just like I should be saying to *you.*" Matthew was annoyed yet unsurprised to see Kasartha behind him. "Thanks a lot for just leaving me like that."

"I don't like to see men cry," Kasartha replied.

"I wasn't crying."

"Oh yeah, you were. Besides, I knew your so-called sad excuse for a friend, Josh, was on his way. Was I right?"

Matthew shrugged. Josh had arrived moments after Kasartha disappeared. In fact, he had followed Matthew to the back of the Bowl-O-Rama and watched from the edge of the parking lot. It was Josh's dad who came to the rescue and delivered Matt to the local emergency room, claiming the boy was crazy and arguing with someone when no one was there. *How embarrassing.* Matthew ran his mind through the events of that hour. After the nurses were convinced there were no drugs in his bloodstream, good ol' Dr. A and Marnie took over.

"Gotta love that Dr. A. She's a brick house, eh?"

Matthew was annoyed at Kasartha's comment but laughed just the same. "Yeah, she's something else. She wondered what my *reality* was. Man, she doesn't have a clue."

"Did she give you her 'treasure chest' of sorts?"

"Oh yeah—a supernatural toolbox!" The two boys roared with laughter.

Just then Karo called out from the top of the stairs. "Matty, who you with?"

"Get lost, kid!" Matthew hollered, and the boys laughed even louder. Then, from the basement window, they watched Arnie get into his car and drive off.

"You and your polyester suit take a jog!" Matthew was on a roll, yelling through the crack of the window.

"Look, I gotta go," Kasartha said as Marnie entered the house. "But I'll be back after your mom is out for the night. Tonight we do Mount Skia. And I promise not to leave you hanging again."

"Truckin' we will!" Matthew replied. "I'm looking forward to getting out of this dumb town."

They heard Marnie calming Karo, who was upset about something.

"Maybe for good," Matt whispered.

CHAPTER FORTY-NINE
ALWAYS A CHANGE OF PLANS

Somewhere in the Cosmos

KASARTHA WAS OVERWROUGHT with concern. He understood the new transaction well enough, but the associated risk was bothering him. If he failed to follow instructions precisely, to carry out the new terms of the agreement, Uncle would surely demote him. At best, keeping his job and being highly regarded for doing it well was all he had left. *I'd settle for that.* He continued to pace back and forth in front of his cavern, kicking his clever "Welcome Matty" mat over the ledge.

Gah, Uncle, you got no faith! Kasartha lamented a gnawing notion that Uncle didn't trust him. *Do something nice for the guy, above and beyond even, and he turns it all around, then threatens me. Me! Like I'm the enemy.*

Uncle's instructions were clear. The two boys were to get above the watery fields surrounding Skia, cut through the ice shelf, and head over to the furtive and shallow bank of the River of Times. Then he was to be "ready to watch." *Ready to watch what?* Uncle would take care of the rest. Kasartha couldn't get over how Uncle had so blatantly taken over his own well-thought-out plan and, in return, had given explicit, detailed orders—with a threat, no less—not to fail. It was a reminder that Kasartha would never be appreciated. Rather, he was just a minion, towing the line.

When the timing was ripe, Kasartha would once again retrieve Matthew. He had already shot an influential arrow of fire toward Marnie's boss, Lance, so pressure at work would spill onto the Decker/Mackenzie home front. By now it should be heating up nicely. Targeting directly and indirectly was his role, and when he carried it out successfully, it brought Kasartha great pleasure. That is, it brought Uncle great pleasure, and when Uncle was pleased, Kasartha's existence flowed much more smoothly.

Soon the deal with Matthew would be all over. "Poor bloke. He hasn't a clue what's comin' his way. 'Course, then I'll simply be assigned a new target." Kasartha held the back of his neck and gave it a good stretch. *Too bad it's ending so soon. I liked working with Matty Boy.*

He studied the towering Mount Skia. He had already memorized the detailed directions Uncle gave him, a path Kasartha had never taken before—a way to get up past the mountain, the waters, and the ice and over to the great River of Times. *Heck, he had no idea a safe passageway existed. Did Uncle know he had attempted to get up there himself, with Matthew?*

Nobody Kasartha knew had ever gotten past the watery border. It was forbidden. *Am I being privileged or punished?* he wondered. The only thing he could be certain of was that the passageway Uncle provided would ultimately lead to a most unfortunate loss— for Matthew—and a gain for Uncle's side. *Too bad, buddy bloke.*

Kasartha turned his attention to the stone in his hand, the one with Matthew's name inscribed upon it. It was fraudulent. "Anybody knows stones can't be removed from the River of Times or its murky shores," he scoffed, "not until one's good-for-nothin' journey's over. Then they collect it, only to commit it either to the king or to Uncle."

He placed it back into his pocket just in case whatever Uncle was planning didn't pan out and he could use it somehow. For a fleeting moment he thought of his own living stone. *If only I never gave it to Uncle. If I could get my own stone back, I would give it differently.* He looked up and sighed. It was too late for that. He had surrendered his living stone to Uncle so long ago. There was no getting it back and no chance to change a mind now. Deep down he hoped he was wrong.

At a glance, a privileged viewer could know the experiential whereabouts of any earth inhabitant simply by the location of the person's living stone. If it was stuck in the mud or knee deep in weeds on the riverbank, they were likely neither learning nor experiencing anything of eternal value. In contrast, one could be journeying merrily along the interior stream, experiencing the harmonious accompaniment of the crystal current. Most of the stones raced along, some efficiently and some chaotically, within the deeper sections, the dark waters, bumping into each other and dodging as much as possible the inevitable murky black swirls. That was a highlight for watchful viewers, watching how the stones coped and escaped those whirly storms. The hopes of the kingdom were such that the stones would shed their imprisoning weighty tar so they could float upward to catch a current that might lead the way to the clear stream. Too often, however, that was not the case, which pleased and excited the rebels. Uncle always encouraged his agents to catch the names of stones trapped in the watery swirls and to target them wherever they were on earth. No sense targeting those stuck in the mud—they're already trapped. But keep a watch! We don't want them loose, he'd further instruct.

Kasartha took a deep breath; it was time to go. *Oh crap, that raunchy smell...*

Alas, the top of Uncle's helmet appeared beside his cavern's ledge, edging up just enough for Kasartha to see Uncle's evil eyes. It didn't matter how often Kasartha peered into those eyes, the fright penetrated his being, top to bottom and inside out.

"Beware. The kingdom guard is aware of your plan," he announced dryly.

Kasartha avoided covering his mouth. The stench was disgusting, but he dared not show how sick it made him feel. Uncle's head moved back down until the top of his helmet could no longer be seen. Kasartha stood for a moment in silence, wanting to be sure Uncle had drifted away before he gagged and coughed.

"Gross!" He spat out the odorous remnants from his throat. "Oh, sure, *now* it's my plan. And how in the space of all blackness could the kingdom's guard possibly have learned about it?" *Go figure. If I fail, I'm the one that's doomed.* Kasartha was livid. *I bet Uncle himself apprised the enemy. But why would he do that?* Kasartha punched the air, but soon his anger petered out into fear. Everything was unknown and unpredictable, particularly his own fate.

Then again, perhaps I'm being too hard on myself. Kasartha basked in a moment of renewed hope. After all, it was entirely possible Uncle was simply testing him. Could he follow explicit instructions and deliver up this Matthew kid to the riverbank?

Hey, if I can, I might actually get a promotion. What a crow that would be.

CHAPTER FIFTY
PLAN IN MOTION

In the Town of Havensight

"MATTHEW!" MARNIE SHOOK him harder. "C'mon, I'm getting tired of this."

Annoyed, Matthew rolled over in his bunk. "Then leave me!" *She's obviously not happy with whatever discussions she's having with Mr. Polyester Decker the demon*, he figured. Then he tossed the "I'm not feeling good" card at her, which she did not accept. He also pondered how stupid he was for believing Kasartha once again, who, by the way, didn't show up after he said he would. *I'm freakin' stuck here.*

"Yeah, my behind you're sick. Get up now!"

Ahhh, she's really peeved. He caught her drift and sat up, deciding he had to fight back. "What's your problem?" he asked, his words like an arrow in her back.

Oooooh, maybe that was a mistake. He didn't like the sudden change in her eyes.

"You!" She marched back toward him. "You're my problem!"

Matthew's core shook, jerking both arms.

"Don't look so surprised, young man," Marnie fumed. "Encyclopedias? Really? Did you think I wouldn't find out? After all I do for you, worry about you, want a good life for you. Do you think I like all this any more than you? Do you think it's all so… so easy for me? You and your sister are all I work for, think about, and do things for. My entire existence is for you and her. And do you care? Do you ever notice? What do I get in return? Hmm? Well, let me see, buying weed at school—oh yeah, that was embarrassing. Bragging and making bets you couldn't win and then scamming me to pay them! I hear you're a bully at school too. And let me tell you, mister, they're tiring of it. The empathy well for you has run dry. Bone dry. Do you hear me? Then there's running out of breakfast when people are only doing their job or trying to help you! And worse, the way you've been insulting your sister lately? She's only four years old, for crying out loud. What on earth is going on with you?"

Matthew choked back as unnoticeably as possible. He had no words to meet his mom's hurtful rant. She started to walk away, then pounced back with a different tone but even more vigor.

"Matthew, I'm doing my best. Do you see any other parent here? Do you? Do you know my boss is losing his patience? Do you know how hard it was for me to prove myself to get that job? Do you have any bloomin' idea? If I lose my job…" Marnie walked away again, caught her breath and then returned. "Well, maybe you'd like the three of us to live in some shelter somewhere. Would you?"

She walked out of the room, muttering more parting shots. "I already get evil eyes from people in this community. I don't need *you* to make it worse."

This time she did not return. Matthew heard her thump down the stairs and yelp for Karo to get down there too. Within a minute, the car pulled out of the driveway, and Matthew was left on his own, drowning in regret.

He sat staring at his closet door for a painfully long three minutes until an urge to get up and take action took over. If he got ready quickly, he could bike to school and not miss too much of first class.

In fact, I could bike every day, so mom doesn't have to worry about driving me anymore. When I get home, I'll clean my room, and then I'll hang with Karo, so Mom can make dinner. Matthew was thinking hard about rectifying this predicament. He didn't like how his mom was so angry, and everything she said struck and hurt. "Paper route job? Yuck. But that's what I'm gonna have to do. I need to pay her back." His mind swirled as he pulled his jeans up and buttoned his vest.

"Doggonit." The front tire of Matthew's bike was flat. Determined to make things right with his mom, he looked around for a solution. Propped against the back brick wall of his kindly neighbor's home was a brand new Schwinn ten-speed. Matt eyed it for a full three seconds before deciding it was for a good cause; he needed it.

In moments he was clipping along at a good pace toward his school and hopefully toward a reconciliation with his mother.

Upon arrival, he tucked the bike into an empty space in the bike rack and then ran into class. "Phew," he muttered, his mind already at ease.

For the rest of the morning, he stuck his attention to blackboards and notebooks, trying not to think about the penetrating attack from his mother. He admitted he deserved those words. His self-punishment would be paying close attention to his teacher and ignoring Josh and Nick. *Yeah, that's a good start.*

"What gives?" Nick cornered Matthew as soon as the lunch bell rang, only to be hit by Matthew's "What's your problem?" face. "Yeah, somethin'! What did I do? Why are you so, like, '*Yes, teacherie, I'm eatin' your cheese*? What gives?"

"My mom's spazzing right now."

"So you become a nerd and then don't talk to me just because the old lady's mad at you?"

Matthew sighed before turning and walking away to grab the lunch he had brought the day before and stored inside his locker, leaving Nick feeling puzzled and disappointed.

Coming in the opposite direction was Phil, who gave Matthew a warning nod that meant "Something's up at your locker, good buddy."

Peering around the corner, Matthew caught a glimpse of Josh and Emerson hanging together in front of his locker, obviously waiting for him. *This can't be something I want or need right now.* Matthew decided to bolt out the side door. Chips and a coke from the drugstore would suffice for lunch.

But when he got outside, the neighbor's Schwinn he had borrowed was gone. Panic set in. In his rush to prove himself good, he had forgotten to lock the bike. In fact, he thought, there wasn't even a lock on the bike. *So, it's not really my fault it's gone, is it?*

His self-mitigation was brief, and his panic tripled when he noticed a community police car parked with its lights swirling a few steps away from the school's front doors. *They know I took it. I was gonna take it back! Will they understand? Pretty sure not.*

Matthew felt sick. His heart sank into his stomach. He debated whether he should stay at school for the rest of the day and play dumb or march inside and report himself to Cooke or, much worse, to Decker. *But the bike's gone now. It's been stolen—for real, and that wasn't me.* He stepped away from the bike rack so as to not draw suspicious looks. If he were to take the blame for a stolen bike, he would be turning himself in on his own terms, not because of some rat pointing a finger at him. He walked briskly to the side of the school, out of site, then sat, leaning against the school's graffiti-covered brick wall. He calmed himself down. Perhaps there was no connection between the police presence and the missing Schwinn.

"You know, I can get you out of this mess."

Matthew didn't have to look. He recognized Kasartha's voice. "How convenient that you show up whenever you want. You're a phony of a friend, you know that?"

"Are you mad because I couldn't get to you on your terms?"

"No. But you shouldn't say you're gonna do somethin' and then not do it."

"Ahhh, so you *did* want me to come back! I was just testin' ya. Hey, congratulations." Kasartha broke into song. "You won!" He smiled profusely at Matthew. "So, come on, let's blow this popsicle stand. Attendance has been taken. Marnie-momma's not going to miss you, so we have all afternoon." Then he leaned in close. "Better not to be around, so you can't catch the blame for those speedy wheels you helped yourself to," he whispered. "I bet you want a set of your own, right?"

Matthew peeked around the corner. He decided he did not want to march into those halls and confess. No one would understand. There was no sense going home either, he would only replay his mom's words over and over in his mind. He exhaled in resignation. "There's no use. Nothin' good is here for me anymore. Let's go."

CHAPTER FIFTY-ONE
AND OFF SHE GOES

Outside the Kingdom

STILL MIFFED AT Megalos, Pipiera paced the "work in progress" cloud arena that she had used once for Matthew's brief classroom visit. She no longer felt like hanging out at the gate's courtyard. That life was behind her now. She thought Megalos was her friend, her confidant, her beloved father figure. He shouldn't have kept such a secret about her family for all those years. "My family! He knew but he said nothing!" She fumed and struggled to let go of the heavy blackness that surrounded her. Was it hurt or anger? A combo of both, she decided. Except now there was more. The authoritarians had called Megalos to another meeting over Matthew's intervention. She couldn't believe she was not invited and that Megalos wouldn't allow her to tag along.

"Unbelievable!" She continued her new routine of pacing. It had taken over the routine of jumping that she used to enjoy so much. "The authoritarians didn't save Franklin, my own brother. I didn't even get a chance to meet him, to know him. Gone. Gone forever. What makes them think they can save Matthew? And why are they keeping me, *me*, out of the loop, unless they're hiding another secret?"

"You okay?"

"Jophiel!" she said, turning to face him. "What are you doing here?"

"Well, uh, they told me to keep an eye on you," he admitted.

Pipiera gave him a stern, wry look. "Oh, they did, did they?"

"They're concerned about you, Pip."

"Oh, they are, are they?"

"And I ask again, are you okay? You seem really, uh, angry."

Pipiera's shoulders were scrunched high around her neck while she stood on her tiptoes to ensure Jophiel could see the anger in her face. After all, he was kind of, sort of one of them. But he looked so seriously innocent and genuinely concerned that her shoulders slumped down, and she fell softly onto her behind and hugged her knees.

"Yes, I'm angry," she squeaked.

Jophiel sat beside her, the core of his frame from the waist up still enormous by comparison. "Talk to me."

The arena's floor consisted of sweet, aromatic fog that swirled around them both like a precipitous hug, reaching as high as Pip's shoulders. She didn't seem to notice.

"Megalos lies to me. The brother I never knew I had is dead. The authoritarians are hiding something from me. And Matthew is still in trouble."

"And you are grateful for… what?"

"What?" Pipiera thought it was an odd and almost insulting question. She knew what he was getting at, but she didn't want to go there right now. She didn't even want to play along with it. "I don't feel like that nice talk right now," she mumbled.

Jophiel remained quiet for a while. Finally, he broke the silence, "Come on, climb out of the pit, unless, of course, you like it."

Pipiera was certain this time—it *was* an insult. She wouldn't stand for anyone bringing her expectations lower than what she believed to be right.

"Your ways are *higher?*" he inquired.

She knew he was referring to the king's ways. "Of course not!"

"Do you really think he doesn't have the best for you in mind? The best for all his citizens and future citizens?"

Pipiera sighed. "Of course he does. It's just… I'm not… well, I… oh, forget it. Why are you here anyway?"

"I told you, many are concerned about you."

"Like they were concerned about Franklin? Like they're concerned about Matthew? Not!"

Jophiel smiled, which made her angry at herself for the sarcasm she had just projected.

They sat together in silence while Pipiera's mind continued to swirl. What should she do next? She studied Jophiel and noted he didn't respond well to her emotional outbursts. "You think I'm just a little girl."

"No, I don't."

"Yes, you do. Well, I've made up my mind."

"Oh?"

"I'm going to Havensight to make things right. I'm going to go there and tell everyone the truth. I'll bring Maggie and Charles into Matthew's life. That should be easy enough. Then I'll straighten Matthew out. Not so easy, but I'll do it. Then I'll come home, and that'll be that."

"Home? Is this your home now?"

"How dare you!" Pipiera stood up. "Of course it is. How could you ask such a question?"

Jophiel shrugged. "Your stone, you're still carrying it around." He pointed to her skirt pocket.

Pipiera wrapped her hand around her stone as if to make sure it was protected. *How dare he think I'm selfish?*

"Call me an escort," she demanded. "And not you!" She was determined to fix the gaps she thought needed fixing, with or without Jophiel, preferably without.

"I'll take you," he replied calmly. "Just let me put it in the schedule." Jophiel turned his back to her and began fiddling with a small floating notepad, which apparently meant he was scheduling himself to be out on duty, but when he turned to give the thumbs down, Pipiera was already gone. She didn't stick around to hear his "Warning! Danger—No Clearance" response. In fact, the messaging and firm instructions to Jophiel were clear: "Under no circumstances may you or any other escort for Pipiera have clearance. Stay put and guard her."

Pipiera's stubborn determination led the way! She was an amazing long jumper, quick and efficient. If Matthew could jump the clearance and land dead center in the main tunnel, so could she. And she did. Perfectly. Pipiera knew she'd have to move fast because Jophiel would be right behind her. She was thankful for that though and trusted he would protect her, but she needed to keep ahead of him, so he couldn't stop her. It was an unofficial plan, but she was determined to make it work!

"I'm not going to fail you, Matthew!" she yelped as she slid down the tunnel at lightning speed.

CHAPTER FIFTY-TWO
BACK OFF

Outside the Kingdom

IF ONLY MEGALOS could shake it off, but he couldn't. His gatekeeper instincts warned him things were not all good, at least not yet. The same team was present as per the last briefing he attended. This time rather than chatting busily with greetings, all were quiet. Too quiet. Megalos stood watch. Othis paced back and forth across the opening, also on guard. Perhaps it was Othis's restlessness that made Megalos nervous.

Megs could tell Othis was anxious to speak, which he would do, hopefully, directly after the meeting's opening routine. There was no kingdom equipment to be brought out this time, another oddity to the gathering. Soogreese, the maintenance guy, was pleading quietly to Katakos, the kingdom visionary, while anxiously rubbing his hands together. When Soogreese realized Megalos was watching him, he tucked his hands into his pockets, backed up, and stood on the sidelines.

"No. I don't like this at all. Something's up." Megalos breathed out the words ever so quietly. Aivy, who was just a few steps away, walked over and placed her hand on his shoulder, which happened to be quite a bit higher than the top of her head.

"Shhh… It's going to be okay, Megalos. You know how these things work. She's going to be all right."

Aivy's words should have consoled Megalos, but they only confirmed his suspicions. Yes, this meeting was supposed to be about Matthew, but there was reason to be worried for Pip. Otherwise, why say *she* would be all right? Being the transition lead, wouldn't Aivy know how things would end in advance? Megalos wasn't sure, but he smiled down at her with a nod of agreement.

Finally, Othis was given the floor. Megalos had just learned from the opening remarks that Othis was the one who had called the meeting. Megalos leaned forward; he didn't want to miss anything Othis might have to say, particularly if it meant his Pip was in danger. Megalos felt added weight to his heart and less breath in his lungs. He also felt a twisting motion in his stomach and muscles tightening across his back. Even though James invited everyone to sit, now was not the time for that. Megalos would remain on guard for whatever came next.

Othis was a man of few words and much action, so it was no surprise he got straight to the point. "War. Rather…" He waved his arms in the air as if to restart. "We've been at war for some time, yes. A new battle is brewing. One that involves…" He looked straight at Megalos. "Pipiera. I'm sorry, Megs."

I knew it! "What?" Megalos said. "This is preposterous! Pipiera is a kingdom citizen. She can't be in any kind of battle!"

"Well, Megs," Aivy said, "she's not officially a kingdom citizen yet."

Megalos stared at her, astonished by what was happening. *A rebel battle with his Pip? Seriously?*

"She hasn't actually come *through* the gate yet," Aivy continued. She cocked her head and tightened her lips. The elephant in the room has just been addressed.

And so we just let her go into battle? Megalos fell into a sitting position on the log behind him. It was true; she hadn't walked through his gate. She had been so frightened when she arrived. She said she just wanted to wait with him a bit before she went in.

He looked up at the faces. All were watching his. "She was so scared," he said meekly. Getting a grip, he sat up straighter. "There's a home for her here in the kingdom. You all know that!"

The other attendees nodded knowingly. "Yes, of course there is," Aivy replied.

"So, what's the problem?" Megalos stood up. "I'll have no more of this." He started toward the opening where Othis stood firmly. *I'll go to her and tell her to stop,* Megalos thought. *She doesn't need to do anything.* He was ready to let Matthew fight his own battles, at least without Pip's help.

"I'm sorry, bud," was all Othis could say. The posture within his suit of arms was perfectly straight—too straight, in fact. His body sent a different message, one that suggested Megalos was a prisoner.

"You cannot just let her go into battle!" Megalos roared.

Othis stood firm.

Betrayal was a heavy emotion. Megs felt it pull his bottom jaw downward. "What are you saying? Surely, you're not going to hold me prisoner." This was absurd. "Get outta my way!" He bolted for the opening. He would tackle Othis. He would do anything for Pipiera. Right now these people were *her* enemies.

The two of them attacked each other like wrestlers, hitting the ground and rolling around, but not for long. Othis was more prepared than Megalos and had him flat, face down, holding his thick wrists. Megalos broke down into sobs. Othis could only wrap his arms around his dear old friend's chest and hold him. "Let us explain," Othis said. After a moment, the two were back on their feet brushing themselves off. Megalos scanned the faces of the others. Each appeared to be genuinely concerned. None posed a threat.

Soogreese seemed much more relaxed, as though whatever he

was concerned about was over. Katakos smiled at Megs and nodded to suggest everything was good, a nod for which he was famous.

How could I think these people were against me? Megs wondered as he hung his head.

Aivy came over and grabbed his hand. She led him to a seat up front beside James who had said nothing so far, neither had he expressed anything since he opened the meeting. Megalos sat down, though secretly harboring a thread of betrayal. He wondered if this whole "Matthew intervention project" had ever been about Matthew. Had they approved his request under false pretenses? Everything had seemed odd from the start. *Why didn't I recognize it? How did I not see this coming? They insisted Pip get involved, and now she's in danger.* He was sorry he was the one who had started this whole thing.

He scanned the faces again, granting a long stare at Bookie. Reflecting back, he wondered about that torn out page, that's what started all this. There must be a good reason, he convinced himself. Then looking at no one in particular, "Well, get on with it!" he boomed. "Tell me what's going on."

It was then that James stepped into the center of the conversation circle with his long lanky legs and a discerning glare. Vanished was his trademark quirky grin. "Megalos," his voice was surprisingly soft, wrapping around Megs' heart like a mother's hug.

Megalos wiped wetness off his cheek. He hadn't realized it was there until a droplet gathered, and he felt it fall. *Dang.* How could he be guard-like tough when he was shedding tears? He hoped this entire situation could be resolved in the next few words James shared. He also hadn't realized how much his little sidekick had become so much a part of himself. He couldn't imagine his job at the gate if Pipiera were no longer there.

Although his own earth journey was considered a rough ride, and he had welcomed thousands of newcomers who also suffered, some terribly, he had never experienced that gut-wrenching, degenerative, hollow feeling of loss. The thought of losing Pipiera was so personal and devastating. Managing a stern stare aimed squarely at James, Megs nodded. "Go on."

"I'll get to the point," James replied.

"Please do." Megalos knew he sounded impatient and ungrateful, but he didn't much care for being transparent at the moment.

James sat down crossed-legged, facing Megalos. "You remember the day of your own arrival, Megs?"

Out of the corner of Megalos's eye, he noticed Soogreese once again wringing his hands nervously. "Yes, of course I do. How could I forget? What kind of a question is that?"

James held his hands up, motioning for Megalos to be calm. Then he eyed Megalos carefully, likely to be sure the words he was about to speak would be truly received. Once he started his explanation, he went on for far too long, at least for Megalos. After all, Megalos had spent decades attempting to forget those days, the ages in his own past. Specifically, his own parting words the moment his earth journey reached completion, a sworn curse. A curse born of rage and hatred, a curse the Book Room Keeper captured so efficiently, the root cause as to why others were suffering, paying the price for him, without an inkling of understanding. Something the king had forewarned and the reason why Megalos requested a gatekeeper role in the first place.

James' voice sounded so distant. "… Charles's attackers still loom about…" Megalos didn't want to hear it, and his ears chose to block much of it out, but James pressed on. "… after Franklin Mackenzie perished…"

No, I don't want to hear anymore!

"… the boy needed a solid king's man in his life. We, er, planted seeds to encourage Arnie to get to know Marnie. He was a good fit."

Megalos partially phased out his hearing again. He knew the visionary role of the kingdom would often implement chance happenings to "encourage" certain relationships for a variety of reasons.

"… course the usual shenanigans and attacks…"

"As if those aren't bad enough!" Othis butted in.

Megalos supposed Othis didn't like the terminology of "usual shenanigans" and "attacks." It sounded so frivolous and far too casual. After all, rebel attacks kept the kingdom's army in a constant warring state. It was serious business. Megs could relate to Othis's objection.

Then he turned his attention back to James. Was he about to apologize? Had they messed up on a plan? Where was he going with this drawn out explanation?

"And then?" Megalos used his bold voice to suggest he was not amused, even though he felt like a puddle of weak uselessness on the inside.

"We had to change course once again," James explained. "So, we brought in a teacher at the boy's school, a phys ed teacher, given that the boy was the athletic type. They would spend at least four years alongside each other, plenty of opportunity to connect and inspire. It almost worked." James lowered his head, signaling for Othis to pick up the thread.

"Rebels got 'im. Came home early."

Megalos recalled Andy Falcon coming through his gate. "I didn't realize he was assigned to help Matthew."

"We had hoped Andy would play a role in our quest to connect the boy to his granddad," James said, "Matthew to Charles, to reestablish the family link and incorporate some healing. But we never quite got there."

"No doubt about it," Othis added, "they are after the boy. They must have figured out we have plans to groom him as your replacement."

Aivy, Katakos, and Soogreese all nodded and looked encouragingly at Megalos while Othis moved closer to him.

My curse. This is all about my curse. I gave them a way in. When will it end? Focus! Megalos scolded himself.

"Megs, we need Pipiera now. We know they've been watching her. They have their eye on her. We need her, Megs."

"As bait? No way."

"She's already in danger," Aivy said, trying to be helpful. "They're watching her carefully. They know she's trying to help Matthew."

"Not as bait, Megs," Othis said, then looked at Katakos to chime in. After all, he had a hand in devising the new plan.

"To be an influencer, Megs," Katakos said. "Your Pipiera puts a lot of effort into those jumping sports. We've all seen her; she's super great at it. That's always been a connector for her and the boy."

Everyone nodded in agreement. Then Katakos allowed the other shoe to drop. "Let's call it, Megs. She's been hanging on to her stone, not giving up to the king, and not coming through our gate. And I, well, we believe and understand it to be a guilt she cannot let go of. She seems to think she didn't do enough during her earth journey and doesn't feel she earned the right to go through. We all know that's not true. None of us feel we have done enough, ever! And we don't earn our right that way."

"Time's up, and everybody knows it," Othis said. "The rebels have called it. She should have offered up her stone when her journey was done. That's the rule." He gave Megalos an annoyed look. "Why *your* adopted descendants think they can break the rules is beyond me."

Megalos held back his desire to deck Othis. *How dare he consider me or my line self-righteous?*

James studied Megalos as he dropped his head in his hands. "This is her opportunity, Megs," he said, softening his tone. "It's perfect, and we really need her. It's win-win. She'll want to contribute, and we will appreciate her contribution."

Aivy smiled and nodded while wringing her hands.

It was true, his Pip should have given up her stone long ago. "She was just a little child," he said. "She wanted to play with it. There was no harm and no question she was home." He hung his head. "This is my fault for not applying the rules. You're right, and for that I am guilty. But using Pip in some ploy and hoping she'll come to her senses just doesn't feel right."

No one responded to his plea because they were right, and he knew it. "And what if it doesn't work?" Meg asked, looking up at them. "I don't want her to feel even more disappointed in herself. And for the king's sake, I want her home, where she can be safe."

For my sake too.

James shook his head. "We thought you would say that. So, we've instilled a stay for Pipiera. She must carry out all of her work here. She may not take any out-of-boundary trips. It would be far too risky. We need her involvement, but she must stay on our side of the river."

"So, Matthew will have to come here."

"Yes."

"How many times?"

"As often as needed."

"So, the risks are on Matthew then."

"Yes. We will monitor the visits and the associated journey and eternal risks. But yes, the risks are heavier indeed for Matthew."

Othis sighed. "Let's face it, there are risks for both. That's why I called this meeting, to make sure we are all ready and paying close attention." He looked sternly at Megalos. "You know she's a bit of a wild card herself. Makes our business a bit more... *interesting*. We must watch every step, and she must listen carefully to our instructions—and follow them. We need you, Megalos, to make that crystal clear to her. She listens to you. Do you understand?"

Megalos understood, but he couldn't help thinking about how angry she was with him right now. *Right now, I'm the last person she'll listen to.* This whole business was clearly not his territory. He struggled to put it all together. *This is all my doing. My fault.* Regret filled his heart, but determination to fix it was even greater.

After an awkward silence, James waved for all the attendees to gather in closer. It was time to get down to business and discuss a much-needed alternate plan.

CHAPTER FIFTY-THREE
CAUGHT IN THE MIDST

In the Cosmos Somewhere

"**B**INGO! WHOOOA, YES!"** Never before had Pipiera heard her own voice echo with such exuberance. She was ecstatic and moving at lightning speed down the main tunnel. Admittedly, it was a foolish thing to do, to think she could transit from the kingdom level to the earth level without an escort. Passing through the ice field was dangerous. It would be just the tunnel wall between her and the harsh cold hollows of blackness, the miles-long thick crust that separated her world with Megalos and the kingdom he guarded from the world the enemy ruled over. Settled within its midst was the fantastical divine River of Times. It was a world in itself, with layers of invisibility and visibility, where struggles were encountered daily by the kingdom army, all for the benefit and protection of those in the midst of their earth journeys. Virtually all tussles and brawls and battles would be completely unbeknownst to the journeyer.

Initially, the free fall was frightening. Pip's mind raced as she counted the good things going for her, a good way to calm her fears. Without question Jophiel would jump in behind her. *Oh, he'll be mad all right, but he'll ensure my safety. He has to, right?* She was full of determination; that had to count for something. *Plus, I'm stubborn. That's an advantage, I'd say.*

The best thing going for her was the tunnel itself. It was well protected, the most-traveled and best-guarded tunnel ever. Pip had heard stories about how it was created long ago for the king, who had taken an earth tour himself. Imagine that. Since then, it had been the safe passage used for necessary kingdom business, for those who had to travel beyond the river. She knew there would be an armed presence at the checkpoint smack in the midst of the ice fields. Many battles had been fought there, the kingdom army guarding the opening and the rebel army ready to capture anyone entering illegally.

She imagined what might happen when the king's army saw her exit the tunnel alone. They would be shocked. *I'll tell them my escort is right behind me.* Pip counted on them being satisfied with that. Otherwise, they might force her to turn around and escort her back. *And sure enough, Jophiel will be right behind me, so, that's not gonna happen.* Then as Jophiel himself arrived at the checkpoint, he would take her the rest of the way through diverse other tunnels, through the eerie darkness of space, the brilliance of the galaxy, and onward to the atmospheric skies in perfect position above the planet where Havensight lay. "All will be well," she convinced herself, brushing any guilt for her foolishness aside.

Her initial unease subsided. She found the tunnel fall smooth and well-paced. Pipiera didn't want to close her eyes for fear of missing any of it. The sparkling crystal lights smiling and dancing around her body brought a warm and tender feeling. She melted into it, envisioning Jophiel not far behind, hoping he was enjoying it as much as she was and not stewing. *But why hasn't he called out to me yet? He's probably still a little miffed. He'll get over it,* she chuckled. Releasing the last bits of tension, she succumbed to the journey and wondered how it was possible there was no dizzying effect.

A sudden chill swirled up from below and encircled her legs. *Hang on, Pip,* she told herself. *We're entering the ice fields. Oh dear, this is where having Jophiel right beside me would have been great.* The power of his presence had kept her warm and well protected the last time. She shivered and hoped she'd get through this section speedily.

But something was different this time.

The comforting twinkles of light disappeared. *I don't remember this part. What's happening?*

Above her, Pip saw only a solid blackness. Wind drifted up from below and choked her core with swirl after swirl, worsening rapidly from breezy to a razor-sharp frigidness. A panicky attack of doubt swelled up inside her. A strong stench abruptly replaced the flowery almond aroma she had taken for granted. It burned her nose and made her gag.

Something outside the tunnel walls forced a harsh jolt, like the swat of a baseball bat. Pipiera felt a loosening of the tunnel's stability. The walls swayed back and forth as though she were a weight suspended from a pendulum swinging back and forth. It was pitch black, and the sulfurous wafts stank.

Still falling, there was nothing to grab onto, nothing to hold. She continued to bump from one side of the tunnel to the other as it continued to pivot and sway. Overwhelmed with fear, Pipiera couldn't manage to call out Jophiel's name. She hoped he was somewhere in the darkness above and would appear soon to save her. She pleaded silently to her king. *Do you know I'm here? Help me, please! I'm so sorry. Please, my king, hear me, see me, help me!*

The tunnel continued to pivot and sway, just as her thoughts swung back and forth between faith and doubt.

The accusations she secretly held against the authoritarians carrying out the king's commands, not just for Matthew but also for her own earth journey, suddenly intensified. *Why cause such pain? And where are they now, right when I need them?* Feelings of raw anger and age-old unforgiveness boiled inside her like magma wanting to spew. Pip wasn't sure which was worse—the stench trying to force its way into her throat or the ripe, volcanic emotions striving to get out.

Missing that penetrating warm, safe feeling that lingered from a couple of mere blinks earlier, conditions continued to deteriorate. The walls narrowed and closed in, eventually squishing Pipiera into a thorny patch and halting her fall. Though stuck amid prickles in cold, smelly blackness, she was relieved that the free fall was over.

A light flickered below before disappearing entirely. She was used to the kingdom light; it doesn't just *go out*. A hollow dripping sound, like condensation falling into a shallow pool, echoed. *Water?* Could she still trust where the tunnel would exit?

She recalled Jophiel telling her a story about how he had once traveled in a tunnel that he compared to a seemingly endless long-stemmed white rose—the luscious and beautiful flower at the top, the roots embedded into the ground at the bottom, and a straight, strong stem. The only difference was, the prickly thorns were on the inside of the stem, protecting something from something, and all with good purpose. She couldn't remember the something from something part and wished she had listened more carefully. *Might that be what this is? I suppose this is normal.* She tried to talk herself into believing everything was okay. *No, this feels so drastically wrong, so horribly inside out.*

Pipiera was not safe, and she knew it.

She felt around the tunnel walls. The thorns grew in size and sharpness. She inched downward. Finally, she found one that was large enough to grab onto, allowing her more stability. It was perfect timing too because the tunnel had begun to sway again, this time wildly, as though it were being tossed around in a whirlwind. *Oh, I'm gonna be sick.* She pled again to her king after she recovered from another long, hard gag. She convinced herself that sobbing would not be helpful.

"What would Megalos do if he were here?" she asked herself with the most calming voice she could muster. "He would look out at the horizon, scan the environment, and come up with a plan." Pipiera minded around despairingly. Everything was black with no light streams from above or below, nothing.

"No horizon here, Megalos!" she yelled, as if he could hear her. *Why no light?* she wondered. The only logical reason she could come up with was a possible shutdown of the tunnel. Tunnel shutdowns were frequent. They happened all the time, but never in that tunnel! It was one of the few main travel routes. The thought was horrifying. *Why would they do that? The tunnel must have been compromised.* That's the only reason why the kingdom army would close it off. *Surely, they would first ensure no one was traveling in it though, right? Of course they would,* she convinced herself. She also knew, however, that no one was ever allowed to travel without an escort. And escorts were scheduled and logged.

Pipiera felt like a fool. She hung her head, realizing how foolish she had been to think she had the right to jump into the tunnel and make her way down without an escort, without waiting for the trip to be sanctioned and logged.

"Fear is my enemy. Fear is my enemy," she repeated over and over. *Think, think, think! Wouldn't they know I'm in here? No, dummy. I didn't wait for clearance!*

Pipiera braced herself between a couple of large, thick thorns to keep from being tossed around. She knew she was close to rebel territory. The viper cold of the ice fields gave it away, not to mention the odor. What was worse was the very real notion that Jophiel was not behind her.

I'm so doomed. She thought about her existence in the here and now, so different than before. *If only I could walk into that rear-view mirror and back things up.*

Regret washed over her, causing her to forget her predicament for a moment. *I didn't need to embrace grief, to be all victim-like, claiming to be unworthy all those days.* Papah Megs had tried over and over to convince her of her worthiness, of her value to the king. That the king himself loved her and that she was welcome in the kingdom. The gate that Megalos guarded so lovingly and diligently was hers to go through. It was so surreal to have all that, such a gift. "But no, I was a fool. I refused!" She yelled into the darkness and then sobbed, feeling like she deserved this prison of thorns and stench and blackness. "Why didn't I go?" She hung her head, feeling so ashamed. *The entire beautiful, jewel-filled world in front of me, mine to take part in, and what did I do?* "I refused it!" She yelled some more before quieting down to sink deep into a dark pool of sorrow. *Who am I to think I had something to offer Matthew? Something to offer Charles and Maggie? Nothing. I have absolutely nothing to offer.*

An ear-shattering snap interrupted her pity party. Her suspicion that the tunnel was compromised was justified. The jolt sliced through the tunnel walls some distance above her head. The portion of tunnel hosting Pipiera hurled through the darkness, powered by violent and rotating winds.

Pipiera's primal thoughts were spinning wildly. It was time to really scold her king. She had a great deal to say to him, whether he wanted to hear her or not.

"Okay, let's be straight!" she hollered, looking straight up. "You didn't exactly help me!" Pip wanted to make a fist and shake it at him, but she didn't dare, not in that whirlwind. Instead, she clenched the thorns tighter, not noticing how they were cutting into her palms. The lack of response from the king ached in Pipiera's heart, so she continued. "I didn't want to hurt them! You made me do it. You didn't have to do that. You didn't care!"

Pipiera lost consciousness but not for long. The motion was unbearable. Upside down on several occasions, the wind whipped her around furiously. "I'm sorry! I'm sorry, so very sorry. Please forgive me!" she begged. "I submit!"

Phew, got that out there.

Those words of anger that she had buried so deep were now revealed. As for those words of desire, she hadn't even realized they were imprisoned. Now they were free.

The winds began to slow before turning into a calm atmospheric wave. Everything was silent, an aching, smelly, dark, bitter, cold silence. Pipiera found herself stroking one of the long thorns. It was so thick and biting that she leaned against its side. She touched the tip, which was dangerously needle sharp, an odd refuge. She was both amazed and grateful she hadn't backed into it. She wiped her hands on her skirt, placed her arms around the thorn, and carefully hugged it for what seemed like forever. She shut her eyes tight and wished she could disappear.

"Let go."

Pipiera sat up. Her king was speaking to her. "Let go?" she asked. Again, a painful silence ensued. She laid back against the side of the thorn, its prickles eagerly waiting for her. Her king was nothing but an occasional voice in her head. *Let go of what?* She had never felt so empty; nothing was left inside her. "What do I let go of?" she asked as she embraced the brambles. "What am I hanging on to?"

More silence.

"Let go?" She demanded an answer just as she realized her tight embrace on the thorn was most likely the culprit. Given the black, hollow nothingness below and above, she challenged herself to let go. *No. No, no, no. How could I possibly?*

"Are you serious?" she bellowed. "How can I do that?"

CHAPTER FIFTY-FOUR
PROMOTION, HERE I COME

Leaving the Town of Havensight

KASARTHA SHOOK HIS head at Matthew's pathetic frame cowering around the corner of his school. *What a fool you are. You don't deserve the king, and he doesn't deserve you.* Smacking a smile on his face, he offered his hand. "Okay then! C'mon, buddy. Let's go." He grabbed Matthew's elbow, and up they went.

Kasartha kept up the chatter with Matthew as much as possible to prevent him from glancing back and possibly yearning for his pitiful, motionless body that was sprawled beside the building, head leaning limply against the bricks. The pair oohed and aahed over the beautiful horizon. A soul could never tire of such a view. Their flight continued upward above several thinned-out layers of clouds and into the beautiful sunshine and deep-blue sky, leaving Havensight and all human communities far behind. Kasartha could see the tension leaving Matthew and noted that he actually had a smile on his face. *He thinks he's escaping it all,* Kasartha thought with a chuckle.

"This is great! Is it not?" Kasartha peeked back at Matthew, who was letting him take the lead without a fight. *This couldn't be any easier,* he thought, smirking to himself.

"Yeah. This is great," Matthew replied, his eyes closed, seemingly smitten by the experience. "I bet there's some really cool things you can do for fun up here, right? Not the black scary crap; real fun. What do you do for laughs?"

Kasartha fought the temptation of thoughts entering his mind. *Imagine him and me hanging out together, doing as we please, the entire cosmos our playground. Now that would be a dream come true. That would be fun.* He stayed firm, deciding to remain mum in response to Matthew's questions. It would be easier that way for both of them. *No, I must deliver him up, and what will be after that will be. Like I have a choice anyways.* He had to follow Uncle's instructions. Or else.

"Where are we going anyway?" Matthew asked after a long, awkward silence. "To get some rocks up your mountain?" He chuckled, making light of their past excursions.

"Nah," Kasartha replied. "Thought we'd play it a little safer. The riverbank is a cool place to hang out. We can skip rocks there if you like. It's a pretty cool place. You're gonna like it."

Kasartha sped up, anxious to get there and get all this "hand him over" business dealt with. Why Uncle wanted to meet at the riverbank in the midst of the ice fields was a mystery. It was not for Kasartha to ask questions though, particularly when Uncle was quite serious with directives. The increased speed forced Kasartha into an even uglier version than Matt had witnessed before.

"Hey!" Matthew yelped. "What's the rush? Slow it down a bit. Your ugly face creeps me out!" He laughed but was serious at the same time. "Why do I always do this?" Matthew muttered.

"Do what?"

"This! Trust you! I keep forgetting all your lies and the trouble you get me into."

"Because I'm your only real friend. And what trouble? What lies? What are you accusing me of?" Kasartha enjoyed their bickering. It was such a refreshing distraction.

"I have friends." Matthew protested, taken aback.

"Yeah, right. Sure you do. Twinkle Toes Nick ratted you out about the bike. Oh, oh, you didn't know?" Kasartha taunted and whirled around for added flying fun. "And Josh. What's he all about? Sucks up to Marnie-momma. He likes to hang at your place on purpose 'cause it makes his parents all peeved up. They don't like you."

Matthew pondered Kasartha's words and then shook his head adamantly as the boys made a wide, twisty circle. What Kasartha enjoyed the most was how Matthew's face twisted all about.

He halted momentarily in mid-space. It was good and black, a perfect place to close the deal and to make sure Matthew felt defeated. "You really don't get it, do you? They use you. They've been using you for a *long* time. Open your eyes, dude." His eyes bulged even more and throbbed purposefully for added drama.

And it worked—Matthew looked revolted and vulnerable.

Kasartha resumed their flight, jolting Matthew firmly toward their destination—the riverbank. But first they had to get past the army and through layers of that unforgiving ice field. Uncle had given specific secret directives to navigate a safe passage. He had also issued a warning: "Sarthie, don't try anything foolish." *He must know I've tried it on my own a few times, once with Matthew.* Kasartha hoped he was wrong and that Uncle didn't think he was a potential escapee, not trustworthy to carry out business as directed.

Kasartha glanced back at Matthew, wishing things could have been different.

Entering the outer edge of the ice field, Kasartha shouted frequently for Matthew to duck and avoid the tiny and nearly transparent ice spears that darted out from the myriad of large, bowl-like gassy formations.

At the next level, it was disks of material shot from mini-planet-sized ice spheres. Then they landed and shimmied cautiously along a shelf just inches wide against a sheer wall of ice. That part was just for fun, at least according to Kasartha.

Uncle was right. He said they'd have no problems if they followed his directions explicitly. Although their surroundings were treacherous, no armies interrupted their journey.

Alas, the spectacular River of Times was finally in view. They followed it around a portion of Mount Skia, both boys careful not to make a sound and risk polluting the incredible beauty. Matthew's heart and mind, dreadfully wounded and discouraged, succumbed to Kasartha's directives. Kasartha eyed the spot along the riverbank that Uncle had described. The narrowest part of the river, he had said, with a rope suspension bridge connecting both sides where Kasartha would see mounds of stones fluttering along the banks. It was far less beautiful on the rebel side, but that was the side the boys landed on.

Fascinating! Kasartha thought, grinning.

For a narrow river, the waves were ferocious and tall, often overtaking the delicate footbridge and causing it to swing wildly. He had never been there before. What a thrill! *If I could only cross that river myself and leave all this behind...*

CHAPTER FIFTY-FIVE
JUST BAIT

At the River of Times

KASARTHA EYED MATTHEW cautiously as he stomped about in the tall, weedy patches. *This is it, bud. It's all over for you. Believe it or not, I'm sorry.*

"It's buggy here," Matt complained. He pointed to the other side of the river. "Couldn't we have landed over there?"

"Yeah, we're close to the living, so there's bugs." Kasartha knew Matthew wouldn't get it and made no attempt to explain further.

Matthew noticed the gasping stones, which were everywhere. One in particular squirmed beneath his foot.

"What the heck?" Matthew yelped.

"Don't touch them!" Kasartha scolded.

"Them? They're alive? Stones? I've never seen stones gasping for air before. What the hey?" Matthew bent over and, despite Kasartha's warning, picked up a shivering, struggling grey stone. He examined it closely. A name was etched on one side. The stone jumped as though it had coughed. It seemed to want to go back into the river.

"Don't even think about it," Kasartha warned. "They had their chance." Kasartha knew once again that Matthew would not understand. Kasartha kicked an ailing stone beneath his feet. "They're on *our* side now," he said fiercely. He glared at Matthew, wanting to add, "as you will be too," but he refrained. He needed to put his mixed feelings aside and stabilize his expression, knowing the kid was gonna have more questions. Of course, Matthew did.

"Why?"

"We're preparing an army. For a war. Nothing to worry about. But it's necessary, trust me." Kasartha couldn't help but add urgency to his next statement. "If you throw those back in the water, they'll carry on their journey and we'll have to put more resources on them." *Plus, dork face, Uncle will lambast me.*

Kasartha could tell Matthew was trying to comprehend it all. He was looking across the river's surface, observing the flow, the rough waves, the shimmers of light where the crystal-clear stream ran through darkened waters, and the rope bridge that was clearly uncrossable.

"You're with me, right?" Kasartha asked. "You're on our side. Together we'll make our world a fantastic place! C'mon, Matthew, you must be absorbing *some* of this." Matthew still looked puzzled, stroking the shivering stone in his hand.

Kasartha peered around nervously. *Uncle, where are you?* The sooner Uncle arrived, the sooner he could pass Matthew over and his part of the mission would be finished. Finished. He would be rewarded for sure—or so he hoped. Even better, once all the dust settled, maybe there was a chance Matthew would be assigned to him for training. Maybe they would even work on common missions, side by side, a short distance apart. Kasartha kept an eye on Matthew to ensure he didn't toss that stone he was so annoyingly petting into the water. If Uncle caught him red-handed, it would spell trouble. Kasartha looked around again and sniffed the air for a potential incoming stench. Nothing. *Uncle should have been here already, or at least close by.*

He checked Matthew again, now perched on a large rock by

the river, still holding the suffering stone. *This is painful*, Kasartha thought. *I want this exchange to be over with before I change my mind!* Perching himself on a rock near Matthew, he cast an envious stare upstream and avoided any glances coming from Matthew's direction.

While Kasartha pretended to be preoccupied with the stormy ebbs and flows of the river, Matthew slipped the stone into a small puddle of shallow water among some weeds by his feet. He watched the stone as it seemed to breathe in deeply and sigh an exhale of relief. Matthew had never thought of these stones Kasartha spoke of as being alive, breathing and giving off a sense of their emotional state, yet there they were. The stone lay still as if it were afraid to move. Matthew looked Kasartha's way. "So, where is *my* stone again?" He'd remembered it being all jumpy and attempting to dive off a cliff by a waterfall. "I've lost track. You have it, don't you?"

Kasartha could tell that Matthew was now awakening to the significance of the stones, particularly his own.

"You haven't cared about it up till now. What's the diff where it is?"

"What's the diff? Where is it? And where am I?" Matthew looked up the river and the various formations within it. With a closer examination he could see test-tube-like structures with flames inside swirling and swishing trapped stones. "Can they get out of there?" He felt empathy for the little guys each trapped in the middle of their own intimate and harrowing storm. Matthew fixed on one in particular, trapped inside a flicker of fire. Its eyes heeded fright, as if it wanted someone to come and dump him out.

Kasartha offered consolation to ease Matthew's mind. "They can get out if they want, but they don't. Don't you get it?"

Matthew pressed harder. "Why are we here? And where's my stone?"

Kasartha pursed his lips.

Matthew looked down, the stone he had carefully laid in the small pool of water had slipped into the deep waters, disappearing. He wondered what would happen to it, that living creature now deep within the River of Times. Where might it be? Where would it go?

A nauseating stench filled the air. Matthew gagged while Kasartha looked around. He knew Uncle had arrived but had chosen to remain hidden. The sound of a marching army approached. They came from virtually nowhere and created a semicircle around the boys, the river their only escape. The waters blackened even more and stirred in a threatening manner. Undercurrents rose and whipped into treacherous whirlpools above the water.

Really, the army? It's supposed to be a simple transfer, isn't it? Kasartha thought. He watched as Matthew became quickly overwhelmed, particularly at the faceless soldiers hidden beneath the dozens of helmets. From their foreheads to their chins, nothing. The rest visible. The stench, now overwhelming, didn't seem to bother the soldiers.

It seemed the pair were trapped.

The presence of the rebel army caused considerable doubt. Kasartha knew Uncle thrived on deceit, but he had hoped it would never be applied to him. Was he himself about to be reprimanded and punished? He considered an option. *Should I run? Nah! Don't be foolish,* he consoled himself. Not wanting his doubt, fear, or guilt to show, Kasartha spoke as in command. "You're late!" he scolded the army's commander.

"We are not late!" Uncle's distinctive voice boomed.

Kasartha felt a raunchy splash of sticky spit along the side of his face and into his right ear, drips creeping down his neck. Uncle had made his presence known. Kasartha wished he had kept quiet. He hung his head, feeling the hot presence of Uncle's breath at hand. *Oh, if I could just pass out, wake up in my cavern,* he thought. But there was no passing out and no more wishful death, only his current pathetic existence. He cocked his head slightly to check if Matthew was watching, and of course he was. Kasartha had a solid brick of pride to maintain, so he spoke in a quiet voice. "Uncle, I have Matthew and am ready to transfer him to you." *Please let's get this over with*, he pleaded internally.

"Do you now?" Uncle said. "I never said I *wanted* Matthew. I merely said I wanted you to bring him to the shore."

"What? But you said… I thought, er, I presumed."

"Silence! You did what I wanted, so kudos to you. Do your ridiculous happy dance and vamoose, would you?"

Vamoose? But I'm surrounded by your army. Our army.

Uncle remained invisible. Matthew and Kasartha stared at the vacant space from where his voice boomed as he continued to speak. "I only wanted Matthew for bait."

"Bait? For what? For whom?" Kasartha was shocked at his own courage to suggest he was privileged for answers. Strategic overviews and end goals were never any of his business.

Uncle unleashed a wet chuckle. "Now *she's* the one who's late."

CHAPTER FIFTY-SIX
WHAT'S SHE DOING HERE?

AN EERIE SOUND whistled above them. Kasartha perked up in time to witness a long, thick, wavy pipe-like structure slam into the ground directly in front of them, partly on their side of the shore and partly in the stormy waters of the raging river.

For once, Kasartha was more concerned for Matthew than himself. *What is Uncle up to?* Though intrigued by this new development, he decided to stay put and watch it unfold. Plus, he was a little embarrassed. *What if Uncle's army doesn't let me pass? How will that make me look to Matthew? Small and unimportant.*

The pipeline structure smashed open upon impact, revealing an interior spine loaded with thistles of various sizes poking about. "Blimey!" Kasartha couldn't believe his eyes. "It's off the main tunnel!"

Never having been inside, many times he had stood afar while kingdom citizens and their escorts emerged from the bottommost opening, well below the river and the ice fields. No doubt about it, a section of the most distinguished travel route was smashed and strewn in front of his eyes. Black water from the river threatened to swallow one end, forcing the other to wave about frantically.

Kasartha was still trying to get his head around the historic impact of the crash when a figure emerged, squeezed out quite forcefully. The figure skillfully regained its balance and cautiously peered at the boys.

Then, oh, another blast of stench. It never got easier. Kasartha wanted to vomit. He wished Uncle didn't have to be so dang close and knew he was about to speak given the warning of hot, stinky air, followed by thick, gloppy moisture dripping down Kasartha's neck. But no words followed. Uncle remained invisible and silent. Kasartha also remained silent while trying to refrain as much as possible from sucking in the stench.

The figure was petite. Matt and Kasartha's eyes were glued to it. Excitement rose within the invisible, monstrous dragon. Kasartha could tell because the breaths Uncle took were particularly heavy and deep.

What? The gate girl? For decades Kasartha had used his special equipment and spare time to spy on Pipiera, fascinated by her fun energy performing all those long jumps in that faraway magical meadowland. He never could figure out why she was spending all her time outside the kingdom gate and not inside its walls. Who would get that far and not go in? *Is this my dream come true? Is she really here?* He had dreamed of this very creature as a representation of his refuge. His ticket out of his current state. Dare he think it was possible?

Kasartha quickly forced the thought out of his mind. Doom would be his only certainty if Uncle had any inkling as to what thoughts were swirling in his head.

Pipiera appeared to be confused.

Obviously, she did not plan for this. Kasartha had heard of tunnels closing up, but he had never heard of one breaking off and crashing, much less with someone inside, and never the main tunnel. *I bet she was on her way to see Matthew. Where's her escort? Surely an escort could have protected her from a crash.*

Pipiera looked around to size up the situation. She focused

solely on Matthew, her eyes widening in amazement. "Matthew?" She studied the ground he stood upon, shocked and horrified at all the stones.

Kasartha watched as she leaped away from the torn tunnel, landing with a splash on the shore. On her tiptoes, she stepped over the weedy edge and headed toward Matthew. Reacting in disgust and horror, she stooped to pick up one fledging stone and then another and then another and carefully secured all three inside her cupped palms.

She shot Matthew an accusing face. "What are you doing here, with him?" She nodded toward Kasartha.

She's here for him. Kasartha retained a straight poker face while battling the despair that plagued him within, his secret hope deflated. *I wish you didn't hate me so.*

"Do you know these earth inhabitants are in terrible danger?" She turned to study the river and its raging variants, her eyes wild with desperation. Kasartha imagined she was searching for the crystal stream. She would know it was somewhere inside those racing waters striving to make its way through time.

Oh no, now what the heck is she doing?

Pipiera tiptoed with an armful of fledgling stones over to the footbridge.

There's no way she can cross that, not without an escort! She's doomed. She really doesn't know.

Pipiera hesitated and looked back at Matthew, angrily urging him to come and help her. *Does she not see the rebel army encircled around her precious Matty Boy, not to mention me? Is she not subject to the stench of my fearless leader?*

To Kasartha's amazement, Matthew sprinted straight through, right smack between two soldiers to where she stood. *When did he become so brave? So loyal to her?* Kasartha could barely hear what she was whispering to him. He inched toward them. The army shuffled forward along with him.

"Seriously?" Kasartha said. "I'm not the prisoner, he is!" He was annoyed with the army and frustrated with the whispers, which he still could not make out. *I bet he's warning her of the danger surrounding them, the danger she seems to be, oddly enough, unaware of.*

Then, one by one, Matthew and Pipiera began tossing the stones into the river, aiming for a particular spot that appeared simply as a grouping of tiny glimmers. *Darn her anyway!* Kasartha scratched the back of his neck. *Is Uncle not seeing this? Why is the rebel army not stopping them? Not doing anything shows such lack of control.* So, he spoke up, and firmly, he knew Uncle must be paying attention.

"We spend countless nights working so those stones end up on our banks. Why are you tossing them back? You will have to pay for this atrocity!" Kasartha shook his fist at the sickening pair he envied so, who were still picking up gasping stones from the muddy bank and tossing them into the water. Neither paid any attention to Kasartha's threat.

"Ignore him, Matthew," Pipiera instructed. "We must free them all, send them onward to continue their journey, and let them have a chance. Quick, keep collecting and tossing!"

"You're unblocking our interferences!" Uncle wasn't taking charge, so Kasartha decided he should. *If I'm not in those books from where she comes, I must stay in Uncle's good pages.*

Alas, Uncle finally spoke, his booming voice again filling the atmosphere. "Stop!"

Indeed, Pipiera stood perfectly still. Only her eyes moved to and fro, searching for the source of the voice.

Finally, she looks frightened. Kasartha was relieved. Pipiera stepped behind Matthew. "Who was that?"

That confirmed Kasartha's suspicions. Pipiera could not see the rebel army or Uncle. Well, for that matter, no one could see Uncle at the moment. Kasartha's confidence in whatever the plan was increased substantially. *She's part of Uncle's plan! Imagine that, my own special gate girl. Maybe I'll get to train her or even keep her in my cavern. Wouldn't that be a ticket to paradise. She'd be even better to have around than Matty Boy.*

Kasartha waved frantically at the army. "You fools! Them!" he pointed to the pair at the shore. "*They're* your prisoners, not me. Go!" But the rebel army didn't move. *C'mon, Uncle, seriously? They're undoing our hard work and you have me captured? Move these minion goons. Please!*

Uncle had other things on his mind. "What about this poor lost stone over here… up that hill?" Uncle's voice was oddly gentle and no doubt scheming.

Pipiera hesitated, looked around, still seeing only Matthew and the Kasartha twerp she didn't much care for. She spotted a stone jiggling furiously up the hill, farther away from the riverbank. She headed toward it.

"No! Don't!" Matthew cried, but Pipiera was already on the move.

"Got it!" She picked up the shivering, angry stone and held it up for examination. But as she turned to head back to the river, the rebel army shuffled in unison to encircle her and, with a blink, made their presence known. She held the stone close to her chest. It looked like a good cover-up—protect the stone to hide her fear.

Whew! Finally. Kasartha could see she had not anticipated an army of faceless goons forcing her to halt. He chuckled, though he was careful to hide his relief and even more careful to hide a big sigh. Secretly, he didn't want to see her harmed. For years he had idolized her, fantasizing that one day she would take him away from his pitiful existence. Although it was more than he could ever hope for, at least if she weren't harmed, he could still hope. Secretly.

The rebels stood with their rifles pointed to the ground. Pipiera glanced at Matthew, peeked at the stone still cupped in her hands, then held her head up and stepped toward the river.

Sharing the same mind, the rebel soldiers maneuvered their rifles to the ready position, their faces still blank, displaying no emotion whatsoever.

Pipiera froze, one leg still bent and held high.

"Oh, dear little Penney, is there anything I can do for you?" Uncle allowed himself to be visible, just enough to see a vague outline of his long skull and oval nostrils.

Out of fear she dropped the stone, even though she knew it represented a precious life in the midst of its tour. Other than recently hearing the name spoken by her parents, no one had called her Penney since the short-lived days of her own earth journey. Was she really staring into the eyes of the dragon himself?

"Surely you're not afraid of little ol' me?" Uncle put on his best charming act, "Am *I* your enemy?"

CHAPTER FIFTY-SEVEN
WHICH HOME?

PIPIERA HELD HER breath. The straps of an army helmet dangled at the side of the dragon's head. She noticed scales and scars as he covered his mouth with gangly piano fingers while gooey drips slipped out and fell upon living stones, causing them to choke even more. Nearby were outlines of wing tips, most likely attached to the curvature of his shoulders.

"The rebel, *the* rebel of the kingdom," she said. "You are surely him."

Megalos had always told her, the smallest in the kingdom was far greater than the leader of the rebels. Pipiera placed her foot down and crossed her arms in defiance. "Yes, indeed you are." Her boldness surprised even her.

"Au contraire, my lovely. Am I not the reason you stayed outside your little gate up there? You simply couldn't let go of me, could you now?" Uncle moved his face closer to Pipiera's, removing his stubby hand and revealing four perfectly even rows of sharp teeth and a terribly crooked smile. And oh, the funk.

Kasartha's face was full of intrigue and confusion. "Our plan is working, hey Uncle?"

Matthew looked at him, appalled. "You planned this?" Matthew may have been overwhelmed, but fury took over. "Get me outta here! All you guys are like doomin', freakin' crazy. I don't belong here. I *demand* to go home!"

Uncle's response was sly and distinctly geared to Pipiera. "The boy can go, as long as Penney stays here."

Matthew was ecstatic. "Great, I'm goin' then." He glanced at Kasartha, assuming he would take him home.

"After everything Megalos has done for you?" Pipiera was short with Matthew. "Could you be more ungrateful?"

"Who the heck is Megosos?"

"Megalos!"

"Look, I don't know who you are. You show up, and I don't get why. I don't know why I'm here, but…" Matthew stalled for words, then changed gears. He eyed Kasartha fiercely. "Another thing: I will *never* listen to *you* again!"

"And all loyalty flies out the window, just like that. Poof." Kasartha made waves in the air to illustrate his point.

"So," Uncle said in a business-like tone, "the kid can go home, and he says he won't listen to my spy anymore. Miss Penney, you appear to have won. Just like you wanted to save that poor little stone you dropped, you have saved this kid. I send him home, and you stay here. Deal, everyone?"

Kasartha was discouraged. Of all the ways this whole scene could have worked out, this was certainly not one he anticipated.

Get a grip, get a grip, get a grip. Pipiera choked out a demand, admittedly a little on the weak side. "Let us both go."

"Let you both go?" Uncle's gangly fingers shook as a result of his unseen belly laugh. "On what grounds?"

"You kidnapped me."

"No, my dearest, I did not. I have witnesses here who saw the same thing I did. You came upon *my* shore."

"It was an accident."

"An accident, was it? Where is your escort, dearest young lady?

A kingdom escort never would have allowed such a landing place for a dear precious one like you." Sarcasm oozed much like his mouth continued to drip. "No, my dear Penney, you escaped your escort so you could come back to me. That's the way I see it. You want to be here. You've been waiting for such a long time, haven't you? I ask again: Where is your escort?"

Pipiera thought of Jophiel. *Why, oh why, did I not wait for him?* She sighed heavily. "No escort."

"So then, you came on your own accord? Then you are fair game."

"I'm a kingdom citizen!" she shouted. "How dare you! You know the rules."

"Tsk, tsk, Penney. Now you are deceiving. Surely, you belong here with me."

Uncle's grin was disgusting, and it irked Pipiera. Stricken with revulsion, she had to look away.

"Come now, you must know how this works, hmm? You came to my shore, Penney. Someone who refuses for such a long time to enter their gate and then escapes without an escort to get to me personally, well, how about that."

The beast demonstrated great satisfaction. Her tears demonstrated great regret. She let them fall, one by one.

"Come now, it's not going to be that bad. I have a special place for you. You can hang out and jump all you want in front of *my* gate."

Matthew squirmed with impatience. "Can I go now?"

"Let him go," Pipiera demanded. "I want to be sure he gets home safely first." At minimum, if Matthew were safe, perhaps that would prove her love for her Megalos. Possibly that was all she had left, a last, valiant act in honor of Papah Megs.

"Sarth!" Uncle shouted. "Take the boy across the bridge."

"Across the bridge? You must be mad!" Kasartha cupped his mouth, then took a stand. "I can't do that. I'm not an escort. Only kingdom escorts can go safely to and fro across that bridge."

Uncle stared him down. Kasartha wanted to run, but, as usual, there was nowhere to hide. He needed to look like he knew what he was doing, so he turned and barked an order to Matthew. "Well, come on then. You're going home, pinhead."

Pipiera knew it would be impossible for those two to get across the bridge; even she could not do that alone. The roaring waves would undoubtedly sweep them away into the rages of time, never to be seen again. Those waters, crystal or black, were not habitable for anything but stones, living reflections of earthly inhabitants.

She caught Matthew staring at her. He obviously sensed the immense danger. A quick memory flash reminded her of how everything in her life was perfectly fine till Megalos got that letter—that ripped-out page that shook him, that message that suggested his precious Matthew was off track. She reminded herself that Matthew was hers too, part of her family, the son of the brother she never got to meet. How this would hurt him, wherever he was. And how this would hurt her own earthly parents, Charles and Maggie. Oh, how disappointed they would be. To lose an infant daughter, a grown son, and now their one and only grandchild? She had to help Matthew somehow.

"Um, is that the way to Havensight?" Matthew asked innocently. He had been through a great deal with Kasartha, but never had they crossed a river as such.

Pipiera carefully considered his fate. Home to Havensight, and he could continue his journey and learn to navigate the waters and the inevitable dangerous swirls that would be sure to suck him in from time to time. The other option? Across the river and home to the kingdom. He'd never get to be a gatekeeper, but at least he'd be safe there.

CHAPTER FIFTY-EIGHT
I'LL SAVE YOU!

KASARTHA CAUGHT PIPIERA'S glances at Matthew. He was suspicious of both of them. Surely, Miss Gate Girl was scheming something. He hoped they were. A diversion would be really helpful. *I really don't want to attempt that bridge,* he thought.

"Come on!" he yelled at Matthew, knowing Uncle was watching and waiting. He hoped Matthew wouldn't budge and Gate Girl would do something brilliant to escape. But truthfully, that was unlikely.

Kasartha knew that he was dispensable too. *Uncle knows I'll never make it across.* No one had ever survived the ferocious abyss of the River of Times. It was meant for depicting and tracking earth journeyers. Only their stones could live in those waters—no one and nothing else could.

He swallowed and blew out the air he held in his cheeks. He glanced back again at Pipiera, still encircled by the rebel soldiers. She was motioning her fingers alongside her head. *What is she doing?* He glanced at Matthew and realized he seemed to understand what she was secretly messaging. *They're up to something.*

The rebel soldiers tightened their circle, probably on a cue from Uncle. *And those soldiers are nothing but dumb arses. They're puppets. I scheme, I plan, I carry out my work, and I deliver! They get safety, and I get thrown to the abyss.*

Kasartha couldn't help but hang his head. Then he picked it up urgently. It would be good for no one if Uncle got impatient. "Let's go, Matty Boy," he said.

Matthew fixed his attention to the bridge. "What exactly is on the other side?" he asked. No one answered, so he turned around and crossed his arms, awaiting an answer.

"He doesn't need to go there yet," Pipiera said.

"He said he wanted to go home, did he not?" Uncle asked.

Pipiera nodded toward Matthew as if to reassure him the other side would be good, that crossing the bridge would be a good move, the better of the options before him at the moment.

Matthew turned to face the rope bridge. Stormy black waters swirled beneath while an occasional large, hungry wave swept over top of it, causing it to swing wildly, impatient to devour anything that crossed. Hints of glimmers were visible here and there in the water. One could only dare to trust the crystal light stream existed in the midst and that its current had to be strong and mighty.

Matthew took several steps backward, nearly bumping into Kasartha.

"What the heck are you doing?" Kasartha scolded before suddenly realizing the boy's plan. Matthew ran toward the bridge. *Crap! He's going to jump it!* Kasartha paused for the briefest of blinks. *Brilliant! If he can do it, so can I!*

Six giant steps forward, and Matthew leaped with his left leg. Uncle waved toward the black waters, which obeyed his command. An oversized wave with devilish eyes formed and roared toward the bridge. It would hit precisely when Matthew was midway across, certain to swallow him whole.

"He will surely perish!" Kasartha was horrified at the thought. *I'm coming, Matty Boy!* Kasartha needed to take action. He stepped back to prepare himself for his own running leap, and then he jumped directly into the wave as it descended toward Matthew.

With a bone-splintering crunch, Kasartha felt his body slam into Matthew's. Together, the pair whirled round and round in the force of the roaring wind and water. Kasartha clung to Matthew's waist, and they became a single mass, both completely helpless.

Kasartha felt a deafening jolt and gasped for breath but instead sucked in and digested a thick, hot, sticky liquid. Then he felt a falling sensation till suddenly he was lodged beneath a heavy weight that felt like a truckload of boulders. Dizzy, confused, and crushed, he heard a distant scream. Oblivious to his surroundings, Kasartha closed his eyes and drifted into blissful blackness.

CHAPTER FIFTY-NINE
AGAIN, REALLY?

In the Town of Havensight

LANCE GLARED. MARNIE knew this was it. The last straw. How many times could she leave clients waiting so she could attend to her despondent son? *As often as I need to.* How many times would he believe her son was in dire need of her? *That,* she thought confidently, *doesn't really matter.*

He shrugged and made a distinctive nod toward the office's front doors. She grabbed her purse and scooted out through the tiny lobby. She barely acknowledged her one p.m. appointment, but she certainly noticed the big grin on her assistant's face. Peg had stepped in and covered for Marnie time and time again and practically knew her entire job now. Marnie didn't give her the usual "loads of thanks" look, but instead gave her one that blurted another message: *You're just eager to have my job.* She slammed the door behind her, only to regret the fit of anger she'd been subduing for weeks.

Before turning the key in its ignition, she hung her head and cried. "How did I get here?" she sobbed, never anticipating her life to be so challenging. Regaining control, off she went, once again, to Havensight's emergency room, where Matthew had just been taken.

The hospital was small, more of a regional medical facility equipped to handle whatever tourists and residents happened to present. Anything from cuts and bruises to major heart attacks, care for terminally ill, and the odd automobile crash. So, Matthew was the talk of the building given his frequent visits and abnormal reasons for being there. Marnie was well known by association, not to mention the unpaid and mounting medical bills.

When she arrived, no introductions were necessary. The receptionist escorted her to the small family room at the back of the emergency treatment section. She peeked in each open curtain they walked past, checking for her son.

"Coffee?" the receptionist asked once they were inside the family room.

"I'd really like to see my son. Is there somebody I can talk to? His doctor? His nurse?"

"Mrs. Mackenzie, I'm sure they will come along as soon as they can. They know you've arrived, and they're glad you're here. I'm certain they'll be here as soon as they can. How about some water?"

"No, thank you." Marnie turned toward the loveseats and decided she didn't want to sit. "And it's Decker. I'm Mrs. Decker." The receptionist nodded and then left the room, closing the door behind her.

Where's that other guy? I liked him better, she thought, thinking about Alan Pine. Marnie walked up to the worn crocheted dove hanging on the wall. It was flimsy and should have been framed. It seemed a little dirty to handle. Regardless, she pulled it down and clutched it in her hands. "So, am I guilty? Are we all guilty? Is that why you're holding an olive branch?" She sighed before tacking it back on the wall.

The door opened, and Marnie turned anxiously for news.

"Hi, Marnie."

"Uh, I'm just waiting for the doctors." Her body language suggested she wanted this visitor out. He was not part of her family's tiny circle, and he shouldn't have been there. She gave him a stern look, but before he had a chance to leave, she unleashed on him. "You should be fired. You can't keep children safe at your school. What kind of place are you running over there? I can't send my son to school without wondering if he's gonna come home alive. Get out of here!"

Harry Cooke lowered his head and toed the edge of the loveseat for a moment. "Somebody's head will roll over this. In fact…" He looked up at her, hoping his news would cheer her up. "That somebody has already been fired."

Marnie was horrified. Had this creep just put all the blame on Arnie? "How could you? You fired Arnie, didn't you!"

"I had to!" Cooke replied defensively. "Do you know he took your son *off* the schoolyard and went somewhere for a so-called chat? There are witnesses who saw your son running away from him. A couple of days later, the kid's, like, suicidal or something. Who knows what Decker did to that boy!"

"What Arnie did? Suicidal? Let me tell *you* somethin', Cookie." She took three steps toward him and practically shoved her finger up his hairy nose. "I don't know what happened today, but I can tell you, my son did not cause harm to himself. I know him better than that. As for Arnie, he was trying to help him. He was reaching out to him, something you need to figure out how to do. You should be ashamed of yourself. Coming here and blaming Arnie and telling me *my son* harmed himself? Get out of here."

Her screaming brought two nurses barreling into the small family room. Harry backed away, a little stunned. Then he nodded and scampered off.

As soon as Cooke was out of the little room, Dr. Bonneville rushed in, bumping into the two nurses, who were just leaving.

"Marnie, I want to talk to you."

She sat down obediently, resigned to the cruel emptiness that reflected a new low for her. "My world is crashing down," she mumbled, but Dr. Bonneville, who was still standing, didn't acknowledge her comment. Instead, he grabbed Marnie's shoulders and shook her until she snapped out of her self-pity and looked at his face.

"This is serious," he said. "I need you to tell me, was Matthew taking any non-prescription drugs? Or prescription drugs? Was he taking anything he wasn't supposed to? Can you think of anything?"

"What? No!" Marnie was shocked at the question. "Is that what this is all about? Did Matty take something?"

"We don't know, but we have to rule that out. Nothing is showing up." After a brief pause, the questions started up again. Dr. Bonneville wanted Marnie to explain the happenings of that morning.

"This is so embarrassing. We don't usually fight like that. I… I… never leave like that. It's just that… ah, crap." Marnie reduced to tears. Dr. Bonneville said he would call someone to sit with her, and he or one of the nurses would keep her updated.

"May I see him?" she asked.

"No," he responded as he stepped out of the room.

Marnie checked her watch. It was 1:55 p.m. She would have to call Arnie to pick up Karo. But if Arnie was fired, she would now have to call him at his house. His new wife would answer. Despite the fact she was nice and all, Marnie didn't want to talk to her. She stared at the picture of the garden gate somewhere in Spain. Arnie used to talk about the kingdom gates and how beautiful he thought they were and that one day they would find out for themselves. "Not now, please! Not now! Do not let my baby in, not just yet. Let him stay with me. Please!" she begged.

Just then Alan Pine stepped into the room, closing the door quietly behind him. He gave Marnie a half smile, with a "Hello again" look on his face. Marnie nodded at him, thankful to see a friendly face. They sat quietly for a few minutes until Marnie broke the ice. "I'm sorry. I don't think I was very nice to you last time we met."

Alan shrugged. "Hey, that's okay. You have no idea what I get sometimes."

"Why do you do it? This must be a challenging job. Sitting with people like me with their emotions all wound up."

"I like to help. Often, truth be told, I don't know what to say, but I like to think just the presence of someone who cares is helpful."

Marnie chuckled. "Someone who cares? Do you know how cliché that sounds? You don't have the faintest clue who I am." She stopped before she said something mean.

"That doesn't matter. I'm not here to judge. I do this because I don't think anyone should have to sit here alone in the midst of dire uncertainty."

"Do you do this all day long? Surely not, I hope! That would drive you bonkers, I would think."

"I come when they call me. My job is flexible, so I can leave it whenever a situation arises."

Marnie was surprised and intrigued. "You don't work here?"

"No," he chuckled slightly. "I own the small grocery market in the tourist section. My wife and I run the shop. I'm a volunteer."

"You're putting me on. You came here for this? You left your shop to come here to be with me?"

Alan nodded. "My wife and I both do this—we take turns. We believe it's just one way we can do good for the king."

Marnie considered Alan's response for several seconds, then offered him a stunned smile. "Thank you. And thank your wife too."

"Can I get you anything?"

Feeling a little more settled, Marnie nodded. "Actually, yes, a good, hot cup of coffee."

They both looked at the empty Mr. Coffee machine and he chuckled again. "Your wish is my command."

Just then, Dr. Alexien knocked and entered the room. Alan took it as his cue to exit. "I'll go to the cafeteria to grab you one," he said on his way out.

Dr. Alexien sat on the couch opposite Marnie, then leaned forward and grabbed her hands. "Tell me what you know, Marnie."

Marnie sucked in a deep breath and wondered where to start. "Matthew does *not* take drugs," she blurted.

Dr. Alexien nodded. "There is no evidence of any unknown substance in his body."

"Can I see him?"

"Of course, soon. We're just intubating him."

"What does that mean? Oh my gosh, he's not breathing on his own? Really? Is that what you're telling me?"

"Stay calm. We're going to figure this out. He arrived with no vital signs, Marnie. He has vital signs now, and we're working to keep it that way. We don't know why he's not responding so well. It's like he's not here." Dr. Alexien eyeballed Marnie as if Marnie was supposed to know what that meant, but Marnie just slumped into herself letting the tears flow. "I have a good feeling, Marnie. About you and Matthew. I think this will turn out okay. I really do."

Marnie wondered what on earth she meant by that. It was an odd statement. But she was getting used to Dr. Alexien's strange comments.

"What about Karo? Will Arnie pick her up?" Dr. Alexien asked. Marnie was thankful Dr. Alexien knew her family well enough to anticipate this need. "Shall I ask Alan, our volunteer, to contact him?"

"Oh, I'd be so thankful if you would," Marnie replied, hoping Alan would also come back and just sit with her while she continued to wait.

"I'll take care of it." Dr. Alexien stood up to leave the room, but before she did, she leaned down and whispered to Marnie, even though no one else was in the room. "If Dr. Bonneville advises you to remove Matthew from his breathing support because there's no hope, *do not* consent. We need to keep him alive for as long as possible." She slipped out of the room without looking back.

Stunned, Marnie stared at the door as Alan entered with two coffees in hand and two Havensight police constables.

What now? she thought. *Please, all this has to stop.*

Alan handed a coffee to Marnie. "These two gentlemen were in the hall. They want to talk to you, Marnie, but I told them this wasn't a good time."

"Detective Johnstone here, ma'am, and this here is Constable Rusch. I think we've met before." He glanced at Marnie out the top of his large, black-rimmed glasses. Marnie barely nodded as she sat there, frozen, waiting for the next shoe to drop. "Can we talk now? We need to ask you a few questions. We'll be out of your hair in a few moments."

Marnie didn't respond.

"Look," Constable Rusch, the shorter one of the pair, said. "We're really sorry for what you must be going through right now." He bent down so that his face was closer to hers. "We want to help you. Really. It's our job to investigate. Anytime something like this happens, we check into it, ask questions, and find out what happened before the incident. We want to help you find out what happened to your son."

"Incident?"

Marnie nodded at Alan, suggesting it was okay and he could leave. He reassured her that he would be just outside the door if she needed him.

By the time the two men left, a full twenty-five minutes later, Marnie was shaking. She had never been so grilled about personal things in her life. The highlight of their interview focused on the rough waters recently between her and Matthew and also with Arnie. They seemed fixed on proving Arnie had done something wrong or hurtful. Marnie wanted to throw up. Although she took her own shots at Arnie, he was a good person and had never done anything to harm her or Matthew, and he totally adored Karo, the child they shared together.

"Oh, what have I done?" she could barely breathe. She wondered frantically at any comments she had made that may have been misconstrued or blown out of proportion, simply to find someone to blame.

Alan entered the room with a big smile. "Look who I found!" He was delighted to have done something helpful for Marnie. Arnie walked in directly behind him. "I'll be nearby in the hallway. Just yelp if you need anything." He exited after picking up Marnie's empty coffee cup.

Marnie leaped up and gave Arnie a big hug.

"You okay?" he asked. "Well, obviously, that's a dumb question." Marnie shrugged as they sat across from each other. "I heard he's on a ventilator."

"I haven't even seen 'im yet." She sounded despondent. "Still waiting. Not sure why it's taking so long."

"Patience," was all Arnie could say. The pair were silent for a few moments.

"They think he stole our neighbor's bike."

"We just have to wait and get Matthew's side of the story. Maybe... maybe he just *borrowed* it."

That suggestion made Marnie chuckle. Another few moments of silence ensued.

"Borrowing the bike would be better than the other thing they're talking about." She looked at Arnie, all teary eyed. "They thought he... they thought he did this to himself." She shook her head. "He would never have." They were both silent again for several moments. "Did you lose your job over this? That's what Cooke implied. Oh, Arnie, I hope not. I know you would never do anything to harm Matty."

"Yeah, but don't worry about it. The dust will settle, and they'll figure out all the pieces. All will be well. I know it, Marnie. All will be well."

"You always say that. Thank you. I really needed to hear that right now."

He stood up. "Well, I should go. I wanted to check in on you before I pick up Karo. Don't worry, take all the time you need. We'll take care of her."

Marnie knew the "we" part of that sentence included his new and pregnant wife. She felt discouraged thinking Karo would likely enjoy being in a home with two parents, protected from the stresses her brother caused and having the excitement of a new baby coming. *How can I compete with that?* she wondered. "Thank you. I really appreciate it," she muttered.

Arnie stopped short of opening the door. Marnie felt his gaze upon her even though she was looking at the floor. "Would you like us to pray together?"

She looked up at him. "You really believe that stuff? That there's another world out there, and those running it actually have an interest in us?" She chuckled sarcastically. "All up there battling away to win us over and whatever else?" She knew she annoyed him when she spoke like that. Marnie talked about God, but the whole thing never really took root within her heart, particularly the king part. She didn't like how Arnie peddled it all the time. That had been a sore point in their incredibly brief marriage.

"I do," he replied gently.

"Perhaps you can do it by yourself then."

"Marnie, you have to believe. Seriously."

Marnie knew if Alan Pine were asking her to pray, she would. The same went for Dr. Alexien. But Arnie? Why didn't she want to pray with him? Why the hesitation? She had asked herself that many times, resolving he was simply too serious about it. He believed wholeheartedly. It wasn't just some righteous cliché or façade with him. *Hmm... no, that's not it. Alan Pine and Dr. Alexien are pretty real about it too.* Arnie knew her too well. Knew she didn't, rather couldn't, truly believe, only pretended to when convenient. Praying with Arnie was too real for comfort. *Frank never held such beliefs. If I suddenly truly believed, where does that put you, Frank? I'd have to question whether you even entered those gates or if you're out there floating around somewhere in that galaxy you loved so much 'cause they won't let you in.* She glared at the painting on the wall. By the time she looked up, Arnie had already resigned to the fact she wasn't interested.

"It's okay. I'll catch you later," he said and then went out.

A nurse came scurrying in. "Mrs. Mackenzie, Dr. Bonneville would like to chat with you."

"Do *not* remove his ventilator!" Marnie's eyes, set deep into a face so pale and tired and sad looking, were steely black and mean. The nurse turned and left the room with an impatient glare, shaking her head curiously at Marnie's angry outburst.

CHAPTER SIXTY
UNWELCOMED

In the Outer Courtyard of the Kingdom

MEGALOS SAT ALONE in his watch post murmuring to himself. Roly and the junior gatekeepers were managing the arrival process just fine, so at least he didn't have to think much about gate-related matters. Roly hiked up the stairs to pop in every third or so arrival to ask a question or debate a fact.

Pretty sure he's just doing that to check up on me, Megs thought.

No one could recall a time when Megalos appeared so despondent. Even kibitzing over measurement details couldn't get a rise out of him.

Hearing a familiar voice, Megalos sat up to peer out the circular window in his tower room. It gave him a perfect view. He could see all the way to the horizon and any arrivals that were coming forth. He could see and even hear the conversations at his post station where Roly and the crew were working, and he could see the family and friends gathering at the picnic tables chatting away. He heard Aivy's distinct voice, and sure enough, there she was, chatting with the waiting families.

If Aivy was out there waiting, that meant *they* had to be

arriving soon. It also meant the new plan was in play. Megalos had adamantly rejected the last-minute revisions, but it was no use. If this revised plan was in fact in play, it meant his Pipiera could possibly now be a captive of the rebel army, and potentially, it called for Matthew to come home early to the kingdom. He sighed and then trudged down the staircase and out the tower's entrance. *Two serious losses. Some plan.*

He took his post at the gate and kept a watchful eye on the grassy waves coming in over the horizon, watching for Jophiel's distinguished profile. "This better work," he muttered.

There was no mistaking Jophiel's form. It was majestic even compared to all the other kingdom escorts. *Look at him. He could bring anyone to their knees if he wanted.* His posture was perfect, his height impressive. When his wings were spread fully, there were no words to describe him. Megalos and Jophiel had met countless times, given the authoritarians called upon Jophiel often to bring an especially precious—or contentious—arrival home safely. He was gentle and kind, but there was a side of him that Megalos would not want to cross.

"Hey," Megalos said, "he's got *two* lads."

"Might one of them be Pipiera?" Roly inquired.

Megalos was hopeful and grabbed the telescope for a closer look. "What? No!"

Aivy sprinted toward the arrivals in question. *She must be just as appalled as I am,* Megalos thought. Aivy's concern was telling; this was *not* part of the plan. *We've already been thwarted!* If what he just saw was indeed that Kasartha kid, the rebellious evil one caught spying on his gate and on his Pipiera, the very one who had caused so much havoc, then why was Jophiel bringing him here? Megalos shot off in the same direction.

Aivy and Megalos intercepted the incoming trio. Keeping their distance, they commanded a halt. "You are not bringing him any closer," Megalos said, referring to Kasartha.

Aivy and Megalos maneuvered themselves on separate grassy waves, attempting to show force that would strongly encourage Jophiel and the two boys to step backwards, so the waves couldn't do what they normally did—faithfully bring the arrivals up to the kingdom gate.

"Jophiel?" Aivy looked up at his face, seeking an answer.

Matthew carried out a complete 360, balancing carefully on the wave he rode aside Jophiel. Megalos could see the boy was in awe. This was not the way Megalos had envisioned Matthew's return, with him holding back the boy's approach to the gate.

"Surely, it wasn't his idea?" Aivy cocked her head toward Matthew, in horror that Matthew could have insisted Kasartha come along. "What happened?"

Kasartha hung his long, lanky neck in shame, hat in hand, revealing a balding, murky green scalp along with a guilty conscience.

Megalos eyed Kasartha's movements cautiously. "I don't trust him."

"Nor do I." Aivy was onside with wherever Megalos might be taking this.

"He shouldn't be here. I command you to get him away from our gate. Remove him from our grounds. He's a danger to all arrivals not processed yet. Get him away from here. Immediately!"

"I cannot," Jophiel stated calmly.

"Jophiel, you know you do not give orders," Aivy scolded.

"He was on our side," Jophiel explained.

"*Our* side? How'd he get across?" Megalos burned his gaze into Kasartha, who stood quietly with his head still bowed. "I know you can hear me," Megalos said.

"Megalos!" Aivy scolded. Megalos knew he shouldn't have been derogatory. There were rules that were normally easy to follow, but they didn't account for situations like this.

Megalos cleared his throat, altering his tone. "Okay, so, young man or beast, whichever you are, just how did you end up on our side of the river?" He glanced at Aivy, who nodded with approval to his newly adapted and somewhat forced attitude. A managed tone was important.

"We saved him," Jophiel said.

"You what?" Aivy and Megalos exclaimed in unison.

"What an absurdity. Please explain." Aivy's tolerant tone was gone. As transition lead, all arrivals came through her, and the vast majority arrived in sync on a perfectly predetermined schedule. Matthew was expected; Kasartha was not. Simple as that. Jophiel had some explaining to do.

Megalos took note as to how much closer they had all drifted to the kingdom gate. The grassy waves were naturally bringing them inward. He caught a glimpse of Roly's concern and motioned to the group to keep a good distance away from the gate. Jophiel picked up the two boys in his arms and in two giant steps was back at least a half dozen waves while Megalos and Aivy jumped them one at a time. Once settled again, Jophiel began to explain.

"I found them on the narrowing, by the footbridge. Matthew was lying deep in the weeds on the shoreline, I picked him up but had to yank hard. This kid had his arms wrapped around Matthew."

This news infuriated Megalos. "Of course he did. He was holding him back. Probably trying to keep him in the murk, trying to get him back on their shore." He looked at Aivy. "We need to imprison him, but not here, down on the lower deck. He shouldn't be up here in the arrivals court."

"Wait," Jophiel said. "If it weren't for this kid, Matthew would have perished. The black waves would have taken him down."

Aivy sought clarification. "You mean *you* didn't escort him across the river?"

"Like I said, he was already across the river." Jophiel paused to allow this information to sink in. No one had ever crossed those waters without an escort. The whole thing sounded rather fluky.

Megalos looked at Matthew. Normally, this would have been a happy reunion, but things were anything but normal. "What happened, son? Tell us everything."

Matthew scratched his neck and gawked around as if to study his surroundings once more before he began to speak an utterly dumbfounded, "Uhh…"

CHAPTER SIXTY-ONE
OTHIS TAKES CHARGE

THREE SHORT, SHRIEKING trumpet blasts sounded from beyond the picnic area announcing the galloping approach of Othis and several of his warriors.

"Thank you, King," Megalos said, breathing a sigh of relief. Othis had come to collect the trespasser on the kingdom's territory. *Othis can take it from here.*

In no time the kingdom army encircled Kasartha, further bewildering Matthew.

"On what grounds will you imprison him?" Jophiel inquired.

Megalos and Othis gave Jophiel a look that he wouldn't much care for, but his question remained hanging, demanding an answer. Why wasn't the usual charge suitable in this case? Charges of intrusion, interference, influencing deceit, anger, pride, and likely a slew of other emotions. There were countless opportunities for charges.

Why is Jophiel questioning this? Megalos wondered. *He's been around a long time, and he knows how this works.* Something was not adding up.

"It appears Matthew was the escort, and he brought along Kasartha willingly," Jophiel explained. "Partway across, Matthew was overtaken by the waves, but Kasartha saved him and brought them both safely to our shore."

Kasartha stood up a little taller, liking Jophiel's description of events.

"How can this be?" Othis demanded.

Aivy decided to take the lead in the inquisition. "Tell me, Jophiel, how much can you testify to as a witness, and how much is hearsay? We need to separate fact from mere possibilities."

Jophiel was on board with Aivy's line of thinking. "Okay," he began, "the main tunnel closed off. Pipiera had already jumped in." Jophiel glanced at Megalos, knowing this information would be hurtful for him to learn.

Megalos was a master at hiding his thoughts, though. For a moment he had forgotten about the danger his Pip was in, and he was careful not to flinch. If only he could collapse to his knees and scream, but he knew that was out of the question. Instead, he nodded sternly for Jophiel to continue. *Why does Pip have to be so stubborn and impatient?* he wondered. *Now she's paying the price.*

"As soon as a new temporary travel way was open, I jumped in." Jophiel glanced at Othis, knowing full well he had disobeyed the temporary stop order. Othis merely grumbled, so Jophiel continued. "I landed in time to see this pair on the shore. On *our* shore, as I mentioned before. The kid beneath Matthew."

"With his arms holding him like a prisoner, as you mentioned that earlier." Megalos wanted to be sure that fact was not left out.

"Yes, the kid's arms were wrapped around Matthew's waist."

"So, why do you believe he *saved* Matthew?" Aivy asked. "I don't understand."

"Well, how was it that they were able to cross?" Jophiel sighed and thought he should start from the beginning. "I headed to Havensight, figuring that's where I would find Pipiera, with Matthew somewhere. She had a plan, a hopeful one." He eyed Megalos. "She wanted to clear matters up. You know, work out a few things."

"On her own," Megalos said. "She thought she'd do this on her own."

"Yes, sir. She was determined, and I needed to protect her." He looked at Othis who nodded in understanding. "I was almost to Havensight when I received orders to go to the river, the narrows where the footbridge lies. I rushed there, thinking that was where Pipiera was. To my surprise, I found these boys instead. At that moment, the rest of the order arrived. It was urgent, directing Matthew's transition here."

"So you brought them both," Othis grumped.

"So I brought them both," Jophiel replied, nodding.

"The orders were correct," Aivy said. "James and I determined that an early return home would be the best and safest option for Matthew. It was urgent and last minute, but we got permission from the king." Her voice faded toward the end. She knew Megalos was disappointed in the plan, including the possibility of an early return for Matthew, and she didn't want to dwell on it.

"Matthew," Aivy said, switching the inquisition toward him, "did you willingly bring this Kasartha rebel across the river?"

Matthew looked at Kasartha, who quickly dropped his head again. "No. I did not." His answer was surprisingly clear and distinct.

"Okay. Just to be clear, you did not bring Kasartha across with you willingly?"

Matthew shook his head. "No."

Megalos and Aivy each exhaled, looking relieved.

Unconvinced, Othis picked up the line of questioning. "What did he do to force you to bring him here?" Othis's army kept their eyes on Kasartha, waiting to take him away as soon as a specific charge could be identified.

"He didn't force me."

Aivy's eyes widened in alarm. "He didn't force you? Okay, then why did you bring him across? This is very important, Matthew. Please think carefully before your answer."

Matthew wasn't sure what all the fuss was about other than he sensed this was no time to be untruthful, nor did he know why he wouldn't want to be truthful. "I jumped across to escape. That girl hinted to me that I should do that."

Megalos perked up. "Pipiera?"

"Uh, yeah, I guess her name was something like that. Penney, I think. She's a jumper herself."

"The gate girl," Kasartha mumbled, attempting to be helpful.

Megalos didn't like Kasartha's reference to Pipiera, and he scowled at him before turning his attention back to Jophiel. "Jophiel, did you see Pip?"

Jophiel shook his head.

"Go on." Othis was getting impatient; he wanted the rest of Matthew's story.

"A big wave overtook me, threw me off my jump. I landed in… uh, it was like black gunk, swirling me around. I knew I was done for. Then this guy," he motioned toward Jophiel, "picked me up. He had to yank pretty hard on account of Kasartha's arms and legs wrapped around me. I'm pretty sure he saved me. I would have drowned in that water, or whatever that liquid was."

Othis eyed Matthew suspiciously. "Who saved you? Which guy exactly?"

Matthew looked from Jophiel to Kasartha and back again. "Well, er, I'm pretty sure Kasartha saved me first. Then the big dude, I guess."

It was evident Matthew wasn't even sure who saved him, what exactly he had been saved from, or even when he was saved. Was it the moment of the bone-splintering crunch, the tussling and wrestling in the gunk, or being yanked up out of the weeds? Othis wondered if it really mattered. He rubbed his chin. "If Matthew was left in those waters, he would have ceased to exist anywhere. We would have lost him."

Few could appreciate Matthew's escape from danger more than

Megalos, Aivy, Jophiel, and Othis. Matthew would have perished from existence had he not been pulled out of the River of Times. Safe crossings were restricted to those identified through kingdom orders executed by Aivy's team and brought across safely by the kingdom's escorts.

"If that's the case, then I kinda owe him," Matthew admitted, nodding toward Kasartha.

The news was good—Matthew had not perished. However, a rebel had saved him, not for the purpose of retaining him for suffering and attacks, but rather to ensure he was brought safely to the shoreline of his homeland. This was extraordinary. "What to do, what to do," Aivy said, drumming her fingers on her hips.

"What if we offer a trade?" Megalos suggested. "This Kasartha kid for Pipiera?"

His head still lowered, Kasartha glared up at Megalos.

Othis shook his head. "They won't want him, he's useless to them. And he's just proven that."

"He has to go back. Matthew, you must go back," Aivy instructed, referring to the need to send Matthew back to his earth journey.

Megalos nodded in agreement. "At least we can all agree on that. I can't process Matthew. He won't be able to go through the gate with a rebel as an invited sidekick! You must get new orders to send Matthew back. As long as he's hanging on to this, er, kid, he needs to get back to his tour." He looked at Matthew. "So you can shake him off!"

"Do we not have a timing issue?" Jophiel asked, anticipating an answer from Aivy. She would know.

Aivy asked Matthew to turn around and swirled her left hand counterclockwise around his back. Atop his head from nowhere appeared a sand clock. She eyed the crystals falling into the bottom chamber and nodded in agreement. Yes, there was a timing issue. The boy must be returned to his physical body before the crystals run out or all this business of planning next steps will be moot—Matthew's tour will be over and with questionable results.

"If he is to get back, I can take him, but we can't delay. We must leave now." Jophiel stressed the urgency.

Othis pointed to Kasartha. "What about him? What'll we do with him? Is there something we can charge this fiend with, so we can hold him?"

"Trespassing!" Megalos commanded.

"Nope," Aivy replied. "Matthew brought him here willingly."

"Spying then. You can make that stick, can't you, Othis?" Megalos hoped this suggestion made sense.

"Nada," Aivy said, shaking her head.

"Nah, not enough to stick," Othis added.

"Uh, we gotta go, guys," Jophiel said. "Time's running out. I'll take Matthew while you guys figure out what to do with this other young... er... man." Jophiel seemed to be the only one with a hint of empathy toward Kasartha.

Kasartha raised his head. "Take me as a prisoner, I beg you. Don't send me back! Uncle will surely torment me and throw me into the river. Please, I... want to... I want to be *here*."

Neither Megalos nor Othis believed him. Both remained stone-faced and silent. Neither provided even a hint of empathy in response to Kasartha's cry.

Aivy paced before suggesting her plan. "Okay, Jophiel, take Matthew back to Havensight." She pointed at Kasartha. "But he must remain here, at least for the moment. We need someone in place as quickly as possible to inspire Matthew, or he'll remain off track and will be an even easier target for the rebels." She paced some more while studying Kasartha. "You *are* the enemy," she declared. "If you're so keen on saving Matthew, what would you suggest?" Megalos and Othis were a little taken aback by her line of questioning.

"He needs to stop listening to guys like me," Kasartha said, his eyes still on his feet. "He likes us. I'm his best buddy."

Matthew looked the other way, squeezing the back of his neck in frustration.

"Hmpf." Aivy pretended Kasartha's answer was of no use, even though it was. "So, then tell him. Tell him right now that he should not entertain you any longer! Tell him you are deceitful and only wanted harm to come his way." Her voice grew louder. "Tell him you targeted him knowing he had a great future in the kingdom. Tell him!"

"I can't."

"Then you're lying! Arrest him, and charge him with deceit." Aivy shouted.

"Wait, no!" Kasartha protested. "That's not totally true. I wanted him to be my friend! I was lonely."

Megalos rolled his eyes.

Othis had heard enough. In response to a slight movement of his right index finger, his army moved in closer to Kasartha, pushing Jophiel and Matthew out of the way. Othis was pleased to see the rebel kid alarmed, now encircled by armed kingdom warriors.

Kasartha held his hands up and gave a "I'm telling the truth" facial expression, which resulted in a head shake from Megalos.

Jophiel squeezed his eyebrows and tapped his right foot nervously.

The expression on Matthew's face encouraged Othis and Megalos to keep silent. They could tell he had become close to this rebel, and if Matthew was to have a successful earth tour, he would have to denounce that relationship on his own accord.

Aivy was desperate to wrap up this situation. "Okay then, Jophiel, take Matthew to Havensight now and then report back."

"What about a new influencer?" Jophiel asked while grabbing

Matthew's waist in preparation for flight. "He's going to need that, and I'm afraid sooner than later."

"Wait!" Aivy said. "Why don't we have a quick chat with Andy Falcon before you go? A word of encouragement, one that will stick with him, a message he'll remember coming out of this ordeal?"

Othis and Megalos nodded in unison, agreeing the message would be valuable despite the precious time constraint.

CHAPTER SIXTY-TWO
ANDY JUMPS IN

A IVY STEPPED AWAY and transmitted a summons for Andy, pulling Matthew's former phys ed teacher away from a soccer game inside the kingdom. In no time, Andy exited the gate, jogging joyfully and expediently. He waved at Roly before jumping numerous incoming waves of tender grasses to meet with Aivy. The pair gleefully shared greetings, and then Aivy quietly filled him in and no doubt requested a task of him; to leave Matthew with an impressionable and memorable message.

Megalos could see Andy was eager to meet with Matthew. Everyone was happy and relieved to see Matthew's face light up once he recognized his favorite teacher had just arrived on the scene.

"Mr. Falcon!" Matthew jumped—practically flew—over a couple waves to greet him with a big hug. "I didn't realize how much I missed you. Is it you? Is it really you?"

Andy ruffled Matthew's hair. "Remember everything I stood for, Matt. Don't give up. You hear me?" Matthew held on to Mr. Falcon even tighter and nodded his head against Andy's chest. "Like everyone else, you're just a pilgrim on Earth, so think long-term.

Think higher. Think big picture. Got it?" Matthew sobbed and nodded some more.

A subtle signal to Jophiel from Aivy, and off Jophiel and Matthew went.

"You've got a grand future, Matt!" Andy called after them. "Hold on to it!" Matthew had tears on his cheeks. Aivy smiled, certain this brief, emotion-filled encounter would be helpful for him. He seemed comfortable going with Jophiel, likely anxious to get back to the home he knew. Best of all, he did not look back at Kasartha with any kind of sadness nor wanting.

"Whew." Megalos wiped his brow. Typically, it was that final moment one remembered if and when such a privileged kingdom visit occurred, so Andy's embrace and simple words of encouragement would be helpful.

Aivy thanked Andy, who was happy to oblige. Knowing he was excused, he jumped toward the nearby gate, signaled Roly, and then leaped back inside the kingdom.

That man's energetic, Megalos mused.

CHAPTER SIXTY-THREE
To Uncle's Gate

O THIS COMMANDED THE group to reposition themselves and jump toward the horizon.

By then several new arrivals riding the grassy waves became onlookers to an unusual sight. They had no idea that a kingdom army encircling an apparent invader was unusual. However, the group was becoming a spectacle. Megalos waved to the arrivals as they passed. Thankfully, Roly would take good care of them.

"Was it really as easy as that?" Megalos asked, snapping his fingers as he referred to the impact of Andy Falcon's encouraging words. Aivy sighed heavily before responding.

"I wish. But no. Of course not." She paced a bit. "We'll have to closely monitor his measurements at all times. We need to get him connected with his earth granddad and to Arnie Decker. I'll work with James on that. In the meantime…" She turned and queried Othis, "Do you have any suggestions for getting Pipiera back here?"

"It'll have to be a military response. I can't see any other way."

"You certain they won't take Kasartha as an exchange?" Megalos asked.

"Yes," Othis replied.

"I know where she is," Kasartha mumbled, cautiously eyeing the encircling army.

Othis raised his eyebrows. "And why should we believe you?"

"Because I really want to prove myself."

"To whom exactly?"

"I don't know."

Aivy, Megalos, and Othis shared glances. None of them believed him, but Megalos rubbed his chin, signaling he wanted to explore this further.

Megalos motioned for one of the warriors to move over, allowing him to enter the circle, so he could probe Kasartha close up. "Okay, where?"

Kasartha remained tight-lipped.

"Just as I thought. You don't know. You're useless to your master, aren't you?"

"Does everyone think I'm useless?" Kasartha yelped in frustration. "Do you know what it's like to be me? Yay, yay, yay, my choice. But you know somethin'? It wasn't! I was tricked! Tricked!" Kasartha kicked the wave, and for a splinter of time the ground swelled and shook. "You'll never get it. You sit up here in your grandiose environment where everything smells so good and looks so good. So freakin' respectful to each other, everybody huggin' everybody before they go in." Kasartha pointed to the gate that Megalos guarded.

"Then tell us." Othis shouted. "Where is she?"

"You have to promise not to send me back."

Othis looked at Aivy, who shook her head. "That is beyond any of us. You will have to consult the king. I don't know what he will do. Plus, reversing choices, as I understand, it defies a great many purposes for earth journeys." She could see he was depressed. "But nothing is impossible with our king. Nothing."

Kasartha studied their faces in turn. "Uncle wants her at *his* gate."

"So, you think that's where they are? *That actually makes sense,* Megalos thought.

Othis wasn't buying it, but this was their best lead. "Can you take us there?"

"To Uncle's gate?"

"No. To Mars. Of course to your so-called Uncle's gate!" Othis was clearly annoyed.

Megalos, still close to Kasartha, decided to play the good guy and changed his tone. "Kasartha, what do you need from us to take our army to your Uncle's gate safely, retrieve Pipiera, and get back here? How do you see all this working out?"

Othis was uncomfortable with the question—asking a rebel how to lead the kingdom army to release a prisoner held by the rebel army on the very grounds the rebels guarded. Granted, their guards would be in place to ensure no one came *out* of their kingdom. The rebel gates were heavily guarded to ensure their citizens remained inside. They were indeed prisoners. The army Othis led guarded the kingdom to protect its kingdom citizens, who were free to come and go as they pleased. Othis rubbed his chin in thought.

Megalos hoped Pipiera was still outside those gates. *Surely she wouldn't go inside, not voluntarily anyway.* He also hoped Kasartha, a rebel kid, was telling them the truth and not leading them into a trap.

It crossed his mind that perhaps their capture of Pipiera was a way to get to him. His earthly father's chilling words from so long ago, warning him he would never escape the evil one's reach, haunted him once again. *Nah.* He shook the thoughts away. Megalos had forgiven his earthly father long ago. Not only had he forgiven him, he had blessed him. But rules were rules; he could not reverse choices made by others. *Everyone must decide for themselves.*

Kasartha looked up. "I need your trust."

"Our trust?" Aivy struggled to hide the same sarcasm Megalos was feeling.

"Your trust. That's all I ask. I will lead you to Pipiera, and you must bring me back here along with her. That's all I ask."

A long silence prevailed. Othis and Megalos and Aivy couldn't even look at each other—the risk was just too high. Then they each nodded slightly. They wanted to retrieve Pipiera. No other feasible plan came to mind. They were resolved to take Kasartha's lead.

"Okay," Aivy said.

"I'll get a crew together," Othis added, falling in line.

"No," Kasartha replied boldly.

"No?" The three stared at the rebel. Surely he did not expect Othis to go in without a battalion of the king's army.

"Him." Kasartha pointed at Megalos. "And him only."

"Oh no. Not happening. Why our lead gatekeeper?" Othis's eyes narrowed as he got in Kasartha's face. "You think we're going to waltz right into your trap?"

Kasartha sighed. "An army will be spotted from miles away. There are spies all over the universal fields. You won't get anywhere near Uncle's gate. Besides, *your* presence says 'I'm a soldier.' His, well, I have a better chance at getting him past the spies as a regular guy kind of thing."

"A regular guy kind of thing?" Othis was bewildered. "We're talking about Megalos, right?"

"Yes. That's the only way I see this working," Kasartha replied.

Othis had to walk away. He shook his head at Aivy and Megalos. "No. We're not doing this."

Megalos stepped forward. "I'll go." All he could think of was bringing Pipiera home safely. Home to him, but this time he would escort her inside the kingdom gate and wait as she handed in her living stone to the king. Then she would become a kingdom citizen officially and not have any further threats to where or who she belonged. Ever.

"Looks like you are the tie breaker, Aivy." Othis was confident she would not agree to this plan. Her vote would stop this whole nonsense of Megalos being led to the rebel gate by some rebel kid thinking they would capture and bring back Pipiera, all without the support and protection of his kingdom army.

"Regrettably, I have no authority over Megalos's decision," Aivy replied, "not as transition lead."

Othis felt his jaw and heart sink simultaneously. That was not the answer he anticipated. Roly's whistle caught his attention. The grassy waves had brought the foursome and surrounding warriors close to the kingdom gate once again. "Get 'im outta here!" Othis commanded. "Get him away from our gate!"

Othis was referring to Kasartha, but Megalos felt a tinge of Othis's anger directed to himself. Although Megalos was the one taking the risk, if anything went wrong, the blame would fall squarely on Othis's shoulders.

Megalos grabbed Kasartha's forearm and squeezed it tight enough for Kasartha to squirm. "Straight there. Straight back. No games."

As Megalos dragged Kasartha past the picnic tables and headed toward the cloud arena to find a suitable travel way, Kasartha glanced back at Othis. "No army," he mouthed.

CHAPTER SIXTY-FOUR
REGRET AND GUILT

In the Rebel Courtyard

"IF I COULD take every decision I ever made in my life back, I surely would," Pipiera mumbled angrily to herself. She was full of regret and guilt. "At least Matthew's okay."

She had seen Jophiel arrive on the opposite side of the river, her side, her old side. He struggled to pick Matthew up, then threw him over his shoulder and stared for the longest time at Kasartha's body. Jophiel couldn't see her waving her arms frantically, calling out to him, "Hey, Jophiel! Over here!" The scene played over and over in her mind.

The demon dragon laughed and laughed, mocking her, saying she should have known better. Now that she was on *his* side, she would be erased from the memory of anyone on the other side. "They won't look for you because they won't even remember you." His sneer of satisfaction made her ghastly ill.

"You're lying," she said as his army needled her away.

Now, with her knees huddled to her chest and her back leaning against a wall made of grey cinder blocks, cold to the touch, all she could do was stare at her toes. They had taken her shoes, preventing her from running away. The ground in front of her stretched out for miles to the horizon. It wasn't much like the rich, grassy waves in front of Papah Megs' gate; here the grounds were flat and hard, full of tall weeds, mostly sharp and oversized prickles full of seed pods. And it was dark, lit only by street lamps lining the wide, trampled path that led into the courtyard where she was huddled.

"So, where's Sarthie? What happened to 'im?"

Pipiera avoided conversation with the kid they put in charge of guarding her. Other than the way he walked, he looked much like Kasartha, only stockier and even shorter. Another thing, he smelled of sulfur a great deal.

"Rumor is he was pushed by Uncle into the black waters at the river, the place of *no* return. Schizzzle!" The goofy character made wiggly movements to suggest Kasartha had been electrocuted in hot water. She continued to ignore him. "Oh come on. You were there. We've got bets on what happened up there." He pointed a long dart-like stick toward her, pretending he was going to jab the sharp metal end into her left temple. She continued to ignore him. He crouched down and leaned in toward her. "You were there. I know it. And you, girlie, are going to tell me. What happened to Sarthie Boy? My cloven hoofs are on the line." She eyed the feet underneath his knees. No hooves, just worn-out soles in desperate need of repair. She said nothing. He spat out a hoarse laugh then straightened up and checked to see if anyone was watching. "You do know," he said, "if he is alive, they'll likely offer up a trade. Him for you."

"They won't remember me to initiate a trade," Pipiera said. *Maybe that'll shut him up.* She knew that wasn't true, technically. *Megalos and all those authoritarians will remember me.* She hoped the king would still want to remember her. She wondered if Kasartha's body was still lying on the shore. The dragon's army had whisked her away before she could tell. *What if…* She shrank deeper into depressing thoughts. *Great. It's totally possible that Kasartha could be there in my courtyard! And I'm here in his.* She wondered if that was his plan all along. *Nah,* she thought. *Even so, it doesn't really matter, does it? I'm here.*

Her fiendish guard poked her again. She believed she deserved it. She should have gone through the kingdom gate a long time ago. *But noooo, I always wanted more time. More time for what?* She had to admit, she had gotten too comfortable with feelings of unworthiness, guilt, and anger. She hid them though, burying her feelings well.

She took a slow study of her surroundings. *Maybe this is where I belong.* Her eyes landed on the rebel gates. Not a single gate, like the one she was used to, but multiple doors, six in all. Suspiciously, not a single one was guarded. Rebel soldiers accompanied individuals along the pathway that led inside. *I suppose they're like our escorts, but why no gatekeepers?*

She wondered if anyone would actually force her to enter. Plenty of unsettled folks were hanging around in the courtyard, much like she was now, barefoot and drowning in agony, some silent and some moaning.

What if Papah Megs doesn't come for me? What if I sit here, waiting and waiting, hour after hour... She broke into sobs, unable to comprehend such rejection. *Should I just get it over with and go in?* She took a few deep breaths and tried to look at her situation logically. *He'll be angry. Of course he'll be angry. Matthew lost his eternal desire. Every time Papah looks at me, he would be reminded of that, I'm sure. No, he may not come for me. I bet Matthew will even become my replacement in his heart. Me and my selfish stupidity.* She nearly regained some control when another horrific thought struck. *What's even worse is the pain I just caused to Matthew's earthly mother. She lost her boy and will never understand why for the rest of her earth journey. I've harmed so many. I should never have been created.*

Pipiera heeded the ugly character charged with guarding her. "I want to go through the gate," she said. "Now."

CHAPTER SIXTY-FIVE
No Way, Man

In the Town of Havensight

"WOWZERS, GO BLOW, he's a goner."

From the back of the hospital room with Jophiel towering behind him, Matthew gawked at his body lying there all stiff and white. He crept forward for a closer peek, maneuvering around the shoulder-to-shoulder lineup of folks in white coats hovering over the bed. Without even a thought to command it, he found himself rising upward automatically to get a better view. He shook his head. "Poor bloke."

Jophiel chuckled. "Get used to it. You're going back in, buddy."

"Ha ha, you're really Mr. Funny today. I'm not going back in there. Are you nuts?" Matthew had regained his sense of humor as soon as he and Jophiel entered the realms of Earth.

"Nope. Not nuts."

They watched a little longer as the shorter balding guy stood up and pulled down his mask, which signaled to the others to cease their efforts.

Obviously, they were giving up. Matthew crossed his arms in satisfaction. "See? It's over. I'm done. Let's go."

Jophiel prodded Matthew. "Come on, I thought you'd be better than this. You've barely started. No wonder they call you a quitter."

"Who called me a quitter? I'm not a quitter! Well, maybe I am sometimes. I just happen to know when to pack it in."

"You really think you should pack in this one and only opportunity? The one you begged for?"

"I begged for?"

Jophiel nodded. "You've got great things awaiting you. But you need to do your part."

"What's my part?"

"Fulfill your duties."

"What duties?"

"You'll figure them out one day at a time. Just stay close."

"To what?"

"You should be asking to whom."

"Okay, to whom?"

"If I have to answer that, maybe you should be packing it in. The king, of course."

Matthew knew this to be true. He watched as a second doctor and a couple of nurses left the room, leaving just one to do a final report of some sort.

Jophiel continued his instructions, presuming Matthew would jump back into his body. "You will not remember any of this. So, hey, it was good to meet you." Jophiel put his hand up to give Matthew a high five. "But there is one thing I want you to recall."

"And what might that be? Oh, let me guess, Pipiera's 'let go' thing?"

"Uh, er, well, yes that too. Let go and *give it up*. I presume you've learned that. That should be part of you now."

"Yeah, I guess it is. I think about it sometimes."

"Well, think about it a lot!"

"So, what was the other thing? If I'm gonna do this, I need to do it now."

"Yes, you do." Jophiel pushed Matthew forward. "Remember your visit with Andy Falcon."

Whoosh, a flurry of high energy ensued and Matthew was gone.

Jophiel stepped closer to the motionless body. "Take care, buddy. See you soon. But with the King's grace, not too soon!"

One of the monitors began a tapping noise. The woman jotting down stuff in a binder at the small stand-up desk in the corner of the room turned her head, then stepped closer. She noticed the boy they just declared as dead twitch his eyes, then one shoulder. She called for the others to come back in.

Jophiel smiled. "Okay, my work here is done." Off he went, hoping to track down Megalos and Kasartha and rescue Pipiera.

CHAPTER SIXTY-SIX
FALLING AND FOLLOWING

Somewhere in the Cosmos

THE JOURNEY FROM the kingdom gate to the rebel gate felt like a continuous, agonizing freefall, from the highest and most divine doorway to the lowest entrance ever to exist for humankind. Megalos wished he could convince himself this route was surprising and shook him to his core, but he couldn't; he had taken it centuries earlier. A few times, actually. He knew the route well. He let Kasartha lead the way, biting his tongue when he knew of side tunnels they could have taken to skirt certain galaxy dangers. Megalos needed Kasartha to believe he trusted him, although he clearly did not.

You think I don't know what's going on? The trip gave Megalos time to consider and prepare mentally. He knew another meeting with the dragon himself was the purpose of this journey. As far as he was concerned, he had already served his time. He kept silent. Just a few more light year markers of measurement, and they'd be there.

A big breath held deep and tight, then an exhale, felt good. There was nothing unusual about their approach. They arrived without a hitch or any fanfare. A strong yet manageable stench wafted past his nose, a telltale signal that the dragon himself was close by but not present. Otherwise, Megalos knew the odor would be unbearable. The ground was rough and hard. Low, wide bushes hugged the surface. Their long prickles were plentiful and healthy looking, bowing gently toward the entrance of six large, ominous gates and positioned well to needle the feet of anyone heading in the opposite direction. A few of the lights on the lampposts flickered as they strolled along the wide path and into the immense courtyard.

Megalos eyed the several hundred saddened souls milling about. *Such mass confusion. Such deceit. Such loss.* Some walked about screaming as though there was someone to scream at, someone who might listen. Some cheered, simply to be loud and boisterous. Most hugged themselves so tight they looked like human spheres, wanting to be left alone.

Megalos knew what it was like to be one of them. He had arrived at this very place as a young boy full of hate. He knew those curled-up souls were thinking how weak they were and how useless, how nobody cared for them now that their earthly clothes have been shed, much less about their whereabouts.

Megalos breathed in silently through gritted teeth. "Oh how I wish we got through to you." His whispered message was directed to every one of them, wishing each of these suffering beings might hear and believe his words. "Don't give in." He hoped they had loved ones they left behind who would persistently make requests to the king on their behalf.

At least a dozen rebel soldiers came charging toward them, bringing along a thickened darkness that Megalos could actually feel with his fingers.

He braced himself. This was indeed a setup. He was convinced it was him who the dragon really wanted. *He knew if he had Kasartha poke Matthew enough times, he would somehow end up with me in his clutches. He's holding Pipiera hostage in return for me. That dragon's a sly one.*

He shut his eyes to steady his thoughts. He needed to strategize and size this whole thing up. He thought of his king, who was so full of mercy and who took him in. He also thought of his Pip, who demonstrated without realizing it what a loving family felt like. *She trusts me. I can't let her down. I must free her, let her go home, tell her she must march through that kingdom gate with or without me. She must not wait any longer.*

A loud cry sounded a few feet in front of him, followed by another and another. They belonged to Kasartha. Soldiers surrounded him and poked him repeatedly with their long, poisonous javelins. Kasartha crumpled to the ground, trying to protect himself, Megalos could only watch in horror and disbelief.

"Why do you treat your own as such?!"

The rebel soldiers paid no attention to Megalos's hollering and continued until Kasartha no longer moaned or stirred. Sickened, Megalos wondered about his calculations. Perhaps Kasartha had been genuine in his desire to help. He felt a pang of guilt, then shook it off. His years of learning had taught him that feelings of guilt in situations as this, are simply another method of attack. The smelly dragon wanted Megalos to harbor guilt and fear in preparation for their meeting.

The rebels disappeared as quickly as they had appeared, taking the thickened darkness with them and leaving Kasartha's body lying motionless. Determined in his thoughts, Megalos stepped over Kasartha's body and headed toward the center of the bleak, crowded courtyard. *You will not impose un-kingly thoughts in my mind. I won't allow it, not this time.*

With his desire to serve his king strong as ever, Megalos began to speak to the mass of shadow-like beings. His robust voice could be heard throughout the courtyard and possibly even inside the nearby gates. "I beg you to beg the king for mercy if you want it, if you, in fact, have sincere regret. Knock on his door and keep knocking till he answers. You'll not gain anything here."

"Not the rules, bloke," someone said.

"They've forgotten us!" another yelled. "Not a single being remembers us."

"Yes, possibly," Megalos replied. "But you have nothing to gain here. Continue to seek the king. Do not enter these gates. With the king, nothing is impossible. Continue to seek him, I beg of you."

Two beings moved closer toward Megalos to hear more, but the rest turned the other way. Hundreds curled up in a fetal position against the outer wall of the rebel kingdom, sitting among prickles as though they were comforting. Others snickered and threw rocks his way.

The stench intensified. Megalos knew his brief public plea would attract the dragon. The two who drew closer to Megalos scampered away and hid their faces while others sought to protect their nostrils and mouths from the nauseating fumes. Astonishingly, anticipation of hope could be seen glimmering in many eyes. *Really? You think he's your leader? That he's going to protect you?* Megalos shook his head in sadness and disbelief and then braced himself for what was to happen next, another face-to-face discussion with the leader of the rebels himself.

CHAPTER SIXTY-SEVEN
SIBLING SQUABBLES

In the Rebel Courtyard

THE LINEUP WAS frustratingly long, but it gave Pipiera a chance to be awed. An enormous circus affair revealed itself as she stepped inside the gate. Tents with food and drink stands, treacherous roller coasters full of screaming beings, numerous gigantic Ferris wheels, each stuffed to the brim with riders. Nearly everyone, except the beady-eyed beasts meandering all over the grounds, were ferociously chewing candy apples of all colors—all colors but red, she noticed. Her eye caught a vendor's hand slamming his counter and screaming at a patron. "There's no ketchup in this place, so stop asking for it!" She scanned the eyes of the faces in the crowd. They looked so anxious, running from attraction to attraction, stuffing their faces and pushing each other, as if they couldn't inhale it all fast enough.

This was not a place she wanted to spend her existence, but what choice did she have?

Those in front of her beneath the "Sieve Hall" sign were anxious, wanting the line to move faster, so they could get in and get at it. There was no gatekeeper, no Megalos-type guy, only numerous long desks, each with a neat pile of forms and a registration official, faces hidden by ball caps. No palms were scanned. Arrivals had to read the form on their own and then agree to pay their price. Once they committed, they tossed their stones into the pile, the turnstile lifted, and voila, they were in—free to enjoy the circus all they wanted for as long as they wanted. *Forever, I suppose,* she figured. She checked behind her. The lineup was getting longer. She wondered if it was always this busy. It was certainly busier than the kingdom gate.

An older gentleman standing at the table reviewing his forms seemed to be suffering somewhat. Sweat collected and beaded on his brow. "Hurry it up!" said another, which only aggravated the old man.

Stupid me. I belong here. I wish I didn't, but I'm not good enough for the kingdom, especially not now. Pipiera hung her head and waited as the squabbling continued.

Finally, she was next in line, until she wasn't. "Hey!" she yelped as a tall figure dressed in a black hoodie grabbed her arm and pulled her away from the lineup.

"Stop it! You're hurting me." But the hooded creature continued to drag her along till they were safely out of earshot from any rebel soldiers. He pressed her against the wall and shook her. "What are you doing here?"

"I belong here." Pipiera was surprised by her own defiant response.

"No, you don't."

Well, that's a degrading remark for him to say, Pipiera thought, *suggesting I don't even belong here!* Then another thought struck her.

"Wait, do you know me?"

The hooded figure became hoodless.

As if that helps. She shook her head. Although he was slightly familiar, she did not recognize him. So, how might he know her?

"You..." He glanced around to ensure no one was paying attention. "You are my sister."

"What?" She stared at his face, his eyes, his slightly pointed nose, his almost egg-shaped head. *There's no way I'm related to that!* "But you're so, er… tall."

He looked impatient. "You've got to get me outta here," he pleaded.

Obviously, this was not a typical family reunion. There was no time for hugging and catching up. Her eyes narrowed skeptically. "Why did you come here in the first place?" She doubted she was related to this being.

"Some ancient guy cursed me. Now that guy is some kinda big shot, has a big role in the kingdom, and I'm stuck down here."

"A likely story. Now let go of me before I call the guards."

"No! You're not getting it."

"What's there to get?"

"Look," he said, inviting her to sit to hear him out while reluctantly releasing his grip on her forearms.

Pipiera hesitated. Then, realizing she had nowhere to be in any hurry, she sat down to entertain this guy's line of thinking. She reminded herself that she had just learned not too long ago, by accident, that she even had a brother. Could this possibly be him? In the short time since learning of his existence, she had pictured him to be kind and smiley, gentle and polite, fun-loving and protective of her. This guy clearly did not fit the profile. She had to admit though, if her true brother was not a kingdom citizen, then he must be somewhere in the rebel environment. She also admitted that at one point, before all this crazy capture business, she had been determined to find him and rescue him. She turned her eyes suspiciously to his. She would be cautious, but she would hear him out.

"Okay, go on," she said, more patience in her voice now, acknowledging to herself there was a possibility this might be the brother she had never met. *Yuck, I hope not though.*

"Well, there's not a lot to the story. Basically, my journey was cursed right from the get-go."

"Cursed? How?"

"A great ancestor of mine…" He paused, his face becoming stern before continuing. "An ancestor of *ours* cursed us, all of us, everyone in our family line. You included."

Pipiera was intrigued but suspicious and doubtful. She didn't like the way his eyes suggested she should know better and urged him to provide more relevant info, but he didn't have more to give, claiming the backstory did not matter.

"Well, you're right," she said, "it doesn't matter. You, dear boy, were responsible for your own tour, just like everybody else, so don't go blaming some old guy who cursed you hundreds of years ago!" Pipiera stood up. She'd had enough of this guy. "I've lost my place in line because of you." She turned to the lineup and sighed. It was long. She'd have to go to the back and wait again.

"Lost your place in line? Are you crazy? Stupid? You should be thanking me. I saved you from your precious place in line."

"You know nothing about me!" Pipiera shouted.

"I know enough. I know a great deal more than you. You hardly journeyed, and yet you lived out your days refusing to enter the kingdom, playing out front, jumping around like you were already a citizen. But you're not. And look, sissy, now you're here. You had it made, but you blew it." His whispered scolding and finger pointed in her face only made Pipiera cower and slither against the wall. Teardrops fell.

He turned his back on her and started to walk away in disgust.

"Wait!" she cried. "I didn't deserve to be there. I hurt them so much." She looked up at him. "I was waiting for my parents, so we could go in together."

"Yeah, they would've liked that." It was a mean grumble. Then he sat down beside her. "I've been waiting here for my son, hoping I could find a way to tell him *not* to come here. That monstrous dragon's been after him ever since I arrived; I know that much."

He unzipped a pocket in his pants and pulled out his stone,

a name etched upon the small, hard rock. He allowed Pipiera to glance at it before he returned it to his pocket and zipped it up. "I won't give it up, not here anyway. Curse that Dimietris anyway."

Pipiera was shocked to hear that name. "Megalos?" she was afraid of the answer.

"Yes, Megalos Dimietris. The guy you've been hanging around."

"No. No. Megalos is the greatest being I know. He's like a father to me. More than a father. He's my family, my best friend. I look up to him!" She hung her head. "And now I've disappointed him."

"You're so full of guilt, you're pathetic."

Pipiera leaped to her feet. "And you're so full of anger, you disgust me." She realized suddenly this had to be Frank. She had learned her brother held a tight grip to the darkness of anger. *Oh my gosh!* She grabbed him and hugged him fiercely, "You *are* my brother." He held her gently and cradled her head into his neck.

"I guess we never had the chance to duke it out as brother and sister before," he said, to which she laughed and cried at the same time.

"So, this means Matthew is your son?"

"Yes, do you know him? You haven't met him, have you? Nah, how could you?" Frank gasped. "He's all I think about. He's the reason I won't commit. He's the reason I wait here, watching in case he arrives. I know he's a target."

Pipiera nodded. "He is a target. I know that. But you're wrong about Megalos. Megalos has gone to great lengths to save Matthew, to keep him on track. Besides…" She switched to a teasing tone. "Your son is a brat. You know that, right?"

"So you *have* met him! But how… and why?"

Convenient, she thought. *He ignored my sisterly tease.* "When we got the message he was off track, I was put in charge of the plan to fix it."

"What? You? Why you?"

"Well, er, hmm… that I could never figure out. Why me? I donno. I'm not in any of those departments, you know, the groups that fix such things. The authoritarians and that team that intervenes."

"I've heard some pretty rough stories, kingdom interventionists up against rebel interference guys."

"Yeah." *Sounds like he knows more about these things than I do. Is that possible?* "How do you know so much?"

"Uh, I hear things."

"But how? I don't get it."

"I've made a few, er, friends. They keep me informed."

"Who are they? Why would they help you?"

"Well, just one bloke actually. Kasartha. He checks in on Matthew for me from time to time. I keep him informed on what I overhear the others say about 'im, and he tells me what's going on over there, with my family. He's kind of a loner."

"No. Not Kasartha! You can't trust *him*."

"Hey, lady, I've been around here much longer than you. I know who I can trust and who I can't. You think I would have survived this long if I couldn't?"

"I'm older than you, remember? I've actually been around longer. I know your creepy Kasartha friend is a fiend, and my Megalos is genuine. *He's* our family. He's on our side."

"Yeah, so why are we both here?" He could tell his question stunned her. "Look, we can settle this once and for all. Let's go tell the guards we want to chat with Kasartha. Depending on who we ask, they won't suspect anything. I meet regularly with him."

"You trust the guards?" Pipiera felt sad for her newfound brother. *He's been so totally deceived.* No doubt about it, his stern jaw and steely eyes meant serious business. *Geez, at least I hope he's the one who's deceived and not me.*

She stood tall and muscled her chin as high as it would go. "Kasartha's not here," she spoke confidently to prove she was in fact the more knowledgeable one. "I saw him in the weeds on the shore of the River of Times. On the *other side*."

Frank eyed her cautiously then yanked her arm tight. He pulled her toward a nearby rebel soldier, one who he had learned to trust. The soldier laughed at Frank's request. "The bloke's a goner," he said, pointing his rifle toward the exit on the far end of the courtyard where Kasartha's body lay crumpled and motionless. "Go ahead and check it out if you don't believe me." Then the soldier chuckled some more and commented on how Kasartha's death had been quite the show. "Too bad you missed it, Frankie." Then he cast a smirk and evil gaze Pipiera's way a little too long for her and Frank's comfort.

Pipiera burrowed her head into Frank's chest to escape the moment.

Must have been brotherly instinct—Frank wrapped his arms around her protectively and held her tight as the pair scurried back to the wall, the place with the opening to the courtyard, fitting for vision by a singular eye. Frank peered first and choked at the sight of a lump, all crumpled up in the prickles in the distance. It was a body, could easily be Kasartha. His instincts on high alert, he knew it was indeed Kasartha, the only being he came to trust. "There's no coming back from the second death," he whispered, his voice hinting a quiet distraught.

Pipiera pushed Frank aside to see for herself. She gasped, not at the mystery of Kasartha's body in the courtyard, which was alarming enough, but because she caught a glimpse of Megalos standing in the midst of it all, arms wide open, seeming to enjoy a thick layer of black fog that was blowing across the courtyard.

Could it be possible? My own Papah Megs cursing me and Frank and maybe even Matthew? No, I won't believe it. It can't be true!

Nevertheless, she was horrified that her brother might be right.

CHAPTER SIXTY-EIGHT
I'm Coming With!

In the Town of Havensight

EACH CELL IN his body grumbled miserably. Laying stiff like a boulder, Matthew strived to wriggle around but his freezer-burned brain wouldn't accept any such command. Something was wrong. His body was a prison and he was its captive. *I'm stuck in here. Who pushed me? I've got to get out!*

Working up a fruitless groan, he caught a glimpse of a broad backside with enormous wings walking away—right through the wall. "Wait! Wait!" Matthew tried to scream, but his lips barely quivered. The man disappeared. Determined to follow him, Matthew squirmed hard till he broke loose. "Jump!" he told himself, then "hey, I'm here. Wait for me!" he called out. It surprised Matthew that he too could literally pass through the wall. He glanced back and noticed his mom coming into the room, white-faced with her hand cupped over her mouth. *Well, someone is with her, so that's okay,* he thought and turned to keep going. He needed to follow Jophiel.

It all came flooding back. Kasartha was in trouble. Penney, Pipiera, whatever her name was, she was also in trouble. Something odd was going on, and it concerned him. *Dad, I haven't found you yet.*

"Wait!" he hollered again. This time Jophiel glanced back.

"I'm coming with you," Matthew said.

"What's your timer say?"

"My timer? Oh, uh, dunno."

"Look." Jophiel pointed above Matthew's head. Most of the pile in the sand clock was in the lower half. Jophiel shook his head. "You don't have enough. You need to go back now. If you run out, you *cannot* go back. Capiche? Besides, you don't want to go where I'm heading!"

Who cares about a timer thing? "I'm coming with you. I've seen it all. Don't ya know? I've traveled the universe umpteen times now."

"Crap, another earthling who thinks he's supernaturally needed," Jophiel mumbled. He grabbed Matthew's arm, and off they went, at least ten times faster than Matthew had ever experienced with Kasartha. "You ain't seen nothing yet, kid!"

The speed at which they flew surprised Matthew, but he supposed, once again, it really shouldn't. Nothing should surprise him anymore.

In mere moments they were approaching the rebel courtyard, Jophiel finding it awkward to locate a safe spot to land due to a black fog that moved about, attempting to block them. Matthew's head also felt foggy. *Where in the dickens are we, and how did we get here so fast?*

They found a large dead stump to hide behind, although Matthew wondered why Jophiel was being so secretive. After all, the black fog cloud was now practically glued to their behinds. Eyes plastered on all sides, it reached out and attempted to snatch Matthew more than once. He stuck as close as possible to Jophiel.

The courtyard was empty except for the large man with his arms raised in the middle. As the man turned 360 degrees, trickles of light emanated from his body, then streams of it, till it became hard to see the man himself.

"He made it!" Jophiel exclaimed. "Megalos made it," he whispered to Matthew, as though that should have made Matthew cheer. Jophiel scanned the courtyard. "Pipiera must be here somewhere."

Matthew was nervous and preoccupied. The fog was armed with several sets of groping arms. *Get lost, would ya?*

Jophiel jabbed Matt and told him to focus.

"Maybe my dad's here." Matthew scanned the outer walls of the rebel kingdom where shadows of bodies crunched against the wall, several with eyeballs glued to the center of the courtyard. A stench was evident and quickly grew to be unbearable. Even Matthew knew exactly what that meant. The outline of the dragon's head and shoulders appeared. "Those tiny arms blow me away," Matthew whispered, only to be shushed and jabbed again by Jophiel.

"You should not get comfortable with that presence," Jophiel scolded. "Now stay quiet, and do as I say."

Seriously? "Uh, which presence, dude? Mr. Googly Hands behind us or the raunchy, stinky space beast?"

"I liked you better when you were stunned and quiet!" Jophiel wished he hadn't brought the sarcastic and foolish boy along.

The light cast by Megalos made it easier to see whatever was about to happen as the dragon and Megalos's voices boomed.

"We meet again, Megalos Dimietris." The dragon spoke his name slowly, letting spittle fly.

I can't believe Kasartha calls this guy "Uncle," Matthew thought.

He hardly knew Megalos, but having to be so close to the dragon's breath made him think no one should have to suffer that. He noticed the outline of the dragon's tail waving in the distance. "He's one big sucker," Matthew whispered, quickly returning Jophiel's fierce gaze, meant to silence him. He didn't want another jab.

"State your business. You are disrupting my courtyard. Be quick. Unless, of course, you're here to beg for your position back, hmm?"

"His position back?" Jophiel couldn't help but blurt out his surprise.

Megalos didn't entertain the dragon. "I'm here to pick up a prisoner. A prisoner your guards have taken and have no right to hold."

The dragon rubbed his chin.

Again, those short arms, they kill me.

"And why are you here alone? Where is your Othis and your army? Seems kind of unusual."

Again, Megalos didn't bite. "The prisoner you hold is one of my descendants. Release her."

"Oh my, aren't we a boss. You don't have any descendants. Do I need to remind you why?"

"I have adopted descendants. Release her."

"Oh goodness, Dimietris, you mean *him,* do you not?"

"Him? Oh, oh, this isn't good." Jophiel jabbed Matthew as if he too should be alarmed.

At that, the dragon ordered Franklin to be released. The blob of black fog raced inside the rebel gate. In no time, out came Frank, surrounded by rebel soldiers forking him into the center of the courtyard, pushing him down till he lay flat at Megalos's feet.

"Dad?" Matthew exclaimed. Jophiel cupped his hand over Matthew's mouth and held him tight.

CHAPTER SIXTY-NINE
WITHOUT PIPIERA

In the Rebel Courtyard

MATTHEW SQUINTED SO hard his eyes hurt. His heart and mind ached to race out and grab his dad. *Yes, that's him! There he is, right there. I found you, Dad, I found you!*

"He's done his time, I suppose," the dragon said to Megalos. "He won't commit. So, he's yours. I'll let him go. You needn't have come in person, but now, no more delay. Off you go."

Is he free? Matt wondered. *Was he a prisoner? Can he come home now? Back to us?*

Megalos stood firm, he didn't budge. In fact the light streams emanating from his presence became even brighter and farther reaching. His brilliance enabled Matthew to see more details. He was horrified at the sight of his late father's drained face and thin, scraggly body. *My gosh, he's lost in his own clothes. That's his Sunday suit, the one mom buried him in. But where are his shoes?*

Hearing the tiniest alarm, Matthew looked up at his sand clock. Only a dozen or so crystals were left to fall. He wondered if he should grab his dad and get back to Havensight right away. They could all be a family again, couldn't they?

"I'm not here for Franklin," Megalos said.

"And here we go…" Jophiel had to hold Matthew back with both arms as the determined lad squirmed to break free.

I'm here for you, Dad, I'm here!

Jophiel calmed Matthew down and assured him the best thing for him and his dad was to remain still and quiet, at least for the moment.

"But I will take him," Megalos insisted.

"Whew!" Matthew sank into Jophiel's arms. "Thank heavens," he whispered. *Megalos, you just became my new best friend.* Then Matt started to feel dizzy and hot. There was way too much he couldn't understand, and he became overwhelmed.

"Pipiera," Megalos said, commanding her release. Jophiel was hopeful there could be no charges against her. He watched attentively, holding Matthew tight, the boy's body floppy and exhausted due to his struggle.

The dragon unleashed a long, eerie hiss at Megalos, followed by a rub of his chin. "Hmm… You arrived as a very resentful fella, as I recall." His neck arched and stretched like a snake in the grass till his nostrils neared Megalos's face. "You still owe me, Dimietris, the infamous gatekeeper. Hmm… you snatched the descendant line from one of my very own. What shall I do to make you pay?" He let out an annoying hissing laugh.

Megalos took a moment before he responded. "All has been put away. No longer do I have any darkness within. No anger, no wrath, no malice, and no slander. The king has forgiven—"

"The king's in charge of his kingdom," the dragon said, "and I'm in charge of mine!" He jiggled his head back and then calmed his voice. "You have so-called relations present right here, right now, eh, Dimietris? Listening. Witnessing. Do they know about your curse, directed right at them?"

Pipiera let out a gasp, then covered her mouth with both hands. She had been watching the entire scene unfold through a tiny spyhole that someone, quite possibly Franklin, had carved in the rebel wall. Still inside the rebel gate but not having gone through the registration process, she was free to run into the courtyard but decided to remain in place, still taking it all in. *Franklin was right*, she thought. *Megalos did leave a curse behind him. For me, even. He cursed me too!*

"I've paid my dues," Megalos said. "Now, hand over Pipiera. And I command you to take Matthew Mackenzie off your target list."

Target list? Matthew tried desperately to keep his attention sharp, but his body felt so heavy, his brain so sleepy.

"You command me nothing. I target who I please." The dragon's eyes flickered with blood-red flashes.

"I am loyal to my king. He has wiped my slate. You no longer have charges against me," Megalos added.

Furious, the dragon blasted flames at Megalos, who stood firm other than turning his head so the dragon's fiery, foul breath wouldn't enter his mouth.

Pipiera ran out from inside the rebel walls and into the shadows of the courtyard. Jophiel was elated to see her in the distance and inadvertently dropped Matthew, the fall shaking the boy out of his stupor.

The dragon cleared his throat, a warning signal that caused Pipiera and Jophiel to freeze in place. Franklin continued to lay still and weak at Megalos's feet while Kasartha continued to lay as if dead off to the side. Matthew twisted his face in weary frustration.

"But you are still guilty without the curse, my dear Dimietris." Even the air stood still waiting for the dragon to reveal his accusation.

"What could the charge possibly be?" Jophiel whispered while picking Matthew up off the ground.

"Just how long has Miss Pipiera been hanging around your kingdom courtyard? Hmm, Megalos? How long? And while you're calculating that, did she, by any chance, enter and commit? Did she?"

"No," Megalos replied calmly.

"Decades of no. That's all you can say, isn't it? So, she is not, in fact, a kingdom citizen and presumably not interested in *your* kingdom. If she was, she would have handed over her stone by now."

Megalos remained silent, waiting for his accuser to continue.

"You blocked her!" the dragon said. "If it weren't for you, she would have entered long ago, possibly upon her arrival. But that did not happen. You, dear Megalos, blocked her. And that is a most *delicious* charge. You see, just before your little advent today, your dear little girl was about to toss in her stone, to *me*. But then you made such a scene."

Pipiera unzipped her pocket and reached deep within. Phew, her stone was still there, still warm and soft and deeply protected. She was appalled at the suggestion that her Papah blocked her.

Matthew felt Jophiel's grip tighten, displaying his displeasure at the proceedings.

"The penalty is three hundred years. Three decades times ten. Three hundred. That's the going rate. Correct me if I'm wrong. Am I wrong, Dimietris?"

The dragon was a bit outrageous with the penalty and cocky talk, Matthew thought, but what did he know?

Megalos remained silent. He had convinced the authoritarians she hadn't entered on account of him, wanting to protect her by moving the risk of danger from her to him. After all, he had made that curse long ago, and she was impacted. It was the least he could do. He was careful not to sigh. He needed to remain firm, confident, and kingly.

"No!" Pipiera shouted. "It was me. It was my decision not to enter and mine alone."

Delighted at her outburst, the dragon kept his fiery gaze fixed on Megalos. "Ah, then I can charge *her* for guilt and shame. She admitted it through her actions and now by her words. She's not a citizen, so she cannot make the loyalty claim as you do, can she?"

If Megalos could have melted in sorrow on the spot, he would have. But he stood strong and firm, silently asking for help from his king. The beast was in his right to accuse her.

Rebel soldiers emerged from the thick, dark cloud to capture Pipiera. They escorted her farther into the courtyard, shuffling in unison so as to not deform the perfect circle they had surrounded her with.

"We've got to get her out of here," Jophiel whispered.

"Uh, yeah, and my dad!" Matthew was annoyed that no one gave his dad much attention. "He deserves to be rescued. I'm not leaving here without him."

Jophiel nodded. "It sounds like they just freed him, so chill. But I will take him with me. You, young sir, are going back to Havensight."

Matthew looked at Jophiel in frustration. "Seriously? This is like some kind of stupid game."

"It's no game, Matthew. Strict laws govern our divide."

"To divide what?"

Jophiel shushed Matthew again. He wanted to make things clearer for Matthew, but knew that was not advisable if he was to continue with his earthly journey, which was the most current plan. "We don't have much time, we need to get you back," was all he said.

A few more crystals of sand had dropped into the lower chamber of Matthew's sand clock.

Determined to save his dad, Matthew broke free of Jophiel's hold and hollered to him. He could not wait another second. None of this made sense. He just wanted to hug his dad and get him safely back to their home, to him and his mom in Havensight. They could be a family again. *Including Karo, of course, I guess.*

Still on the ground, Frank goggled cautiously, thrilled to hear his son's voice. Then Frank scrambled to his feet and ran toward his charging son.

Matthew had been hoping for a moment like this nearly every night for the past five plus years. In fact, he'd dreamed about it so many times he almost couldn't believe it was happening, him and his dad together again. He ran faster, but it felt like he couldn't get to his dad fast enough. *Why is this taking so long? I'm running and running and running...*

With black foggy patches looming, he tripped over something and went head over heels. He scrambled to get back up, only to notice he had tripped over a body, which lay heavy and motionless. "Oh, bogus. Kasartha!" Matthew didn't think his heart could beat any faster, but it did. *Kasartha saved me when I was down and out. I can't just leave him. He didn't leave me alone on that shore.*

"Kasartha. Buddy." He stood up and glared at the dragon. "What did you do? Did you kill him? Really? He worked so hard to please you, but you didn't even notice him. Some uncle you are."

Matthew's rant brought a crooked grin to the dragon's face, which halted Frank frozen in his tracks.

Pipiera peered around one of her captors' helmets. She too felt a shivering wave of horror. Was Matthew so attached to Kasartha that he would challenge the dragon?

Jophiel caught her attention and motioned for her to check out Matthew's sand clock. Only three crystals of sand left! If Matthew didn't get back to Havensight to join his flesh and bones, he would die his first death.

Matthew felt the danger of the frozen silence. Glancing back in hope of support, he saw Jophiel looking extremely uncomfortable. Much worse was the glare of horror in his dad's eyes, which were glued upon him. Megalos lowered his head.

"What did I do?" Matthew whispered. He had a feeling he might have just blown the whole operation. *Okay, stay calm,* he reassured himself, *I just have to get out of here now with my dad. That's all I need to do. Focus.*

"So convenient to have so many witnesses, my dear young boy," the dragon said. "You are loyal to my nephew, which means you are loyal to his family, yes? So, you and your auntie shall stay here at my gate's entrance. And Dimietris, enough of this. Off you go!" The dragon's grin was wide and sickening. "Two potentials for the shaft. Thank you, Dimietris. Always a pleasure doing business with you. Now get out of my space!"

My auntie? Who the heck is he talking about? Matthew stole a quick glance around and got his answer: Pipiera. She was his aunt. *Huh. Who'd a thought?*

"I'm not leaving without my son or my sister," Frank said firmly.

"Well, well..." The dragon chuckled, returning his attention to Megalos. "Looks like you made a fruitless trip. They're *all* staying now."

"Let the three of them go in exchange for me," Megalos commanded.

"No!" Pipiera shouted. "Do not accept that offer!" She signaled with her finger to Matthew.

Does she want me to jump over something again? he wondered, a puzzled look on his face. But no more signals came. Matthew felt sick to his stomach. *Think, think, think! I just messed this up. It's all my fault, all of this.*

He gaped angrily at Kasartha's lump of a body. *No, it's not my fault, it's yours!* He couldn't hold back. "You got me into this. This is all because of you! You're a liar, and I don't feel sorry for you. Not anymore!" As soon as Matthew released those words, he felt a sense of freedom. "Yer just playing dead," he declared. "I can tell. Doesn't matter. As far as I'm concerned, you are dead. Dead, dead, dead. Dead to me!"

Matthew peeked at Pipiera. *Oops, I made a scene.* But she was grinning in approval.

Feeling empowered, Matthew glared at the dragon. "Let go of me. Do you hear me? I belong to the king." Where had that latter part come from? *That felt so good, so right!* "And by the way, I'm taking my dad. He's free. You said so yourself."

Now it was Megalos's turn to crack a grin. "Well, then, I think we're through here." He turned to his people. "It's time to go. Shall we?"

"Hold on just a minute," the dragon blurted, pointing to Pipiera. "She is not free to go, not by law."

Pipiera was inspired by Matthew's boldness and shocked at the same time. She had no idea of the real power her teaching message to Matthew would bring one day. She stood firmly. "You shall let go of me as well," she declared.

"Really?" the dragon replied sarcastically.

"Really," Pipiera said. "I'm letting go of you!"

"You still owe me." Uncle bellowed before blowing tongues of fire, knocking both Megalos and Matthew off their feet. The fiery blow distracted the rebel soldiers who had encircled Pipiera, but not enough for her to make a run for it.

Frank ran to Matthew and held him tight. Matthew felt a chaotic whirlwind and watched a massive flurry approach. He felt claws grab him, lifting him, his dad, and Megalos. It was Jophiel. "Rad!" Matthew was overwhelmed by the power in his lift and his swiftness. Jophiel had swooped in to grab those who were free to go. In the blink of an eye, Matthew, Frank, Megalos, and Jophiel were safely out of the rebel courtyard and traveling into another atmosphere, Jophiel carrying two passengers and Megalos hanging on Jophiel's side, expressionless.

"Oh, Dad!" Matthew was breathless as he held on tight, his eyes glued to his father's gaunt face. His dad shushed him and smiled. "Everything's gonna be okay now, son. I promise."

Pipiera wasn't with them, but Megalos knew they had to hurry. He saw there were no sand pieces left in Matthew's clock. Whether they could make it or not depended on Jophiel getting them to Havensight in a flash. Megalos could not dare command that they go back to get Pipiera, not when Matthew's future was at stake. He had no choice—Matthew was the priority. They would rescue Pipiera later, as soon as possible.

"Dad, we're going home!" Matthew was ecstatic.

CHAPTER SEVENTY
DID I SEE A GHOST?

In the Town of Havensight

MARNIE WAS THANKFUL for Dr. Alexien. The two of them, hands locked together, remained kneeling at Matthew's bedside for over fifteen minutes. Marnie rested the side of her head close to her son's chest. Marnie could not feel a heartbeat, but Dr. Alexien swore she could feel one, ever so slightly. Dr. Bonneville did not disguise his disgust at Dr. Alexien's behavior. The machines had already been turned off, and he had declared Matthew deceased over twenty minutes ago. *There is nothing further we can do, Mrs. Mackenzie,* rang over and over in Marnie's head. The fact that he could never get her name right reduced his credibility, so it was much easier to place hope in Dr. Alexien, who would not give up. *It's like she knows something.* Marnie wanted to believe she really and truly did.

A warm breeze swooshed by. Looking up for the briefest of moments, Marnie was certain she saw her deceased husband, Frank, put their beloved son Matthew into his body so tenderly as if he were laying him in his bed and tucking him in. Marnie sat up immediately. "Frank?" she whispered.

Dr. Alexien stood up gleefully. "A beat! I get it! There's a beat now!" She motioned for the nurses to get back into the room, instructing the monitors be hooked up immediately. Dr. Bonneville simply watched from a distance, shaking his head, and could be heard mumbling "not again."

Marnie got closer to Matthew's face, and sure enough she felt a slight exhale from his nostril. She jumped up and down. "Yes, yes, yes!" Again she bent over her son and called his name a few more times. She could not have been more ecstatic. Sure enough, the heart monitor registered a beat.

A weak whisper came from Matthew. Marnie leaned in.

"Dad," he said, his voice barely a whisper. "Dad?"

"It's okay, son. Mom's here."

"No! No. I want to stay with you, Dad." Matthew's words may have been quiet, but they were clear and full of passion and determination.

"He may be having a vivid dream," Dr. Alexien said. "Let him work through it. There'll be plenty of time to fill him in later. Let's give him a few moments."

Marnie wiped some reddish-brown wisps of hair off his forehead and kissed it. She whispered to him that he was safe and that everything was going to be okay. Matthew drifted off into a deep sleep again, only this time his heartbeat grew stronger with each breath.

Marnie couldn't stop the swirls in her mind. Had she actually just seen the ghost of her dead husband? "Oh, Frank!" she whispered. "You haven't left us. Oh, my dearest, you *are* taking care of us!" Tears continued to wet her face, only this time due to indescribable thankfulness.

Dr. Bonneville strode into the room. Wanting to take charge, he asked Marnie to leave, so her son could get some rest. He said they would monitor his vitals to be sure he couldn't "slip away" again. Marnie hesitated until Dr. Alexien nodded that it was okay.

Alan Pine had remained in the hallway the entire time. He

escorted Marnie back to the family waiting room and sat down with her. They discussed what a miracle Matthew's recovery had been. He was pleased to see Marnie actually speak from a place of joy instead of the dreary grey reality she had adopted as of late.

CHAPTER SEVENTY-ONE
GOODBYE AGAIN

TEARS STREAMED DOWN Frank's face. "I really let them down," he squeaked, staring at his son lying in the hospital bed after his overwhelmed wife left the room. "She looked so, so tired."

"She is," Jophiel confirmed.

"That didn't help," Frank muttered as he cast another glance at the oversized dude with wings. He had never met anyone like Jophiel before, but somehow felt he owed the guy a deep, and truthful, explanation. His long-time adopted emotion of hard anger was churning into mushy guilt. He had been wrong about Megalos, the other towering presence hovering behind him. *I can't face him, not just now anyway.* And Penney was Pipiera, Megalos Dimietris's beloved friend. What's more, she was his sister, the girl he had heard about but never dreamed he'd get to meet. Now she was a prisoner, not just trapped in the courtyard of the lost, but actually accused and in danger of being imprisoned. He knew too well the challenges she would face. *He's gotta be cursing me all over again. How can I possibly ask Megalos for forgiveness?*

"Uhrrrrrgh, that Kasartha, I can't believe I actually trusted him." Frank forced a quick look at Megalos, hoping for a signal of assurance that Megalos would know he was truly sorry and that his expressed words would be received as the start to an apology, or perhaps even justification, for the hatred he had harbored for so long.

Megalos stood firm, his expression unchanging.

"Obviously," Frank said sheepishly, "I need to explain in detail. I owe you a big apology." He kept his eyes on his son. "I do thank you. All of you. Everyone in this room. I didn't deserve any of you."

"That's how the kingdom works," Megalos replied, although his mind was on Pipiera.

Frank burst into sobs. He didn't really understand Megalos's comment, but he was full of remorse and shame, though he felt empty, like someone had turned him upside down and dumped his insides, including all of his thoughts, right out. His guts felt like they were all over the floor. He thought of his little family, his boy lying there fighting for his life, his distraught wife, now in another room, hanging on to hope. "I got it all wrong," he whispered.

"In so many ways," Jophiel whispered, but Megalos stomped on Jophiel's foot to keep him from saying any more.

Frank was thankful for his rescuers, Megalos and the big dude. The room was full of great awe, and he intended to hang on to that feeling, along with love and forgiveness. And grace, he hoped.

Matthew and the doctors and nurses were oblivious to the threesome as they milled around. Jophiel wanted to hang out a bit longer, indicating he needed to ensure Matthew wasn't going to attempt another surprise pop out and chase after them.

The comment made Frank chuckle. "Yup, that's my son," he said. Then he turned and faced Megalos. "Forgive me, Megalos. I cursed you for decades. I blamed everything on you. But I get it now. I think I do, anyway. I realize I blew it. I'm so grateful you never gave up on me!" He hung his head. "I'm so sorry I listened to and became friends with Kasartha. I really thought he was pulling for me."

"Doubts and suspicion aside," Jophiel said, "I think Kasartha's the one with the most regrets."

Megalos choked back a tear, unsure why he felt remorse over Kasartha. Plus, he couldn't put a troubling doubt aside. "I think so too," was all he could mumble.

Three nurses were tending to Matthew, and he seemed to be settling well into his body. Jophiel decided it was time to leave, to return to the kingdom. He held up the sand clock with a sign of victory, happy they had conquered within the allotted time. His expressed look at Megalos was a definite, "Wouldn't want to come that close again!"

Megalos grinned. The kingdom was always chasing passages of time. It was the authoritarians' way of life. Everything had to happen in perfect timing.

"Wait!" Frank exclaimed. "Is he gonna be okay? I can't just leave him again."

"He'll be fine. Eventually. He needs to mature though. He's got a lot of storms in front of him," Jophiel replied.

Frank considered what that meant, his face twisted with anxiety.

Sadly, Megalos agreed, they should get straight back to the kingdom. There they would deliver Frank, then gather with the authoritarians to reflect and strategize. This intervention was not over yet.

CHAPTER SEVENTY-TWO
FAMILY TIES

In the Rebel Courtyard

P IPIERA SURPRISED HERSELF with how quickly she turned to hatred, just like how the stone still deep in her pocket had turned black. Yet, she refused to give it up, to toss it in the pile behind the registry. She remained in the bleak corridor tucked in between the rebel wall and the registration desk, guarded by two goons shaped much the same as Kasartha. Instead of jumping in fields of applauding flowers, she sat huddled in the place where she once conversed with her brother and spied into the courtyard through a peephole he had carved.

Him, the brother she never knew she had. Him, the one who had taken her place in the kingdom. *How I wish I never met you either.*

Yet she found comfort sitting where he had sat for so many long years, pining for his son to arrive. She wondered if Matthew had made it back to Havensight or if he might arrive one day soon. If so, to which gate will he arrive?

Pipiera had plenty of time for her mind to churn and ache. There was no shield to stop the negativity, the accusations, or the wild, imaginative cursing thoughts that flowed through her head in a continuous racing stream going around and around in circles. This was her prison, and she was too exhausted to escape.

The carnival behind the registration desk was always active, never a dull moment nor a quiet phase. Just run, run, run. Everyone went from one attraction to another. Why it appealed to so many and why they scrambled to get in puzzled Pipiera. However, she had to admit the aromas of the sweet concoctions were tempting, and the squeals of the crowds drowning in excitement aroused her curiosity. Wandering circus masters circulated about, handing out free tickets and vouchers, tossing them into the air and laughing as the crowds clambered about to pick them up.

Pipiera realized the difference between them and her. *They all want to be there. If I go in, it's not because I want to; it's because I have to. I'm not good enough to be where I want to go. It's not like I have a choice. And besides, they just left me.*

"I owe the dragon? Really? C'mon, like what? Please somebody tell me, what do I owe him? They just believed him... and... and they left." She shook her head in anger and sadness.

Pacing the inside wall, she felt the eyes of the rebel soldiers on her. They would ensure she didn't escape. She reimagined over and over what she saw with her own eyes, challenging her accusing thoughts to open-mindedness. Megalos, his arms stretched out. *Was he praising the king from this dark place, or was he being sneaky and in some type of partnership with the dragon? Perhaps Megalos owed the dragon, and he paid him off with me.* She was so torn. Never before had she felt so betrayed. She vowed, for her own protection, that she would never believe him again. Hope simply meant betrayal, she surmised.

She eyed the courtyard through her spyhole. *What's going on today?* Same as the other tenfold times she had checked. Greyish air, shadowy figures milling around. There had been no stench since that day, so she knew the dragon had left the rebel soldiers in charge. She particularly eyed the group of his agents, his so-called "nephews" high-fiving each other, tossing stones in the air for each other to catch. They commended and praised Kasartha for his fine work. "Yes, you Kasartha." She eyed him accusingly, assuming he couldn't see her through the wall. "You're going to pay for this." He had tricked them all. "The deluder faked his death. I bet he's done it umpteen times." She walked away from the wall. "I can't take it here!" she screamed, only to receive a few looks and laughs from rebel soldiers nearby.

She crouched against the inside of the wall. *Oh, Moolos, I can't hate you. How I miss you*, she admitted deep inside. A soldier came by offering crackers and a dirty glass half full of water. She shoved the fruitless circuit of her innermost thoughts down as far as they could go.

"Hey, I don't get it," he said. "You're mad at all your so-called friends, who left you here. I hope that wasn't your family." The look on her face was reply enough but he continued anyway, "Oh, geez, I'm sorry. I'm sorry they all left you. So, like, seriously, give them up. They left you, so now you need to leave them. Look…" He pointed beyond the registration desk. "There's good food in there and lots of friends. Make a new family. Why persist out here in such misery?"

She didn't respond, nor did she accept the snack he offered.

"Okay, have it your way," he said, strolling away. She knew she would have to take the bland, unclean food offering eventually. She was growing thin. Her knees were becoming narrower and tender to touch. There would be no more jumping even if she wanted. Her knees reminded her of Franklin. *If he could hold out here in this dark space for all those years, so can I.* She wondered how he must have felt when she walked in for the first time. *He recognized me as a member of his family. It must have been an exhilarating moment for him.* She thought more about his suffering. He had sat right where she was now, waiting for his son to arrive, so he could warn him not to register, not to fall for any of this. *Yet he himself had befriended Kasartha.* She shook her head and felt his pain, only to have it transform into anger. "Go figure. I spend decades hanging out at the kingdom gate, not ready to commit, and he's hanging out at this rebel gate not ready to commit. Now, he's there, likely being crowned this very moment as a kingdom citizen, and where am I? Right freakin' here! Some brother he turned out to be!" She sobbed yet again and wished she could close her eyes and disappear, float away into nothingness. That would be a better existence than this.

Someone sat down beside her and elbowed her side.

"Get lost!" she exclaimed, not caring who it was.

"I've wanted to hang out with you for a long time," the boy said. "Can we be friends? As long as you're here, we might as well." He jabbed her again, gentler this time, teasingly.

"I said, get lost, capiche?" She turned her back on him.

"I didn't mean for you to get hurt," he said, piquing her curiosity. He leaned back on his elbows. "I would love it if you could teach me how to jump like you do, 'cept you need a little more meat on those knees."

Pipiera whirled her head toward him in horror. "You!" she exclaimed. "How dare you talk to me!"

Kasartha grinned. When she didn't respond to what he believed to be his boyish charm, he got serious. "Look, we do what we have to do here. If you follow orders and do a good job, you don't have to—"

"Don't have to *what?*" She dared him to continue with his explanation. Why had he ruined her life, not to mention the lives of practically everyone she knew?

"Hey, hey, calm down. I'm just calling it as it is." He hung his head, deciding to ignore her glare. "As I was sayin', if you carry out a job, you can get outta here. Like, not spend your days hanging around here."

"And just what is that job? To ruin people's lives like you do?"

"What? No!" He sat up, full of pride. "I target as commanded. All commands are sanctioned. Well, most of 'em. Sometimes some of 'em, sometimes not. But basically, it's not a bad job. I've had worse, believe me."

Pipiera didn't want to hear any more.

"You should try working the elevator shaft; that prison's the worst," he mumbled grumpily.

She wasn't interested in a job there or hearing about what Kasartha did or what jobs he had done in the past. Totally disgusted with him, she decided to give him a piece of her mind. "You know, you off-roaded Matthew. Then there's a whole chain reaction after that, and because of *you*, I'm here."

"Uh, no, little girl…"

"Don't call me little girl."

"Okay, okay, touchy, geez. Okay, young lady, you're the only one who can get yourself here. No one else. We may carry out trickery and games of all sorts, but in the end, honey girl, it's all you." Kasartha leaned back against the wall. "Believe me, we can bring no one here unless they either commit or, like you, they display a lack of commitment for that…er…king up there."

Pipiera studied Kasartha's eyes.

Frustrated, he tried to make it clearer. "Like, either they add their living stone to Uncle's pile, or they keep it in their pocket and just, uh, hang on to it. Just sit on the fence. But do what you did, hang out in front of that there gate up there and refuse to go in? Do that for too long, and baby, you're up for grabs, I'm tellin' ya."

Pipiera didn't know how to defend herself. Choosing an offense was much easier. "You faked your own death!" She was still so astonished. How could he be so deceitful and do it so well? "And you're still at it. Deceit, deceit, deceit. You and your stinky dragon don't bother me." Pipiera wasn't sure how she got to be so brave in her talk. "You can leave now."

"Really?" He laughed and shook his head. "Okay, Matthew,

and yay, okay, Frankie. He didn't get it. But you, I thought *you* would know better." He pulled out a big orange along with a fresh beef sandwich from a backpack. "Here, it's on me."

"Not a chance," she replied, though she was so hungry. She couldn't help but sneak a peek at the tantalizing orange. *My favorite.* Not nearly as aromatic as what she was used to in the kingdom courtyard, but it was still inviting.

"Look, just because you eat this doesn't mean you like me. Come on, I bet you like this combination. It was Frankie boy's favorite. And look where he is now. It's not going to harm you."

She grabbed the sandwich, then the orange and peeled it ravenously. "What was Frank like when he was here?" she asked. Not because she liked Kasartha, but rather because she really wanted to know more about her brother, like what he did all day long when he was here.

"Much like you," he took a bite of his own sandwich. "Feisty, adamant he didn't belong, yet... " He munched away. "He was full of..."

"Full of what?"

Kasartha made funny motions with his long fingers "Evil thoughts! He let them take over his mind. Just like yer doing."

"I'm not doing that!"

"Okay. If you say so."

"And what if I am? What's it to you?"

He put his sandwich down. "Don't you get it? I can't believe you spent all that time up there and still so... so duh like."

She had no words and could only stare at him as he continued.

"You let all those thoughts in. You had a gatekeeper up there, but you didn't use him. You refused his protection!"

She still appeared dumbfounded, so he continued. "Look, here there is no gatekeeper. Symbolically, lots of ugly thinking lives here. They worm themselves in, and you have no way to kick those guys out. You haven't noticed?"

"Noticed what?"

"The keepers, the soldiers, all the workers here, they work to keep you in, not let you out. So, pressure builds and builds and builds... and your own thinking gets more... uh," he wiggled his fingers again, "evil. So you sign on and join up. Or," he glared at her, "you wise up and kick *them* out." At that Kasartha stood up and turned away, leaving Pipiera to contemplate her orange.

"Wait!" she called after him. "Why are you helping me?"

Kasartha's face transformed into a twist of emotions.

Is that hatred or might he actually be trying not to cry? Didn't matter what he was feeling, Pipiera pushed. She needed to hear his reasoning.

"Because I can tell. You will never commit," he choked out.

Suspicious at the twisted and all-sad-like facial expression he dished up, she scrutinized his body language carefully. *What's he getting at?* "So?" she said.

Kasartha said nothing.

She didn't flinch and kept up her glare. "I'm waiting."

He spilled. "Because once you were one of my very own. Can you blame a guy for wanting family around?"

CHAPTER SEVENTY-THREE
WHO'S TEACHING WHO?

THE STRUGGLE TO keep her mind and heart in check with each other was disputatious. *He's lying,* she told herself over and over, unable to shake the thought of her being a part of Kasartha's family. *Absolutely not true. No way. No how.*

On the other hand, it did explain why he toyed with Frank so much; he wanted him around. It could also explain why he was after Matthew. He wanted the boy to end up with him, in his world. Who wouldn't want that, to be together forever?

She peered out the spyhole. *There he is. Slapping hands and acting so tough with his colleagues.* "He is dangerous." Realizing she announced the declaration aloud, she quickly looked around to be sure none of the guards overheard. She sat again with her back against the wall, hugging her knees. Eager to release, she cupped her face to catch the pool of pent-up tears. Too many though, they overflowed. In no time, the drops turned the hard ground into a muddy mess. She twirled the murky clay with her finger. "Guess we're meant to be together," she sniffled, feeling sorry for herself. "I've made such a mess of my life. Huh, I've made you. Nothing but an ugly mess."

The clay mixture awakened, two tiny eyes glared at her, then four. "Good heavens!" Pipiera was startled and frightened. She jumped up and stepped away, careful not to step into whatever it was. "You're living!" She dared a closer examination, "And you're evil." It horrified Pipiera that it had been her own tears that made up this mixture. "Living stars, I made you....no, no, no!"

A guard edged closer.

She turned to face the wall. A hint of her reflection in a shiny block stared back at her. *Smarten up,* she scolded herself, *stop feeling sorry for yourself. Stay on track, get back to your mission.*

She looked behind her. The guard had strolled away.

Having that mission felt like my purpose. It was my purpose! I've never felt purpose before.

Yet another guard strolled in her direction.

I've got to get out of here and warn Matthew. She wondered if that were possible. How might she escape?

Oh, Papah Megs, will you ever receive me again? That seemed even less possible.

She whispered aloud, knowing Kasartha would never hear her, but she hoped somehow he could know. "I'll pray for you, Kasartha," she said. "If what you say is true, then you lost your descendants, all of them, to Megalos. You will never escape your pain. I wish things could have been different, but you can take solace in knowing Megalos watches over us."

The guard passed her and kept going.

She urged herself to switch gears, it was time to plan. What had Megalos told her countless times about new kingdom arrivals? *If I'm to be one, it'll serve me well to remember.* He said they had a comforting wisdom about them, that they shed the hard covering that had to be discarded. *Like your oranges,* he had said, *the good stuff is on the inside.*

She looked at the orange in her hand, the one Kasartha gave her. She peeled it, revealing the fruit and discarding the peel. Separating the pieces, she took a bite. *Ugh!* It was bitter. She threw it on the ground. "I suppose Papah Megs used the orange analogy because he knew I liked them so much." But in the kingdom, the fruit was ever so sweet, aromatic, and delicious. "Those new arrivals at the kingdom gate were only rarely bitter and angry, like I've been."

Pipiera wondered if the fruit inside of her was sour or sweet. Glancing back at the clay pile, its eyes fluttering to keep open, she guessed sour. It reminded her of Matthew's childhood dream, the image of the soldiers coming to get him, to take him away and cause him eternal harm. He was on the outside and needed to get safely inside his house, into his basement, the deepest, structural part of his dwelling. But it was full of men who wanted to kill him. He'd have to clear them out so he could get in and have a safe place to be. *Huh,* she thought, *who'da thought changing sour to sweet would be such a battle?*

A light bulb went off. "Whooo," she said, waving fists of victory. "I need to clear out my mind, so I can have a safe place to be. The place where I was created to be." She looked around. Thankfully, no one was watching her, nor could they tell what she was thinking. She sat back down, allowing her thoughts to settle back to Matthew's dream. "I'm just like him, and I didn't recognize it. I have fear too, I didn't even know I had it, fear that kept me from going through that gate, the gate Papah guards, *my* gate."

She paced quickly, wondering what to do with this illumination. "Matthew had a helper in his dream, a calm, bright figure. The king himself. And what had Jophiel told her? Make a detour when you meet a trouble spot—ask and wait for instruction, then keep going." She pursed her lips, then inhaled excitedly. "Oh my gosh, oh my gosh, I know what to do now. I know how to get outta here!"

Eyes closed, she reveled in how her chest rose, feeling satisfied from another deep inhale. *Focus.* She wanted to be real, with a personal and silent request. Stilling her breath and feeling the pounding of her heart, she invited the king to work within her, to clear out the enemy's destructive thoughts. Pushing out her breath and her face upward, a sunbeam glimmered in the distance. She smiled and continued. "Plus," she confessed, "I need to be better at gate keeping. I just wanna let the good in. Will you be my shield?"

She laughed as she thought of her Papah Megs. He would be so proud she had figured this out. He had once told her, in order to truly know the king, one had to pursue him. "I'm sorry," she whispered to her king. "Please, please forgive me. Please, I need your help to get into my own house, along with you. I know you are right behind me, so please join me in my home. And please go also in front of me, I need your help to squash and get the fear and guilt out once and for all. Will you remove them from me?"

She smiled and leaned the back of her head against the wall. Somehow, she knew she no longer had to worry. She knew where she belonged and had just accepted it. As for all this business with her current entrapment, it would sort itself out. She was confident of that. *Keep focused on the kingdom and the king, that's all that matters. Everything else will work out! How foolish I've been. I've known that my entire existence and never put it to work. Funny, I thought I was teaching Matthew, but it turns out he was teaching me.*

CHAPTER SEVENTY-FOUR
AIVY DOES A DANCE

In the Outer Courtyard of the Kingdom

MEGALOS MADE A pounding motion to his head with his fist. *I blew it*, he scolded himself over and over. *I should have known.* It was obvious to James and Roly, the two most concerned about his behavior, that he was hurting, and deeply.

Jophiel's few words over Kasartha's regret had twisted Megalos for days until finally James confirmed it. Kasartha was the long-ago forgiven by Megalos much prayed about father. The pa he once hated had been targeting his own family line, the very line the king took away once he made that dreaded commitment to the rebels. *He just couldn't overcome the evil; he hung onto it, like he'd lose himself if he let go. So opposite to the truth.*

Instead, the family line was given to Megalos, a precious gift. *All I had to do was watch over them and greet them upon their return. They were so blessed and so cursed at the same time.* Cursed by Megalos himself. He remembered it well. "I curse you and anyone or anything you ever create!" he had shouted in agony and disgust at his pa, seconds before the final blow. The curse had to be dealt with, the king told him gently. And so it was.

Megalos blamed himself for the kingdom's loss of Pipiera and thumped his head more between sobs. *Kasartha will do anything and everything in his power to keep her there. I should have seen this coming.*

The dragon's accusation haunted him. *I blocked her. Did I? And now I've just left her. I left her there with him! To figure it out all on her own. I abandoned her. I don't deserve her. I don't deserve any descendants of my own! I'm just a fool.*

Technically, James had declared, although loved and welcomed, Pipiera wasn't *legally* a member of the kingdom to lose.

That word made him shiver. *What does "technically," "legally," and "officially" have to do with anything?*

James checked in on Megalos daily, encouraging him that not all was lost. In each visit he found a way to gently, but firmly, remind Megalos to dare not leave his post again. The authoritarians forbade him to make another trip to that "other" gate. As far as Megalos could tell, Roly was put on watch to ensure that didn't happen. So, Megalos spent a lot of time alone, stewing in his lonely room atop the watch post.

As much as he knew, Pipiera's name had not gone through the Registrar of Rebels. *At least I have that to be thankful for. Hang in there, Pip.* Megalos groaned. He begged James to reconsider, to let him go back for another rescue attempt. He asked Othis to send his army out to collect her, and if not to please just check on her. Met with absolute no's all around, he relished in despondency.

The times were confusing. Even Jophiel stopped coming by, unable to take the sadness that streamed from his once-favorite inspirational hero. Megalos claimed he didn't miss the visits. After all, Jophiel had turned him down too.

When Megalos could remove himself from harmful emotions and painfully summed it all up, the same calculations prevailed. He nearly lost Frank, it appeared he had lost Pipiera, and who knew what would happen to Matthew. He looked out the window and witnessed Roly doing a superb job. Megalos contemplated an early retirement, which meant he would have to resign, no longer be in a watchful position over his descendants. *I've disappointed you, my King. I'm sorry.* He penned a resignation letter, folded it up, and stared blankly at the lush, gentle waves rolling in toward his beloved gate. One more good look before collapsing back to his bench.

Soundbites from below rose and swirled into his window. It was a fireball of commotion to say the least. Megalos couldn't tell what the root of it might be and he didn't bother to look. Despite the intrigue of it all, given his heavy heart and exhausted mind, he stayed put. The old Megalos would have spiraled down the staircase in no time to check it out. If it was caused by something not anticipated on his agenda, he had a responsibility to be in the know. Loud, excited voices chirped annoyingly. Then he heard Roly's yelp in the midst of it all. "Hey, Megs, get down here!"

Megalos stuffed his resignation letter into his trouser pocket and sauntered down. If a member of the authoritarians were among those making the commotion, he could hand deliver his letter right away.

Sure enough, it was Aivy excitedly brandishing a scroll with both arms waving about. She was so excited she jumped into Megalos's arms.

"What the hey?" *This is so unlike her.* He swung her around only to prevent himself from falling back. *Whew!* He placed her on her feet to stop the nonsense. He wondered how it was possible her tiny figure had nearly bowled him over, but then he caught a lightning flash of elation in her eyes. *Could it be she was bringing some good news about his Pip?*

"Yes, yes, yes!" She must have known what he was thinking. Springing away from his arms and waving the scroll, she danced around the courtyard. Megalos laughed for the first time since that dreaded day of the partially successful rescue attempt. Well, non-successful in his view.

"You have news?" If Aivy had a scroll, it would be a daily list of the new arrivals needing pickup arrangements and apprising her to get prepared with individual training plans and itineraries for each one. Aivy grinned and nodded.

"Really?" He looked at her with hope. "No! I mean, yes! Oh, come on, I can't stand the suspense."

She jumped up and down, screaming. "Yes!" She came closer to Megalos, so he could see the list of names along with detailed instructions and precise arrival timing for each. He held the scroll close to his face. "Oh, my." He started a merry dance with Aivy.

"She did it. She did it! She's coming home! She's coming home!"

Then Aivy stopped, left hand on her hip, right index finger scolding a wave. "Now, didn't James tell you to be patient? Didn't he say it would be best if she determined with her own will to come here, for real, for good this time? No jumpin' around, pardon the pun. She's going to be a citizen, Megs! Much better than any ol' rescue plan we could have schemed up."

Megalos was so relieved. "Yes, I guess James was right." His shoulders slouched. "I should have had more trust in the process."

"And patience," Aivy added.

"And patience," Megalos admitted joyfully.

Aivy smiled and burst into a little happy dance again. "Well, I gotta go. I have lots to do." She looked admiringly at Megalos. "It'll sure be nice to have the normal you back."

The nod he gave her was slight, but his appreciation was deep.

"It won't be long. I'll be arranging her pickup right away." Off she scampered back into the busyness of the kingdom.

Megalos felt so much anxiety, guilt, and sadness leave his body. "I shouldn't have doubted." Roly overheard and came closer to hear the rest. "But she's like my closest family member. Like my own daughter." The two hugged, and Roly urged Megalos to help him by getting back to work. Megalos was eager to do so, it would make the time go by faster till Pipiera came over the horizon, riding a wave toward him. Toward her new permanent and eternal home. The thought couldn't have pleased him more.

CHAPTER SEVENTY-FIVE
PIPIERA'S TURN TO WHISPER

In the Town of Havensight

"DO NOT, AND I mean do not, breathe a word of this to anyone!"

"I won't, I promise, Kasartha. I… I don't know how to thank you. I don't know why you did this for me, but I thank you." Pipiera steadied herself on Matthew's roof. "Ha! I never thought I'd see the day you'd be my escort," she added.

Kasartha hung his head, then raised it proudly. "I am what I am, and don't think that I'm suddenly on your side or anything. It's just you I helped. And just this once." Kasartha released her hand. "I trust you can get home on your own. You just have to call someone, right?"

She nodded, then narrowed her eyes and scrunched her nose. "Now, don't you go bothering Matthew anymore, you hear me?"

"All's fair. I just might," he warned and took a long look at her face before taking flight and disappearing down the highway toward a field of fresh lavender blooms.

She was astonished that the hurt she felt for Kasartha ran so deep. However, she did not like the sly grin on his face as he left. Pipiera hoped she wasn't being tricked again and reminded herself always, always to be on guard when outside the kingdom. After all, it was in Kasartha's best interest for Matthew to remain in his earth journey. That way the battle for loyalty could continue. Kasartha could still have a chance for a go at Matthew and possibly win.

Alone in the dark, with a view of Warmud Street, she whispered to her king. "Please do your work through me. I feel you want me to be here, to finish my mission." *The one and only one I've ever had,* she thought. *I've got to get this right!*

She snuck into Matthew's room and found him out cold on his bottom bunk, a side table full of prescription medications, half-full glasses of water, milk, and some kind of juice. Scattered on the floor where his arm flopped were piles of used tissues. An annoying, low-key buzz came from a transistor radio tucked under his bed. *Perfect, he's sound asleep.* She crept up close to watch him breathe. It felt surreal. It made her smile to realize that, yes indeed, she did have love and compassion for him. *Megalos was right. You're my Matthew, too.* She leaned in to whisper in his right ear, knowing he wouldn't remember much of what she'd say, so she'd have to be brief and to the point.

"Matthew," she whispered, "you are loved, you are wanted, you are needed, and you have a purpose. Be patient through it all. Be as faithful as you can. Work at it! It'll be worth it. I'll be waiting for you, and so will Megalos. The king, Matthew. Focus on our king, your king, and his kingdom. Stay focused, you hear me? That's all that matters."

She looked at him. He hadn't moved or twitched or anything, but that was okay. *Hmm… that wasn't so brief, was it?* She leaned in once again to sum it up, get it drilled into his heart and mind. "Focus on the king and his kingdom. The rest will follow."

Pipiera watched Matthew sleep so peacefully. "You're brave to be here. I'll keep an eye on you," she whispered. Turning to leave, she recalled the snide grin on Kasartha's face, that "I'm gonna get him yet" look. She bolted back to Matthew's ear.

"Listen, Matthew, and listen carefully! Those swordsmen in your night terror… you need to kick them out. Lean into him, the man, the true light standing behind you. Lean into him. He's your king. Enter your house together; you'll be safe. I promise. *Do not* let Kasartha get in there ever again! Please, please promise me that."

Despite a lingering mishmash of emotions, she was satisfied her work here was done, for the moment, anyway. *Okay, onward to Maggie and Charles.*

She stopped short when she heard her king speak. *It is time.*

No! I must continue! Her shouted thought was followed by an agonizing silence.

She sighed and challenged herself. What had she just shared with Matthew? That he must trust the king.

And so shall I. He's got this covered. He can handle what I cannot, and only he knows what we need. Pipiera knew instinctively she must obey and trust. It was time to come home, no delay.

Two escorts, neither of which were Jophiel, appeared instantly behind her.

CHAPTER SEVENTY-SIX
THE ARRIVAL

In the Outer Courtyard of the Kingdom

*B*REATHE DEEP—SWALLOW IT, *out the nose, slow it down.* Pipiera's efforts to control the badgering of her heart were futile. *Shoulders down, head up tall, look straight ahead.* She had spent thousands of days in the kingdom courtyard in front of Papah Megs' gate, but today was her turn to approach. She took in the familiar scene only from the opposite side, Papah's magnificent gate in the distance. The same eagle carriers she had once sent for Matthew released her and waved goodbye. She toed the soft, lush grass. *Oh, how I missed you.* The nearby flowers bent over to greet her, their stems delivering a curtsy as if she were royalty. *I feel so unworthy.*

A tear trickled down one cheek. She wiped it away. Her falsely placed sense of guilt was behind her now. From now on, her innate desire to please would be directed to her king.

The watch post was in the far distance. *Even above you, my dear Megalos, is my love for the king. But,* she chuckled, *he's always been your first love, so you get it.*

She knew very well that with visual aids and informed announcements, those watching from the gate knew exactly who to expect on the horizon each and every hour. A burst of laughter busted out. No doubt Megalos was at the other end of that telescope watching her every move that very moment.

Breathe! You're going to be crowned! Her self-encouragement and self-realization were pleasing.

Rather than jumping the waves as she so loved to do, Pipiera decided to just enjoy the ride. She stabilized her footing on a large rolling wave and soaked in the beauty of her surroundings as it swayed her forward with a gentle rocking motion, onward to the ultimate destination, the home she knew the best and loved the most, *her home. Only this time, I'm going in!*

Even from a distance, Megalos looked so handsome and stately. Still feeling a tinge of remorse for not trusting him implicitly, she admired him and enjoyed the smiles they shared as she got closer and closer. She fought the anxious urge to run and jump toward him. *Nope, this day is different. I'm going to enjoy my arrival ride.* She fixed her eyes upon him. Closer now, their eyes locked in a mutually admiring gaze. Pipiera exhaled and whispered a command for her tears to stop.

Finally, she arrived.

His body language seemed different. She no longer felt like the little girl who totally belonged to him, but rather like a young woman. Yes, a mature being with a sense of wisdom and knowing. *I belong to my king now, as you do.*

He held his hand out for her to clasp while releasing a loving sigh of approval.

Not listening to her own command, more tears soaked her cheeks. *It's okay*, she reassured herself, *these are good ones. Sweet.*

"I was so afraid I would never see you again," they said at the same time.

"Okay, you first," Pipiera said with professional politeness and refrained excitement.

"Welcome, Miss Penney, you have arrived," he said, using the same tone.

Jubilant silence.

Pipiera considered the moment—the tiny blue petals weren't playing music. *Why not?* "What's wrong?" she asked them, each with big blue eyes and long lashes, watching her every move. Pipiera giggled. They knew her well, and she knew them all. She nodded and smiled. They giggled and then got on with the orchestral harmony prepared specifically for her. Eventually, Pipiera faced Megalos and spoke.

"Thank you, Mr. Gatekeeper, I appreciate that." She curtsied. They both laughed dotingly and then hugged, a long, endearing hug. Long stems of flowering plants bent toward the pair to capture and delight in the tears that dropped.

"Seriously though," she said, spilling her thoughts first. "I'm sorry. I disobeyed. I doubted. And I realize now how selfish I was, feeling pity for myself, feeling guilty for doing what I was destined to do, holding on to anger, pretending all was..." she choked, "perfectly fine."

He shook his head and cupped his oversized right hand atop her petite left shoulder. "I enjoyed having you here with me so much. I should have encouraged you more. I know better. I knew better. I-I-I am the one to say sorry." They hugged again. Then he pulled away, ready to make a deep confession. "It's true. Before I completed my earth journey, my last seconds, I cursed you. I cursed an entire line of descendants, people I didn't know, not thinking I would ever meet them or that they could even be important to me. I . . I... I..." He lowered his head.

She grabbed his right forearm. "It's okay. I'm not angry. I get it. It must have been an impossible time for you." Another hug, this time a hug of reassurance, one that clearly meant it's all good. "The king forgave you, and so do I. And hey, you're officially my ancestor now. Papah for real!"

A comforting and serious quiet readied Pipiera for another confession. "You know, you told me many times, it's not till many despair in darkness before they search for the light." Megalos made no comment, just watched the emotions in her face churn as he knew her mind was swirling, as it always did and as it always will. That was who she was, how she was wonderfully made. "You shoulda bonked me on my head a little harder, made me listen!" Teasing now, she shook her finger at him.

Another bout of silence ensued till she spoke again, her voice gentle. "So, you know about Kasartha then? Who he was?"

Megalos nodded slowly, full of regret. "Yes. A man who once owned me and ruled me. A man I once looked up to, called him Pa. A man I once loved and relentlessly tried to please."

"I'm sorry," she whispered. Her Papah appeared to suffer genuine agony over this knowledge. "Our king heals, remember that." *You'll be okay, Papah, your loyalty will heal you. I know it.*

He nodded, a teardrop slipping down his cheek as he produced an enthusiastic smile. "Hey! With Matthew still on his journey, my—your, well, *our*—descendant line continues!" He wiped his brow and composed himself. "Let's get on with it, shall we?"

Megalos had a formal process he needed to follow, the same for each new arrival coming to his gate. Upon completing the scans and the sincere welcoming messages, letting her know what she might expect next, she promised she would come back to visit him regularly. Once she received her official citizen papers, that is.

"I can't wait. I want to see those papers myself—personally!" he exclaimed, making note they'd reveal what she already knew to be her kingdom name. Pipiera.

"I promise you will." It amazed Pipiera how calm and mature she felt, a feeling she hadn't known before the entire "Project: Matthew Intervention" business began. She shuddered at the thought of how close she came to entering the rebel gate. *I have many people to thank.*

She took two steps before she glanced back at Megalos. She knew he'd be watching her as she headed closer to the entrance.

The king first and foremost, and you as well, Papah Megs. "Thank you, Moolos."

"We're family," he said. "Now get in there! Your great aunt is waiting for you."

She stopped abruptly. "My great aunt? I have a great aunt?"

Megalos laughed heartily. "Oh my, you do, and…" He faced upward as though to calculate something. "As I understand it, she might be a great-great-great-aunt." He chuckled. "There's no question the two of you are related! She convinced the authoritarians to let her take on a little assignment of her own, just to help you out."

"Oh, wow. Seriously? I wonder how." She flashed a puzzling grin. "So, I have a family in there?"

"Oh, yeah," he nodded again. "A big one."

She shook her head before cocking it to one side. "You know, I'm so much richer now than I ever was. There are people in there who I never knew existed. Family!"

"You've just scratched the surface, my dear."

She looked gingerly at Megalos and took a step closer to him. She needed to ask. "Do you know that Kasartha, that…he still lives?"

Megalos nodded. "So I've been advised. It simply means our work must continue."

It was her turn to nod and she smiled one more time at her Megalos. He polished off the beaming glow he gifted back at her with one of his infamous winks.

Bookie was right there, waiting anxiously for her. "Come on, come on." He urged Pipiera to hurry. "First things first. Then you can gander."

A young woman came sprinting over from the picnic tables, worried she might have missed the greeting of her great-great-great-niece altogether. "Hey!" she yelped, waving her arms crazily. "Pippy dear!"

Pippy dear? Now that's a new one. Pipiera hadn't expected a waiting party for her. *Who is this woman? She does look familiar, but from where?* The woman grabbed Pipiera and hugged her excitedly. Pipiera hugged her back. *I must know you from somewhere.*

The girls held hands. "Okay, I know I know you," Pipiera said.

"Of course you do!" the woman teased. "And I came to watch you enter our gate. Don't worry, once you get through, it'll all come back to you. We'll *all* come back to you."

"We? All?" Pipiera was still digesting the "big family in there" revelation.

The woman grabbed hold of her and began escorting her toward the anxious book room keeper. "Your family, my dear. Generations and generations of family." She looked straight at Pipiera and gave a little curtsy. "Allow me to introduce myself. I'm Alexien, one of your many aunts. Of course, me and Serena are your favorites, right?" She winked and got a little closer. "Say it. C'mon say it. Me and Serena are your favorites."

Pipiera blushed.

"We pulled a few strings—hope you don't mind." Alexien stepped back. "We've all been waiting for you! And *you*, my dear, are a *hero*."

"A hero?"

"Don't be silly. You did your part so well, your actions helped to bring Franklin home. He's waiting too. Now get in there, would you? I have a little something yet to do and will be along shortly." She released Pipiera's hand. "Oh, I almost forgot! I must deliver this letter to you. It's from Jophiel. Give it a read. You made quite an impression on him, you know."

"Oh, Jophiel, I so want to see him! Is he around? I need to apologize… and explain myself."

Alexien shook her head. "Nope, you missed him. But along with the letter he told me to, and I quote, 'jab you and shush you'!"

Pipiera laughed and held the letter fondly. *Why a letter?* she wondered. *Is he not here? Did he go somewhere?*

She opened it and read.

My dear Pipiera,

I am so proud of you. If I were there, I would join you on this glorious day of your arrival. As it is, I am not, and it is your fault, I dare say. You have inspired me to sign up and take the fall. My application for a humankind tour was approved almost immediately. You know we are not the ones to determine our time or our placement, but I did ask for somewhere close to Havensight and thought you would be happy to know it was granted. If you are reading this, then that is where I am right now! I know how tough these humankind tours are, I have seen plenty enough. But witnessing your courage and love for struggling members of your family inspired me. I do not know what to expect, but I rest a little easier knowing I might have you watching out for me. I look forward to seeing you again when I too can become a kingdom citizen instead of a kingdom escort. Please watch for me.

Our King lives forever!

Yours, Jophiel

Pipiera leaned back and enjoyed the love that surrounded her. *I'm home. And yes, Jophiel, I will keep a watchful eye over you!*

CHAPTER SEVENTY-SEVEN
SHE'S GONE

In a Town Next to Havensight

HONK, HONK! THE taxi driver tooted his arrival. He was in the driveway and ready to sweep them away. It was their usual food shopping excursion, and he was their usual chauffeur. He could lean back now, pull his cap down and catch a couple zzz's. The couple was lovely indeed, but they certainly moved slow. Shuffle, shuffle, shuffle. He was used to taking little catnaps while he waited for Charles and Maggie. In fact, he rather looked forward to them.

"Charles," Maggie called out, "cabbie's here. 'Bout ready?" She slid the kitchen curtain panel into its place across the window rod and carefully smoothed out the wrinkles even though there were none. Course she knew he wouldn't be. He was always in charge, always the boss, always telling her what they should do and why. But when it came to preparedness, he never quite got it.

"We pay'im. He can wait," he called back from the next room as he debated between his favorite well-worn wool cardigan or the newly purchased spring jacket while fussing at the reflection the front hall mirror offered in return.

Maggie opened the screen door to give the cabbie a wave, to

let him know they'd soon be out. "Oh, he's havin' his nap," she chuckled aloud teasingly, till she heard a crash coming from where Charles just spoke. "Charles?" she called. No reply. "Charles! You okay?" *Course he isn't. My gosh, he's fallen.* The rattling clang spooked her, making her nervous. No time to grab the cane. Every foot drop felt achingly slow and her body weight uneven. She scampered as best she could to reach him. She found him on the floor, leaning all crooked and bent up against the couch. The floor lamp horizontal instead of vertical. He was breathing heavily, eyes open with an excited weariness about them. *Phew! Thank heavens,* she whispered to herself, *you're still here.*

Charles had stepped backward, lost his balance, and grabbed the lamp on his way down. She leaned over and crouched as best she could and stabilized herself on both knees, knowing that getting back up would most certainly present a challenge.

The look on Charles's face was strange, posing an unfamiliar expression. He made a sweeping motion upward with his right arm. "Wooosh," was all he said.

"Woosh? Woosh what? How'd you fall? Com'on, we've got to get you back up." He didn't appear hurt, yet the shaking of his head suggested no, not just yet. Maggie took the moment to sneak a relaxed breath. *I thought you dropped dead, you big lark.* In a gentle voice, she prodded for more. "What happened?"

Still shaking his head, he smirked a chuckle. "You won't believe me." He paused, "Well, maybe you will."

"Com'on, out with it."

He nodded toward the closet. "I was standing right there, and… whoosh," he made the same arm movement again. "Penney. It was Penney."

"Penney?!"

He shushed her and took a deep sigh. "It caught me by surprise. It was so quick, so brief. She's gone, Maggie. She's gone."

"Oh Charles, Penney's been gone for years. You know that." It was a scolding remark, she couldn't help it.

"No, no, no. Course I know that! Help me up." The pair maneuvered and twisted and leaned on each other till they both were stable, standing face-to-face and holding on securely. She studied his face with the expectation to hear more.

"It's like she was inside me and suddenly, whoosh, she left. I didn't know I was carrying her. Inside me, all these years." A genuinely puzzled look blanketed his face. Maggie smiled empathically. She motioned to cup his face but hesitated, not daring to loosen the grip on his forearms. "She just left. She's free now, Maggie," he announced.

"No, dear. *You've* been hanging onto *her* for all these years. To guilt. You've been hanging on to guilt. I think it's *you* who hasn't been free." She didn't like the discerning look on his face but announced her opinion anyway, though she would have to let him be in charge. "You let her go, Charles. You let her free. You've let yourself free." She smiled lovingly. *Something you shoulda done years ago!*

Charles smiled in return. This time it was an expression she was quite familiar with—the '*I know better than you look*'. "Well, I don't know about that," he declared. "But, she's home now. I feel it. She's finally gone home."

The pair embraced, still leaning on each other for physical support. Maggie couldn't be confident what really transpired other than her husband's fall was mysteriously sewn with some sort of healing thread. She would be happy with that.

Honk, honk.

"He'll have to nap a bit longer." They both laughed and cautiously readied themselves for their morning shop and for whatever else might come their way in the days to come.

CHAPTER SEVENTY-EIGHT

A New Time Marker

In the Town of Havensight
Six Months Later

"I'M REALLY GOING to miss you. I wish you didn't get transferred." Marnie and Dr. Alexien enjoyed an hour of tea and conversation on the final Saturday afternoon of each month. To Marnie it was therapeutic, and Dr. Alexien had become such a good friend, a friend with a tolerant ear to hear the same stories over and over. She released a deep sigh. "Do you think you might come back to Havensight from time to time?"

"Oh, I so wish, Marnie. These transfers tend to consume every inch of my being. I barely have enough time to start a proper life for myself. But you… *you* have a lovely life going for you. Find and keep the joy in it. Please promise me that!"

"I will." Marnie smiled. Yes, indeed, she felt fortunate. During the last six months she had experienced a great deal of change. All wonderful changes, or mostly anyway.

Marnie was in a much better place. She realized how she had become stuck in her grief. "After seeing Frank ever so briefly, and maybe it was just my imagination, but you know, it doesn't matter. After seeing him putting Matthew into bed, with the coincidence and all of Matthew waking up just after that, well, I just feel Frank is truly alive and watching over us. He's not dead to me anymore. I'm not mad at him anymore either. I will keep an open mind from here on out."

Dr. Alexien smiled in relief.

Marnie scanned Dr. Alexien's office. "I'm always so stunned at how neat and tidy your office is. Your desk is always cleared off and wiped clean."

"I know, I know. I'm a bit of a neat freak. I like to be sure all things are perfectly tidy. So, how's Matthew doing?"

"So much better now. Goodness, I practically don't recognize him sometimes. He loves his new part-time job at the bicycle shop. Too funny how that came about—our neighbor's friend owns the shop and loaned him that Schwinn to try out and, well, you know what happened to that bike!" The women shared a good chuckle. "Wouldn't you know it, Matthew went to apologize to the owner of the shop, and the owner was so moved that he told Matthew to come by after school each day to wash the bikes and do cleanup in the shop in exchange for the whole bike fiasco. Crazy! Sometimes I can't believe how good things come out of bad." Marnie continued to express how happy Matthew was, especially since it had turned into a paying job. "He's got pocket money and is saving up for his own Schwinn. I bet he'll have enough by next summer." Dr. Alexien was equally thrilled for Matthew.

"He's so much better at relationships too. Well, actually, so am I. But Matthew, well, when he learned it was Josh and that Damien guy who moved the bike and reported it stolen, he told them he understood why they did it, that they were all in kind of a battle over friendships and reputations, I think. You know how boys can be; everything's a competition. I was shocked, but those boys, ha ha, you wouldn't believe it. They were speechless at first. And now? They're all friends!" This was one of Marnie's favorite stories. She would go on and on about it to Dr. Alexien, particularly when Dr. Alexien asked if she could share it with future clients.

Wanting to focus on Marnie for the last couple of minutes, Dr. Alexien changed the topic. "How's that new job going? Still having fun?"

"Oh my gosh, I love it! The owner of the boutique is so wonderful to work for. You know, she made me assistant manager last week? Imagine that! So quick, too. I've only been there five months. Quitting my old job was the best thing I ever did. I love being creative with flowers and being part of the community. Imagine that, *me*. I deliver many of the arrangements myself. We take pride in our personal service. And I'm not so rushed in the mornings. I have the time we need as a family to do the breakfast thing before getting Karo and Matthew off to school. And I'm getting to know some folks around here, which is kinda nice. Now, what about your new job? You haven't said much about it. Another hospital, I presume? You didn't say which community."

"Oh, it's a good three-hour drive away. Pretty much the same thing as here. I love my work too. So, what about Frank's parents? You said you were going to have them over for dinner again. How did that go?"

Marnie smiled. She knew Dr. Alexien was prodding her more, wanting to be sure all was well with her and her family. Even though there was a seemingly clinical component to their relationship, she respected it and appreciated it. "Did I tell you how thankful I was for your friendship?" Marnie asked. It was a true confession from her heart.

"Thank you, Marnie." Dr. Alexien smiled, comfy in her straight-back chair while Marnie was on the edge of the big comfy chair, excited to share the latest news. Dr. Alexien was the only person Marnie shared the secrets of her feelings with. She wondered what it would be like once she left.

"That coincidence still blows me away." Marnie cocked her head as if that would help her portray its mystery. "I told you how Matthew kept dreaming about his teacher, the one who died suddenly earlier this year, remember?" When Dr. Alexien nodded, Marnie continued. "Well, in these dreams, Mr. Falcon—Andy Falcon—encouraged Matthew to keep up with his athletic abilities. I guess he felt Matthew had some talent there. Anyway, Matthew couldn't keep up physically, not yet of course; he was still healing. But long story short, he asked the new gym teacher if he could still be involved. Lo and behold, they invited him to be a junior judge for the regional games! And there he was. Frank's dad was the retiree judge, the one they invited back year after year as their honorary judge. Can you believe that? Frank never even told me his parents lived a short drive from Havensight. They hadn't spoken for years, had a fight when he was a teen, and then broke ties. Frank refused to talk about his parents when we were married; I never ever met them." She leaned forward even farther. "Frank was a great guy, but he sure was stubborn and could hold a grudge." She sat back up. "Anyway, I had never met them, and neither had Matthew, but there they were, sitting together in the judging box, side by side. Frank's dad actually recognized Matthew. Bizarre."

"And now?"

"Now we have family. Imagine that. And they're so wonderful and so genuinely interested in all three of us! I can't believe some stupid argument kept Frank estranged, so many wasted years. But Frank could be stubborn, as I said. But oh my gosh, this reconciliation has been *so* good for both kids. They actually have grandparents now. I can't say enough how amazing that feels!"

"I hope you get the chance to grow close to them," Dr. Alexien said. "It's nice to have a support system."

"You know, Arnie's been good too. He and his wife, Cilia. My gosh, they have both been so kind to us, and she doesn't seem to mind me. I'm so grateful that I can get to know her. I really like her. In fact, they need a sitter for their little guy, so they can both attend some weekly thing at their church on Friday nights. He's just a little over three months old now. Karo and I thought it would be fun to be their Friday-night sitters. It's been great for Karo, and I'm enjoying it too. I bet Matthew will start hanging around with us on Friday nights." Marnie chuckled. "He and this little Joppha character seem to have a special bond. Matt just has to walk into the room, and the little guy smiles and kicks his little legs like crazy!"

"And how is little *Joppha?*" Dr. Alexien grinned sheepishly.

"Yeah, funny name, eh? Arnie says it came to him the instant the little guy was born. Unusual, but they love it, and that's what counts. Oh my gosh, you should see him!" Marnie cupped her mouth to cover a giggle. "He's got the cutest broad shoulders and extra-long feet. But look at the time. I best be getting home."

The two ladies took their last sips of tea and hugged, wishing each other well, Marnie hoping she would see Dr. Alexien again, and Dr. Alexien promising Marnie she would.

"One fine glorious day, Marnie, we will meet again."

CHAPTER SEVENTY-NINE
PASS THE BALL

"HEY, IS THAT your mom?"

Matthew checked, and sure enough, his mom's Pontiac was turning up their road, just as he got hit in the head and knocked on his butt.

"Hey!" Matt laughed and jumped up eagerly, putting a good spin on the football as he threw it back at Emerson. Emerson caught it and ran to the far end of the front boulevard on Warmud Street, past a marker, and jumped up and down. Touchdown! Nick blew a whistle, and the three boys gathered, slapping hands.

They were friends now, Matthew Mackenzie and Emerson Damien, in the second year at Havensight Collegiate, both getting ready for junior football tryouts. Nick preferred to play the role of coach, referee, linesman, and overall boss, while Josh was lucky enough to have a home console and be enamored by Pong.

It was Dr. Alexien's idea, back in the early days of summer, for Matthew to call on Emerson at his home. "Invite him out for a game of catch or something." Matt thought she was nuts, but she convinced him. "The payoff could be great. You could gain a friend and close this chapter, have some fun this summer, and stop stewing." When she dared him to do it, Matt finally worked up the courage.

Nick blew the whistle again, instructing the two boys to head to their respective ends of the boulevard. Matt smiled as he jogged. He had learned a great deal about Emerson, especially the common challenges they faced. Sure, Emerson had a dad, but he was absent all but one weekend a month. His dad had a big job and *another family* in another city, so it was just Emerson and his mom most of the time. Matthew grew into a supportive role for Emerson, and the two became inseparable. So much rejection and anger diffused through simple acceptance.

Matt waved to his mom as she pulled into their garage. Yes, it'd been cleaned out. All his dad's stuff had either been given away or organized, so a car could fit inside the garage again.

Nick and his whistle; there it went again. Emerson put a good spin on the football. Matt dove to catch it, rolling across the ground. The cold hardness of the ground reminded him of his crazy experiences earlier that year, experiences he swore were real but refused to talk about. He lay on his back for a moment and gazed into the sky, which threatened snow one day soon.

"Dad," he whispered, "I know you're good now. One day I wanna have my own family, just like you have. Just like Arnie has too. And don't worry, I'm gonna take care of Mom. Thanks for bringing me home."

"Hey!" Emerson yelled. "Get up, dude! C'mon, toss 'er back."

Matt jumped up, sprinted down the boulevard, and pushed off into an extra long jump. While in midair, he tossed the football to Emerson with perfect precision.

"Showoff!" Nick and Emerson yelled in unison.

From the Desk of Interventions

Somewhere Inside the Kingdom a File Is Closed

THERE YOU HAVE it. File closed. This one anyway.

Can you see now why I jumped when Megs came to me, all concerned about one of his descendant young'uns? How great that was, an opportunity to work a bunch of things together, all for the good. All for the king.

It wasn't just Megs' Matthew boy we helped. I mean, sure enough, a new page was written for him. He got through a pretty hurtful and grievous phase, that's tough enough for anyone. I was quite impressed with his practice of relationship grace, and he even built some character! But consider who else grew. The boy's mom, Marnie, she's a good sum more open and curious. And his friend, Emerson, got more than a little boost to help his own healing and soften up. Then there's Charles. He loosened up his grip, shook out some of his own guilt which kept him so darned angry all those years. But the one who crossed the finish line? Well, that would be Pipiera. She's my favorite part of the story.

Sometimes it's plain and simple—we learn the most in the dark. That's when we shouldn't walk away, no, sir. That's when we figure out what to let go and whom to seek. Yup, faith and emotional health, they're intertwined, I'd say, on account they grow together like a beanstalk, reaching for heights unknown. And until that day whence all the targeting is banished, and all the houses safe and full of light, I suppose me and my intervention team, we'll keep on doing our thing. Help'n to keep folks on track.

In case you're wondering, Pipiera is having a blast now that she's official, a kingdom citizen and all. And she's famous, too—earned herself a "known-around-the-kingdom" reputation as the amazing courtyard jumper. Yeah, "that's my gate girl," as Megs would say with adoration in his voice.

And Megs himself? Well, he's still in his role, as strong, dependable, and thankful as ever. He sure misses his sidekick, but rumor is they meet at the picnic tables every so often and have some good chuckles. Of course, he's thanked me a thousand times, unnecessarily. It's not just my job—it's my pleasure. Gotta admire him, my Megs. He's kept every single one of those descendants gifted to him safe, meaning kingdom citizenship granted after their tour. At least to this point anyway, trouble is always brewing. Kasartha's still out there, still watching, still wanting, still targeting.

As for me, you know it. It was a long wait for my chance to make a difference in the life of my ole neighbor buddy, Megalos. I knew the king would grant me that desire one day. What I learned myself through all this, given my own yearning to intervene? Patient endurance, my friend, patient endurance.

Come by again!

Coming next

GATE GIRL

Pipiera's next adventure is in the works!
Interested to be notified once it's available?

Drop a note to johanna.z.frank@gmail.com, or

Send a tweet to Johanna Frank@Johanna_Z_Frank